Fiennders Keepers

A Londoner by birth, Jean Marsh has spent most of her adult life in Oxfordshire and New York. She is best known for her role as Rose in *Upstairs, Downstairs*, which she co-created with Eileen Atkins, and has acted in a wide variety of shows on stage, in film and television. At the age of twelve she made her West End debut in *Land of the Christmas Stockings* and ten years later appeared for the first time in New York in *Much Ado About Nothing*. Since then her performances have included works by Shakespeare, Shaw, Ibsen and Coward.

Articles by Jean Marsh have appeared in the *Sunday Times*, *New York Times*, *Los Angeles Times*, *Washington Post* and the *TV Times*. She enjoys good food and walking.

D1464852

Also by Jean Marsh

The House of Eliott

Jean Marsh

Fiennders
Keepers

PAN BOOKS

First published 1996 by Macmillan

This edition published 1997 by Pan Books
an imprint of Macmillan Publishers Ltd
25 Eccleston Place, London SW1W 9NF
and Basingstoke

Associated companies throughout the world

ISBN 0 330 34987 2

3 5 7 9 8 6 4 2

A CIP catalogue record for this book is available from
the British Library.

Phototypeset by Intype London Ltd
Printed and bound in Great Britain
by Mackays of Chatham plc, Chatham, Kent

For Michael

I would like to thank Margaret Munday of The Bell
Book Shop in Henley for her help with research and
the generous use of her private library,

and

My editor Susan Hill for her faith, patience, affection
and advice.

1878

MARY HESITATED AT the edge of the wood: she was tempted to follow Master Richard into the cool leafy depths. She could hear the snapping of dry twigs as he pushed his way through the beeches. There in the centre was the special place, their special place, a glade where the wood had been coppiced and the trees didn't meet at the top, letting the sunlight slip through. It reminded her of the church in the watercress village where the sun shone through the coloured windows and lit the dust floating in the air.

'Come on,' he shouted, sounding impatient.

'I shouldn't,' she called back.

'Come on,' he shouted again. Already, at fifteen, his voice had a natural, easy authority. She retied the strings of her cotton bonnet, pulling the pleated edge forward to shield her face from the overhead sun. It was the heat as much as his command that changed her mind and, following his path, treading carefully, she joined him in the glade. He was lying on his back squinting up at the sky.

'We shouldn't come in here this time of year.' He ignored this, still squinting through the tiny circle he had made with his forefinger and thumb. There were grass stains, she noticed, on his white shirt and a few leaves clung to his thick brown hair. 'You look like the Green Man.'

'There's no such thing, that's a folk tale,' he said dismissively.

Laughing uneasily, she repeated, 'We shouldn't come in here this time of the year. My father doesn't like his birds disturbed when they're nesting.'

'Not *your* father's birds, I think. My father's, wouldn't you say? So I can disturb them whenever I like.'

She stood her ground, though a slight flush coloured her pale skin. 'Mebbe, Master Richard, but 'tis my father what cares for them and you ought to be minding their welfare.' Her slight local accent was always more pronounced when she was upset. He jumped to his feet, ashamed to be corrected by her and, as he knew, justly so. He touched her shoulder in a conciliatory gesture, smiling gently at the serious little face.

Funny thing she was, he couldn't remember not knowing her. She was like a chap, really, a trusty friend, more so than any friend at Eton and much better than most girls, or at any rate better than young ladies like his three sisters. He thought with distaste of their incessant high-pitched girlish giggles and irritatingly coy manner with the occasional school friend he invited to stay. Friends they professed to despise and threatened to ignore, although their scorn and lack of interest took the form of constant dramatic appearances in frequent changes of clothes with breathless enquiries of, 'Oh, so you're here?' 'Have you seen Mamma?' 'Was that the dressing bell?'

Mary pushed off her bonnet, smoothing the wings of

silky, straight, milk-blonde hair, wondering why he was observing her so silently.

'That's horrible,' he said abruptly, taking her hand and examining it. 'Your nails are really quite disgusting.'

She snatched away her hand, putting it behind her back. 'I can't help it! It's the grates – I've been doing the downstairs fires since the other Mary was sent off. It's black and oily, the cleaning stuff.'

'I've never seen you in the house. I thought you worked in the dairy at Home Farm.'

'Well, you wouldn't see me, would you? I've finished and gone before seven o'clock so's I can get to the dairy.'

'There's something wrong here,' he said, teasing her gently. 'Cleaning *our* fireplaces makes *you* dirty.'

She relaxed a little, looking at him with a half-smile. 'And that so is the truth. To make most things clean someone has to get dirty. That's why I'd rather work in the laundry or the dairy.' Suddenly she glared at him, her pale eyebrows arched above the deep tawny brown of her eyes.

'And why do you light the fires anyhow when it's still so hot?'

'The house is cold in the evening, I suppose.' Her directness and simplicity pleased him. At thirteen she was a touching mixture of maturity and innocence. Always strong and capable, she had taken care of her younger brother and sister when her mother worked in the big house. She could cook, and helped keep their cottage clean. Long before she was ten she had adult responsibilities, even looking after the hen yard, capable of killing and plucking chickens and skinning rabbits. In the shoot-

3

ing season she dealt with partridges, pheasants and wild ducks quickly and efficiently.

Richard had seen her in the vegetable garden behind Keepers Cottage, helping her father hoe the neat lines of potatoes, onions and carrots and carrying heavy buckets of water. But although she seemed strong she didn't look it: her slight frame was still small-breasted and girlish and, unlike most of the red-faced hoydens from the village, her skin had a delicate pallor – except for the tip of her nose, which escaped the protection of her bonnet and was browned by the sun. Her demeanour was usually quiet and self-contained but she still had the impulsiveness of a child. When they met for the first time each holiday she would smile broadly and run to hug him, her greeting warm and unselfconscious.

They left the wood hand in hand and, heading for the farm, skirted the fields, the corn a hot yellow nearly ready for harvesting . . .

'I'll speak to my mother about the fires, Mary. It isn't correct for you, especially being the keeper's daughter—'

'No, no, please don't do that,' she interrupted hastily. 'She'll think the less of me for complaining and there's a new girl coming soon from London, as soon as she's twelve, and she'll be the tweeny.' They reached the granary set high on staddle stones to protect the corn from rats.

'Let's see how much you remember of your Latin,' and standing on a milking stool Richard reached up into the beams and brought down a Latin primer. On the fly-leaf was written R.O.O.F., his initials, but it belonged to Mary. He had given it to her when she left the dame school one year earlier. She should keep up her education, he'd said, though there was no question of keeping up with Latin for she'd never started it. Reading and writing she'd learnt, sewing, of course, and simple arithmetic, but it hadn't been possible for her to go to school every day: if her mother was needed at the big house then she was needed at home.

Leafing through the book, he said, 'Do you remember anything? Have you looked at it?' Richard's attention to her education was less generous than Mary thought: he did it because he had found that teaching her helped him to remember.

'It's like a mystery,' she said, biting her lip and trying to explain. 'When you're told a tale and nothing seems to be what it ought and then . . .' she paused making an effort to be clear, 'then suddenly, just one little thing you can understand and after that each bit gets plainer until at the end you don't know why it was a mystery in the first place,' she finished triumphantly, and settled comfortably in the corner holding the book. When he failed to join her she looked up at him. There was a moment between them, not speaking, not smiling, a moment to which they were accustomed, when they were companions, friends, and more, when there was a depth of feeling neither shared with anyone else.

They arrived at their separate homes in time for the midday meal, Richard for a formal luncheon with his parents, sisters and a clergyman from a neighbouring village. This gentleman, who was at least fifty, was still considered by his sisters worthy of the effort of curling their hair with tongs, reducing their waists with the tight-est of stays and pinching their cheeks to a flush of unnatural health. The meal was longer and more elaborate than the usual family luncheon. It consisted of five courses and three wines: a madeira with the clear soup, hock with the mackerel and gooseberry sauce, and a good claret with the simply roasted capon. The claret was good but not one of Thomas Fiennders' best. There were rules concerning his cellar; the very best was served to him alone, except on extraordinary occasions – and in Richard's memory none had happened. The more people present the lesser the vineyard and the vintage, although Thomas's cellar did not contain any wine that he would not drink himself. The Reverend Algernon Grant-Ingram was a second cousin of Richard's mother, Ann; his stipend was poor and his private income small so the Fiennders' felt it their duty to entertain him once in a while. He was a good guest, amusing them with all the local gossip, attentive to the ladies and with some well-told ribald stories for the gentlemen with the port. Today he was behaving quite roguishly with nineteen-year-old Isabel, teasing and complimenting her on the large ringlets that hung either side of her face looking like bell-pulls. It was absurd, Richard thought, observing her high colour and listening to her shrill excitable voice. His sisters only existed when there was a man around. Without one, they were fretful and bored. And Algernon Grant-Ingram, of all people! Didn't they realize *why* he was unmarried at the age of fifty-one? Perhaps, though, he wouldn't have recognized it if he'd been educated at home. At school that sort of thing was quite clear – which masters were interested and which boys were available.

'Ruthie, Ruthie, wake up, you haven't said a word.'

Jessica poked him in the ribs. Richard pushed her away, muttering, 'Nothing to say, said nothing.' He noted that the hair tongs had been used, more circumspectly, by seventeen-year-old Jessica and just a few flat curls had been contrived on her forehead.

'Ruthie?' The Reverend Mr Grant-Ingram raised an amused eyebrow and pursed his lips. 'My dear Richard, when did you change your name and why?'

'That's what they call him at school, poor darling,' his mother, ever his champion, explained. 'It's Roof, you see, R-O-O-F, Richard Oliver Ormerod Fiennders.'

Algernon realized that his reaction to 'Ruthie' had been a little arch – it wouldn't do for the family to be aware of his tendencies. Not that there would be any trouble with Richard, nice boy, and nice-looking, with his mother's dark blue eyes and his father's narrow patrician face, but no, there was only one person in this household in whom he was interested, and unfortunately Algernon was aware that the interest was shared by his hostess.

Keepers Cottage, built of local brick and flint, with its neat thatched roof hanging like heavy eyebrows over the upstairs windows, was set on a track away from the village of Findlesham, half-way between Home Farm and the Manor House. The track was known as Drover's Lane, it being the route by which both the shepherd and the cowherd drove their animals to the market town of Wellsbury. The cottage was small but the family, too, was small, with only three children, and it was well looked after. The stone floors were covered with bright rag rugs made by Mary's mother and grandmother. They had used any bits that came to hand, regardless of colour, and the impression was of a floor strewn with the faded brilliance of wilted flower cuttings. The fire, though laid, was unlit, the late summer days still warm enough to save the precious wood for evening cooking and colder nights. Emma Bowden was trying unsuccessfully to set the table for midday dinner and calm six-year-old Albert, who was racing round the large scrubbed table banging a spoon and shouting, 'Tally ho! View halloo! Come y'ere, Daffodil, y'ere, Bluebell,' and any other cries he could remember from following the huntsman working his hounds.

'It's hot so 'tis only boiled potatoes and cheese, and you could pull a lettuce, Mary, and get a jar of beetroot from the larder.'

'Oh, Mam, I'm sorry, I should've been here before to help. Quiet now, Albert, or I'll not take you with me this afternoon.'

The child, his face red and shining from his boisterous play, quietened, but only for an instant. 'Nooo,' he wailed. 'Take me, take me, Mary, for 'twas you that said you'd pull me home in the cart from the village.'

'Hush, yes, and I will, but only if you're good and quiet till we leave.' Albert sat at the table with an exaggerated stillness, his finger on his lips. Laughing at her mother with her back to her brother, Mary said, 'I'll get the lettuce now, Mam, after I've been to my privy.' She opened the back door, where the thatch almost reached the ground, and made her way through rows of climbing beans and a neatly laid out vegetable patch, pausing to scratch the pig who had come out of the shade of his lean-to hoping for scraps.

The privy was a small wooden structure at the bottom right-hand corner of the long garden. She had said 'my' privy and indeed it was hers, and treasured. The family privy was an identical structure in the left corner. Years ago, her parents had discovered she was using the spinney at the end of the bottom field. They had seen her walking back to the cottage in the half-light of an early winter evening soaked by the rain, and unlike her usual obedient self she had stubbornly refused to use the family one. That John Bowden loved his daughter, his eldest child, was natural, but he also admired her, her strength and willingness to work, to do any task however distasteful and he decided to indulge her fastidiousness. On the eve of her tenth birthday he had stayed up most of the night, building a privy for her own private use. Starting work on it the second his beloved Mary was in bed, he dug the hole, fetched the planks he'd cut and polished for the seat and assembled the shed.

It was the best present she'd ever had, the best present anybody had ever had, she thought, as she always thought when she used it, and nobody else, ever, was allowed to use it. Not even Queen Victoria if she happened to be passing by would be granted permission!

She pulled up one of the last of the lettuces, and broke off the root and outside leaves and responded to the pig's oink, oink by tossing them into its run. They should really have gone into the chicken bucket but the pig's days were numbered: soon he would be flitches of bacon, cured hams, blood puddings and joints of pork.

When she returned with the lettuce and beetroot her

parents were arguing in hushed but angry tones. It had been this that had finally cowed Albert. Hearing her they stopped but she'd heard enough to know it was the old set-to: her mother's need for money to put aside for a rainy day against her father's wish for them to live as the keeper's family should. Better off than most of the villagers, except for the innkeeper and the Jacksons at the forge, John Bowden was proud of his position: a tied cottage, not big but bigger than most, a good piece of garden and always something for the pot, a rabbit or a hare or bird in the season. They had a dignity that he felt was undermined by Emma's unnecessary fears of the poorhouse.

They sat to eat their meal in a silence punctuated only by requests for 'A little more home-brew, Mother,' from John; 'Can I sup some, Da?' from Albert, aware that the answer would be no, and a soft, 'No more, thank you, Ma,' from Mary, in reply to her mother's gesture at the large piece of cheese covered by butter muslin to keep the flies off. Equally quietly, she asked, 'Should we be keeping some potatoes for Hannah after school?'

'No, no need,' her mother said. 'I'll be boiling a suet pudding with a bit of bacon for our tea.'

Mary pushed her chair away from the table. 'I'd best be getting the hand-cart loaded up if we're to be off to Findlesham.'

'We're not,' Albert wailed. 'Bogger it.'

The stunned silence and three shocked faces that greeted this stopped his cries and he looked anxiously at his sister. 'Done wrong?' he said, in a frightened whisper. His mother made a very odd noise and left the room quickly, covering her mouth with the corner of her apron.

Was she crying, he wondered, sounded like it. Couldn't have been laughing, no.

'Where did you hear that, son?' His father made an attempt at being stern.

'You said, Da, you told Mam, we wasna to go.'

'The other bit, Bertie.'

'Bogger it?' he said innocently. 'It's what you say when fox has been at your chicks.'

Pushing the cart loaded with produce from the garden, a sack of potatoes, one of turnips, onions, leeks, and jars of her mother's justly famous apple chutney and pickled cauliflower, Mary watched her little brother skipping ahead raising the dust on the dirt track that led to the village. Life was truly strange, she thought. They were doing this only because he had said a terrible word, but that word had made her parents laugh and made them the way they ought to be – more loving, like. She had seen her father gently touch her mother's laughing face, and later he had said with a sigh that she could go to Findlesham but not to tarry at the Bull and Butcher. Deliver the vegetables and chutney, count the money carefully and leave. She wasn't to accept lemonade or ginger-beer, however tired and hot she was. The back parlour of the inn was used as a shop, the only one in the village. Her father drank at the inn occasionally and knew it to be a decent place, but he didn't think it fit for a young woman to be seen in an ale-house. The only women ever seen there were those whose age and plainness guaranteed respectability. He also thought it not fit for his daughters to be seen in the fields collecting stones, the same fields that had yielded the flint that helped to build Keepers Cottage. Mary and Hannah – if she could awaken her – would be out in the fields before dawn when they could please both father and mother: they collected the stones but they weren't seen . . .

'Oh, oh, Mary, horse, ducks, baby horse, oh, oh, Mary.' Albert's excitable little face was contorted with desire and indecision, and he ran back and forth, tugging at Mary's skirt. What to do? The pond beckoned him with the ducks in their sleek white plumage with egg-yellow beaks, but opposite stood the forge, its wide wooden doors open to the sunlight. From inside you could hear the clang of iron and catch a glimpse of George Jackson by the smithy fire as he moulded a horse-shoe, keeping the fire bright with the bellows. Outside stood George's younger brother Billy, shoeing what Albert had called a baby horse but which was, in fact, a donkey. The pond was forgotten in the excitement of seeing the donkey bucking and rearing, managing to knock Billy to the ground, braying loudly as he did so. George appeared at the door holding a hot horseshoe with iron tongs. 'You're too fast, Billy. You can't do nothing with a horse or donkey till he's your friend. When he trusts you, then you can become his master.'

Billy picked himself up, grimacing and rubbing his behind. 'That's more like a mule than a donkey.'

'Here, you put this back to fire,' George said, handing him the shoe, still a dull red from the heat, 'I'll calm Neddy down.' He put his hand, palm up, to the donkey's nose and let him smell it. 'Nice to see you, Mary.'

'And me – and me, George.'

'Nice to see you too, Bertie, but don't be jumping up and down, lad, till I've quietened Ned here.'

Albert froze, afraid of being sent on his way and missing any excitement. George rubbed the donkey between his ears, talking softly to him and blowing gently up his nose. By the time Billy reappeared, George was sitting on an upturned bucket holding the animal's foreleg, prior to shoeing it.

'That's beautiful, George.' The donkey was now standing peacefully, putty in the smith's hands. 'You've really got the feeling,' Mary said admiringly.

'Naw, 'tain't nothing but practice.' He was blushing. 'I should be able at my age, I'm nineteen next birthday, you know, and horses have been my life's work.'

His blushes increased as Mary laughed, but Billy chimed in, 'No, 'tis more than that, she be right, you do have the feeling, even Pa say so.'

Albert looked intently at George, at the strong sunburnt face surmounted by a thatch of dry, spiky, corn-coloured hair, and, carefully stepping out of range of the donkey's legs, he said, 'Nineteen, George. Are you old, then?'

'Not so's you'd notice, Bertie, and not when I look at your pretty sister.'

Mary dismissed the compliment. 'Yes, well, you'll likely be seeing his pretty sister Hannah soon on her way back from school.'

Looking out of her bedroom window at the distant hills, shaded in a lavender-coloured light, Ann Fiennders was bored at the thought of the long morning ahead before luncheon and bored at the thought of that meal without guests. She had wanted to ride with her son but he'd taken his horse before she was up, the groom said, and had gone towards Wellsbury. He was probably visiting the Osmunds at Wellsbury Manor – their son Andrew was at school with Richard – which meant he would not be home for luncheon, selfish boy. But the stable lad, speaking up from the adjacent stall where he was brushing the new grey gelding, had said, 'No, m'lady, Master Richard, he turned left, out towards the farm and Downhill Covert.' The boy always called her, m'lady; it was beyond his comprehension that such a house and its estate could be owned by anyone other than nobility. Anyway, there would be no catching Richard now even though she had the better horse and was the better rider. Odd, that the groom had been so angry with the boy for contradicting him. He had even flicked his whip at the boy's head, which was just visible over the partition between the stables. The boy had thought it a mite odd, too, and had hardly been enlightened by Charles, the groom, who had tapped his nose slyly, saying, 'There are reasons and reasons.'

Ann turned back from the long window and tugged at the bell-pull. If she wasn't going out then her maid might as well loosen her stays. She waited impatiently, hands on hips, looking at her image in the long looking-glass. Fretfully, she kicked her slippers across the room. She wasn't displeased with what she saw but she had always gained more pleasure from the reaction of a man than the reflection of a mirror. She sat for a moment, trying to relax, but the regency satinwood chair was as formal and uncomfortable as it looked and was rejected roughly after a few seconds' rest.

As the maid knocked and entered she heard the clip-clop of horses' hoofs outside in the yard. Maybe it was Richard, home early. She peered out of the side window. No, it was Thomas with Bowden. They were probably going to inspect the pheasant chicks and shoot pigeons. Her husband looked in good humour. He got on well with the keeper who, she noticed, was mounted on Seamus, her old hunter. She felt a twinge of guilt. She hadn't seen Thomas this morning – they always break-fasted separately but he'd sent a note to her room asking to see her, and she had forgotten. It must have been about the horse. Bowden was welcome to ride him, he had good hands, and in conferring this favour on her husband she would earn some needed goodwill. Another twinge of guilt. She hadn't been to the nursery to see Tommy, her younger son. 'My dear Davis, I'm sorry.' Her maid had coughed quietly. 'I've changed my mind.'

'Madam?'

'I don't need you, after all. Just put out my grey lawn before luncheon. I'll change myself.'

Spinning girlishly about the room, she took two cachous from the delicate pink-and-white heart-shaped porcelain box on her boudoir table, put one in her mouth and the other in a silk drawstring purse. Then she picked up a fine bone comb and some tortoiseshell hairpins and took from the drawer of a satinwood smallboy two linen handkerchiefs, all of which went into the purse. Leaving her bedroom, she hummed a tune she'd heard one of the footmen whistling on the servants' stairs.

Criss-crossing the paths that led away from the house,

she saw that, in spite of the Indian summer, the grass was still wet with morning dew, glistening silver in the pale sun. Treading carefully, she stepped lightly from flagstone to flagstone to keep her highly polished kid boots dry. Usually her visits to the garden were made in the afternoon, when Thomas, somnolent from the effect of luncheon, had retired to his study. There would be discussions about the kitchen garden and how to deal with the invasion of the nuttery by the beautiful but voracious red squirrels. Vegetables would be ordered for the next day's meals and flowers chosen for the house from the cutting garden. As she approached, swinging her basket, she saw the head gardener outside the long greenhouse, talking to the estate carpenter. 'Good morning, Turner. Good morning, Mr Reade.' Head gardener Sam Reade's status in the hierarchy of the employees of Fiennders Abbey entitled him to his title. 'Look, Turner,' she held up her basket, 'one of your excellent baskets.'

'So I see, madam. That's from coppicing Old Barford Wood.' The carpenter was pleased at the compliment. She notices things, he thought. Doesn't only see to womanly things like flowers, sees to all things on the estate, just about. He touched his forelock and left, pushing a wheelbarrow full of planks.

'Jim Turner's quite taken to the idea of the gazebo. It's brought out the artist in him.' Sam watched the retreating figure. 'Anyways it's more of an interest than the usual repairs to the stables and like.'

'A little more than a gazebo, I'd thought.' Ann looked up at the tall strong figure.

'A folly then.' He turned and caught her gaze.

It was her turn to laugh.

'A folly?' she said lightly. 'Oh, surely not.'

He pointed to the smaller of the greenhouses. 'If you were looking for grapes to eat today the Muscats are ready.' They looked perfect, and Ann took the secateurs he offered her and reached up to a large ripe bunch, purple with a dull grey sheen on them.

As she stretched he admired the shape of her bosom, clearly defined in her dark riding habit. He thought, not for the first time, what a pretty woman she was. Masses of dark curling hair surrounding a face whose features all turned up a little, dark blue eyes, a small nose, and a mouth that was full and curved. He took the basket and scissors from her, wondering why she was here in the morning and dressed for riding.

'Would you take me to the clearing where the folly will be built? I want to be quite sure.' Initially disappointed, he walked ahead, the house and its formal gardens left behind as they made their way through a new plantation of beech, ash and elm trees. A hen pheasant flew up, startling her. 'Only protecting her young,' he said.

She leaned back against a young sapling, looking at him, and he put his hands on her shoulders then ran them down over her breasts. 'Ah, Ann,' he said as he embraced her, putting his arms around her and the young tree, pressing himself hard against the compliant body. He never addressed her as madam in public or in private. He called her Ann or nothing at all. 'Shall I take you here?' he whispered, as he kissed her neck above the primly buttoned jacket.

'Here,' she responded.

Kissing her slightly open mouth he tasted the sweet

scent of the cachou she had been sucking. He lifted her heavy skirt, caressed her thighs and touched her. He had never touched her without finding she wanted him. The modesty of her high white collar and the inaccessibility of the rest of her body excited him and he was soon inside her, stifling her little cries with his mouth. It was only when they were in the clearing discussing the folly that they both thought of their own folly, indulging their passion with so little care for discovery. He shivered: the sun was not as warm here and fear, too, made him cold. It wasn't fear for himself – he would always be all right. He could go to the border country or Wales where he had connections. His work here was admired, and he had no reason to be modest about his talent and achievements. But what would happen to her, so used to her position as wife to the county's leading landowner and mistress of Fiennders Abbey?

Ann stood in the centre of the clearing, turning slowly as she examined the dead trees, ancient hawthorn and juniper bushes. Sam was looking cold and aloof, she thought. It had been a good idea, though, to meet in the morning. He'd had no chance to sample his produce, which habit included taking bites out of an onion as if it were an apple. The cachou had been unnecessary.

'Trees will have to be cleared away, we'll need more light, and then there will be a wonderful view to the Downs.' We! She had said we! He smiled, the cold and fear forgotten.

Walking back to the house, carrying the almost forgotten basket of grapes, she felt like one of the swallows swooping and soaring, circling the rose-red brick, the earliest wings of the house; light, airy, happy. Her happiness was not coloured by guilt and she felt no shame. She thought herself an honourable woman. Her marriage was not loveless, and, indeed, she had grown to care for her husband deeply – but without passion. He hadn't been her choice, but when the offer of marriage was made she knew it was her duty to accept, and brought to Thomas not only her beauty but a good dowry of money and land. A believer in the rightness of dynasty, breeding and family, unlike some women in loveless, practical marriages, she had been faithful to her husband through five children, though his embarrassed and inept fumblings in bed had never roused her. After the last difficult birth, Tommy's, it was unlikely, the doctor had said, that she would have more children and Thomas, with no show of reluctance, had slept alone ever since. Ann suspected that he was as relieved as she. It was then that she had felt free to take a lover.

'How could you, you stupid girl? What did you use?'

Mary looked down at her hands, which were red and sore with bloodied nails where she had tried to clean them with a knife. 'Soda and spirit of hartshorn,' she mumbled, trying to stop her tears. His anger had shocked her.

'Soda? Caustic soda?' He looked at her in disbelief. 'Why don't you wash your face with it as well?' he shouted.

They had been sitting precariously on top of a half-made hayrick in the corner of a hot, still field. The horse on which he'd been teaching her to ride was tethered to a sloe tree in the hedge and was whinnying softly to a team of horses pulling a plough two fields away. She twisted her hands in her apron. 'Maybe I will for nobody cares what I look like,' she said defiantly, not asking for sympathy. 'And my hands will always be wanting, for they're collecting stones at dawn and scrubbing the dishes at dusk.'

Suddenly she pushed herself to the edge of the hay-rick, slithered down, and began to run across the field. He caught up with her at the top of Paradise Hill, leading his horse by the reins. 'I care,' he said, folding one of her mutilated little hands in his and putting both in his pocket. He couldn't look at her – he was overwhelmed with a feeling he couldn't understand. Years later he was to remember that feeling, a feeling he had never had for the handsome, high-coloured woman who sat opposite him at the dinner table.

They walked on in silence, down the hill, which was surrounded by a patchwork of fields growing oats, barley, wheat and lucerne all set in their own thick hedges. 'Do you know why this is called Paradise Hill?' she asked.

'Because it's high, near to heaven?' He was intrigued.

'No.'

'Because it's beautiful?'

'Noooo.' She drew out the word, teasing him.

He thought for a while. 'Got it!' he yelled. 'It was owned by a man, a father, pa, who had red eyes. Pa-red-eyes Hill.'

She laughed and pushed him. 'You silly.' Carefully she explained, 'It's really called Sparrows' Dice. You see lots of sparrows here and they dice, they play.'

'Lovely, Mary, I like that.' He took her hand and laid it gently against his cheek.

★

'Ho there, John,' called one of the old cottagers as the keeper passed, pointing to the leather bag slung across his shoulder. 'You've got a nice brace or two of partridge there, no wonder.'

'Ay, I have that, Jack, and I dursay you've had one or two in your pot, thanks to your grandson's slingshot.'

The old man winked and cackled, the cackle turning to a cough. He knew John Bowden wouldn't miss a bird or two, as long as it was for the pot and not for selling to outsiders, townfolk and the like, and as long as the shot was clean. The keeper loved his birds but accepted their death as part of the yearly cycle. What he would not accept was a wounded bird. The old man's daughter appeared at the cottage door, two young children clinging to her skirts.

'You doan' wanna mind him, Mr Bowden, he's daft in the head, doan' know what he's talking about.' She smiled nervously, slapping at the two children. 'Leave me be, you two.'

John Bowden was embarrassed. She was welcome to an occasional bird, as far as he was concerned. Sally was a twenty-three-year-old widow with those two little ones and no income. Her father a permanent invalid with farmer's lung, she had to manage with what little she could earn from stone-gathering, mending sacks and other odd bits of farm work. John had seen her at the harvest, working alongside the men, them with their scythes and the few women with their sickles. The gleaning after the crop was in must have seemed like a holiday after that. She had a large family of sisters scattered all over England in service and they spared a few coppers when they could, but it wasn't regular.

The garden was ill-kempt, a few potatoes, turnips, parsnips, that was all, and they needed hoeing, no sign of a flower except for the dog rose gradually being choked by the creeping columbine. Had she not been a pretty plump woman, the cottage wives would have allowed their husbands to turn a hand in the garden – they all thought of themselves as good neighbours – but as it was, a young widow with a pleasing way, no, too dangerous. 'Don't you worry.' He smiled at her. 'Just you make sure it don't become a habit and tell the young 'un to stick to rabbits.' He shifted the weight of the leather bag on his back, tucked his gun in the crook of his arm, and walked on down the lane, the russet, red and gold of the autumn trees darkening to amber and purple in the twilight. It had been a good day's shooting, first of the season, and he was pleased with himself, the quiet satisfaction of a job well done, and appreciated too. The master never stinted with his praise when all went well, and he'd been mightily pleased, and amused as well, when Lord Colcroft had offered in jest to double the keeper's wages and halve his hours if he'd come over to Colcroft Park. Later, after they'd all eaten their lunch, brought up from the house by cart – the gentry served in the long barn with steak and oyster pie, the beaters and loaders taking their bread, cheese and beer leaning against the wheels of the cart – Lord Colcroft had suggested it wasn't all in jest. John had laughed and been bold enough to say, 'Poaching is poaching, m'lord, whether it's a partridge or a person.'

The flickering light of the fire from the forge reminded him of his own hearth. Young George Jackson was working late, but he was toiling for himself, just about: when old George was gone the business would be his, and rightly so. John sighed and quickened his pace, he was looking forward to his supper and the warm cottage, but not to sitting there in the cold silence. It was more than two weeks now since their terrible row, one of their worst, and always, always, about the same thing: money, security, work. She would never say how much she had saved or where it was, and their exchange of words had been bitter. He'd accused her of degrading his position and the whole family, especially Mary. The bad feelings had gone on, affecting them all, Albert confused and crying, Mary nervous and quiet and Hannah off with her friends, dawdling home from school, and out of the house as soon as she'd eaten. Usually he was able to manage Emma but this time his anger had overcome him, when he remembered how she had treated Mary.

He had seen his daughter sitting against the far hedge in Netheracres field, her bonnet pulled forward. The other women and the children were all eating but Mary seemed to be examining her hands. She looked up as he approached, hearing some of the women calling to her good-naturedly.

'Look you, Mary, your dad's here for to help.'

'Well then, keeper, are you come to give us a hand?'

'Now then, John Bowden, gleaning is woman's work.'

One of the younger ones shouted to Emma further up the field, 'Aren't you got enough that your old man's come to help?' But her voice softened as she addressed the keeper himself, a handsome man in her opinion. 'Mr Bowden, sir, leave us our leazings, pray.'

Mary jumped to her feet and groaned, putting a hand to her back. 'Why aren't you eating, child? Are you not hungry?' She looked down at her lunch, unwrapped but forgotten. 'I am, yes, Pa.' She picked up the slab of bread thickly spread with rosemary-scented lard and started to eat.

He was concerned, she was looking at her hands again and had winced. 'Do your hands hurt, Mary? Are you tired?'

'Not really, Pa, don't you worry.'

'You don't have to do this, you know. I'll speak to your mother, you do enough.'

'It's all right,' she said, frowning, watching her mother and Hannah, their lunch finished, working further up the field. 'I don't mind doing this, it's friendly like, all of us.' She gestured at the women and girls, who were chattering even while bent over the stubble swiftly picking up the wheat ears with one hand and transferring them to a growing bunch in the other.

'You don't mind *this*, you say. What *do* you mind, Mary?'

'Nothing.' She turned away. 'The stones,' she wanted to cry, 'the stones, they're heavy, they cut my hands,' but the little money from clearing the fields meant so much to her mother, pleased her, and she didn't want to be the cause of another sad fight between her parents, so again she repeated, 'Nothing.' But her father had guessed from her unconscious glance at the flint-strewn earth.

'I miss the corn when it's cut,' she said, looking at their cottage a few fields away. 'It's like a huge yellow blanket shining through our windows.'

'Where's Bertie, then?' He squinted against the sun up the field where his wife was working with Hannah, gathering what had been missed by the horse-drawn rakes.

'He's off yonder,' she pointed to the far hedge, 'with the Middlecombe boys, picking crab-apples and sloes.'

'I see, your mother's got him working already,' he said sharply.

Mary smiled. 'Don't take on, Pa. Bertie'll work at anything that'll end up in his tummy.'

It was later that evening after tea that the badness happened. Bertie had seen Mary and Hannah leave by the kitchen door carrying a bucket. 'Where are you going?' he asked sleepily.

'We're collecting snails for the pig,' said Hannah. 'Ugh, slimy snails,' she added.

'Why, Hanny? Give pig tea, Ma.' He beamed at his laughing mother, pleased with his idea of sharing the cold bacon and currant and apple duff they'd been eating.

'Well, son,' she said, kissing him, 'that wouldn't be very kind, we don't give like to like.'

Bertie was confused. 'Pig not like our tea? I like it.'

'The pig likes snails,' Mary said as she left. 'He'll eat all he can get and then be nice and fat for all our teas next year.'

'Wait, wait,' he called, his sleepiness forgotten. 'I'll help.' Pausing at the door, he looked anxiously at his parents. 'Can I help Hanny and Mary? And the pig,' he added, as an afterthought.

'You go on, Bertie,' his father said. 'Not too late, mind, and tell the girls, not too far. As the man, I'm putting you in charge.'

'No, John, he should be up to his bed.'

'Just this once, Emma.' Bertie stood waiting, exploding with excitement and pride, not daring yet to believe his luck. 'Shoo, Bertie.' He was gone before any further discussion could take away his new manhood.

'Not like you, John.' Emma sat in front of the dying fire, but her husband lifted her gently and took her place, sitting her on his lap.

'It's good to be alone together for a change. I want to talk to you, my love.'

The moon was only in its first quarter but the warm apricot glow was enough to light the hedgerows. Mary put out the light of the lantern to save the wick and the oil. The snails had left clear silvery trails in the moonlight and they were soon filling the bucket. Bertie, unused to being out at this hour, was distracted from the search by the owls hooting to each other and the mysterious difference that night made to his familiar countryside. 'What's that?' He clutched Hannah's arm, pointing to a large dark shape looming in the distance.

'That's only the sheepcote, silly.' A couple of shadowy figures appeared from the cote.

'Big sheep,' Bertie said, trying to control his quavering voice.

His sisters laughed, but Mary put her arm protectively round his shoulder. 'Them's no sheep,' Hannah said, giving Mary a knowing look. 'They've been courting.' The shapes disappeared back into the cote.

Sheltering in Mary's arms, Bertie spoke in his most manly voice, 'Not too far, Pa said.'

'No, all right, love, we'll walk back the other side of the hedge.' The three made their way home, easing off the snails that clung to leaves and twigs like suction pads.

Small bats whirled above their heads; like the owls, they ate late and were looking for supper.

They could hear the raised voices only yards from the cottage. Instinctively Mary took Bertie's hand, making a face at Hannah. They stood behind the hedge, too frightened to go home.

'You sold the harvest goose,' they heard their father shout. 'It's a mark of our position, Emma, that the farmer gives it.' They couldn't hear her reply but he continued, 'That money brings shame on us, as do the coppers my little girls get from the field stones and I forbid it, woman. My master—'

They heard her reply to that, in a shrill voice that was hard to relate to their usually gentle and loving mother. 'Your master, you fool, won't keep you when you can't be keeper.'

Bertie trembled and clung tightly to his sister's hand. 'We must go in soon,' Hannah whispered. 'Let's go back aways and start singing so's they hears us.' They retraced their steps, then ran down the grassy lane, Hannah with the bucket and Mary with the lantern, swinging Bertie between them and singing 'All Things Bright and Beautiful'. They were hot and breathless when they burst into the cottage, but John knew they had heard for Bertie's little face was near tears, and after feeding the pig, Mary and Hannah scurried to bed.

John Bowden turned the corner from the lane into the track that led to Keepers Cottage, dimly lit in the distance. To his right across Threeacre Field, an old tithe barn was illuminated by the gibbous moon; it would be a full one by the end of the week, he reckoned. A well-trodden footpath led to the barn and then across the field, after which it became a green lane skirting the side of a beacon hill, then a proper made-up road which led to the new turnpike and thence to Oxford. Before his marriage, that path had been the promise of escape, Oxford, the word that meant freedom. But escape and freedom from what? This countryside, so beautiful, in which he worked with pleasure? The natural feeling of the land and its care, put back what you take out, knowledge passed from father to son? Freedom? Escape? Those were a young man's feelings. Now he had responsibilities. He looked again at the barn – full of what? Straw for bedding down animals? Hay for their feed? Flax from the delicate blue-flowered linseed? No, he remembered, it was mainly barley – he had taught Bertie to recognize the curving grass-like leaf – with some hay. He hastened his step home. He had made up his mind.

The cold, stern figure of his wife turned away as he stooped and entered the cottage. 'Mary, Hannah,' she called as she went to the fire, 'your father's home.' She took four earthenware dishes, which were warming on a trivet by the hearth, and ladled soup into them from the black cauldron hanging on a chain over the fire. The girls appeared from the back door; they had been plucking and cleaning two cockerels, slaughtered that morning. They were hungry, their father later than usual, but their greetings were subdued. Only Mary asked him how the first day's shoot went. 'Well,' he said, with satisfaction. 'It went well. Four hundred brace shot and look . . .' he opened his game bag, 'two brace of partridge and a good hare.' The sisters were surprised to see him smiling and in a good temper, though he didn't address his wife. For the last two weeks the animosity between their parents had been painful to observe, the tentative overtures of father to mother being received with silence or a few curt, dismissive words.

'And good tips too.' He slapped his pocket, making the coins jingle. Emma set the four dishes on the table in silence and cut four slices of bread while Hannah hung the game in the larder. 'Bertie asleep?'

'Yes, Pa.'

'How did he get on at school?'

'All right, I suppose.'

Hannah picked up her spoon and started her pea soup. She had forgotten Bertie had been at school in the excitement of preparing for the harvest festival. Wheat-sheaves were being woven, baskets of apples polished and bread baked in plaits, all to decorate the church. 'You must give eye to him, Hanny,' John said, dipping his bread in the soup, 'as Mary give eye to you when you started.'

Mary laughed. 'She needed more than an eye, did Hannah, she needed four eyes, or better still a rope to tether her.'

Her sister wasn't put out by this. 'True, Pa, I was worse nor than the boys. All the same, though, my sums is good.'

Mary nodded. 'Best in school, Miss Crewe says. You come to it natural, but you work too, Hanny.'

'You too, Mary, your roots is good,' Hannah said, 'leastways your Latin ones.' She didn't know what she was talking about but wanted to return the rare compliment: roots, as far as she was concerned, meant parsnips, carrots and turnips.

John pushed away his dish and addressed his wife for the first time. 'I see you've finished too, Mother.' He turned to his daughters. 'Your mother and I are going for a walk. You clear away now, won't you, and then up to bed.' He rose from the table and fetched his jacket. 'Get your mother's coat and shawl—'

Emma interrupted, 'No need, either of you, I won't be going for a walk.' She started to clear the dishes. 'This time of night, pitchy dark and cold too.'

'Get the coat and shawl, Mary, please. It's not so cold, Emma, and the moon's high.' He used a tone of voice there was no brooking, and Emma banged the dishes back on the table and accepted the shawl ungraciously.

She walked quickly, a pace or two ahead. 'We're going to Adams' barn,' he said, catching her up. 'Can't talk out here.'

He didn't take her arm, or look at her, and she was surprised by both his force and detachment. 'Nothing to talk about,' she said coldly.

They reached the barn in silence. Rearranging some of the sweet-smelling hay, he gestured for her to sit. He examined her face dispassionately. She was a good-looking woman still: the same milk-blonde hair as her daughters, though less bright, somehow, and the same surprising brown eyes. The face was spoiled by a mouth once delicately curved but now narrow-lipped and downturned. 'If you think, Emma, that after fifteen years of marriage we have only grudges and silences, then it's clear we have no marriage.' He made the statement as a matter of fact and as if the fact didn't bother him.

Startled, she jumped to her feet. 'What are you saying,

John?' It was the first time she'd used his Christian name since the night of their vicious argument.

'I came home tonight because of my children. I was tempted on the way, but I put them first.'

She shrugged, and said automatically, 'Trust a man to put the ale-house before his family.'

He hadn't been thinking of the Bull and Butcher but more of the appeal of young Sally. 'No, woman, you can't accuse me of spending time and money there.'

She knew it to be true and sank back on the hay, drawing her shawl around her. She felt an unaccustomed stab of fear. 'What, then?' Her voice faltered.

'I was a contented man today, pleased with my work, knowing my lot to be fortunate.' He paused, opening the barn door a little, surveying the fields lit by the golden hump-backed moon, now at its highest, causing the trees to cast long, feathery shadows. ''Tis beautiful here, by God,' he murmured softly. Turning away abruptly from the beguiling scene, he spoke harshly. 'But that soon changed when I thought of the evening ahead with you,' he shook his head in disbelief, 'the woman I had loved.'

She echoed the past tense of his last word. 'Loved, John? No more? If it's because of the stones, that's done with, for Mary herself has refused.' She rose, brushing strands of hay from her skirt. 'Oh, I can see you talk behind my back,' she said bitterly, 'turning my children from me.'

'No, woman, you do it yourself.' His voice was raised but he didn't shout. 'I thought, once, you was careful, a good manager, fine things in a wife, but it's become a sickness, Emma. I'm frightened for you.' He stepped away from her, examining her as if she were a stranger.

'Oh, I see now, of course, it was always there. "Frightened of the dogs", you said, but no, you weren't frightened. If they were kennelled up at the big house there'd be no cost for feeding. Selling the game I have by right for feeding my family, keeping to the flint and tinder box instead of matches. You even made money from the miller and sold him our flour after the gleaning.'

'Mebbe,' she said, defending herself, 'but 'twas I that broke my back in the fields and 'twas I that threshed the corn.'

'It was you right enough – and the girls.' Now he was shouting. 'But the girls got no money for their pains. Good God, woman, even the poorest cottager uses the oil or candles and you, you, in the name of thrift, still use a wick in a saucer of tallow when I'm out of the house, I know it . . .' he grimaced with disgust, 'for I smell the fat. No mother you've been to Mary, making her a slavey, and no wife you've been to me.' He knew that was unfair, that he exaggerated, but he wanted to keep a distance from her, to remember the coldness, the secrecy, the penny-pinching, not the girl that still existed in her, the way she stifled her laugh at little Bertie's odd ways, and not the memory of her welcoming his body before the practicality of their love-making had made him indifferent. 'I've put out my hand to you, Emma, time after time, to heal the breach but—'

'I know, I know.' Her voice was muffled by the shawl she held over her mouth.

'But it's too late.'

'Are you leaving us, then?'

He was surprised at the question. 'Of course not, I couldn't leave the children with you.' This cruelty frightened her more than a blow would have. Trembling, she stuttered, 'Could not leave . . . with me . . . I've done it all . . . for them . . . for you . .' Her voice trailed away. 'What do you want, John?' Still trembling, she let her shawl fall to the ground and clumsily pulled at the buttons on her bodice. 'Is it this?'

He looked at the creamy whiteness of her exposed breasts with the delicate blue veins that he used to trace lovingly with his finger. 'Were that all I needed, Emma, I could lie with a woman when I wanted. I understand, you know,' he said sadly, 'but all those bad times were long ago and your grandparents dead and buried. Cover yourself, my love.' She looked up at him pathetically, unable to move. 'I haven't been the man for you,' he sighed, 'not given you what you needed – safety, I don't know.'

She shook her head violently. 'Not so, John, I wouldn't have had other.' Strands of her fine hair fell loose from her bun as she tried to rebutton her bodice. He removed her hands tenderly and fastened the buttons, but it was the gesture of a friend not of a lover. She stood defenceless before him, but she said with some dignity, 'I would like you to stay with us, John. For me as well as the children. And if it be I would try to start anew.'

Mary sat at the window, straining her eyes to the far horizon. She was tired and cold but knew she couldn't sleep till they returned. Perhaps it was a good omen that they had been gone so long. Hannah was fast asleep and Bertie, too, in his little bed in the corner, his thumb still firmly in place in his mouth. She had banked down the fire with the ashes: it would be safe but warm when they returned and the embers would last all night. Her head jerked up from near sleep. Were those shadows moving? She rubbed the window-pane where her breath had misted it. It was them – their shadows were as long as the trees. Her mother was wearing her shawl over her head, it must be really cold now, and his hands were deep in his pockets. Not holding hands, that was sad. Mary drew back from the window, out of sight, but not before she'd seen her father pat his wife's shoulder affectionately before opening the door. She slid quietly into bed alongside the still sleeping Hannah and, turning on her side and raising her knees, she tucked her long flannel night-dress round her cold feet.

Downstairs, Emma knelt at the fire, chose two small logs and placed them safely at the back. John smiled. He'd never known her let the fire stay in all night. She put up a hand and pulled him down to her, embracing him and lifting her face to be kissed. He whispered to her softly, feeling the breasts which hadn't tempted him in the barn. 'You're not doing this to please me?'

'No, John, it's for to please us both.'

He was awake long after she had fallen asleep. The moon had set and their bedroom was dark, the optimism of the previous hours was fading away. But he would keep his part of the agreement and hope she would keep hers. He'd had sense enough to give as well as take, allowing that she should keep the money she'd saved for it would be like taking a crutch away from a cripple. He was to use his tips from the shoots for the pony and trap, offered by Mr Fiennders at a good price. The girls were not to be sent for maid's work at the big house, only at Home Farm dairy, but, like Emma, they could do fine needle-work when wanted. Reluctantly he'd seen the sense of selling the extra vegetables and jams but had insisted the money should pay for herrings and the like when Fishy Aitkens' cart called in the village, and for dresses and boots, not hobnailed, for his girls. 'Use your needles for yourselves,' he'd said.

The scent of the burning logs, applewood from the orchard, drifted up the stairs, he turned to face the back of his sleeping wife who reached for his hand in her sleep drawing it around her. Had the battle really been won – or had this been just another skirmish?

Thomas Fiennders held the coins in his hand: two sover-eigns, six crowns, florins, shillings and coppers, it amoun-ted to eight pounds. He had asked thirty guineas for the pony and trap, a fair price, but not unduly generous.

'Thank you, John, I'm glad you've decided to have the trap. It will make life easier for you and your family. Living away from the village has many advantages but some drawbacks, especially for the ladies.' The keeper and his master exchanged a conspiratorial smile. They both had strong wives who were wilful in their different ways. It seemed that Bowden had overruled his wife's usual parsimony for what could hardly be called a luxury. The dignity with which the keeper conducted himself com-pared favourably with the cunning, cap-in-hand attitude of Farmer Adams this morning. He had complained, rightly enough, about the reduced grain prices, but had used that as a lever not only to get his rent lowered but to obtain easements for various repairs to barns and fences that Thomas felt would not be carried out. Sly, that's what Adams is, he thought. Would he have been as loyal as John Bowden? Charlie Colcroft had told him rather shamefacedly about the keeper's reply to his offer, 'Poaching is poaching whether it's partridge or people.' Good answer, good man.

John waited for his master to speak again, comfortable, though, in his silence. He liked this room. It was – right. Not like the long drawing room he'd glimpsed, with its painted pink and green panelling and dainty furniture.

'So, sir, if it's agreeable to you, I'll take the trap home this evening and the rest of the thirty guineas will be yours by quarter day.'

Thomas picked up one of the documents lying on his heavy oak desk; the feel of the smooth, ivory-coloured vellum gave him almost as much pleasure as the contents. 'You see this, John?' He handed him the scroll. 'De Fin. My name, the family name in the thirteenth century, when the Abbey was still an Abbey.'

The keeper handled the paper carefully, conscious of his rough hands. 'That's a wonderful thing to have, sir. You know houses can last, but a man's writing, well . . . that's more wondrous. Writing by your own forefather.'

Thomas Fiennders pointed to the papers on his desk. 'Maps, lists, documents, it's all there. Farms, fields, woods, cottages, the dower house, all there. Changes to this house. More changes to come, no doubt.' He got up and walked to the long casement window. 'Thirty guineas, did you say, John?'

'Yes, sir, thirty guineas,' he said anxiously. He wouldn't want to be indebted for more.

'Look.' His master beckoned him over and pointed to the view outside the windows. 'See those fields? They'll be planted with vetch near the house, barley up along twelve-acre, linseed above the brook, and corn where the horses are, but that is *this* year. Next year . . .' His voice trailed away. John wondered uneasily what this was leading to. He knew times were bad for farmers, but the usual reckoning was that good times tided over the bad ones. 'Next year, Adams will have to take a lot of this out of cultivation.'

'More pasture, will it be, sir? Increase the dairy herd?'

'No, I think he'll let it lie fallow.' He glanced at one of the ledgers lying open on a side table. 'Bloody stupid, importing cheap foreign grain. It kills the value of land.'

'Are you worried, sir?'

The man's reaction was that of a friend, Thomas thought, with his simple question and look of concern. 'Not so much for myself, for farmers, Adams, of course. And landowners like Lord Colcroft, the Osmunds, Jack Bexley-Wright, Berreford. Their incomes, you see, are based on rents.'

John was puzzled. 'The Duke of Berreford and the likes, sir, don't they have a bit put by?'

Thomas remembered seeing the rather large 'bit put by' lost at the gaming tables by Ralph Berreford. 'Not enough, I fear.' He slammed the ledger shut. 'Fortunately, my income isn't solely yielded by my holdings in Buckinghamshire and Oxfordshire. My wife brought into the family lands in Shropshire and Nottinghamshire.'

'Ah, yes, sir.' John was knowing about that. 'Coal

mines, that's a good thing.' Thomas left the window and returned to his desk.

'Those coal mines have been added to this inventory, pit shafts next to Larkspur Meadows.' He looked again at the coins on his desk and arranged them in neat piles. 'Well, John, the beauty of Shropshire is sacrificed to the beauty of Oxfordshire.'

'Mebbe, sir, but it brings good with it, employment for the miners, coal for our fires, and it keeps the mills and foundries working.'

'Well put, John! We can't be sentimental.' He pulled the green onyx inkstand towards him, chose a new nib and slotted it in the head of the wooden holder. 'Master Richard will be home for Friday to Monday, so he'll join us on Saturday. Get him a good loader, won't you?'

'Yes, sir.' John sensed the conversation was over and walked to the door.

'Not thirty guineas, you know, that was your mistake.' Thomas Fiennders spoke without looking up. 'Thirteen guineas, and yes, by Lady Day will be suitable.'

The pony was a young, high-spirited chestnut, barely broken in. He was trying to throw off the shafts of the little carriage as if they were a blanket. Emma sat in the passenger seat with Bertie on her lap. He was squealing, but with excitement not fear. John had laid the reins gently on the pony's back and jerked the bit, but neither had persuaded the animal to move forward.

Mary broke a long stick off a hazel tree in the hedge and handed it to her mother. 'You smack its rump, and me and Hanny, we'll run ahead holding the harness.'

When she and her sister were ready at either side of the bucking pony, she shouted, 'Now.' Emma smacked, they ran, and the pony took off at a gallop. The little trap splashed through the puddles, rocking in the deep ruts, and was soon nearly out of sight. The girls chased after it, their skirts hitched up to their knees, laughing and stumbling, but when they turned the corner into the long lane leading to the village it had disappeared.

'Thank the Lord for you, George, else we'd have been in Wellsbury instead of Findlesham.' Emma handed Bertie down to young Billy.

'Give us the reins, Mrs Bowden, and jump down. He's all right now, wore out, I expect.' George took the sweating pony out of the shafts and tethered him to an iron ring by a horses' trough, where he drank greedily. 'He's young, a bit raw, but he'll do nicely. A new shoe needed there on his foreleg, that's all. It's a funny old thing this, though.' He took a good look at the trap. 'More of a contraption than a trap. Looks like they was making a cart and changed their minds half way through.'

'Traption,' Bertie nodded, agreeing.

'Do you think it dangerous then, George?' John was disappointed. 'I had thought Mary could use it when she brings in the vegetables, 'specially with winter coming on.' They all walked around what was forever to be known as The Traption, in Bertie's translation.

'No, it's a rare thing, but well made, useful. I wouldn't like her taking it out yet, Mr Bowden, not before I've had a chance to break in the pony to the shafts and give Mary a lesson or two.'

'That's kind, George. It would put our minds at rest, wouldn't it, John?'

'Here she comes.' George pointed down the lane where the girls were approaching, half running. 'They must be worn out.' He untethered the pony and threw a blanket on him. 'You stable him, Billy. It's coming on to rain, I reckon, so you must all come in to tea.'

Emma started to refuse, 'No, no, George, thank you, but we'll get back home,' just as John knew she would. She never had accepted invitations: it would mean returning the hospitality, and that cost money. One of her sayings that saddened him was, 'What you don't get, you don't have to thank people for.'

'Well, Mary, Hannah, you see everyone's alive,' George made an expansive gesture to include the pony, 'and you're coming in for your tea.'

'Now then, George,' Emma tried again, 'it wouldn't be fair on your aunt at such short notice.'

George ignored this. 'You two young ladies,' he said, admiring the colour in Mary's usually pale cheeks, and the tendrils of hair escaping her thick woollen bonnet, 'are in a lather, much like the pony, so I says you're to be tethered, watered, blanketed and given some oats.' He roared with laughter, pleased with his joke.

'You wouldn't get away with treatment like that, my lad,' John Bowden warned, 'these fillies are unbroken, they might kick.' Even Emma laughed at that.

A pitter-patter of rain settled the matter and George ushered them through the forge and into the house. 'Aunt Biddy will be glad of the company, Mrs Bowden.'

Emma was flustered: now there was no choice. 'It's good of you, George, but we must return the kindness.

John, you must get a couple of brace of pheasants for the Jacksons after the shoot.' Mary winced, ashamed at her mother's lack of grace.

'I'm not against the barter system, Mrs Bowden, if it makes you more comfortable. There's many a piece of iron that's been wrought and many a horse shod here that's been paid for in kind.' He put his hand lightly on Mary's shoulder, guiding her, and was rewarded with a grateful smile.

The pony took them home at a sedate trot. It wasn't easy for him to go any faster now that he was pulling the whole family. Bertie slept, lying across his sisters' laps in the back as they whispered about the unexpected treat. In the front, their parents caught occasional excited words.

'Jellied beef on an ordinary day.'

'D'you think . . . every day?'

'Rice flummery, mmm.'

'With cream.'

Emma pushed away a little pang of guilt, remembering that Biddy paid for the food in exchange for the roof over her head.

'They were my jellies Aunt Biddy served.'

John pressed her knee. 'They're the best in the village, that's why.' He carefully guided the pony round the sharp bend. 'Home, Mother. You take the lantern and get in before it rains again, I'll unhitch the pony and let him into the field.'

He leant over the five-bar gate, thinking about the evening, the easy hospitality of the Jackson family, money not much of a worry for them, owning the house and forge, not affected by those Enclosure Acts. He smiled in the darkness, thinking of Aunt Biddy, her own woman, all right – the little nest-egg gave her independence. Lucky the Jacksons were to have her when Nelly died so sudden – she was a good kinswoman. All that talk of hers, interesting it was, about Joseph Arch, the farm-hands' champion. It was the only time old man Jackson came alive, speaking against Arch and his like, and Emma joining with him, both of them feared at the thought of a revolution, like in France in the last century gone. But Biddy knew more and spoke well, too, although, as she said, money gave you freedom of speech.

'The labourers will need a champion, especially now. Don't you think the likes of Thomas Fiennders will suffer from low corn prices, no, not as much as Farmer Adams and he not as much as the hands.'

'And you not at all, Aunt Biddy, so give us men some home brew for we're suffering from thirst.'

John felt in his pocket for the tract she'd given him when he left. Better not worry Emma with that.

She was alone in the dairy at midday, having chosen to finish churning the butter rather than join the family for lunch.

Mrs Adams had been grateful enough to make her feel guilty. 'You're a good girl, Mary, a bigger help nor than my own family and the girls too grand for the dairy.' She had bidden her take a jug of cream home when she'd finished. Working fast, but with care to make sure the butter wasn't over-churned and watery, she finished the two large churns of cream and took a small pail of buttermilk into the cold room that separated the milking parlour from the dairy. She put the pail on a well-scrubbed pine table next to the window, turned back her cuffs and rolled up her sleeves. She looked out of the window to make sure nobody was about, then put her hands deep into the buttermilk. When she withdrew them little creamy globules clung to her skin. She rubbed them into her hands. Dipping her hands in again she smeared them on her face looking at her barely visible reflection in the window.

The sudden sound of the dairy door opening made her snatch a pile of butter-muslin and hastily wipe her face and hands. She carried an old chipped china jug through to the dairy, expecting to see Mrs Adams or one of the young maids. 'I've finished now,' she called, 'and I'll be taking – Richard!'

'I'm glad you've finished because I want to talk to you.' Mary flung her arms round him with her usual enthusiastic greeting. 'Where shall we go? It's too damp and misty to be outside.'

'Don't know,' she said doubtfully. 'The granary's full, and the barns. How long are you home? It isn't Christmas, so why? And Mrs Adams says I'm to take cream home.' She held up the jug.

'In order,' he said grinning. 'Until Monday. It's an exeat, and get your cream quickly – come on.'

She ladled the thick yellowy cream into her jug. He was carrying a parcel, she saw. Maybe it was another Latin primer – good, the old one was out of reach now until the granary emptied.

They walked through the wet leaves; the mist had thickened to fog in patches and the acrid smell was intensified by a wetly smouldering bonfire. 'It's a sort of garden house, Pa said,' she felt for the word, 'a gabbo, a gasbo?'

'A gazebo.'

'Yes, that's it, the carpenter's making it for your mother,' she said, calling over her shoulder.

'She didn't say anything.' He held the parcel carefully, shielding it with his arm against the moisture dripping from the few leaves still left on the trees, as he followed her. She was walking awkwardly, the jug of cream under her cape. 'Do you have to hurry back for your dinner?'

'No, they're out. Mamma, Issy and Jess are in Oxford, shopping, and Papa took the carriage over to Great Giddesly to see the steward.'

Mary accepted all this. She knew about exeats, that was Latin, not hard, really, just like exit. That the Fiennders ladies would buy shoes, hairpins, materials in Oxford was not surprising or that the coachman would drive them in the coach and four. That Mr Fiennders would take his shiny, comfortable, well-sprung carriage pulled by two horses to visit the man who took care of his estate was not unusual either. Had any of these references been to herself or the Bowden family, that would have been rare, as rare as hen's teeth, she thought, and laughed so much she nearly spilt the cream. 'There, see?' She pointed to a pretty wooden octagonal structure on the edge of the clearing. 'It's like one of your gatehouses only smaller.' They peered inside.

No panes of glass had yet been fixed in the windows and only a plank blocked the doorway, but otherwise it was nearly finished. There was a fireplace, already laid for lighting, two comfortable chairs and a garden table with an oil-lamp sitting on it.

'It's a strange place to have a gazebo, so far from the house,' he said, looking around. 'Sit down, Mary.' He wound up the wick of the lamp and lit it. The light glimmered softly through the pale rose of its glass shade.

'Give me the matches and I'll do the fire.' She knelt at the hearth, reaching up to him for the matches.

'Sit down,' he said firmly. 'You should *not* do that.' He bent and struck a match. The fire caught immediately. 'You see,' he said, delighted with his success, 'I'm good at fires.'

'Oh, no, Richard, whoever laid that fire is good at fires.' She stretched out her feet, in their heavy boots, towards the flame.

'Rubbish,' he said, sitting opposite her. He leant forward and shyly put the parcel on her lap.

'For me?' He nodded.

'Another primer?'

'No, not a book. Open it.'

'I don't understand.' She looked puzzled.

'It's a present, that's all,' he said, with a shrug. 'Open it.'

Inside the plain brown-paper wrapper was more wrapping, this time a deep blue paper with gold printing: ANSON & BROOKS, HIGH STREET, WINDSOR, and a little drawing, which she didn't understand, and V.R. It was tied with delicate gold cord, the knot stamped with navy blue sealing-wax. 'Open it,' he said eagerly, his veneer of sophistication gone. Carefully she broke the seal and painstakingly untied the cord, which itself was a present to her. She folded back the paper to reveal a slim leather case and glanced up at him, her wide eyes copper-coloured in the firelight.

'Open it,' he insisted, leaning forward and releasing the small gold catch.

'Oh, no, I can't believe it, Richard. It's really mine?' She didn't want to look at it again, until he'd confirmed her ownership.

'It's yours, you goose, it's yours, Mary.' The case was lined with soft, cream-coloured chamois leather and contained different silver implements with ivory handles, all neatly slotted in their own compartments. She removed the nail file and smoothed the end of her thumbnail. Returning it, she took out a tiny plump chamois cushion, backed with ivory, and hesitated. Taking it from her he held her hand and buffed the top of her nails until they shone. Then he extracted what looked like a tiny silver shovel which, he demonstrated, was for pushing back her cuticles. Gradually they experimented with all the little tools, and replaced them in the case.

'For me?' she repeated. 'For me?'

'Who else?'

'I don't know.' Her voice hovered between tears and excitement. 'I can't get used to it. Maybe your sisters.'

He snorted derisively. 'Not them. Look at it, all of it – the case I mean. You'll see it's for you.' Examining every detail carefully, she finally discovered, behind the top left-hand corner of the chamois leather, M.B., embossed discreetly in a dull gold.

Sam Reade had seen the wisp of smoke curling through the damp leaden sky. It could have been a signal, but the potential signaller was in Oxford. And the smoke wasn't from a bonfire: the floating grey column was too narrow. He approached the garden house, noiseless on the carpet of wet leaves, circling it from the cover of yew trees and holly, still green among the bare branches of deciduous oak and ash. There was someone in there, all right, a couple, a woman it looked like, wearing a white bonnet, funny that, this time of year. Reading, it seemed. And a man, was it? Difficult to tell. You could hear laughter, young they sounded, and the man, yes, it was a man, touched the woman's face. Sam smiled. The world was full of lovers. No harm done, they'd never know, or find it, even the carpenter hadn't found it. The secret within a secret was for him and his love, his lady – his lady-love as she should rightly be called. The couple were standing now, damping down the fire. The woman, more of a girl, really, had a jug as well as the book. They must be leaving. He melted back into the woods, out of sight but still able to see.

Richard replaced the plank against the doorway. 'It's nearly dark. I'll walk with you to the top of Drover's Lane.'

'No, don't you bother, I know my way well enough.' She tried to hitch up her skirts to clear the wet earth but was afraid of dropping the case and spilling the cream.

'Here, let me help.' She held out the jug, thinking he was going to take it, but he dipped a finger in the cream and drew a stripe down the centre of her nose.

'Yes, yes, I can see the difference. Amazing! The beauty of Findlesham women will be known far and wide. You'll be known as the Buttermilk Beauty.' He stopped laughing and took the jug from her before she had a chance to throw it at him.

'You are a – a – a churl . . . a *foul beast*. I should never have told you.'

'My dear Mary, with your hair festooned with gobbets of buttermilk you had to tell me.' He wiped the cream off her nose with his sleeve and took her arm companionably. 'Come on.'

Sam stepped out of the trees as he saw them disappear into the twilit woods. He exhaled, his breath hanging in the cold damp air like vapour. I don't like that, he thought, the keeper's daughter with young Richard. It hadn't been a white bonnet, it was the flaxen hair misled him. Still young 'uns they were, growed but not growed up. Beautiful little creature, she was, like a picture, a church picture, not quite womanly yet. But she was as good a daughter as a man could have. Now, if he could get one of his sons down from Ludlow to work with him, see what happens, she'd make a fine daughter-in-law. But no, none of that was likely, he couldn't see that pretty little thing with his big hobbledehoy sons. And he couldn't see his mother letting her grandsons go: she was too used to the company and the money coming in, now all three were working. And, for himself, it suited him well to have no ties now. He pushed his hand down into the deep pocket of his heavy corduroy trousers, feeling the delicate lace-trimmed lawn handkerchief crumpled there, and sighed pleasurably. He'd have trouble, John Bowden, marrying that girl off. Not for the likes of the Fiennders son and heir, and not for the likes of the young ruffians in Findlesham.

'I'll see you at Christmas, then.' Richard handed her the jug of cream.

'Shall I fetch you a lantern to see you home?' Mary asked.

He looked down the lane at the cottage. The light from an oil lamp was flickering in the windows and he was tempted to invite himself for tea. He had as a child, but now he was too old. The older they got the more secretive they had to be. He didn't question it, but sometimes, as now, it confused him.

'Lord, no, I'm going to cut across Old Sheepwalk. The house can be seen from there, gaslight don't forget.' He looked back down the lane at the cottage – the last time he'd been there the room had been lit by home-made candles and rag wicks in saucers of fat. He rubbed his broad brow, pushing the unruly hair aside, sensing a sadness, an unease.

'You're frowning,' she said. 'What's the matter?' He didn't reply, his head still turned away. 'My nail, hand, my nail-set case, Richard, thank you, today and every day, for ever.' Leaning forward she kissed his cheek awkwardly, aware of the jug in one hand and the case in the other.

'Manicure. That's what it's called, a manicure set,' he said, holding her head against his face. 'It's a French word but it comes from the Latin *manus* meaning hand and – go on, you finish it.'

'*Cura* means care,' she replied, feeling the warmth of his face against her own.

'Good for you, Mary.' He laughed, releasing her. 'You're a scholar.'

She watched him walk briskly down the lane till he cut across the fields, obscured by a hedge studded with red-berried holly and copper beech. She put the jug in the game larder at the back door and ran up to her privy. This was where she was going to keep it, her beautiful present. She had to hide it: nobody would understand such a costly present, her manicure set.

'Snow!' Bertie came scampering down the crooked, uneven stairs, falling the last four steps but jumping to his feet unscathed. 'Snow!' he yelled again, unlatching the front door before his mother could stop him.

The snow, which the wind had blown into a drift, fell into the room. The soft white pile of snowflakes lasted for one pretty minute before it melted in the warmth of the well-banked fire.

'Snow,' Bertie repeated dolefully, as he watched it turn into water.

'Shut the door, for goodness sake, you little monster.' Emma put the porridge she was stirring on the new stove to one side, slammed the door and cuffed the little boy. 'Get Hannah in to mop that up.'

'Where is Hanny? And Mary? And Pa?'

'Your father's gone off to see to his pheasants and the girls are stacking up the wood pile.' The water was spreading across the floor and wetting the rag rugs.

'Pick the rugs up first.' He stood, tottering with the

weight of them. 'Throw them over the banisters and then call Hannah.'

He opened the back door slowly, hoping another avalanche wouldn't fall in. When it didn't, he banged the door behind him and rushed out to savour the first snow of the year.

'Here, Bertie,' Mary called him over to the hen-house, 'take the broom and sweep away the snow here, make a run for the chickens.'

'The chickens don't like snow?' He was dumbfounded.

'Like, or not like, I don't know. What I do know is it's deep enough to bury the bantams.' He took the broom and started to make a path, sweeping the tight bundle of twigs vigorously, covering himself in snow.

'Hannah, Mary,' he heard his mother shouting, 'the porridge is ready. Where's Bertie? He was to call you.'

He sped to the woodshed where his sisters were piling logs into a wheelbarrow. 'Come in now, she's cross, all the snow is water, the rugs are wet and the porridge is ready.'

'Go and tell her we're coming, love.'

'No, I'll wait for you, I'll help you.' Stooping, he lifted a heavy log.

'No,' they shouted in unison as he threw it on top of the wheelbarrow, dislodging their careful arrangement.

'Stupid boy.' Hannah pushed him away.

Bertie hung his head. 'Why is everybody always cross?'

'More jam please, Ma.' Hannah reached across the table and took the jar of blackberry and apple, spooning it on her porridge. She looked up at her mother apprehensively.

It wouldn't do to take it for granted. Things had been much better lately, but the years of scrimping and saving had left their mark. Catching the look of fear Emma pushed the jam towards Mary.

'More jam for both my daughters. It's the least you deserve.' She smiled at them both. 'A day's work you've done before church.'

'Church?' Hannah dropped her spoon, dismayed. 'We're not going to church in this?'

'Of course we are, the traption will get through this easy. We are going, aren't we, Ma?' Mary looked anxiously out of the window. It was still snowing, but the wind had died down and the snow was settling.

'Finish your porridge, Mary. We'll decide when your father gets back.'

Hannah regarded her sister with suspicion. Why was she so eager to go to church? It wasn't as if she needed to get out, what with her work at the dairy and taking the vegetables into Findlesham. Pa had even let her take the trap to Wellsbury, once George had said she was as safe as houses in it. George Jackson! That was it. 'Well, then, Mary, will you wear your new navy merino for George?' She said it slyly, but her sister's reaction showed that she didn't know.

'For George?' Mary was genuinely surprised. 'I'll wear my new dress, but why for George?'

Emma smiled. It was good to see Mary caring about the way she looked. They had made the dress for her fourteenth birthday, fitted it was, quite grown-up.

'It won't be seen anyway, love, too cold in St Michael's to take your gloves off let alone your cloak.'

There was only a slight gradient leading up to St Michael's church, but it was enough on a day like this to create problems for all the horse-drawn vehicles, whether it was the squire's coach and four, its polished surface now bespattered with mud and snow, or the tinker's ramshackle donkey and cart. Most of the carriages had tried and failed to reach the porch, and new arrivals, learning from their failure, were leaving their conveyances in the deeply rutted lane. Some, though, in an attempt to get nearer, had approached across the snow-covered field. This, John Bowden could tell, had not been wise. The snow had stopped and a watery sun was breaking through the pewter-coloured sky. Those carriages in the field could be up to their axles in mud and ice by the time the service had finished.

He called to his daughters at the back, 'Reckon we're best off passing this lot and leaving the trap beyond.'

'And walk back to church in all that slush, then back again after?' Mary didn't like the thought of exposing her new dress and boots to the inches-deep dirty and melting snow. 'I could get it up to the church if you all got out,' she said.

'Not fair, Pa,' Hannah whined.

'Yes, it is. If I can do it you won't have to walk back. Please, Pa.'

'D'you really think you can, love?' He was amused at the confidence and daring shown by his usually modest daughter.

'Nothing lost in trying,' she called gaily. The family all dismounted and Mary took her father's place, guiding the pony so that the trap faced the church, while John called to everyone to clear the path up to the porch.

Cracking her whip in the air to make a loud whistling sound, she laid the reins on the pony's back and leaning forward yelled, 'Go to it, Bucky.' The pony, hardly needing the encouragement, leapt forward from a standstill, nearly upsetting the trap. Mary guided him zig-zag fashion across the ruts with the slightest movement of the reins, pulling him up inches from the porch.

'Well done, woman, well done.' George and Billy Jackson, who had walked to church, joined in the cheers from the enthusiastic onlookers, the noise drowning the church bells pealing out an unmusical carillon as the ringers were missing one of their number, delayed by the weather.

George helped a flushed and excited Mary down. 'You get inside, Mary, I'll lead this here 'traption round the back.'

'You're in the wrong business, George.' The Bowden family had arrived, having trudged up the hill in the wake of the dashing Mary. 'Would you take me on for lessons?' John continued.

'And me, and me.' Bertie, looking like a fat robin, swathed from head to toe in brown except for a bright red woollen scarf crossed over his chest, was bouncing up and down like a rubber ball.

'Make way!' somebody shouted, as the Fiennders' coachman carried Mrs Fiennders up the path, followed by a footman strewing the way with straw for the rest of the family, with Master Richard and little Master Tommy bringing up the rear. The villagers bustled ahead into the church, seating themselves, so as not to be in the way of Squire and his family. Mary followed her parents to their usual pew in the centre of the nave, where the other estate craftsmen were, taking care to sit at the end. The Adams family took their rightful position ahead of the gamekeeper, head gardener, stonemason and carpenter, and behind them the innkeeper and the Jacksons, except for Aunt Biddy who went to a Methodist chapel – an enviable religion this Sunday as the service was always held in the cosy parlour of the old schoolmistress's cottage. At the back of the church were farm-hands, under-keepers, and gardeners, stable-boys and old man Webb with Sally and her noisy young sons. When the Fiennders family had taken their places in the front pew, the service could begin.

After the first hymn, 'Away in a Manger', a carol, it being the last Sunday of Advent, Mary slid her hands back inside her muff. It was a poor home-made thing compared to Mrs Fiennders' white ermine trimmed with grey fox tails, but it matched her dress and was lined with rabbit fur. She hadn't looked at Richard as he walked down the aisle – turning your head and gawping at the gentry wasn't the thing to do – but he would face her as the congregation stood to let the Squire's family leave first. And she thought she'd heard him hum 'The Galloping Major' as he passed. During the long sermon she let her gaze wander discreetly around the church, admiring the strong blues and reds of the stained-glass window with the shield of the Fiennders family arms. She could just see the altar table, with its carving of wheat and grapes where soon she would receive the bread and wine of communion. Her eyes travelled back up the aisle over the monumental brasses and memorial stones, glad that it wasn't her turn to clean them, encrusted as they were with mud.

The wheezing of the hand-pumped organ and the shuffle of the congregation as they stood for the next hymn brought her back to the present, and she joined in with her light true soprano, 'Once in Royal David's City'. Little of this was heard, though, it being drowned by the young members of the congregation, who, led by the fidgety, bored young sons of Sally Webb, kept up a low susurrus of impatience and discontent. The individual noise wasn't enough to earn the sharp slaps that crying or talking would have, but the combined sound overwhelmed their parents' singing and produced an unChristian glare of disdain from the vicar.

Standing in their places at the end of the service, everybody waited to give the Fiennders' precedence, after the vicar, to leave. Some were favoured with a smile or nod of recognition, which was greeted by a bob from the women and brief tug of the forelock from the men. As Richard approached, Mary took off her mittens and slipped her hands out of her muff, dislodging the cloak from around her shoulders. Ann Fiennders turned back to acknowledge the Bowdens, remembering her husband's story of the keeper's loyalty, and saw the look pass between her son and their daughter as the girl raised both her hands; an odd thing to do, she thought. She took in for the first time how attractive the girl was, her long straight white-blonde hair falling down her back, enhanced by the navy blue of her dress. Clever of the creature not to have a white collar – it wouldn't have suited her pallor; instead it was a dark yellow trimmed with narrow navy braid. Her tiny waist was accentuated by the neat little bustle, a waist that Ann doubted needed the help of a corset. During this brief but thorough appraisal she noted the look on Emma Bowden's face. So, both mothers were worried! She took Richard's arm and moved down the aisle, now crowded with the rest of the congregation, anxious to get to their hot dinners. At the font she paused briefly to greet the vicar, 'We'll see you at luncheon, David, what a good sermon,' but she spoke abstractedly, for Richard had slipped away.

'Ah, yes, well, thank you, Ann.' The vicar was a little surprised: his sermon had included exhortations to share one's wealth; the wealth of nations and of individuals. He didn't actually believe his words: a place for everyone and everyone in his place was what he believed, and the poor should be grateful for having an easier access to heaven, not having to worry about the unlikely comparison of inserting a camel through the eye of a needle. Occasionally, though, he felt he had to compete with the Methodists or lose more of his congregation.

'You don't want to be making a show of yourself, Mary.'

'Now then, Mother, if it wasn't for Mary we wouldn't have the trap right here at the church.'

'All very well and good, John, but she's had her moment and now we want to go home properly and driven by you.' Emma knew she wasn't being fair but the exchange of looks in the church had upset her. A fool she was not to have noticed before. That they had been friends since little ones she knew, no harm in that, but by now with young Richard away at school they should have gone their separate ways. His face now, eyeing our Mary, there was more than should rightfully be there, nothing ungentlemanly, but too much regard, affection.

'What? What did you say?'

'I said I'll walk, Ma, it's icy now, I'll take Bertie for a slide down Longbarrow on the way home.'

Ann Fiennders, warm and comfortable in the coach, wrapped in a fur rug, could see no sign of Richard. He wasn't with the Bowdens, who were leading their trap round to the path, and would probably walk home in the cold bright sun. Suddenly she pulled two long pins from her hat and then tugged it off.

'My dear, what are you doing?' Thomas Fiennders looked at the misshapen piece of felt trimmed with birds and their feathers that now rested unattractively in his wife's lap.

'It doesn't suit me, it's stupid, it isn't becoming.' Thomas agreed. These over-decorated masculine-style pork-pie hats didn't suit any woman, but he had supposed fashion superseded attraction. 'You can wear anything, Ann. And so can you two,' he said, realizing that his elder daughters were wearing similar hats, if anything more elaborately trimmed, and Jessica's particularly, which sat on hair so teased and padded that the birds looked as if they'd landed on a nest.

Mary was pulling Bertie along on the icy path by the long red scarf, which she'd tied around his waist. From behind the quickthorn hedge she heard a low voice intoning, ' "My horse, my horse, my kingdom for a horse." ' Richard appeared at the next gap in the hedge, and swung Bertie high above his head. He shouted, 'Aren't you proud of your sister? Not only the Buttermilk Beauty of Findlesham but the Champion Charioteer.' Set-

ting the delighted child down he mouthed to her over
his head, 'Gazebo tomorrow, at half-past twelve?' She
nodded, then watched him march away. Always a new
person, each time she saw him, taller, or his voice had a
new depth, a graveness, quieter. She braved the cold and
looked at her hands: they were different too.

'What do you mean, we're not supposed to drink it?'
Isabel toyed with her roasted pheasant, pushing it around
the plate, pouting so that her over-full lower lip looked
like an engorged worm.

'You said, didn't he, Jessie . . .?'

'I said . . .' Richard held his napkin to his mouth,
laughing helplessly, 'I said . . .'

'Well, Richard, what did you say?' Madeleine Touche-
Forster turned from his father on her left, more interested
in knowing what the young people were laughing about
than what their elders were being earnest about.

Richard cleared his throat and drank some of his
burgundy. 'It's easier to say,' he said, turning to his neighbour, 'if I don't look at them.' He gestured at his sisters
dismissively. 'You see, I told them before I went back to
school this term that . . .'

'Yes?' Madeleine smiled encouragement, with a hint
of flirtation.

'That buttermilk was . . .'

Now she began to laugh with him, though she had
no idea why.

'And I had noticed that they had both got, well, rather
bigger, and . . .'

'And?' Madeleine looked across the table at her husband who, although engaged in conversation with Ann, was clearly aware of her laughter and disapproved of it. Oh God, she thought, he should be the Vicar of Illsbury, not Wellsbury.

'All right, I'm all right now, but it's better that I don't look at you either.'

Her eyebrows arched above the slanting, laughing eyes. 'Thank you, Richard, charming as ever, but do go on.'

'Buttermilk is good for your skin, that's what I told them.' Everybody at the table was paying attention now, attracted by their laughter. 'But they've been drinking it instead of rubbing it on.'

Under cover of the general laughter, Madeleine leant across Richard and patted Isabel's hand, 'Dear Issy, out or in, it has been good for your skin, your cheeks are bloom-ing. And you too, Jess,' she added, looking across the table to the younger sister, for whom buttermilk had increased the size of her breasts to that of melons. Ann was grateful for the distraction – it had been an awkward hour or so since the bombshell in the morning room before luncheon.

'That explains everything,' she said. 'You were both expanding while your appetites shrank. Now tell us, Richard, where you heard this beauty advice. If it is on good authority, I might try it myself.'

'You don't need it, Ann, my dear,' the vicar said mechanically.

Her son blushed a little. 'Oh, you know, at school, history, er . . . Cleopatra, wasn't it?'

'That was ass's milk, dear.' She decided not to pursue it. Obviously the Bowden girl had told him – after all, she worked in the dairy. Signalling to the butler to clear away and bring the pudding, she turned to Algernon on her left, David now doing his duty by Jessica on his right. 'Did your parishioners get to Little Bewdley through snow and ice?'

He answered her with a veneer of his old humour and confidence, although he was now well aware that his days as a welcomed guest might be numbered. 'All Saints is right in the village, don't forget, Ann, unlike St Michael's. Nevertheless it was a very Little Bewdley.'

She smiled dutifully and helped herself to the frangipane, waving away the cream. She sensed his nervousness, which was justified, but he need not fear that her displeasure would be shown. That would only compound the damage he had done. 'We expect you for Christmas, Algy, but what about Boxing Day? The meet is here as usual, but we'll be drawing Rollright Covert, nearer to you. Perhaps you should join us there, keep your horse fresh, don't you think?' So that was how he would be punished. How shrewd she was. Nothing that Thomas would notice. The usual offer of an extra hunter and a groom was to be withdrawn and he would have to make do with his own horse.

'Ah, that does sound wise, Ann, but wisdom should never interfere with pleasure. I enjoy the meet as much as following the hounds. I'll drop out when my horse is tired.'

'As you wish, of course. Now, do tell David and Madeleine that extraordinary story about the blackamoor and the governess.' While he was 'singing for his supper', telling a story based on a modicum of truth, which had been enlarged, embroidered and re-embroidered to reach the status of a music-hall monologue, she tried to work out how best to repair the hurt he had caused. They had been scattered in groups of twos and threes, the morning-room fire was lit, not with wood but coal, too hot for her, and she had sat in the embrasure of the window with Richard, and Sybil, the girls' governess. They had been talking about, what? music, she thought, all the composers whose names began with S. Thomas and David were near the fire and Algernon was entertaining Madeleine, his tongue loosened by several glasses of sherry. Thomas was proudly telling, yet again, the story of the keeper's loyalty at Charlie Colcroft's attempt to poach him. What had happened next was very clear; her mind had recorded it perfectly. She could hear again David saying, 'As it should be, Thomas, you know what they say, "The Keeper is the Master's Man and the Gardener is the Mistress's Man." '

Thomas had seen Algernon's reaction, as had she, a smug knowing smirk. The tiny dart of pained surprise on her husband's face had been succeeded by a nod of acknowledgement. 'Yes, indeed,' he had said, 'but Bow-den's refusal was both civil and witty, good man, good man.' He had covered the moment but had sat heavily in an armchair, not speaking again till luncheon was served. Algernon, too, floundered in his conversation, aware that his unguarded reaction had been seen by both of the Fiennders'.

Algernon finished the tale of the blackamoor and the governess, which since its last telling had grown to include a maharajah, a stolen ring and a foundling. He was a good raconteur but less amusing when his performance became professional. Ann caught Thomas's eye for the first time during the meal, smiling at him and shaking her head imperceptibly, indicating disbelief. He returned the look, but his smile was a joyless one, not even wry. It wasn't the usual look of conspiracy. She joined in the general amusement and surprise but was thinking, And no more little sums of money to tide you over, cousin dear.

Thomas retired after lunch to his study, ostensibly to work on bringing the archives up to date but no doubt to include in the afternoon's work an hour or so of rest. Ann hoped he would sleep and not brood on the morning's unpleasantness. Maybe in time he would think he had been mistaken, that he had misinterpreted that stupid smirk of Algernon's. An idle afternoon lay ahead of her, though: the girls were walking over to the farm to collect yet more buttermilk, this time to pat on their skin not put in their stomachs, and Richard was playing the piano in the drawing room, one of the new composers, not something one wanted to listen to. However she spent the afternoon she must not only *not* see the gardener but she must be seen not seeing him. Out of the window, beyond the reflection of lights from the house, she noticed that the cold platinum-coloured sun would soon be setting. The music drifting down the stone-flagged corridors increased her melancholy. Perhaps she would have an early nursery tea with Tommy and Maud, the daughter whose existence Ann often actually forgot. No! She had a better idea than that. She would get one of the young grooms to help and maybe the cook's son, the pot-boy at the inn.

Thomas Fiennders had left the maps and ledgers undisturbed and he hadn't slept. The incident this morning had distressed him. That odious and pathetic man had started an unwelcome train of thought. He knew he hadn't been Ann's first choice – he who had been dispatched to America by her parents, bribed with a small income which would cease if he saw her again. Nobody had known about *his* first choice, a cousin, ten years older than he, who had seduced him when he was sixteen. She had been considered plain, mousy, but there was nothing mousy about her as a mistress. She had organized everything, taken the initiative. He had never again found the sensual pleasure of being the taken and not the taker. It was she also who had found the archives, started his interest in his heritage. She had, as it were, introduced him to his past. He turned up the wick of the oil-lamp on his desk and noticed the figures outside in the snow. Ann and the young children were surrounded by a ring of burning faggots embedded in the crisp snow. They were building a snowman.

How dear of her. She was being a 'good mother', near enough to ensure that he saw and would be reassured. Well, he would join them, be a 'good father', show her his genuine affection and understanding. After all, this morning's incident, true or not, affected his pride, and only indirectly his marriage.

It had snowed again in the night and then the temperature had dropped to freezing point. She had even risen at an early hour to put more coal on her dying fire, but now, wiping condensation from the window, she could see it was going to be a glorious day and felt invigorated by the thought of sun and snow. After breakfasting downstairs and acquainting herself with the arrangements of the rest of the family, she had made careful plans.

Thomas, who was sitting on the bench at Woodstock Assizes, had already left in the coach which would take him to Wellsbury, where he would get the steam train the rest of the journey. The coach would return and take the girls and Sybil to Starveall Hill; they were to stop at the Bexley-Wrights on the way and invite them to join in the tobogganing, and a picnic in the barn at the foot of the hill. Richard had been particularly vague about his plans but had made a half-hearted promise to join everybody for the picnic luncheon, hoping, he had said, that he wouldn't be the only man there. A hope echoed by Isabel and Jessica. Nanny thought it too cold for Maud and Tommy to go out, having disapproved of yesterday's snowman. 'We don't want colds on Christmas Day, do we?' Davis, who had appeared with a raw red nose and running eyes, in Ann's bedroom to dress her, certainly had a cold and had been sent back to bed.

After instructing the cook to prepare the picnic, intimating to Sybil that she would join them at some point, and giving Richard the vague impression that she was taking a groom with an extra horse to Findlesham to have a loose shoe replaced on her hunter, she felt she had laid tracks too shadowy to be pinpointed. What she would do was take the groom, leave her hunter, and ride the extra horse back through the woods to the bottom of the park and look for Sam. Later she would discreetly join what would probably be a large group at Starveall.

★

Sam leaned back comfortably in the snug hide he had made during the morning, leisurely smoking his pipe and thinking about the two different problems. On waking at his usual early hour and fetching in a load of logs, he had startled a small herd of fallow deer. Emboldened by hunger, their usual vegetation hidden by the snow, they were nibbling the bark on the young trees and would no doubt make their way, if undisturbed, to the Abbey's gardens and wreak havoc on all his hard work, eating and trampling vegetables and flowers alike. And the rose-bushes especially. Why couldn't the buggers look at them and let be! The hide was made of bales of straw, carefully stacked logs and interwoven branches of white cedar; the sweet-smelling younger and softer branches made a dry carpet inside. He would bring his gun out early tomorrow, long before dawn – those deer would surely be back. He ought to speak to the keeper, more his job truly, but John could join him if he so wished, the hide was big enough.

Sam took the pipe from his mouth, tensing as he heard the sound of hoofs. He didn't have his gun – they must be hungry to return at midday. He took up his field-glasses, holding them with care and affection, and raised them, a gift from her, to his eyes. Focusing through the thinly planted wood he picked up the movement of an animal. Not headed his way? No, it was moving at a canter along one of the tracks made over the centuries by man and beast. Canter! Of course, it was a horse.

'Ho, there,' he shouted, 'who is it?' It could be some-body from the house. He had no right to accost a member of the family but he felt protective about the gazebo where the horse was headed. Lowering the field-glasses and tamping down his pipe he emerged from the hide as the horse and rider appeared.

'What are you doing here? Why did you shout?' Ann leant over the horse's neck, patting and quietening her mount.

'Didn't know it was you. Not your usual horse, is it?' He lifted his cupped hands for her to use as a dismounting block. Keeping her feet in the stirrups, she said, 'Why don't I see you at the gazebo?' The horse edged away nervously and he took the reins.

'No, that won't do, somebody there already. Jump down and I'll tether this with my nag in the lean-to.' She watched him walk the horse over to his cottage, simple late-Georgian clapboard but its simplicity made it beautiful, perfect of its kind. He led the horse into the makeshift stable that he'd thrown up and never completed. When he returned he found her in the hide, leaning back against the straw, but the familiar crooked little smile was followed by a frown. She was torn between desire and anxiety. Who was in the gazebo? And how did he imagine Algernon knew about their meetings? Listening to her questions, he used a branch of the cedar partially to cover the opening, then he lay beside her, putting his arm behind her and lifting her to lie across his chest. It would be wiser, he thought, to speak about the Reverend Grant-Ingram first, for the knowledge of who was in the gazebo might temper her desire; that was something they might not see eye to eye about. He'd opened her heavy top coat and was slowly unbuttoning her jacket, neither of them heeding the cold. He explained about Algernon's visit to his greenhouses in the summer.

'He told me you'd sent him, after lunch it was, that he was to have beans, tomatoes and the like.'

'I suppose I did, I tell any visitor to—' She gasped as his hand covered her bare breast, his fingers caressing her nipples.

'He asked to see the kitchen garden, the roses, then we went back to the long greenhouse, but I felt, you know, not right, I wanted him gone.' He buried his face in the mass of dark curly hair brushing it off her neck and pressing his lips against the curve of her spine. 'I realized it wasn't my raspberries he was after.' She sputtered with laughter and turned to face him. They suspended interest in the Reverend Algernon's horticultural or other needs as they made love, the movement of their bodies disturbing and accentuating the scent of cedar.

She sat up, adjusting her dress, her voice changing from its breathy sensual quality to amused practicality. 'So, he was interested in more than your raspberries,' she laughed, 'but that doesn't explain how he knows about our, well, us, and Sam,' she tried to put her next question modestly, 'how did he make known his interest in you, and how – let me see – how did you deflect it?' His face was flushed, quite red; with embarrassment, she supposed. Ridiculous! How could he have lain with her, his hands, his mouth, every part of him penetrating her, and receive a question like that so awkwardly? He was embarrassed, but not for the reason she supposed.

'He's not a fool, Ann, and neither am I. It was clear what he had in mind and clear that, well, I wouldn't, didn't, respond. And he don't know about us – it's a good guess, I'd say. You and me, we'd been together the day afore in the long greenhouse, and you must have dropped your handkerchief and, well, you know . . .' He was stumbling with his explanation partly because it wasn't quite the truth and also because the memory reawakened his desire.

'You dropped it, Sam, I think.' She also remembered the delicacy with which he used the flimsy wisp.

'Mebbe, yes. Anyways, he saw it, folded up in one of the seed trays.'

'How appropriate,' she murmured.

'He went to pick it up and I was rather sharp with him, I remember.'

'Mmmm, yes, I can see,' she mused. 'He could easily make something of that.' Remembering her other question she stood up quickly. 'And who is in the gazebo?' What a fool she was, letting this passion overcome discretion again. Relieved that she had accepted his explanation, Sam told her slowly about her son's visits to their new trysting place.

'Not that they've found our room, and it's all innocent, Ann, nothing to worry about.'

'The very reason *to* worry. If he was using her, a little fun, a bit of amusement, experience,' she shrugged, 'it wouldn't matter, and if things went wrong, well, we would see the girl looked after – but—'

'But, yes, but . . .' He tried to control his rage. 'That's not like you, Ann, words I might expect from an ignorant cottager.' He caught her hand before it reached his face and pinioned it behind her back. 'But if "things went wrong", you say, you'd "see the girl looked after". And the bastard, Ann? I mean a baby, by the way, not your son. "The girl" is not a whore, not a plaything.' His anger suddenly evaporated and he felt only a sadness. 'She's a fair young creature, a decent girl, you know that right enough.'

His head was turned from her and she felt a pang of deep jealousy. Trying to wrench her hand from his, she spat, 'Like would defend like.'

'Well, now,' he paused, ' "Mrs Fiennders," you pay me a compliment.' He let her go suddenly. 'They are not lovers, they love, that is all. All. They will have pain enough when they find that they love. Don't meddle now, don't harm the girl.'

She had staggered back against the straw bales at his sudden release of her and he bent to assist her. This time her hand did strike his face – hard enough to produce a deep red mark.

'You think that you are, in your position, qualified to advise me on matters of upbringing? I think not.' She was trembling with anger but underlying this was a desire even now to be taken by him again. She wanted to punish him for his interest in the girl but she also wanted to have his weight heavy on her body and feel him moving inside her, a proof of his passion and of his greater interest in herself.

But she knew immediately that she had misjudged him, for, looking at her dispassionately, he said, 'You should be careful what kind of man you hit, Mrs Fiennders, a gentleman might hit you back.' He threw aside the branch of cedar blocking the opening and called over his shoulder, 'I'll fetch your horse.'

Mary could see George Jackson outside the forge: he was holding a chestnut horse, beautiful, but difficult to control. She couldn't see the man he was talking to, who was concealed by the horse; big, she thought, at least seventeen hands. She slowed Bucky to a walk and stopped the trap by the village pond – she didn't want to disturb the excited animal.

'Well, Mary, I suppose I'm lucky this creature hasn't galloped off to Gyddesden Row, where it comes from. I think this Christmas present is a way of my parents saying they wish rid of me,' Richard put out a hand to help her down, 'though the sight of you, Bucky and the trap would be enough to scare off any horse, broken or not.'

'Not fair, not fair, Master Richard.' A grinning George also held out his hand, which he had wiped carefully on his old leather breeches. 'I don't know any coachman more able than Mary, she could handle the Devil in harness.'

Pleased with the compliments, she smiled down at them both. 'I can't stop,' she said, refusing their hands. 'I'm to Wellsbury with some goods, and Pa likes me home before nightfall.' She nodded at the chestnut pulling at his tether. 'He looks frightening, but splendid.'

'Yes, a good one, isn't he? George here is going to help me break him in, he's barely off the lunging rein.'

'Are you to Wellsbury alone, Mary? I'd send Aunt Biddy with you but she's laid up with an ague of sorts.' George crossed back to the horse, now bucking and rearing. He spoke softly, breathing on the animal's face, calming him.

'Not hunting today, Richard? Ground too hard?' She spoke wistfully – they hadn't seen each other since church on Christmas Day, and that had been brief, her mother pushing her into their pew first. And apart from that marvellous picnic that they'd had in the gazebo, foods unknown to her, meats and fishes, smoked, devilled, roasted, jellied and potted, with the fire lit but no lamp-light and lots of talking, their only other encounter had been in the dairy. That hardly counted: he had accompanied his sisters, and the Adams girls were there too, working alongside. When the Fiennders' had gone, the Misses Adams had been full of stories about the big house. Guests from all over, hunting, shooting parties, the Osmunds had ridden over for a dance and stayed the night. There had been much talk of the Hon. Florence Osmund's French lady's maid and her way with clothes and hair. All this they had got from a disgruntled Miss Davis.

George returned from pacifying the horse. Richard said, 'Yes, ground too hard,' and there was no opportunity to make a plan. He had been kept too occupied to miss her but now, seeing her again, he felt the usual need to talk, hold her arm, just be with her.

'Why are you going on your own?' he asked, with a violent wave of anger that he didn't understand.

'My mother is sewing up at your house, Hannah is working in the laundry, and because I'm old enough and wise enough.' She tapped Bucky lightly with her whip and encouraged him into a trot, waving at the two young men as she left, glad to escape their questioning. Awkward, everything was, it wasn't 'quite right' to travel alone and deal with the tradesmen in Wellsbury. Kind, though, of Richard to care. And George, of course.

★

Emma sat in the low comfortable chair examining the dark green woollen dress. She was ill at ease: this was not the usual work for which she was required and it would be difficult to achieve such a major alteration, and as if the woman needed it! She who could order six new green dresses of any stuff or style. It was those marks and stains, she supposed, that had to be tucked or pleated away and seams let out to compensate.

'Excuse me, madam, but how will you be able to walk, if it's to be so narrow at the hem?' Ann Fiennders had been sorting through her day dresses looking for one she wouldn't mind being spoilt.

'It seems walking is going out of fashion too, along with the bustle.' Looking at the woman increased her bad temper – she was so like the daughter, except for that narrow, compressed mouth. Emma dropped her head, turning the dress over, examining it again. Unpick the back seam, she thought, but why is she asking me? She usually worked in the sewing room, repairing embroidery, copying simple blouses, attaching feathers and ornaments to velvet bands for headwear. This sort of thing Miss Davis could do better.

'You seem reluctant, Mrs Bowden. I had thought a challenge would interest you and there would be payment for your time and what we hope will be your expertise.' That should arouse her interest, though she had noticed that, of late, money was not such a guiding principle.

Emma was puzzled and worried: Mrs Fiennders was in a strange mood, switching between charm and irritability. She stood and held up the dress against herself, looking in the long mirror. Had she planned it, the effect on Ann Fiennders couldn't have been better. The green took what little colour Emma Bowden had from her face and made the pale hair look lifeless and dull. Turning her back to the mirror, Emma smiled ruefully. 'Oh, what a change! On you this dress, this colour, is like a jewel, it sort of . . . No, you sort of gleam.' She took another peep at herself. 'But I look old – dreary.'

'It isn't your best colour, no.' Smiling sweetly now, Ann held the dress against herself: her vivid colouring, the dark curly hair were accentuated by the rich green. She remembered wearing it only a month ago, walking in the scented garden – that had been Sam's idea, the garden, full of freesia, night-scented stock, nicotiana – when she had held the train of her dress over one arm revealing her leg two inches above the ankle. He had continued to discuss the planting, suggesting winter-flowering jasmine, but he had stared at the revealed leg with a half-smile and she could see that he wanted her. But did he still? She hadn't seen him alone for nearly two weeks. At first she had punished him, seeing him regularly as usual, but always with somebody else, Issy, Jess, a guest, but now it was he who was never alone and all because . . .

'Why don't I unpick the back seam and pin it on you, Mrs Fiennders? If it doesn't work, no harm done.'

'No harm done,' Ann repeated softly. Again she seemed cold and distant: there was something unsaid between them. Emma sat, unpicking the seam. Nothing was right here, she knew, and she could only guess at the cause.

'How old is Mary?' There it was, the unsaid thing.

'Fourteen, madam.'

'As much as that? She looks like a child still.'

'Looks, maybe, but she's a responsible girl, a good girl to me.'

'And so she should be. Yes. You could have sent her into service. She could be married.'

Emma laughed. 'That would be a bit previous.'

'Twelve, isn't it? One can be married at twelve?'

'That is so, madam, but – now could you hold this round you and I will pin it accordingly.' Emma placed a box of pins on the floor to augment those already stuck in the velvet pin-cushion fastened to her wrist, then helped Ann Fiennders adjust the dress.

'But? Emma, you were saying . . .?'

'Oh, nothing, only that there be twelve and twelve. Young Dolly Minter, that worked below stairs that you had to send off, she was a woman early, and that groom couldn't rightly be blamed, but my Mary . . .'

'Yes, yes, but she isn't twelve now, she's fourteen.'

Emma knelt on the floor, shortening the skirt at the back to take up the length the bustle would have used. 'Even so, who would she marry? There's a shortage of young men in these parts, both high and low. There's your girls now, older than my Mary and no suitors.' These observations were dangerous, Emma knew, bordering upon impertinence. 'And lovely young women,' she added, as an olive branch.

But Ann was keenly aware of her daughters' plainness and the barb hurt. She twisted suddenly away from Emma, spilling the box of pins. 'Hardly as worrying. They're not likely to form any unsuitable alliance.'

Emma finished picking up the pins and stood up. 'As I doubt my Mary would,' she said coldly, with a hint of warning. The unsuitability of the alliance to which Mrs

Fiennders indirectly referred concerned her, as much as the other woman. 'I think I should wash my hands before continuing. They're dusty from the floor.'

'Of course. There is a wash basin now along the hall where the small night nursery used to be.' What a tangled web, Ann thought, while the woman was out of the room. They both had a certain power over each other and needed a mutual discretion.

'Oh, the running water, and hot too!' Emma had forgotten her displeasure on her return. 'It's worth a king's ransom, especially in this weather.' In case this sounded like a complaint, she added, 'We're lucky, though, having our own well.' She knelt again to pin the skirt. 'As tight as this?'

'Tighter.'

'No wonder, then, it's called the "hobble".'

Ann had other, less sartorial matters to air. 'You get all your water from the well, Emma?'

'Most times. A long dry summer, then could be we'd need the village pump, but else – still narrow all the way to the waist?'

'Yes, like a tube, I think.' Ann patted her hips. 'Leave room for these, though. The village pump – how inconvenient for you.'

'Only people in Findlesham who have water laid on are the Sharps at the inn, and the Jacksons at the forge.' The sentence hung in the air. The two women exchanged a slight smile. They had shared oblique confidences before. At the advice of Ann Fiennders, Emma's small savings were placed securely where her own secret income was invested. Torn and dirtied clothes had been cleaned and repaired by Emma Bowden that would normally have been given to Davis.

In the case of the Jackson family, Emma had always kept Billy in mind for Mary but, on becoming aware of George's interest in her daughter, she had switched her allegiance. That she hadn't promoted it yet was partly selfish: she would miss her Mary and the help. But it was true, she *was* a young fourteen. Now, though, it was time to encourage them to be suited. A man like George wouldn't want a wife who was smitten with another, and he would, like enough, catch on before Mary herself. All the time he had spent helping her drive the traption was handy, but it wouldn't do to let the friendship get too brotherly. It was hard to change a friend into a lover – harder than turning a lover into a friend, perhaps. Not that she knew, her John was both to her.

'Old George Jackson was our farrier when I came here, and now young George looks after all our horses' shoeing. And your son, Emma, we hope he will be Richard's head keeper one day. Thomas thinks highly of your husband, you know.'

Emma stood to finish the last of the pinning at the waist. 'I know, Mrs Fiennders.' She was able now to speak without guile. 'And John has the greatest respect for him.' She examined the effect of her work, unhappy with what she had created.

'And I think my husband would agree with me that his head keeper should have amenities equal to those of the innkeeper and the smith.' Ann looked at her profile in the mirror. 'Your cottage, Emma, should have running water.'

Emma was frowning slightly. 'That would be most

kind. We would be grateful, Mrs Fiennders. But whatever you call this style,' she forced a laugh, 'it's beyond me.'

Ann shook her head. 'Oh dear, it isn't what I imagined.'

'I'll remove the pins, Mrs Fiennders. You give it to Miss Davis. And no harm done.'

Ann smiled. 'And no harm done.'

Mary sat huddled against the tree, her cloak wrapped tightly around her. Looking out across the young green of the woods and the distant fields, some with lambs so new born they tottered after their dams, their bleating carried on the soft wind, she tried not to remember the last time she had been on Paradise Hill. She wished she couldn't remember anything. All her memories this year were confused. How had it happened? Every moment leading up to it she must have been thinking contrariwise to everybody else.

First there had been laughter and fun, teasing Bertie and swinging him high, flattering Hannah with nice words, such good humour with all. With the arrival of running water Ma had forgotten all the old scrimping, people had come to tea, cakes baked, home-brew and cider for the men. The fire kept in, the cottage warm. Walking with George in the crystal cold, his arm over her shoulder, that had been comfortable, like. Evenings at the forge. Aunt Biddy and Pa with their talks: the rights of man, a working man's rights. Ma, all pretty and flushed, arguing but gentle with it. She had never known a time before when her family had been this pleasant together and it seemed it would always be so. Even that day when a serious Pa had asked her if she was sure about George: 'sure' in her head had meant trust. He had taken over teaching her how to ride from Richard and his quiet encouragement helped her to believe she could. Of course she was sure, she'd replied. 'George is a good fellow.' And then it had been too late, he had asked for her father's permission, which had been granted, and before the halting proposal to herself her mother, like a town-crier, had informed every cottager, the Adamses, the estate workers and the family up at the big house.

Holding her hand and mumbling, unusual for him, he had said he thought they would be happy. His looking at her hands had been her last chance to see clearly.

'You have fine hands, Mary,' he'd said, 'like a lady's. You take care of them, but you're not afraid of using them, hard work.' She had smiled happily, thinking of Richard and his beautiful present, her manicure set: *manus*, hand; *cura*, care. She could hear his voice, feel his hand on her face pressing it to his. Then grief had suddenly filled her. Why hadn't Richard come home at Easter, and why hadn't he been expected either for any exeats? She had used George's words and arms for comfort. He had been strong and warm like Pa, even kissing the top of her head like Pa. Kissing. She shivered. It was colder up here, felt more like March than May. Twisting the narrow gold ring on her finger she noticed how loose it was.

Time she went home, the sun was high, it must be nearly midday. If only she could really go home, back to Keepers Cottage, but she must return to George's forge, he liked her calling it that, and help Aunt Biddy. Cook something special, keep Father Jackson company, darn

Billy's socks, tell George a funny tale about the morning, be helpful, amuse, please: be in the daytime what she couldn't be at night, a good wife. She ran down the hill, her hair flying, the wind whipping the tears off her cheeks.

'You'll get used to it,' he'd said. 'It's right for a decent young girl to be nervous at first but then it'll come natural.'

Never, she knew, *never* would she get used to it! It was wrong, like a sin for her, not natural. And not just the pain.

Sam Reade saw the girl, breathless, at the foot of Paradise Hill. She looked more like a child not less, as one would have expected, since the marriage. He had wanted to help her, hoped this would be as good a match as it seemed – sensible but with heart in it. Too fast for his liking, the whole thing, but he had seen them walking and laughing on Swainshill, young Jackson, an arm on her shoulder, protective. He was a good man yet she was looking too thin now, those big brown eyes filling her face. Funny, the way she'd eyed Sally when he'd been working the Webbs' garden – curiosity, she hadn't tried to hide it. He had sensed a need for women's talk and wanted to leave them be, but she had gone on her way. And no talking to Ann about it. They had made their peace, but that wasn't the word to use if the names of other women cropped up. 'It's not the rutting season, Ann, and I don't go scavenging. I'm not the man to lie with the lady of the manor, a needful young widow-woman and a half-formed little lass.'

She had accepted that, but it wasn't only the bedding she feared: it was his care for them, and that wasn't going to change. He liked women, their company. It wasn't for him to use them, though he had, maybe, young and careless before marrying his Flora. A shrewd woman Ann was, practical. He respected that in her. He loved her all right, he knew her too. The water now, that had been a clever move. In the greenhouses with the little one, Maud, and the nanny – let the child choose a flower – all open it was. Head estate men were to have water piped in. Himself, George Nichols the groom, and the keeper. And now the keeper.

He had gone to the gazebo that afternoon and up to the secret room. She appeared as he guessed she would. He had taken her quickly without speaking, with no care for her clothes or her well-dressed hair. At one point she had clutched protectively at the pearls around her throat, but he had removed her hands firmly and stretched her arms back above her head. 'I'm not to be had for running water you know, Ann.' He stroked her face and, removing the pearl drops, kissed her ears as she lay beside him. He examined her body with tenderness and passion, for they were rarely able to be naked with each other. She had spoken about the girl. Old Jackson's son at the forge was taking an interest in her and it seemed to be returned. And Richard, he was to go to Italy at Easter. She had spoken gentle, quiet, wanting his approval. 'Wait and see, Ann. Don't go too fast, let things run their course, or you'll be making trouble all round for the future.'

'The future,' she said, and sat up quickly, banging her head on the low ceiling. He rubbed it gently as she spoke, all excited about the new plan for her secret money. Sam had suggested she invest it in America, for that was where the world was beginning to shop for its corn. If the Fiennders' were to lose money farming in England, why not invest in their competitors who were winning? She had spoken to the right person in London and written to the right person in America. 'And you, Sam, you must have a commission, a percentage, it was your idea, and—'

'I'm not to be had for a bushel of corn either, Ann.'

It excited her, the money, the planning, the *secrecy* – although that wasn't necessary any more, she had her rights now. That Married Woman's Property Act had done it. But, even without Parliament, he reckoned Thomas Fiennders would have allowed his wife her due. Not the sort of man to do wrong, even with right on his side.

The only conveyance available at Wellsbury station was enclosed and, as it was too fine a day to travel inside, he let the cabby load his luggage and sat up in front with him. It had been a last-minute decision to come home from Scotland where he had been shooting since the middle of August with his Ormerod cousins. The weather had finally crystallized his vague feelings of loss and home-sickness. The Glorious Twelfth had become the glorious thirteenth and fourteenth and on to the glorious twenti-eth. The Chiltern Hills beckoned, the Thames, the beechwoods, Findlesham. He had a graw – a need – for home. A *graw*, wonderful word, he'd got it from his O'Neill family in County Wicklow – his mother's dashing Irish relatives.

Between Eton and Oxford his parents had arranged for him a busy and exciting year, or, rather, his mother had, he supposed, although his father had stumped up the money. Italy, with the Osmunds and a tutor, had given him more than he had expected. Robert Browning and other poets had prepared him for the countryside and architecture, the colours – so many shades of terracotta. The sculpture, paintings, he had known of, seen in country houses in England, his own, in fact. Latin had come alive: the Georgics were no longer Virgil to be translated but, like John Clare's 'The Shepherd's Calendar', it was a startling and real replication of rural life. What he hadn't expected was the music. The tutor had taken him to La Fenice, the little opera house in Venice, concerts in Rome and recitals in private houses – something he wanted to start at Fiennders Abbey.

Back at school he had enjoyed his music, studying, playing the piano, even trying the organ in the chapel. He had been occupied constantly and hardly thought of home until Andrew Osmund had mentioned his sister's engagement. 'Makes you feel old, you know, Roofie, I could be an uncle next year.'

As they approached Findlesham he looked about him. It was more like travelling than coming home. Eight months. He had forgotten some things and others had changed. The old wattle and daub cottage, set back on the corner of the ancient London road in what was once Great Findlesham, had gone; tumbled down or pulled down, probably both, the white limey soil the only sign that it had ever existed. 'Stop, if you would.' He swung himself off the high seat and jumped to the ground before the cab driver could help. 'Take my things, will you? To the Abbey – someone will see you all right there.' He walked off across the fields, climbed the hill through grazing cattle to the windmill and looked out over the patchwork of multicoloured fields and hedges, woods and hamlets, most of which he owned – or would eventually. With his arms outstretched he turned slowly, breathing in the warm air scented with horses and woodsmoke. He wanted to fling his body onto the earth in an act of worship. I'm a pantheist, he thought. C of P, not C of E. Mary would understand. He would see her now, had to see her, speak to her. She would be at the dairy. He ran down the hill towards Home Farm, stumbling and tripping over tussocks, in rabbit holes and on mole hills, then changed direction. He would go home first, fetch the silk he had bought her, tell her the funny story – what a fool he had been.

Nobody was at home except the servants. His luggage had been delivered and put in his room. He rummaged in his trunk for Mary's present and when he found it unwrapped the tissue paper. The palest blue silk slithered between his fingers; it had been bought to match her eyes. He had been pleased with himself and only noticed his mistake when, visiting a dimly lit damp church in Trastevere in Rome, he had looked at a ravishing painting on wood of the Madonna and Child. The Madonna was wearing a delicate white coif – pale as Mary's hair – and she had brown eyes. Returning to the shop, he had found some shot silk that seemed to be woven from a dozen different shades of brown and bought that too. He reached into his trunk again and found it, comparing the two colours. Now he saw her face clearly, pale skin, even paler hair and the fought-against sun-browned tip of her nose.

★

The groom was startled. 'Don't know about that, Master Richard. That Ferocity needs some riding. He don't go out regular. Why don't you take the grey or the master's other hunter?' He shouted, to the stable-boy, 'Get Greyling saddled up – and today not tomorrow, d'ye hear?' Without lowering his voice, he added, 'He's good with the horses but a bit slow.'

'Yes, all right, the grey.'

Sensing that his young master was displeased, the groom explained, 'You've not been back now for some months, see.'

'I thought the smith was going to work him.'

'Ah, well, he did early on, and me, and young Mary . . .' He paused. 'Early on, yes, but to be straight, Master Richard, I should have kept it up, I know.'

'Mary Bowden. Yes, she has good hands.'

'Young Mary, yes.' The groom looked uneasy.

'Good hands and a fine nerve,' Richard added, remembering her icy canter up to the church. The stable-boy helped him up and adjusted the horse's girth. 'I'll take Ferocity out tomorrow, and you might lunge him this afternoon.'

'Yes, Master Richard, I'll do that.' The horse trotted off, its hoofs clattering on the cobblestones.

'Her be Mary Jackson now,' the boy said, gazing at the retreating figure. 'He should know.'

'And you should know to mind your tongue.' George Nichols cuffed the boy automatically. 'The world is all upsides.' He, too, stared sadly after the horse until it disappeared, turning right under the arch.

★

Hannah was aware of somebody in the yard. She had heard the horse and then the thud of somebody dismounting. She stopped churning to have a brief look out of the window. It was Richard Fiennders, smiling and carrying a parcel. He saw her and, thinking she was Mary, raised a hand in greeting but dropped it as he approached the window, his smile vanishing, and turned back to his horse.

Hannah returned to the butter. Poor Mary. This was going to go hard with her, but whatever was in the parcel couldn't match the present Mary had shown her in the privy. It was *her* privy now. Ma had thought *she* should have it when Mary was wed but it was in Mary's gift, it being made for her by Pa. There had been a coldness in her sister when she denied Ma the key. She'd taken Hannah's hand and run out of the house shouting, 'It's not for you, it's for Hanny.' They had sat together, laughing, in there, and she'd been more like the old Mary till she talked about being wedded and asked questions, all red and awkward. Funny to sit in a privy with your older sister and give advice about that sort of thing, and her with a husband these two weeks or more. Funny, too, that Mary didn't want to do it and had to, whereas she wanted to and mustn't.

'From what I can tell, Mary, you does it a lot early on when it's all new and loving, for an instance. More in the winter when it's cold. You can figure that out by so many birthdays in autumn. And not so much at harvest-time because the men's out working all hours and tired.' Mary looked worried. 'You don't do it at all your last month with child,' Hannah added, to cheer her. 'And then you can reckon, when it's all settled down, once a week when he comes back from the inn.'

She had thought to make her sister laugh, but Mary had nodded and whispered, 'Thank you. I'm going to trust you with something, Hanny. Here . . .' She reached up to the broad ledge and brought down a school book, it looked like, and a parcel that turned out to be the mannycue. 'I can keep the Latin, but I must leave this, Hanny, for it wouldn't be understood. I've never even told Pa. You must keep it here and care for it and I'll come sometimes to use it and clean the silver.' She handed it over. Never said where the beautiful thing had come from or who. No need.

It had been two or three weeks later that she'd had the great idea. Ideas did come to her but she couldn't often carry them out. This time she would, for her sister. Whenever Mary came now to collect the vegetables for selling, Aunt Biddy was with her. George didn't like his wife going alone to the inn or Wellsbury and Hannah could tell that Mary worried the old lady, so thin and quiet. The idea would be a surprise, cheer her. Phelim, the young Irish footman, had got the card for her, in exchange for a kiss – and a little bit more. When Mrs Fiennders paid calls, for those who weren't in, and most weren't, she left a card with the corner turned down. It all seemed daft to Hannah. Why call on people you didn't want to see and who anyways was out? Mrs Fiennders would stay in the coach while the footman presented the card. At Whitley House on Tuesday morning, he kept the card. Hannah had rewrapped the leather case carefully in the blue paper and gold cord and attached the card and, for another kiss and much more, Phelim agreed to deliver it. The Fiennders' were all off to London for a while so there'd be no chance of, 'Very nice, so kind, thank you, madam', and Mary could write a letter of thank you – and throw it away! She stopped at the forge for some tea on her way back home after school. George was there, full of pride. Mary was told to show the present. 'Wedding present', they called it.

'It's used, of course. Mrs Fiennders' own, no doubt, but none the less for that.' Aunt Biddy touched the delicate silver pieces. 'Funny idea, though, for a wedding present.'

'Oh, I know why and so do you, Mary.' Hannah put a piece of walnut cake in her mouth while the Jackson family waited for the explanation. 'It's for all those times you went up of a morning to do grates, when the other Mary was sent off sudden.'

'She don't be doing that any more.' George patted Mary's shoulder. 'My wife's no skivvy.'

'Course not.' Hannah stuffed more cake in her mouth. She didn't want to look at her sister whose face had been laughing secretly with her, but which had now resumed the pinched, haunted look.

She started churning more vigorously, her sturdy arms working swiftly and rhythmically. Now the real giver of the present was back and what would pass? For no man could give such a thing to a girl and not mean something, and if he was looking for Mary here then he didn't know yet that she was no longer M.B.

He had slept with all his windows open and the curtains tied back. It had been comfortably warm in the night and he wanted to use all of the day. The light woke him at five o'clock. Before the sun was half-way up, he was down in the kitchen ordering his breakfast. Maids he had never before seen scurried away from him, their hands holding brass polish, blacking for grates and jugs of hot water for the servants' ablutions at the top of the house. He remembered Mary's poor hands, happy that she no longer did the rough, early-morning tasks. The cook, Mrs Bunn, hadn't yet descended. She was one of the recipients of hot-water jugs but an under-housemaid, sleepy-eyed in her pink cotton morning dress, set to preparing the poached eggs, ham, toast and tea that he'd asked for.

Waiting in the morning room, he savoured the scents of warm sun on grass and flower-beds and, pushing the long window further open, picked a tendril of honeysuckle curling round the sill. He could hear the stable-boy clanging his bucket as he washed down the cobble-stones. He breakfasted alone, enjoying the food which had all come from his father's estate. Eggs from their own poultry yard, often laid at random under hedges and hidden in the bales of straw and haystacks. Finding the most was a game he'd often played with Mary as a child. Perhaps little Tommy and Maud and Bertie Bowden did the same now. The ham had been salted from a pig up at Home Farm. Toast from bread baked in the ovens here from flour threshed up at the miller's from wheat grown – and growing again – in fields he could see from the window. The blackberry jam had originated on wild tangled brambles around the park, the milk in his tea from the prize Guernsey herd at the farm, and even the tea could have come from a plantation in which the family had an interest.

He lifted the bell to ring for more toast but, anticipating his needs, Mrs Bunn appeared carrying toast and hot water for the tea. Somehow, with both hands full, she managed to knock on the door and open it. Shutting it was a simple manoeuvre – she pushed it with her buttocks. 'I bring it myself, Master Richard, for I wanted to see you with my own eyes.' She went to embrace him but thought better of it. 'Seven month it's been, or longer, I 'aven't set eye on you and there you are, home, all tall and grown-up and no warning.'

'No warning about growing up, Bunny? Didn't you expect it?'

'You knows what I mean, and what am I to do for your luncheon?'

'Fatted calf will do.' He held out his arms and hugged her, enjoying her affection. Even at this hour he recognized the smell of flour and spices and lavender water. He knew she had been correct to stand back from initiating the embrace. He had crossed the line between child and man. It was no longer appropriate for a servant to greet him like that, any more than they would his father. Had he heard her minutes later in the kitchen, this would have been confirmed by the change in his title.

'Young Mr Fiennders likes mayonnaise so we'll have the sewin poached and cold and I'll make a soufflé. You get down to the farm, girl, and fetch more eggs.'

Ferocity, although still skittish and difficult to manage, was a wonderful ride. He had taken the five-bar gate and then the narrow stream in two beautifully collected jumps and raced on, willing to jump the shoulder-high hedge.

Richard pulled him up and slowed him by cantering in a circle. On the other side of the hedge was a ditch and life was too good to risk either his neck or the horse's. He leant across Ferocity's neck, patting him. 'Good boy, good boy.' He was barely sweating.

Isabel and Jessica were delighted to walk to church with their brother in such a good mood. Teasing them gently he was surprised to find that they were no longer the silly geese he remembered from last year but quite reasonable young women. Their thoughts were still mainly occupied by young men and their effect on them, but they were happy to welcome him home, pointing out changes and holding his arms affectionately. Late, they joined the few stragglers outside the church, where the conversation consisted of variations on the themes of 'Fine day' and 'Welcome home'. Walking down the aisle behind his sisters he saw her seated against the wall in a bench pew behind her parents. Her pale hair was coiled in a loose knot on the back of her head, showing her long, slender neck, the flat untrimmed straw hat tilted forward, casting a shadow on the profile of her face. She lifted her head from her hymn book and he could see the sharp line of her jaw and cheekbone. She was thinner. Her shoulders, too, showed the lines of bones jutting out through the thin fabric of her dress. He would tell her to drink more buttermilk! It must be nourishing stuff. The service droned on, the usual mixture of beautiful readings badly read and hymns sung lustily by people pleased with the sound of their own voices. A sermon from the Reverend David Touche-Forster neatly combined the necessity for gratitude for one's earthly lot – even if it wasn't a lot – with the advantages of hard work to better oneself. This to the background of the boot-clad feet of young lads kicking the wooden pews, at least one old man snoring and the hum of wasps buzzing around the communion wine. Richard felt only rightness in this and deep happiness; almost euphoria.

He was delayed after the service by more well-wishers, more 'Welcome home, you brought fine weather with you.' As he made his way out, he saw that she had gone and quickened his step. Ignoring a greeting from the minister he spotted her walking away, flanked by the two Jackson boys. 'Mary,' he called softly, prepared to mouth, 'The granary.' She turned, the large sad eyes filled with dismay. Their gaze held until she dropped her lids and he saw the pathetically thin breastless body, its stomach swollen in its light summer dress.

1890

Algernon wasn't sure that the shop would be open but he could get George Jackson to look at the horse's hoof. The animal was a bit lame, only a thorn, he hoped, so he wouldn't have had a wasted journey. A joint of beef, his housekeeper had asked for, well hung, and, failing that, get them to kill a couple of chickens. He hoped there would be beef and that it would be well hung. He liked eating chicken but didn't like the responsibility for their deaths. Ann's letter delivered this morning by that insolent footman, he winced at the memory, proposing her visit this evening, had been a surprise. Superficial their friendship, based on consanguinity and a mutual need for distraction and entertainment, remained as close as ever, but for years now it had depended upon Ann's sufferance. He was invited to Fiennders Abbey only on occasions when his absence would be noticeable and, since Thomas Fiennders' death, he had presumed that even these visits would cease. But his social ostracism meant less to him now that he had a friend and a future. Since meeting the schoolmaster in Wellsbury his life had a meaning and a permanence it had lacked before.

The shop was open – and at lunch-time! No surprise, really: Hannah Reade and Mary Jackson had inherited their mother's famous thrift. It was needed, the situation being what it was. The younger sister was there, he saw, as the jangling bell brought her out from the back. 'Mrs Reade, good morning. Or is it afternoon?'

'Both I should think, sir. Morning if you haven't had your dinner, afternoon if you have.' Hannah smiled, waiting for his order. She was lovely, he thought. Not as interesting, perhaps, as her sister, but more womanly, and bright as a button, sharp. She did all the calculating in her head, only wrote the prices down when it was for an account. They had everything he wanted and more. Examining the shelves of the small shop while the girl was fetching the beef, he was taken by the extraordinary variety of goods, all home-made or home-produced. His favourite peppermint creams flanked by marzipan balls and vanilla fudge; jars and jars of jellies, jams and pickles; stacks of circles of cotton crochet of every size edged with bright beads – to keep flies off everything from a bowl of dripping to a glass of sherry; small rag rugs; besoms made with twigs from the local woods; always a flitch of bacon, and cream cheese made weekly from sour milk. There was a bake-oven, used by the villagers to roast their Sunday joints and by the Jackson family for bread and lardy cakes, which they also sold. Even the shop itself, extending from the forge, had been built by the family with help from the estate carpenter, its clapboard painted a shiny white.

'Where are the children?' he asked, as she wrapped the meat and measured peppermint creams into a funnel of paper.

'With my mother, sir, till Mary gets back from the school and takes over.'

'Useful having a willing mother.'

'Ah, well, she made us work hard enough when we were young,' Hannah said, with a wry smile.

'Young, Mrs Reade? *Were* young?' Algernon looked with envy at the twenty-two-year-old's clear skin and bright eyes. He was not looking forward to his birthday next month.

It was this dread that had foolishly encouraged him to flirt with the footman. Misinterpreting his lingering hand as he offered the letter, he had taken him by the wrist and drawn him nearer, but the young man had made it clear in the coarsest of three- and four-letter words that what he'd had in mind was a tip and not a tup, him not being a ewe.

Hannah misunderstood his brief frown. 'Don't look so worried, sir. That's for the likes of me – an old married woman with two children.' The horse waited at the stone mounting block as he attached his bag to the pommel and swung himself into the saddle. A new shoe had been necessary. More expense. A bicycle might be the answer – no oats! He waited for a cart, being pulled at a fast trot, to pass. It slowed, however, and came to a halt outside the shop, perfectly controlled and manoeuvred. He moved off, then looked back briefly over his shoulder at the girl. He didn't want to linger and seem to be prying. George Jackson was still uncomfortable with him, after all that had happened.

Mary jumped down before her husband could come out to help and lowered the back of the cart for unloading. Algernon found her looks breathtaking, though he knew his admiration wouldn't be shared by all the conventional young men in Findlesham. The severity of her costume, the beautiful head with the milk-blonde hair scraped back and the lack of adornment served to emphasize the high cheekbones, long neck and narrow body. At a distance she could look like a boy, which was probably a partially deliberate attempt to render her sexuality invisible.

Hannah ran out of the shop to help. 'Why didn't you collect the children, Mary?' She picked up a box of potatoes, earthy with some roots still attached, and carried it in.

'Thought you'd like the afternoon free.'

'Free? I've got to clean the cottage and do dinner for Sammy and us.'

'You go home, then. Sorry, Hanny. I'll pick them up later in the cart, bring them over and stop for my dinner with you. All right?'

She had planned it, Hannah knew, nothing she could say. Mary spent one evening a week with the schoolmistress, learning what to teach, one with Ma and Pa and one with Sam and her. Mornings she was at the school, afternoons in the shop, meal-times Aunt Biddy and Billy were there. That was her life, it suited everything fine. She didn't understand it wasn't how others lived. Sammy and her found precious the hour after putting Betsy and Bobby to bed. Taking their time eating, sitting close by the fire, walking a little way on a fine evening. Making plans for the cottage, making love. She had revised her opinions about that: knowledge had come from experience. Making love didn't depend on an evening at the Bull and Butcher or a cold winter night. Four years after their marriage they were as loving as they had ever been when they were tumbling together in barns or clasping each other lying on warm grass on a summer night.

'All right?' Mary repeated.

'All right.'

The housekeeper had gone to bed. They could help themselves to more beef from the sideboard, and a steamed pudding, redolent of lemons, was keeping hot on the low flame of a warming plate. They were drinking a delicious burgundy which the Fiennders' had sent him years ago when her gifts and money were more forthcoming, and were on to the second bottle. Ann was amused but just a little irritated by her cousin's false naïveté. 'Algernon, dear. I don't know how to put it more clearly. Something was said by one of the undergardeners to the effect that not only had you helped officiate at Thomas's funeral at Findlesham, but you were poaching other funerals from poor old Touche-Forster.'

'Was the information gleaned from an under-gardener called Samuel Reade?' He raised an eyebrow reminding her of a previous occasion, long ago, when his archness had caused trouble. 'Sorry, Ann. That was uncalled for.' He wasn't *very* sorry. He had lost her patronage, but honesty might regain her friendship.

'No, it wasn't called for, and I don't gossip with the sons of my employees.' He watched her struggle to find a way of questioning him without betraying undue interest. She pursed her still prettily curved mouth. 'There is talk, you see, about a woman in the village and . . . er . . . children, and the father of the children – or fathers – and then, are they the sister's or not? And if so why wasn't it buried wherever whichever sister it was lived. And, either way, why is the wife concerned?' Ann was frowning at the end of this muddle.

'More to the point, Ann, why are *you* concerned?' It was delicious to have her floundering like that, in need of him, and he laughed. 'This conversation,' he said, 'has become so oblique I've almost forgotten what we're talking about. I presume it must have something to do with your relationship with Sam Reade.'

He remembered the summer afternoon in the greenhouse when he had discovered their affair. It had been hot and Reade had fetched from his pocket a kerchief to mop his face. It hadn't been a large coarse piece of cloth but a delicate lace-trimmed piece of linen enfolding a silk stocking. The flush on the man's face had not been brought about by guilt or embarrassment, but by remembered desire.

Honesty served him well. She pushed her glass towards him and smiled thanks as he filled it. 'Not directly, Algy, but I do feel some responsibility for the people concerned in an indirect way.'

He raised his hands, shaking them, still laughing. 'No, no, no, Ann. I will answer your unasked questions if you will only be quiet and stop confusing me with your serpentine sentences.' She sipped her wine, turned the sip into a gulp and joined his laughter. 'You are talking about the Jacksons, yes?' She nodded. 'They should never have married, the girl was too young,' Algernon said.

He admired her too, she could tell that by his tone. 'Too young? She was fourteen.'

He turned his head to the darkened window. Beyond his garden, in the pasture, he could see pinpricks of light

– men with yokes on their shoulders carrying buckets were walking towards cows to be milked by the light of their lanterns. 'Too immature then.'

It *was* her concern; that girl frozen in adolescence. She had some responsibility, Ann. But what? 'I would guess that their physical relationship stopped after the birth of the boy. In due course, young Jackson . . .'

'George?'

'Yes, George Jackson, took up with a pretty widow in the village, Sally Webb, with the tacit approval of his wife. Not sure he was aware of their friendship at first.' Algernon remembered the anger and confusion of the man confronted by this, what, friendship? Expediency? 'Naturally, over the years the woman went through pregnancies. Three in all. When she was close to her confinement she would go away to one of her sisters and bring the baby home as a child of that sister.'

'Quite usual, you know, Algy, and many a mother is bringing up her eldest daughter's child as her own.'

'I'm well aware of my parishioners' peccadilloes, Ann. I rarely marry a couple who haven't already taken the necessary action to becoming parents. And I don't consider myself to be in a position to cast the first stone. Anyway, the last child was born sickly and the Webb woman was none too well either. She had travelled down from Staffordshire alone. When the baby's colic worsened she put up at a place in Stanford-in-the-Vale and sent for Mary Jackson. The baby died. Mary laid it out and brought them both here for what they hoped would be a discreet funeral – obviously not discreet enough.' He was angry that people making generous accommodations with their sad problems should be gossiped about. 'How do you know about it, Ann? Not through Hannah and young Sam? And why is it your concern?'

'Emma Bowden heard something of it and asked me to help.' She would tell him some, but not all, of her involvement. It was curious that the two women of whom she had been jealous – Mary Jackson and Sally Webb – should be sharing, as it were, a husband. Her jealousy had been unnecessary but it had helped to create the unfortunate ménage.

'And?'

'And I owe her a . . . good turn, one good turn . . . many good turns, actually.'

'The mother didn't know her son-in-law had a mistress? She must have been burying her head in the sand.'

'Those who are closest often don't know.'

He turned his head to the window, embarrassed. Not at the difficulty he had once created for her, but at any pain he might have caused her husband. The flickering light from the cowherds' lanterns was slowly proceeding to the farmhouse.

'Don't worry about that, Algy. What Thomas cared about was the parentage of his own children and he knew he was their father.'

'Good. I'm glad.'

'It's young Albert Bowden who is the problem.'

'Little Bertie? Rather a comical little lad, I remember.'

'Yes. But not so funny when he's a strong young man of six foot who wants to avenge his sister's honour.'

'An honour which she didn't value, Ann.'

He collected their dinner plates, put them on the gleaming, candle-lit sideboard and placed the dessert plates in front of them both.

'Nothing for me, Algy. I'm fat and fifty.'

'Are you? Fifty, I mean?' He set the pudding in front of her with a broad silver knife and spoon.

'So you, too, think I'm fat?' She examined her body encased in black silk trimmed with jet beads, the crisp white pie-crust frill at the neck the only relief from black. She was in mourning for her husband and might mourn for ever. Black was very becoming.

'How discourteous of me, Ann. Not at all. You are as shapely and attractive as you were at half your age.' He cut into the pudding, revealing a whole lemon in the centre and handed her the spoon.

'Mm, the smell, delicious. Pond Pudding. It's one of the few things our Bunny can't do well. I can't resist it.'

'Good. Mrs Roberts made some crème Chantilly. I know it's gilding the lily, but this lily should be gilded. The lemon makes it a little sharp.' Now, he decided, it was time to pump *her*, having been pumped successfully himself. 'Why does David Touche-Forster care about the funeral of a baby born out of his parish? Very little cash or cachet.'

Ann reddened a little. 'It's all a bit awkward. He takes everything very personally. We adore Madeleine but he's become rather difficult, sees demons where there are none.'

'I hear he has a habit of stopping sermons in the middle, forgetting his subject. Mrs Roberts's daughter said he actually went back to the beginning of the service after the bidding prayers last Sunday.'

'Yes. Madeleine says it's a form of dementia or premature senility, poor man.'

'Not all that premature, surely?' He knew he must

tread carefully. Years ago it had been understood that he would be given the very good living of Findlesham were anything to happen to David Touche-Forster, but since his estrangement from the Fiennders', he hadn't counted on it.

Inconsequentially she said, 'It would be much better if they lived in London. Doctors, hospitals, that sort of thing. Madeleine would prefer it too.' Before he could get any ideas about the new incumbent and embarrass them both, she added quickly, 'And then we would give the living to Isabel's husband. The rectory at Bickley is far too small.'

Ah, well. He hid his disappointment. Not unexpected. 'And how is Richard?'

She brightened. 'He took over the reins immediately, has great plans. He loves the place, always has done.' She smiled and licked her lips. He didn't think it was the Pond Pudding she was savouring. 'And it seems likely that an announcement will be made soon.'

'Who?'

'Caroline Colcroft.'

'Ann, my dear, I *am* pleased. Lady Caroline. What an asset. Money, land, title, and very good-looking. We must celebrate. I'll get a bottle of champagne.' No wonder she was so pleased. The dower house was very near the gardener's cottage.

When they were beyond the outskirts of Wellsbury Mary slowed the horse to a walk, relaxed the reins and put an arm around her brother. 'I insist we speak about it, Bertie. It won't go away.' He stiffened under her embrace and flung her off. 'It's the way of the world, my love. People don't always live happily ever after.'

'It's true, then?' He punched her arm viciously, but regretted it immediately, and rubbed it gently. She encircled him again. This time he accepted it and, leaning against her delicate body, cried, muffling the noise in her cloak.

'Can you imagine how you've upset Pa and Ma? No Bowden has ever been in the lock-up before, Bertie.'

'He called you names. Said no wonder he looked elsewhere. What man wants a bony schoolmarm in his bed?'

She ignored this. 'Why were you in such a dreadful inn, anyway? What's wrong with the Bull and Butcher?'

'Didn't want to see people.'

She took away her arm and lifted his head. 'My love, if you're to be angry with anyone 'tis with me. Don't go drinking with strangers and fighting with friends. This is hard for you today, maybe, but next month, next year, it will just be part of everything. Forgotten, or accepted by all who know, or who think they know.' She jerked the reins. 'Gie on there. We must be getting on. Ma and Pa will be anxious till they sees you.'

'Why is it you, Mary, that I should be angry with? Why you?' he shouted. 'It's George! It's George! He's done this to my Mary.'

'Be quiet, love. We're nigh on the new cottages, then we'll be in Findlesham.'

'Passing *her* house.'

'Listen now, Bertie, you're old enough to understand, see. We love each other, George and I, but not in the way of Ma and Pa or, say, Hanny and Sam. I never did. I think he felt those sort of things but I didn't so . . .' She felt the cold, sad pain again. It didn't come so much now, not in the last year or so.

'Is that why your John is all?'

'That is why.' They were through Findlesham and around the sharp bend nearing Keepers Cottage. She pulled up the horse. 'Bertie, I've been thinking.'

'So have I, Mary. But you go first.'

'Well, all right then. It's that I have been at fault. I tried to make amends to George in the best way I could. Now I see that I put all that before . . . well . . . the worst fault is I've been hard on Ma and . . .' She understood her mother better, now that she herself had to earn money so that George could take care of his other family. 'Look, I want us to go in loving, like, to Ma and Pa. There's hardly a family in the land, high or low, that doesn't have its troubles. And in this very shire our family's troubles must be little, considering.' She regretted her coldness to her mother and the cruel accusations. '*You sold me for running water!*'

He nodded. 'And, Mary, I'm sorry about the lock-up. I liked getting drunk and I really liked punching Arthur Redding. But I know it's wrong. And . . . if I ever get married – for I'm not sure I will – then I'll test all the girls first to make sure they want to have babies.'

The lantern she had brought for the journey home was unlit and the moon was behind a cloud now, thank goodness. She hadn't been seen. Crossing the fields on the old green way, stony and hard-earthed, baked by the sun, she had been glad of the moon's silver light. As strong as the gold of the sun. 'One rising, one falling. The calling of night and the ending of June.' She had intended to use the picnic for George's birthday on the first of July as an excuse for the visit. An excuse was necessary now. She had been aware last Friday of an awkwardness when she had called in and had left early, forgoing tea. This evening her feet had been silent on the grass. The hens were already shut up and the garden gate was ajar. Her noiseless approach to the little cottage meant she had caught them unawares.

Hanny's hair, a long silk sheet, was loose to her waist and she and Sammy were coiled together in the large armchair, as one. As it should be, she thought, without envy, as she slipped away. Too early to go home. She always tried to make sure George was home just before her, the same as she left before him; then there was no need for his badly told stories and half-truths. There weren't many places to go to pass the time. Ma and Pa would worry if she went to Keepers Cottage more than once a week, and on a summer's evening like this, courting couples might be found in every barn, granary and sheepcote. She didn't venture into the Abbey's woods and gardens unless she'd heard that Richard was away, and now that she knew exactly why the gazebo had been built, that also was out of bounds, whether he was away or not. She thought of her privy and laughed aloud. It was seldom used now that her parents had an indoor water closet. A gazebo for the lady of the manor and an earth closet for her.

Sam Reade heard the girl laugh as he smoked his pipe leaning against the still-warm walls of his house. He had been listening to the nightly sounds of death; an owl with a mouse, a fox with one of the ducklings, a stoat with a rabbit. What was she doing wandering out alone at this hour? Perhaps she wasn't alone. He waited for the sound of voices then, through a gap in the silvery poplars, he saw her walking slowly up Princes Ride. So as not to startle her, he strode firmly through the copse on the dry, cracking twigs. 'Ho there! Mary, is that you?' She heard the soft call and ran to meet him. 'You been to see young Sam and Hanny?'

'Not really.' She grinned. 'I see them but they didn't see me.'

'Oh?'

'They was all lovey-dovey. I could see through the window – not spying, like.'

'Course not.' He took her arm companionably. 'They are lovey-dovey. Nice, isn't it?'

'Oh, yes, like a fairy-tale.'

'Not many of those, Mary, in these modern times.'

'No, Mr Reade. So I crept away. Leave them be, I thought to myself.'

'Ah, that's right.' They reached the clearing in front of his house. 'Come on in, then, and I'll make us some tea. The kettle's always on.' He gestured to the open front door. 'That was the best leg that ever was broken.'

'Broken leg. Why?'

'Well, Mary, if I hadn't broken my leg, young Sam wouldn't have come here to help out and . . .' He handed her a delicate blue and white porcelain cup and saucer.

'Thank you, Mr Reade. And he wouldn't have met Hanny.'

'Right.'

The cup was pretty. Not like a man would have. It must be hers; she must come here. Mary laughed and replaced the cup carefully on the sturdy kitchen table. 'You're right. It *is* funny, a broken bone bringing lovers together.' She must control herself, stop laughing. It wouldn't do for him to guess that she knew how the leg had been broken. Falling out of the secret room in the gazebo, that's how it had happened.

'Now then, Mary, I've got an idea. You need somewhere to study your books of an evening, your French and all that, and I know just the place.'

She tilted her head, the little face looking even more angular in the light from the large, white-shaded paraffin lamp. 'Where would that be, Mr Reade?'

'Back of the shop. We should've thought of it before. Add on to the store-room there, it's more of a cupboard right now, put in a nice comfortable chair. Bit of peace and quiet for you. What do you think to that?'

She felt tears pricking her eyes. What a good friend he was. He understood everything, always had. When Aunt Biddy had suggested the shop, it was Sam Reade who had organized it, seen it through. True, she had paid for it, Aunt Biddy, and Pa had helped with the work, but Mr Reade had got Jim Turner and Jim Turner had got the wood. He had shown her where the trees had been blown down in a storm, then kept to dry and season before being planked. She jumped up and hugged him, tucking her head under his chin against his broad chest. He folded his arms around her, feeling the bird-like bones across her spine.

'You're not crying, girl, are you? I wouldn't like to be the cause of that.'

'No, no.'

'What are these tears, then?'

'They're not crying tears, they're pleased tears. Do you see?'

'I see the tears, and yes, Mary, I think I see what you're saying. Now, I'm going to get us a bit of supper here. There's cold rabbit – a present from your dad, the rabbit. Jellied it is, with parsley. I'm going to have some home-brew and you're going to have a nice glass of madeira, no argument.'

'I'm not going to argue.'

'I mean about the madeira.'

Her brown eyes gleamed like topaz and twinkled. 'So do I.' That must be for *her* too, she thought. 'Shall I tell you an easy way to cook a rabbit that the tinker told me?' She didn't wait for a reply. 'You clean it in the usual way, stuff it with breadcrumbs, chopped apple, suet and parsley and thyme, cover the whole thing, fur an' all, with clay and bake it in the embers. When it's cooked you break the clay off and the skin comes too.'

'And then what happens?' he said, putting a plate and glass in front of her.

'You eat it, silly!'

He saw her off, having lit the candle in her lantern. 'Safely home, Mary. Don't forget, any worries, come to me, talk them out. I care for you, child, like you was my own.'

She hardly needed the lantern-light; the moon was high above her in an unclouded sky, dotted with the fierce brilliance of stars, perfect in their purity. The shadow she cast was like a friend leading the way. The new room would be a good idea, especially in winter. She made a hop-skip-and-jump, clearing the ditch, forgetting the maturity of her twenty-five years. Most of her worries were sorted out; they could be managed. All but Bertie.

It was a nicety of George's to drop in at the Bull and Butcher on his way home from evenings with Sally. Half a pint of cider or shandy was all he took but it meant they could speak openly about his absence, and George, too, would bring talk from the sages at the inn. This evening, though, he hadn't, and waited for Mary with unaccustomed irritability. His aunt sat at the open window making use of the large oil lamp to read her *Daily Chronicle*. The moths were also using it to singe their wings and from time to time, she would grunt in annoyance, but whether from news in the paper or at the intrusion of the moths, George couldn't tell.

'What's the use?' she muttered.

'What's the use of what?' he said impatiently.

'Farm-hands having the vote and then not using it.'

'They use it, all right, they just don't vote the way you want them to. And the same would happen if they give the vote to women – not that they'd be daft enough to do that.'

'And you think, do you, George Jackson, that you use your vote rightly? That your great brain entitles you to your vote better nor than me, or Mary, or Aphra Behn, or Emma Bowden, or Queen Victoria, or Patty the fishman's daughter who won the scholarship, or—' Incoherent with rage, she ran out of examples.

He shuffled away from her, surly and confused. 'Alf Bean, whoever he is when he's at home, is a man.'

She stifled a laugh — not right to sneer at him. He was a good man, by and large.

'There's Mary now.' She pointed to a bobbing light making its way across the meadow beyond the pond. 'She's late, George.'

'No, I'm early.' He turned from the window, adding thoughtlessly, 'I forgot to go to the inn.' It had been a bit contrary-like at Sal's. They'd chatted, the children were put to bed and, it being Friday, he gave her the money. The curtains were drawn as usual. They always were after five, whether it was one of his nights or not, so as no one could put two and two together. They'd chatted a bit more, of the model farm and the new cottages, how the hired hands didn't take kindly to the changes in old tried ways. And then he'd felt tired, wanted to go home, really, and, truth be told, didn't want her. Couldn't rightly tell her why, wasn't clear himself. Something to do with this morning.

He'd woken to see Mary standing by the window, the pale early light penetrating the thin cotton of her nightdress and revealing the naked body underneath, the shape of which he had only been able to guess at until now. They slept in the same bed, kissed goodnight on the cheek, held hands sometimes when she was frightened in a storm, but otherwise their touch was accidental: turning over in sleep, stretching a cramped leg. He examined her body through half-closed eyes. If anything it was more child-like than when he had taken it in marriage eleven years ago when she was fourteen. The slightly swelling breasts were flat now as was the stomach; even the shadow of hair between her legs had diminished to just a token of womanhood. He had forced himself inside that body over and over until she got with young John. And he had wanted her still over the years, not so's it had bothered him once he'd taken up with Sal. But now he felt a freedom. It must have been happening for a while and he not noticing. He loved her, yes, he loved her. More, maybe, but didn't want her any more. And therein was the strangeness of it all, for he didn't want Sal either.

'Hello, love.' He took the lantern from Mary and locked the door. 'Did you ask Hanny and Sam if they want to come with us on the outing?'

'No, I thought it would be nicer like, just the three of us, you, me and our John.'

Biddy folded her newspaper carefully. 'Quite right. You don't see enough of him. And I'm getting a bit old to be serving all day in the shop on my own, you know.' To emphasize that, she groaned as she stood and stretched her back.

'Not too old to walk five mile there and back to hear the lady preacher in Up Gadstone!'

'That, George, was inspiring. If you light our candles, I'll turn this lamp out and we can all go up.'

'John asleep all right, Aunt Biddy?' Mary whispered, as she mounted the creaking stairs with care.

'He's not here, Mary love, he's staying over at Keepers Cottage. Your pa's taking him out before sun up, checking traps.'

'Did you hear that, George?' She had already slipped quickly into her side of the bed when he joined her after bolting the back door and locking up the forge. 'No wonder she said we don't see enough of the boy.'

'It's good for him, Mary. He's got a choice, don't you see? Your father says he's got a real way for it – quiet, notices, cares for the birds. Keepering will always be here but I don't know about the forge.'

She was nearly asleep when he got into his side of the bed. Over the years the good comfortable double bed had become hardly distinguishable from two singles. 'The forge? That'll be here for ever. A farrier will always be needed even if cast iron takes over from . . . your iron . . .' She reached out a hand to meet his. 'Good night, love.'

It was Bertie she thought about just before sleep came. Her son was usurping the rights of her brother. Poor Bertie.

'Well, that's it, then. Let's do it soon so that we're back from the honeymoon and don't miss the whole season. I'm longing to give my new mare her head, let her show her paces. We can hunt, of course, in France, Chantilly. I know you think of Paris, but a day or two, well, a week, then. You do your music, I'll do my fittings, Fontainebleau is near, then back to Paris, my clothes will be ready. Train home. And your mother will have got into the dower house. Marvellous woman, I'm jolly lucky, she seems really quite pleased.' She paused through the tumble of words and plans, her lovely face shining with gaiety and enthusiasm.

'So you are sure, then, Caroline?'

'*I'm* sure. Does that question mean you're not? No, of course you are. Hellfire, Richard, it's all absolutely perfect. We both know what we want and what we're getting.'

'So far you're getting a mare, some dresses and good hunting.'

She marched to the windows and gestured out expansively. 'I love this bit of the county as much as you. I like your ideas for the estate. The house suits me, not too big.'

'Fourteen bedrooms,' he murmured, amused.

'Quite. If you can count the bedrooms it isn't too big. I don't want to interfere with your music, you're marvellous. Everybody says so and it's useful too at parties. Not all the gloomy stuff, but . . . you know.'

'And me?' He said this with only a slight edge of irony. They did suit and they did know what they were getting. He knew her, physically, rather well – the creamy full bosom partly revealed in the fine lawn of her afternoon dress had been fully disclosed to him. He had explored her body, pleased and excited by the soft skin and the willingness of her response to his hands. Her desire certainly matched his, and so had her inventiveness in satisfying each other – short of penetration.

She saw his eyes half close and interpreted the lazy smile correctly. 'And you have sown your wild oats to very good effect.' She took his hand and slipped it inside the neck of her dress. Through the house they heard the reverberations of a gong. 'That's the second dressing bell, isn't it? We had better go and change.'

Desire had instantly left her but he caught her hand and pulled her towards him. The face, which was always faintly flushed, was even warmer now. The natural red of her mouth was deeper and the ruddy brown wavy hair looked Titian in the light of the setting sun filtering through the windows. 'You are a funny girl, Caro, passionate and practical.'

Her voice held a rare note of uncertainty. 'That's good, isn't it?'

'Oh, indeed,' he said. Refusing to release her, he pressed his knee between her legs and kissed her, remembering a different sort of kiss last night.

Charlie Colcroft, sitting at Ann's left, was twinkling at her. Even allowing that he was in his cups, could he be so conceited as to imagine that she would entertain the idea of a liaison with him? She was responding flirtatiously, but it was a game. Why would she choose to sleep with this pot-bellied unattractive man, with his bloodshot eyes and skin the colour of the port he drank so freely, when she had the tall, strong, clear-eyed gardener, no doubt, waiting for her? It was good to be back in the fold but Algernon knew he could be exiled again and guarded his expression. He continued to survey the long, gleaming oak table on which every piece of plate and glass gleamed as well. Exquisite silver, all made by Thomas Chawner over a hundred years ago. An array of crystal glasses, a flight at each place, filled, half-full, empty but for a stain of amber from the oloroso, gold from the Montrachet, pale blackberry from the burgundy and now the intense rich yellow from the sublime Chateau d'Yquem. Ann treated her guests as she did herself. Not wanting to relinquish an unfinished wine from a previous dish, she did not allow the footmen to clear the glasses until the end of dinner. The light from the branched candelabra accentuated the match of the colours of the wines to the jewels on the women's wrists, fingers, ears and necks. Amber yellow topaz, deep red rubies, pale diamonds, golden chains. And the blue of the sapphires echoed the Bristol-blue of the glass salt-cellars, the green of the emeralds – the green of the emeralds? Algernon was determined to find their match. Nothing on the table? No, he looked again at the wearer of the emeralds. Her eyes, that would have to do. A choker was a mistake for that neck, it emphasized a tendency to thickness not counterbalanced by length. She was a gorgeous creature, though, and well-mannered. Gave the first half of dinner to Isabel's husband, the Very Reverend the Hon. Boring-Kimball, with no indication that he wasn't the most fascinating man in England – and was now doing the same to Arthur somebody, the new man at Hazely Magna House.

'And where is the youngest of your lovely daughters, Ann?' Charlie Colcroft was really making heavy weather of his compliments, Richard thought, though his mother didn't seem to mind. It had hardly been flattering to compare her with the portraits of her predecessors, which were hung about the dining-room walls. Most of the Fiennders women had lashless, swollen eyelids and a lower lip upon which you could balance a candlestick. Richard looked at his mother appreciatively: she had brought money and looks to the family.

'Maud, my dear Charles, has eaten in the schoolroom with her governess. She is too young to join us.'

Richard caught her eye and grinned. She was amusing to be with alone, but her sharp tongue and lack of grace made her no asset at a dinner party such as this.

'Too young. How old is the little minx, eh?'

'Fourteen.' Ann signalled discreetly to the butler, indicating Lord Colcroft's empty glass.

'Fourteen? Not too young to marry and have children but too young to dine . . .'

Richard didn't hear the finish of his future father-in-law's remark: a pain, cold and sharp, attacked him. Fourteen. Not too young to marry and have children. The image was there again, clear, isolated from the people surrounding her. The huge brown eyes dominating the pale, heart-shaped face, and the distended stomach looking so at odds in the immature body. He had never seen her since. She didn't go to St Michael's any more. George Nichols, the groom, had told him she went to the Methodists with the aunt. Perhaps if he had seen her that image would leave him.

He was unaware that he'd been silent for some minutes and that Algernon, guessing the reason, had covered the awkwardness with a hastily invented story about arranged marriages for babies in the subcontinent and the likelihood of children being widowed before they reached double figures. 'And, Richard,' he said, leaning across Lady Berreford and gently nudging him, 'your marriage was certainly arranged, if not in heaven in the saddle.' This *double entendre* got a few guffaws from the men, a good open laugh from Caroline, and Richard's attention.

He smiled at Algernon, grateful for his intercession. Funny man, he was looking quite avuncular. 'What do you think, Caro? Arranged in heaven? By our parents? Or natural selection?

'Preordained, I'd say.'

★

'Now look here, Richard.' He was kneeling by her bed, she could see him reflected in the triple mirror on her dressing table, his head bent over her body as he kissed her breasts. One hand was under the bedclothes caressing her thighs as he parted her legs.

He raised his head. 'What?'

'I've talked to your mother and she agrees with us.'

'Us?'

'Yes, you know.' She gave a little start as his hand explored her further. 'It's a bit soon, it's true, after, well, your poor father's . . . whatsit.'

'Death,' he said firmly.

'Er, yes, death.' She preferred any euphemism to the word death – 'passed away', 'gone,' 'taken'. 'But she agrees that we should just say it was all arranged, before his . . .'

'Death.'

'And I was thinking . . . Oh, God, Richard! That *is* good, don't stop.'

'What were you thinking?' His touch was light, almost teasing.

Haltingly, between gasps, she said, 'If we have a long engagement, don't get married for six months, well . . . Oh, please, yes, oh, please, we ought to be careful but . . .'

'But?'

'If we get married soon, six weeks say, well . . . Oh, God, more, yes, like that . . . there's no reason why we shouldn't do it now.' He took his hand away and pulling back the bedclothes opened her legs wider and slowly entered her. She was small, a virgin still, but oh, Lord, it was wonderful. She certainly wanted him. 'No reason at all.' Her face, dimly lit by the bedside candle, was beautiful in its abandonment.

'I don't know. Caroline thinks All Saints is far too small. St Margaret's, Westminster, if they decide on London, or Dorchester Abbey is what she wants.'

Ann shrugged. 'It makes no difference to us, Richard darling. The responsibility and choice are theirs, except for giving them our guest list, which I have already done, and organizing the tenants' party—'

'Already given them our list?'

'Don't look so shocked, Richard. I've known for months and so have you. It was clear to everybody. Even Felicity Colcroft has put plans, things, in motion. Reluctance to give up your so-called freedom held you back from what was a forgone conclusion.'

'So it really was an arranged marriage? Stop worrying, Mamma, it's all right. I really am . . . pleased, well . . . happy.'

'Good, of course you are. I wonder if it's true about Felicity and Charlie.'

'Not from observing his behaviour with you last night.'

'Oh, that was just politesse. It could be politesse with Felicity, too.'

It was amusing, but Richard felt reservations of disapproval. 'Is this a part of modern society I've missed, Mother? It's polite, is it, to sleep with your dead wife's sister?'

'Don't be so pompous, Richard. Felicity assumed the role of Caroline's mother. The role might have expanded over the years, that is all.' They walked back to the house having seen the Colcroft carriage bowl away in a cloud of dust. 'What are you doing today? I will be busy until dinner. Then tomorrow I must go to London to order my dress for the wedding.'

'I'm amazed you haven't ordered it already, Mamma. I notice you've started work on the dower house, and as for the gardens!'

'You may tease, Richard, but six weeks only. It's as well I do think ahead.' And, thinking ahead, she gave a little shiver of delight. Two days in London, and two nights, which was quite unnecessary, but half of that time would be spent with Sam on the way back. He would collect a boat at Staines. Windsor would be more convenient, but it was too near Eton and Tommy.

'Will you take Maud?'

'Certainly not.'

'Oh, come on, Mamma, she's not as bad as that and she, too, must have something to wear.'

'Not from Monsieur Donnez she mustn't. Our woman in Wellsbury is quite good enough for the child.'

'It's interesting how Maud's status changes,' he said. 'As Charlie noticed last night.'

'You won't address him as Charlie, will you, dear?'

He brushed this aside. 'She's a "young woman and should behave as such", then "too young to join us at dinner", "old enough to know better" and now a child for whom the local dressmaker is good enough.'

The attack was unexpected and hurt. 'Did you want to be alone, darling? She won't get in your way. Little Rosie from the kitchen will be busy with her, to start packing her winter things, you know. We are bringing her on to be Maud's maid.'

'No, I'll dine with her tomorrow, teach her some manners, and I promised I'd look at her rooms at the dower house, give her some ideas.'

'That's very good of you, Richard. We're going to use some of the stuffs, the wall-hangings, you brought back from Florence in the drawing room. My bedroom and sitting room will be William Morris carpets, curtains and wallpaper.'

'I hope the men who hang it will have "joy in their labour".'

Good Lord, he was in a strange mood.

'Why should they not?'

He relented. Why be unkind, when she had had neither his education nor his experience. 'That's what he believes, William Morris. Pleasure shouldn't be separated from work, nor art from craft.' He walked past the front door, heading towards the stables.

'What a good idea,' she said brightly. 'What *are* you going to do, Richard? Today, I mean.'

'I'm going to start saying goodbye.'

'But *you* are staying.' She laughed uneasily. 'It is *we* who are going – Maud, Tommy, Davis, me . . .'

'Little Rosie,' he added.

'Yes, little Rosie. And Caroline. She will be leaving Gadstone Park, her home.'

'Nichols is saddling up old Ferocity and I'm going to say goodbye to my memories, that's all.' Not that all of his bachelor memories were here. Some of the bad ones had been erased, or at least eased, in Oxford. By Madeleine. He was glad the Touche-Forsters had gone to London. It would have been difficult sitting with Caro and Madeleine at the same table. His fiancée was shrewd, and she might have guessed who had been responsible for making him a good lover, where he had sown some of his wild oats. And Madeleine... He wouldn't have liked her to have felt like an old, discarded mistress.

'Good morning, sir. Perfect day. He's saddled and ready to go, ready for a good gallop. It's a treat for him. You've neglected him in favour of Darkling and he knows!'

'What are you going to ride, Nick?'

'Me, sir?' George Nichols's smile split his face like a sliced melon. 'Am I to accompany you?'

'I'd like you to... unless... I mean, it's a bit selfish of me. Do you have work to do? No, damn it. I want to talk to you. Come on, saddle up Matchmaker over there.' Richard could see the gelding had been groomed. He was a good horse, younger than Ferocity and easily his equal.

'Yes, Richard – sir.' Lovely, Matchmaker. Very considerate of the young master. Or master now, more like.

After racing up Princes Ride, galloping between the spruces laid out like the aisle of a church, they slowed to a canter along the bridlepath leading to the foot of Paradise Hill. Richard led them round the side of the hill and, putting his horse to the low bramble hedge into Deadman's Copse, cleared it easily, as did Nichols. They walked their horses through the path made by centuries of deer until they reached the almost dry dew-pond. Relaxing the reins, Richard let the horse's head stretch down for water. 'Nick, I want to tell you something you may have guessed, but I want to tell you officially. There

are two reasons why I want to tell you and talk to you.'
George Nichols was flattered to be treated as a confidant
but not surprised. There'd been times before when it'd
been needed. 'I'm engaged to be married. Lady Caroline
Colcroft. In six weeks – my word, you do look pleased.
Hadn't you guessed?'

'It's a relief, sir and aye, I'm pleased for you. You
might have been telling me you were off again, going
round the world, and that do take such a long time.'

Richard held out his hand. 'So you congratulate me?'

'And Lady Caroline, too, sir. She's a lucky lady.' He
wiped his hand on his jacket, though it was probably as
clean as his master's. 'Very good, Richard – sir, very good
and time enough now for you to settle down.' The horses
were quiet, nibbling lazily at the reeds around the pond.
The two men, their hands clasped, looked at each other.
Remembering.

'Tell her, Nick, will you?'

'I will.'

The groom recalled when his help had been needed
before. He had known it would happen, wished it hadn't
happened like that. He had been at the church and seen,
so he wasn't too surprised when after his Sunday dinner
he found Master Richard had gone off with the young
horse. Not a good mount to take when your temper
might be careless. He had ridden Seamus out to try to
find the lad. Sure enough, he'd taken a tumble down by
Grimm's Dyke. The horse didn't seem to be hurt, thank
the Lord, just standing under a tree quietly grazing, but
the lad was holding his head and making a terrible noise,
sounded in pain. He was crying, though not like any
crying he'd heard before. 'Nothing to be done, Richard

lad, nothing to be done.' He'd held him in his arms, quietened him. Couldn't take the pain away but could give him a shoulder, be a friend.

'Trust me.' He had said it that time before too.

The horses stirred, shifting positions, and the men loosened their hands. 'I'll ride over to the schoolhouse now and have a word when she's finished.'

Richard nodded, his head averted. He was too old at twenty-seven to have tears for something childish and long lost. 'Then, meet me at the Barley Mow, will you, Nick?' Alone, he thought about Caroline. He *was* a lucky man, she would be an absolutely splendid wife. He guided the restless horse away from the pond and its cloud of hovering midges. If he made her happy he would probably be happy himself.

The farm looked almost deserted. No Adamses there now. Debt had driven the family away, pride preventing them from renting a cottage in the village, too big a come-down. They had gone up to the Potteries and taken a smallholding. What would he do with the farmhouse? Find another tenant, a 'hobby' farmer, somebody who didn't need the income as a living. It was close enough to the railway station and then London to be a convenient second home for one of those City people with money but no land. The farm ran itself at the moment. The same hands, the same foremen, all living in tied cottages on the estate.

The house itself was beautiful and had more architectural integrity than Fiennders Abbey, whose successive inheritors had all added or subtracted from its fourteenth-century origins. This building hadn't been altered since its construction in the early eighteenth century. The faded rose bricks, marked with blue here and there, had been fired in a kiln just a few miles away on Middlecombe Common, where they were still being manufactured in the same way. Perhaps in a few years Tommy would like it. It was in Richard's gift – it all was. Giving the living of Findlesham to Freddy Baring-Kimball to ensure Issy's comfort, and Jess, with her laird in Scotland, land rich but money poor, had taken a decent dowry to her marriage, courtesy of him, even if it had been part of the holdings his mother had brought to the Fiennders'. Ann's amiable acceptance of her lot had surprised him; he would naturally pay towards the refurbishment of the dower house and give her an allowance, but nevertheless, it was good of her to relinquish her role as *the* Mrs Fiennders so graciously. Those mysterious words of his father, when he was dying but still rational, hovered unexplained. Smiling he had said, 'Don't worry about Ann. She won't be lonely and she won't be poor.'

The clank of pails preceded the appearance of a buxom, red-faced young girl at the door of the dairy. 'Do 'e mind these, Fanny, or I'll skuttle 'e,' she called, to no one whom Richard could see. He turned his horse and trotted away, from memories dear and painful. There was just time to face the challenge of the gazebo, unvisited for years. That, too, was his now. Then a long canter over Paradise Hill – Sparrows' Dice – round the old Roman earthworks, and he would see Keepers Cottage across Threeacre Field. He was getting used to meeting John Bowden now with the boy. He didn't look like her or the smith, more like a son of Bowden's than a grandson. The man's grief at Thomas Fiennders' death had been shaming. Had any of his own family felt like that?

Richard doubted it. The meadow led to the parish boundary. Skirting Upper Bewdley he would be at the Barley Mow to meet Nick.

George Nichols had caught her leaving the schoolhouse surrounded by spirited, noisy children all leaping and squealing like untrained puppies off their leashes. This was the dinner hour and somehow they would manage to play every game ever invented involving a ball or a skipping rope, undo and make undying friendships, graze knees, cut hands, bruise foreheads, tear aprons, dirty clothes – especially anything white or clean on today – and even find a minute or two to eat whatever had been given them that morning. This varied from a cut off the Sunday joint, to bread and scrape.

'Can I have a word?'

Mary detached herself from a group of the younger girls, all chattering and pulling at her skirts. 'Miss, miss,' they cried, sad at the loss of her attention.

He noticed his own daughter, Flora, hanging back with the bigger girls, their heads together whispering, for all the world like a gaggle of women at the village pump.

'Everything all right? Pa all right?'

'Yes, oh, yes. I didn't mean to fright you. No cart today?'

'I walked. I didn't need the cart for carrying to the shop, and I'm not such a lady that I ride to school, you know.'

He held Matchmaker's reins a little tighter – the horse was fussed by the capering, shouting children. 'If we just walk on aways, Mary, he'll calm hisself and then you can get on him if you like and I'll walk home with you.'

'Oh, I can't go home.' She laughed. 'I'm a working woman, Nick. I have to get back to the forge and the shop.'

Poor old George, he thought. More than ten years they'd been wed and still she thought of Keepers Cottage as home, but hers was the sadder story.

'If it's about Flora, you and Dorcas aren't to worry. Miss Crewe is trying her with some old spectacles of hers and, like I told you, she's not slow or backward, just a bit behind with the reading.' The horse was calm now and walked steadily alongside the two as they left the school and all its clamour behind. The lane was a pleasure to walk on now that it had been surfaced. Only two years since, it had been ankle-deep in mud in the winter and ankle-deep in dust in the summer. 'We're to go to the river on Saturday for the whole day. It's George's thirtieth birthday and we're taking a picnic and the old trap.'

'Lord help us, Mary! Is that old thing still going?'

'It is, and very well too! It's been resprung and is as comfortable as any grand carriage.'

They were only half a mile now from the forge. How could he bring it up? He was a fool. What if there were tears and she so near to what was her home, like it or not? 'Who'll keep their eye on the forge, then? Saturday's a money day, passing trade, horses, carriages and the like. Even a coach maybe.'

'Billy's coming over for the day and night, from Edge-combe. He's been due time off for a while now.'

'All that machine learning. It'll come in handy round here, you know, Mary. What with the new Model Farm, and up at the house . . . Look.' He led her to the edge of the field, ripening through colours of the palest green to a strong yellow like a sunflower, under the hot midsummer sun.

'Up at the house?' She peered at him, looking more than ever like a startled fawn, from under the brim of her calico bonnet.

'They're getting a mechanical reaper,' he said, with the pride of ownership. 'You won't be seeing two men on a scythe hereabouts no more. And there's to be a threshing machine! What about that, Mary? No more flailing. All in time for this year's harvest. All this,' her eyes followed his gesture up the field, 'will be reaped and stacked in half the time – *quarter* the time.' They stood side by side gazing at the wheat that would soon be gathered, and so quickly. He took a clean red handkerchief from the pocket of his baggy corduroy trousers, wiped the back of his sweating neck and, folding it with unnecessary care, placed it in the pocket of his drill jacket. 'Yes, it's hot,' he murmured. 'And, the young master, he—'

'The *master* now, Nick.'

'And the master, he and Lady Caroline . . .' His voice trailed miserably away.

'Are to be married.' She finished the sentence he had been too cowardly to complete.

There were no tears. She was holding up her hands, observing them. Clean and pretty they were. He took them both in one strong, brown hand. 'He asked me hisself to tell you, Mary love. Just half-hour ago I see him and he asks me to tell you.' He would like to be gone now, a good fast gallop to the Barley Mow and a pint of strong ale.

'You saw him this morning. A half-hour gone. I haven't seen him, Richard, the master, for ten year and more.' She pulled away her hands. 'Did I tell you we're going to the river? Saturday. We're going for the whole day. We're taking a picnic. To the river. George's birthday. He'll be thirty. On Saturday.' She was still speaking as he watched her walking down the lane.

The big bright blue and white doors, newly painted every year, were wide open to the forge. Outside, a large shaggy-hoofed carthorse was backing into the shafts of a hay-cart, also painted blue but faded, with red wheels. The carter and George were laughing and chivvying the horse. 'Not the handsomest horse I've shod today, Frank. Nor the brightest.'

'You'm be careful now what you sez about this 'ere hoss, George, my lad. It's my bread and butter and means a sight more to me than my missus.'

'Bread and dripping, more like, and you being the sight you are, your missus, no doubt, returns the compliment.'

Mary smiled and waved at the two men, who were laughing, well pleased with their banter.

'Have you had something to eat, Mary? We didn't wait on you, we was all hungry.'

'Yes, I did. Sorry I'm a bit late, George. Did you give Frank a bite?'

'A bite and a beer, missus, thank you. And your smile, Mrs Jackson, 's a sight for sore eyes.'

Her smile broadened. 'I'll wash my hands, George, and then let Hanny go.'

'Well, George Jackson, nobody but a turnip-head would choose a carthorse over your Mary.'

Opening the centre drawer of the walnut table, shaped like a kidney-bean, a wedding present from Aunt Biddy, she took out the case. The leather was even more beautiful now, polished with beeswax to protect it, softer with age and use. Folding back the cream chamois for what must have been the thousandth upon thousandth time, but always felt like the first, she examined the little silver instruments, cleaned and gleaming, their ivory handles ageing from a creamy white to the colour of the tobacco-smoke-stained ceilings of the inn. She chose the little shovel shape and started to push back the cuticle of her forefinger. The room was warm, the heat at the window attracting bluebottles that buzzed and dashed themselves against the panes. She pushed harder at the skin until it split on both sides of the nail, the blood dripping unnoticed on her apron. Manicure. What she needed was *dolor cura*.

Emma was in her front garden tying up the brilliant blue delphiniums and staking the hollyhocks which were 'every colour and shade of pink except what folks would call pink'. She raised her hand to shield her eyes from the still bright setting sun. The sound of the rattling cart was coming closer. Off along the path to the turnpike, she'd thought, but here it was turning the corner of Drover's

Lane. Now she could see it clearly. It was Mary's and Mary was early. Was that a bad sign? And on a good warm evening like this she usually walked.

Then after supper she might take the traption home if the weather turned.

With the big horse stamping impatiently, the argument continued, though as arguments go it was subdued. 'There's Ma in her garden, George. We can't suddenly stop here, she'll wonder.'

'It won't take more than a minute or two, woman, if you'll pay heed. I won't have it, Mary, and no come-back, mind. You're clever at all the sorting of words and you turn mine around till I don't know what I'm saying.'

'I only try to make it all clear, love.'

'Ah, that's just it, that's what's wrong. It should not *be* clear. You and Sal and the talking together. It's indecent. I'm not some heathen from over the seas with, well, er, two . . .'

'Two wives?'

'Be quiet, now. How do you think it is when all knows all, and all knows that you, you know . . .' He paused, uncomfortably aware that the little smile held a hint of mockery. 'You say it's all right. No man it makes me, that my wife has no care.'

Giving him a quick kiss on his cheek she said, 'I do care for you, love, and if you want it all under the carpet that's where I'll sweep it. Now please, George, let's get a move on.'

'Good.' He wasn't sure he'd made his point and wasn't really sure what his point was, but he knew that the day the baby was buried had changed everything. He'd been sad, right enough, about the death, but most of all he'd felt foolish. The vicar, Sal, Mary, they all seemed on one side and he on another and like there was a secret that he couldn't know. This little trip, though, this was to show he wasn't ruled. He, George Jackson, would take his wife to visit her parents and take their son home. And all these women weren't going to flummox him with – what was it the vicar had said? – 'all their sense and sensibility'. It wasn't Christian.

'What a lovely surprise!' Emma couldn't conceal her astonishment at seeing them together. 'There, now, I'm that pleased. Will you stay for your supper or are you come to take John home? They should be back soon, just finishing up at the warren, they were.'

George lifted his wife down carefully. 'Rabbit pies, then, Mrs B.?'

'Pies, and spiced potted rabbit for the shop.'

'Does that finger still hurt, Mary?' She had winced as he took her hand.

'What have you done, Mary? Burnt yourself?'

'Just a bit of a cut, that's all, Ma. Nothing to make a fuss about.'

'Make yourself some hyssop water. It's a good thing to keep handy, cuts and bruises, what with George and the horses – what have you got there?'

'Well, it's like this, Mrs B., we *have* come to collect young John, but we thought we'd all have our supper together. Take the other handle of the basket, will you?' They carried the heavy hamper into the cottage. 'And it's to say thank you for helping Biddy this coming Saturday and, anyway, in this humid weather we have to eat up the stock!'

Her mother was really happy, Mary could tell. The family together — and all the food free.

'Leave the front door open, will you, George? We need a draught. I'll pull some radishes and a lettuce if you'll start laying up, love.'

From the little vegetable garden at the back of the house, Emma could just see them unpacking the basket together and setting the table. She turned her back on the scene, holding the lettuce and radishes with their earthy stalks carelessly in her apron, and pressed the back of her hand to her mouth to stem the tears. What had happened? Was it young Richard's wedding? Had that freed Mary's feelings?

'The marriage hasn't taken,' Biddy had said, all those years ago. 'It won't take, not ever.' Perhaps she was wrong. After ten years lots of marriages go wrong. Maybe it took this one ten years and more to go right.

George slowed the carthorse to a walk as they passed any dwelling place; the rattle would wake any hard-working early-abed people. John sat between his parents only half awake, their bodies keeping him warm and upright. It was good this feeling. Something he usually felt only with his grandpa. Maybe the day on the river would be good, after all. It had been difficult pretending excitement when all he wanted was to be in the woods here, alone or working alongside Grandpa. 'Thank you,' he murmured, as his nodding head jerked him awake.

'Thank you?' Mary wondered if she had spoken aloud. 'What for, John?'

'Special evening, staying up late.'

George eyed her across the boy's head. Smug. It had all been his idea. But why? She subdued a sigh. He hadn't been to Sally's and that was the second time. No asking him, though. Have to find a way to see Sally, find out what was wrong. She held her aching finger, newly dressed in hyssop-soaked clean cotton by her mother, and gently kissed her son's sleepy face.

'Whoa there, Muffin.' Pulling up the tired horse easily, George leant forward, straining his eyes in the twilight. 'What's that there in the pound, love? A sheep I can see, black it looks like, but there's a . . . a pony or summat.'

'My Lord, it's Bertie.' Forgetting her sleeping son, who fell forward off the seat as she jumped from the cart, Mary ran over to the pound. 'Bertie, Bertie, is that you?'

'Of course it's me.'

'Of course it's him, Mary. Who else but your brother would join the animals in the pound?'

'There's no need for you to mock us, George. I found this sheep cast at the edge of the barley field and it took a devil of righting.'

'No need to mock at all, George.'

'Quiet now, Mary. I can fight my own battles. And then I had to prod and goad it along here into the pound, see.'

'Yes, I see. I was only teasing, lad. Have you been visiting Aunt Biddy?'

'No, I haven't. I've been working. Cutting wood for the extra to the shop. And now I'll get on home.' All very well for him to tease. He, Albert Bowden, could do a bit of teasing himself, if he had a mind. Not that he'd do it in front of Mary and the boy.

'Get in the cart, Bertie. Go on, all of you. Squash up

together. Do you reckon you can ride Little Dancer home bareback with a rope, Bertie? Because if you can, you're more than welcome and then just let her be and she'll trot back here. What do you say?' All three passengers were silenced with surprise. Little Dancer was a cherished possession, as yet untrained to the shafts. 'So then, Bertie?'

'Yes, George. I reckon I can. And I thank you for the trust. The honour.' His brother-in-law smiled in the darkness at the formality of his speech. He was an odd lad all right, but not a bad one.

Only an occasional light flickered in windows in the village street as they approached the forge, but Biddy could be seen at the lamp, looking out for them, and the wide doors were open ready for the cart. John, now fully awake, jumped down and held his arms up for his mother, holding her weight for a few seconds, aware of her fragility.

'Don't drop her,' Bertie warned as he tied the rope halter round the neck of the constantly moving and aptly named Little Dancer.

'Don't be stupid, Bertie.'

'Uncle Bertie. Right, Mary?'

'I suppose so.' She laughed at the thought. 'Be off with you now, brother Bertie.'

George patted the horse's rump. 'And don't forget to send her home.'

'That was good of you, George.' She reached up to kiss him. 'Give John a hand with that basket, will you? Even empty it's quite heavy.'

'If the picnic Saturday is as good as tonight's do we'll

do well, eh, John? Let's hope the shop don't do too well Friday!'

'George Jackson, I'm indignant that you should think I'd give you left-overs on your birthday.'

'Well, Mary, I don't know what you are when you're indignant but I know you're tired. To bed, both of you, and tell Aunt Biddy to leave the lamp. I'll wait up for Little Dancer.'

He had finished half an ounce of his sweet-smelling tobacco when he heard the little mare trotting down the lane. Tapping the bowl of the pipe on the heel of his boot and emptying it, he waited for the horse's recognition and attention. She nuzzled him and sniffed the air, still scented with the smoke, and as he led her to the stable she whinnied softly. 'Yes, yes. You'll sleep tonight all right and so will I for I have made up my mind.'

'He were a terrible burden towards the end, leading my young 'uns a-wrong. Your dad was saintly, turning a blind eye to their poaching. Put up to it by him, they was. Not your dad, mine, I mean.' Laughing, the two women patted down the earth at the foot of the small cross.

Mary was relieved to see Sally's tears forgotten. 'It might not take, this cutting. Sam said it's the wrong time of year, but if it does it'll be here to mark the grave long after we're gone and that's nice, isn't it? . . . Sally?'

'Oh, yes, yes, and thank you,' she said heavily, laughter gone, the sweet, round, pretty face near to tears again. 'You came this year 'cause he didn't, right? You know this was how we really met, for they died the same week, my dad and old man Jackson.' Sally stood, stretching her stiff back, aware of the coarse cotton of her dress sticking to her damp skin.

'I know. I remember the funerals being hard upon each other. He didn't ask me to come, Sally. It's just that he was up betimes, working through the day and late, for we're going to the river tomorrow.'

'Because it's his birthday?'

Mary nodded, embarrassed.

'Thirty?'

'Yes. Oh, Sally, love . . .'

She was crying again, holding her new apron up to her eyes. 'Do you think, Mary . . . do you think . . .? Oh, damnation! Do you think he's got another woman?'

'But, Sally, you *are* the other woman.' Mary's response, so earnestly put, made the two women smile and they embraced across the grave.

'Shall us sit in the porch out of the sun?' Suddenly she kicked up some earth on the grave, showering the rose cutting with fine dry soil. 'In truth, Mary, he was a right old bugger, my dad. You know my mam had nine children, all girls we were.'

'Nine? I thought there were only six of you.'

'Three died, of course.'

'Of course.'

'And he treated her as if it were all her fault, and all were sent off by twelve year of age into service, 'cepting me, for I were the youngest. And her dying with the last, I were for to be taking care of him. Do you know, every fortnight on a Saturday he'd have a skinful at that ale-house, the Beetle and Wedge, down the road from the lock-up in Wellsbury, kick up a rumpus, hollerin' and swearin' and the likes, and get put in the lock-up for the night. Good breakfast in the morning, then home in time for his Sunday dinner. It were only the last twelve month of Mam's life that he gave that up, for they got a new constable and he said he'd have him up at the Assizes and no quarter given. And, Mary, he told all who'd listen, he did it to get away from us!' She kicked the dry earth again mutinously, half laughing through a fresh outbreak of tears. 'The *shame* nigh on killed Mam, let alone the milk fever.'

'Shame? Yes, I was more 'shamed than angry when our Bertie was took there. Taken there.' They sat under the shade of the large elm tree, leaning back against its broad trunk, eating the bread and cheese Mary had brought from the shop, with watercress picked and washed in the clear fast-running brook that wound between the end of the old village and the new one growing up around the Model Farm.

'Mary, I know I haven't the right, but ... do you mind ... let's see how to put it ... Do you mind if I ask if you and George ever, now ...?'

They both stared out at the wide meadow dotted with creamy brown Guernseys grazing in the shade of huge ancient oaks.

'You do, too, have the right.' Mary thought with fear of what might be the consequence of a rift between Sally and George. 'And the answer is no.' Nervously, she fiddled with the strings of her bonnet. 'So, is that part of it, love, he doesn't come down to visit so often and you ... you don't ...?'

'No. Not for, well, not since – weeks,' she whispered.

Aware that her worry was for herself as much as her distressed friend, Mary was shamed. ''Tis all my fault,' she blurted out. 'I should never have married him. Then all this . . . It was a mischief, a misdeed, would never have happened. I've spoilt everybody's life. George has no wife, you have no husband, young John has no brothers and sisters, and . . .' Her voice trailed away, angry and sad.

'You ought not to have married him, Mary, but nor he you. And your mother had no call to push yous together.' She waved her hand stopping the disclaimer. 'Yes, she did, and all knew it were wrong. You're like Bertie, a bit behind in some ways and forrard in others.'

'That is a truth, Sally, and more so for being a truth twice told. Sam Reade said the selfsame thing only days ago.'

'No good crying over spilt milk. What's done is done. You can't turn back the clock, and we just have to make the best of a bad job.'

That would interest Miss Crewe, Mary thought. Four little sayings in a row. Perhaps it was tautology as well.

'Sam Reade, you say. Now he's a good sort. She's lucky for all her being a fine lady. You couldn't find better nor than him. Does my garden when he can. "Lupins and leeks, poppies and potatoes", that's what he always says.'

Astonished, Mary scrambled to her feet. 'How do you know about Sam and . . . you know? Did *he* tell you?'

'Course not. How do you know? Did he tell *you*?'

Mary shook her head. 'No.'

'Not that all knows, they're right canny about it.'

She wasn't going to tell Sally that the vicar at Little Bewdley had almost told her, hinted, trusted her with the tale. It was 'to illustrate the accommodations people make in an imperfect world'.

'What do you reckon, then, Mary? Will he be dropping in tonight?' Glory, it made her feel old, that clear skin – even in this heat she wasn't sweating. No damp patches spreading across *her* back or, come to that, armpits.

'Oh, yes. Leastways, I think so. I'm baking a surprise for the picnic and he said he'd be off out of my way once he was finished in the forge.'

Sally rose, brushing crumbs from her apron. 'I just made this,' she said, indicating the vivid green-, pink-and yellow-flowered cotton. 'It's the latest, you know. It's called a – a pompydoor, cut into a triangle and pinned up at the front, see? Well, *you* can see, I doubt no one else will. Not so fortunate with men I am, what with me dad, then my Will, him dying of malary in the Indian whatsit and nought now remembers even his name – I'm Mrs Cooper, you know – and now George see-you-sometime Jackson. Oh, my Lord, Mary. Sorry to be rude. Your husband and all and . . .' Laughing she banged her chest with her fist. 'I've got hiccups, I have. Fancy complaining to you, of all people . . .' She bent over, clutching herself. 'Hiccups. I'll wet meself in a minute. Thank you for the bread and cheese, Mary,' she panted. 'Would you give my back a good thump – ooh, that's better – and thank you for being so good about . . . letting me talk about . . .'

Smiling ruefully, Mary said, 'Our George?'

Settling back under the shady old tree again when Sally had gone, she looked up at the few clouds visible between the leaves. They were like vanishing puffs of steam from a train. She had been to the great railway station at Wellsbury. She had seen people get off the train and people get on. A train had arrived, one had departed.

Idly she wondered whether if *she* got on and departed, left for good, would everything sort itself out? Not likely to, no. And how could she leave John, Bertie and her parents? The shop, too, after all that Aunt Biddy had done? Miss Crewe and the school, she was needed there. No, she would live and die here, buried in this graveyard, perhaps in a coffin made of the wych elm under which she was resting. She lifted her head, puzzled by the sound of music. Somebody must be playing the organ in the church. It was good, not as good as Richard had played but a distant lovely sound escaping through the solid old walls of the church, the organist unconscious of his solitary listener. Sam Reade had a phonograph. He had played for her what he said was 'Handel's Hallelujah Chorus' but it was only a little piece and so scratchy it could have been Joe Jenkins playing, 'Fair Maids All' on his fiddle, for all she could tell. Funny that, Sally of a mind with Sam about Bertie. Oh, pray God all would go well tonight! Even though it was an ungodly thing to pray for your husband to sleep with his 'other woman'. And there she was 'tidying people up' again, as Sam had put it to her.

'You and Emma have made the boy, Mary. So pleased was she with a son. And with all her knowing ways she didn't have another child. Her duty done, she went off and left you to mother and love him.'

'Went off? Ma never left home.'

'Went off, earning, little plots and plans, making money her love and not the children. Between you two, he became Bertie instead of Albert. Too much love and too little. Anyways, he's a lot like you, if you care to see. An old soul in a young body.'

Frowning, she said, 'I don't see. I don't see how you can look inside me and see my soul at all. Young or old.'

He leaned against the huge white china sink, his arms folded, smiling at her. 'I only want to do what's best for him. Don't ask me why, Mary, but you're like a daughter to me, my own, so your Bertie is kin too.'

The sink was full of unwashed dishes, probably from lunch with *her*. *She* wouldn't know how to wash a plate or scour a pan. 'Get out of the way. I'll deal with all your washing-up.' She pushed him aside, not speaking in case she wept.

'Don't try to tidy everybody up, Mary love.'

'I'm only trying to help.'

'And grateful I am for it, but it's not just the dishes. It isn't given for us all to march forward in step. If Bertie's a bit behind in some ways now, so be it.'

She paused, the rattle of crockery ceased and in a low tone she said, 'You don't think he's a simple then, Sam Reade?'

His large warm hand patted her shoulder. 'You've been bold and brave, Mary, for it can't be easy to talk of a loved one like this. He's not a simple. Poor old Mother Hocking's son, he is, and there's a difference. You can tell, can't you?'

'Yes, well . . . I think so.'

'Look at what he does well, child, and not what you want him to do. Look at those haystacks. He's been thatching them, beautiful shapes and patterns, for, what, three year or more?' Mary nodded. 'There's a clue, a guide. Lead him on, don't hold him back. It's not in him to keeper. Let your John be keeper, if that's right for him, and let Albert find his own way. Your life was tidied up for you, Mary, and no favour was done anybody.'

. . . The music had stopped, she hadn't noticed when. What if it *were* Richard? Jumping to her feet and lifting her skirts, she ran to the iron kissing-gate and was half through when an imperious voice called, 'Girl! Girl!'

Having reached the safety of the meadow side, Mary turned to respond. Over the iron gate, which George was always proud to point out had been made by a Jackson forebear in olden times, she inspected the distant figure. Had it not been wearing skirts she could easily have mistaken it for Richard as a boy or young man, quite tall, a bit thin, and the face – an oblong with deep blue eyes. She breathed deeply, and her heart stopped thumping.

'Girl, here!'

'What does she think I am, a dog?' Mary stood her ground, taking in the impatience, the arrogance, exactly like Richard, but rather more irritating in a snip of a girl. If she came across him now, would it be less attractive in him, too?

'Why did you run?' The girl took a step towards the gate. 'Don't see why *I* should frighten you.' The voice had lost a little of its command and Mary felt the step taken by the figure would satisfy her honour, which had been bruised by the appellation 'girl'. They met half-way across the churchyard. 'Oh, I see, you're the keeper's daughter, aren't you?' It was that hair. Maud had seen only one other person with hair that odd colour.

'Some might say I'm the smith's wife.' Mary carefully avoided calling her 'miss', because 'girl' still rankled.

Maud examined her boldly. No surprise she had thought her a girl, she was bony and flat-chested, though she must be quite old, at least twenty-five. A quarter of a century. 'I look like my brother, don't I?'

The question startled Mary and she answered defensively, 'Well, as I haven't seen your brother for ten years or more, I wouldn't know.'

'And that is why you were running – you did not want to see him?'

Neither noticed, in the distance, the new sound of a mechanical reaper being tried out to the half-jeering, half-admiring shouts of some farm-hands.

'Oh, I knew it wasn't him playing the organ. You're good . . .' She decided to qualify this, the impertinent little miss looking her over like that. 'Well, quite good, but not as good as he was.'

'And as you haven't seen him for ten years presumably Richard has got even better.' That little barb and the mention of her brother's name made the woman blush. She had upset her.

Mary dropped her guard. 'I have not *seen* him for ten years or more but I have heard him. I heard him play, not the organ but the piano at your house.'

'Spying, Miss Bowden?'

'Mrs Jackson. No, 'twas by chance, walking home one night, a warm night, from my sister's, I heard – the windows must have been open in the long drawing room.' Remembering the beautiful night and the music and from whom it came, she trembled.

'You're familiar with the architecture of my house?'

'I did grates there for a while when I was your age, Miss Maud.' For the first time she used the girl's correct title but with no respect in her tone. 'I'd thought him away,' she murmured.

Maud continued to stare at her. What a lot she knew about this woman. What a lot she knew about most people. She had been treated as a wall when a child, thought to have no sense, no hearing. Everybody, Davis, Bunny, the footmen, the grooms, her mother, they had all spoken indiscreetly in front of her. Even the keeper's wife. For a long while Mary met her stare.

'If you looked at me like that in my classroom, I would call it dumb insolence and take away your slate.' She tried to recover her equilibrium.

'You're a school teacher as well as the wife of the smith and the keeper's daughter?'

'And I own the village shop and run it with my sister.'

'No children, then?'

'Yes, indeed. My son John.'

'Low on your list of priorities, I notice. Not unusual and not exclusive to the lower classes.'

Oh, to smack the little madam's face! 'On the contrary, I'm proud of my son. He is to be . . .' She was foolish, she knew, to become so heated. The girl, unpleasant as she was, could affect their livelihoods in every way. The job of keepering and its cottage was dependent on the Fiennders', and although the shop and forge were owned by the Jacksons, they needed the custom of those up at the big house and at the dower house, and the farm too, and where *they* went the estate workers, farm-hands and villagers followed suit. And never forget, George always said, there was a good farrier over Upper Bewdley way. Even her work at the school could be taken away for she had no certificates.

Maud saw the colour come and go in the young woman's face and was aware of some nervousness, anxiety.

Why had she teased her so? Jealous of her beloved brother's old friendship? That tutor friend of Richard's from Oxford would say it was bad manners to taunt where it couldn't be returned. 'Mary.' The young girl held out her hand impulsively but with a certain inbred condescension. 'I would like to say I'm sorry for . . . er . . . oh dear, well . . . teasing you. You see,' she said, with what she hoped was engaging candour, 'I'm in a frightful temper with my mother about our move to the dower house. I hate her anyway, don't you? I mean, don't you hate yours? And the organ didn't help for, as you succinctly put it,' she laughed, 'I *am* only quite good. I know that and I mind.'

They shook hands, Mary smiling gently. Nevertheless, she thought, I will be careful of you, young lady, should you come my way again.

'And you must forgive me for staring but, you know, you have a very odd face. You may not be beautiful, but you are certainly the next best thing.' She waved her hand in goodbye as she walked away. 'I'm expected home for luncheon. See you at the tenants' party for Richard's wedding.'

Mary watched her untether her horse, a beautiful glossy bay, from the hitching post. Mounted, she dug her heels sharply into its flanks and urged it from a jog-trot to a gallop in seconds. 'I, too,' she wanted to shout, 'am expected for luncheon.' Though to be honest, George expected her for the midday meal, which for Billy was dinner. As Maud vanished, after clearing a five-bar gate, she did shout, 'And you won't be seeing me at the tenants' party for I'm not a tenant.'

★

Looking out of the back window, she watched as he made his way along the edge of the field at the bottom of the gardens. He always did this, walked away from the village till he reached old Juniper Corrigan's hovel, the oldest cottage thereabouts. Juniper being long dead it was derelict now, its downstairs used for hay and straw, its upstairs not used at all, there being no staircase and gaping holes in the floor. The shaggy thatched roof had been colonized by glis-glis, the local edible dormice. Most of the people who lived in Findlesham had eaten dinners made from the residents of old Juniper's roof. He usually turned at the old cottage onto the lane and made his way back home, stopping at the inn for a half-pint. She doubted he would tonight, having drunk cider with her. Cock-of-the-walk, he looked like, short strong body held erect, powerful arms swinging, strutting jauntily; his pace was quicker than usual, less furtive. Did he know she always watched him till he was out of sight? Couldn't do. He'd hardly look so confident, wouldn't let her see his relief at his escape. That had been rude, insulting, how he'd washed hisself in cold water straight away, not waiting for her to boil a pan. 'That don't make any difference to my decision, Sal,' he'd said, dressing quickly, not looking at her. 'I shouldn't have done that, but you must allow you led me on.' She had, too, and deliberate. Arriving late, as Mary had warned, he'd put the envelope, larger than usual, on the heavy, old ship's timber that served as a mantelpiece and said he couldn't stop. Shifting uneasily from foot to foot, he had reluctantly accepted a tankard of the scrumpy her sister Rose had brought up from Somerset on her last visit.

'What is it, George?' She'd had to ask for, like most

men, he hadn't the nerve to speak. The silence, the awkwardness, the sighs, they were to force you to say, 'What's wrong?' Then, after an unconvincing 'Nothing', followed by her 'It must be something', it turned out to be everything. He had sat in the comfortable chair, leaning back away from her, holding his cider. She had waited till he'd drunk some, then sat on his lap and, taking the tankard, kissed him.

'What do you mean, love, "It can't go on"? What has happened?' He let her weight push him back and trap him as she slid her hand inside the thick cotton shirt, feeling his broad shoulders, the muscles in his arms, developed from a lifetime of hard work.

He struggled half-heartedly, turning his face away from her kiss. 'It's not good, all this, not right.'

She eased her hand into the waist of his breeches.

'Everybody, see, everybody – even old Mrs Turch, the other day, she said, "How's Sally?", for all the world – and she's a church-goer.'

It wouldn't do to go up to the bedroom, let him get away, so lifting her skirts, she pushed down hard on him.

'We're not Frenchies,' he said feebly.

It was good, as usual, for both of them. It always had been. Easy and natural. There, she leaned out of the window, craning her neck as far as it would go. He was turning left into the overgrown garden, more like a small hay meadow, scattered with poppies and cornflowers. The girls. She ought to collect the girls from the Quinns'. They'd been there for their tea. Nine children they had. 'Two more never makes no difference,' Aggy always said. Picking up her cider from the windowsill, she drained it and belched. Least when you were on your own you had the freedom to be natural. She hadn't cried yet. She was too angry. '*I*'ve decided,' he'd said. '*I*'ve got nothing more to say.' Nothing to do with *her*. After nine years. It had taken him nine years to decide: 'It's wrong, not seemly.' She picked up the little packet she had folded into best tissue paper, begged from the drapers in Wellsbury, where she had only bought a paper of pins. Months she had saved for this, for his thirtieth birthday. Three large, pure, Irish linen handkerchiefs with 'G' embroidered in the corner. One by herself, one by Cora and one, a bit straggly, done by little Gwen. She had planned it carefully so as not to offend. He would think of them when he used a handkerchief, but no one but *himself* would know. Even *he* wouldn't know now. Waves of self-pity engulfed her. When she thought, all she'd done, sent her boys into service, for what? True, young Bill was doing good, out of the butler's pantry, waiting at table; fine uniform, he said. Oh, dear God! If she went off right now, went to the Quinns', she wouldn't be able to let go, not give in, for the sake of the girls, *his* girls. With the curtain pulled back, sweet-scented evening air filled the room: old Seb had been scything the small field. The envelope on the mantelpiece had been forgotten. She opened it. More money than usual. Enough for a month. And a note in his usual printed letters: money would come every month until the girls were both fourteen. And that was that.

John Bowden appeared at the forge sharp at six in the morning. He had driven the traption carefully to preserve its pristine exterior. If he had bowled along as briskly as the bright crisp day tempted him to, dust would have clung to the early morning dew and undone all the hard work. The trap had been cleaned and scrubbed, all its parts oiled, any brass polished and the pony groomed, its tail plaited and threaded with red ribbon by Albert. The large doors of the forge, big enough to admit a coach, were open wide and hooked back; even at this hour it was boiling hot from the heat of the fire. Billy was bending over the anvil. Receiving unnecessary last-minute instructions from George, he nodded, smiling. 'Yes, yes, I know. I done this before, don't forget, *and* you've already told me, brother. Now get away from the soot in your fine clothes.'

The trap was packed with a hamper, wet-weather coats and blankets, feed for the pony, fishing tackle and a flat box carried carefully by Aunt Biddy. Everything was ready by the time Mary appeared, self-conscious in her new dress, a fine creamy lawn so pale as to be almost white. It had a pleated front, to give an impression of a bosom or, as she hoped, to hide the fact that she hadn't one. The collar, small and square in front, was cut like a sailor's at the back and trimmed with the same ivory silk grosgrain as the little chip straw hat. She twirled in front of the group and then started to put on her sensible tough holland coat.

'Not yet, Mary love. Let us enjoy looking at you.' Her father embraced this immaculate, elegant creature, careful not to ruffle the delicate dress.

John nodded approvingly. 'You look all right, Ma.'

And George hugged his wife, lifting her off the ground and dislodging her hat.

'Now then, George.' Billy joined them, wiping his hands on his long apron. 'This is how you kiss a lady.'

He bent forward, his hands behind his back, and kissed Mary with a satisfying smack on the cheek. 'You gets what you want, a kiss, and she doesn't get what she don't want, all crumpled.'

The old people and Billy watched them out of sight, waving, the little pony kicking up clods of dry earth which splintered into dust. Billy went back to the anvil, anxious to get some work done before the sun was high and the heat in the forge slowed him down.

'You sentimental old fool.' Biddy pulled at John's arm – he was staring off into the distance, a slight smile on his face. 'Come in and have a cup of tea.'

'You're a sceptic, Biddy, you know that.'

'And you're a head-in-the-clouds.'

'Not so. They looked happy enough.'

'That they are. Happy enough, considering.' He was a dear man – Biddy led him into the kitchen, still warm and smelling of the spices and flour from baking – and wise and practical in many things, but not in this instance. He couldn't accept the little tragedy that was his daughter's life. And why should he? Briskly, she fetched the tea and placed a pile of leaflets in front of him.

'Tea and pamphlets, Biddy? I'd rather have tea and toast.'

'You have a look at that top one, John Bowden, while I take Billy his tea.'

It was impossible to guess at any one moment what would be at the top of the pile for Biddy: the Workers' Compensation Act, the vain hope of women's franchise, Home Rule for Ireland, the Fabian Society or Republicanism. Today it was the dockers' strike. John chuckled as he realized he was drinking his tea from a commemorative mug: 'Queen Victoria's Fifty Glorious Years'. Funny that, from a republican. No doubt something to do with the monarch being a woman! Still, the milk was in a jug celebrating the repeal of the corn laws in eighteen-forty-something.

'Biddy!' he called, gulping his tea. 'I'd best be off, or Emma will think the worst of us.'

'If I was a bit younger, you wouldn't be saying that in jest.' She dug him in the ribs, her rosy, apple-like face twinkling.

'And what's this, Biddy?' He waved a piece of paper taken from the pile.

'Gas, Light and Coke Company. They're putting it in in Wellsbury and maybe it will come as far as Findlesham.'

'No, absolutely not, Biddy. I will not have my daughter living in a house with gas, especially with the forge.'

'The Fiennders' have it. Don't you be so old-fashioned, man.'

'The Fiennders' have their own machinery and staff, outside.'

'If they want to light up the streets you won't be stopping them.'

'This here, Findlesham,' he waved to the window, 'this is no street. This is a lane. I can't see for the life of me why anybody wants to see at night beyond the moon and a lantern. Typical it is of modern times, change for change's sake.' He strode into the forge, agitated. 'Good day, then, Billy. 'Tis good of you to come over this long way to help them out.' He stood in the lane, his head thrown back, feeling the sun on his face. Gas lamps here? Daft. 'Goodbye, Biddy. Thank you for the tea. I will come to the talk at the Assembly Rooms next week. Workers' compensation, it's a just cause. The Turners' son, that was an eye-opener.' He wanted to be home, in his cottage, away from other buildings, with nothing to be seen but an old barn or two, pasture with animals grazing, golden fields nearly ready for cutting, and woods. His woods. Damp and cool, with his chicks, gaudy pheasants and discreetly plumed partridge. Woods, where he could find his way by feel and smell without lantern – or gas lamp.

There they were, two dots were all they looked like from up here, but if you concentrated, the dots grew arms and legs, and then one dot had corn-coloured hair and the other dark brown. They were sitting by the little river Thame, a tributary of the big Thames itself. George was teaching young John how to fish. That he had been fishing no more than three or four times in his life did not seem to stop him being an authority. The rods were beautiful, long and slender. They had belonged to George's grandfather. As the two whipped them over their heads, they bent, curved to an extreme, but the willow never broke.

They hadn't wanted to walk or explore. George had an ale in Dorchester allowing John a sip, and both had only reluctantly entered the Abbey. Some interest had been shown in the stone knight drawing a sword from his scabbard and they had imitated him in a mock fight, but no interest was shown in the ancient stone and stained-glass window of the Jesse Tree. The Bible, they had shrugged, a church, what else could you expect?

George had been more interested in the coaches and phaetons that sped through the broad main street. Some of their horses had been stabled at the George, a hostelry too grand, they felt, for supping their simple beer. That had been drunk at the Hare and Hounds, a small ale-house near by. But the ostler at the George had been friendly, once he knew George's trade, and respectful when Mary joined in the talk. Her husband was amused. He could see the ostler thought he had married above himself. He presumed it must be her dress. But young John knew different. His mother spoke like a fine lady: it must be something to do with working at the school with Miss Crewe.

'Just as well he didn't see the traption,' George chuckled. 'He wouldn't have given us the time of day.'

'Pooh, I don't care, Pa.'

'And neither do I, my boy. It got us here, didn't it?'

The pony accelerated its high-stepping gait and added to the noise of the Saturday traffic, trotting through the village. They had found a quiet spot to picnic, right by the river at the foot of the Sinodun Hills – the two Wittenham Clumps. A cloth was spread on the grass and the special birthday dish was placed on it with care while George tethered the pony on a long rope.

'What's that, Mary love?'

'A fish, of course,' she said proudly. A perfectly shaped pastry fish which enclosed a mixture of cod and shrimps, which Fishy Aitkins would have her believe were rushed from the sea to the forge only with George's birthday in mind.

A little sauce was seeping from the slightly broken tail. George scooped it up with his finger. 'My word, Mary, you've really done something beautiful here – to taste as well.'

'We knew, we knew!' John shouted, with unusual animation. 'We all knew. Fish. It had to be fish. Ma baked it last night when you were at—'

'And,' Mary interrupted hastily, 'wait till you see your birthday cake.'

They were to have the cake with their tea before they set off home. About three hours the journey would take so she had better hurry if she wanted to find Aunt Biddy's tree. 'Climb the middle of the hill opposite the church', which was where she stood now, 'then turn east downhill to the second smaller Clump.' On the far edge of the wood, which had grown up on the top of an Iron Age fort, was a beech with a poem carved in the bark. It had been done in eighteen-forty-something, Aunt Biddy said, for she had seen it herself in eighteen-fifty when she was fifteen, by a young local farmer she had heard. There was a path of sorts, just visible, leading through the wood. She clambered over a large fallen oak, careful of her dress and thankful she had thought to bring her boots. Perhaps the beech tree with the poem had fallen, too. She was nearly at the edge now, where the lines of the fort were clearly visible, circling the hill. Ahead she could see the river winding its way through villages and towns where Cromwell had fought when Charles I was in Oxford, and beyond the river, Roman earthworks and Dorchester Abbey. She must have missed the beech. Disappointed and tired, she leaned against the nearest tree. Her fingers touched some deeply etched letters. There it was! Quite clear too, to feel and see.

> *As up the hill with labouring steps we tread,*

'I did, I did, *I* did,' she cried, exultant.

> *Where the twin clumps their sheltering branches spread,*

Fifty years later they still did. She looked up at the sun, filtering through the pale green leaves.

> *The summit gained, at ease reclining stay,*
> *And all around the widespread scene survey.*

She had surveyed. Feeling a shiver of excitement, she put her finger inside the next words, tracing them.

> *Point out each object, and instructive tell*
> *The various changes that the land befell.*

She turned slowly towards the west. That must be the little village of Didcot. Not nearly as important as Dorchester, its only claim to fame being a train halt on the railway line from London to Oxford.

> *Where the low banks the country wide surround*
> *The ancient earthwork formed old Mercia's bound.*

Oh, how terrible to be alone up here. If only. If only? If only Richard were here. He would understand, be excited. Guilty, she peered round the tree, down across the fields where she imagined George and John might be.

> *In misty distance see the furrow heave*

It wasn't misty today. She could probably see four, maybe

five counties. Oxfordshire, Berkshire, Buckinghamshire, Wiltshire definitely, but maybe Hertfordshire, even Gloucestershire.

There lies forgotten lonely Gwichelm's grave.

She must find out who that was: ask Miss Crewe.

Around the hills the ruthless Danes entrenched
And the fair plains with gory slaughter drenched.

Pity she couldn't bring the children from school. The boys would enjoy the 'gory slaughter' and it was a history lesson much more enjoyable than scratching the dates of all the kings and queens on their slates.

While at our feet where stands that stately tower
In days gone by up rose Roman power.

That stately tower must be the Abbey and where 'rose Roman power' were ramparts where sheep grazed now and vegetable-filled gardens flourished.

And yonder there, where Thames' smooth waters glide
In later days appeared monastic pride.

Just like Fiennders Abbey. That, too, had been built out of monastic pride. Oh, she must try to remember at least some of this.

Within that field where lies the grazing herd

Still grazing, bred out of the same animals most like.

High walls were crumbled, stone coffins disinterred.

Was that the civil war? The puritans? Could it happen again?

Such, in the course of time, is the wreck which fate
And awful doom award the earthly great.

That was it. She shivered, but she not being one of the earthly great her grave would never be disinterred. Nothing had changed since Aunt Biddy was here. Good. She would come back again, not alone, maybe, next time. Perhaps she'd return in fifty years' time. Seventy-five, she'd be. The climb might be a bit hard, nineteen hundred and forty. There would be some changes, naturally. A few more cottages and most people would have gas by then. If Aunt Biddy had her way, women would be able to vote! Aunt Biddy would be dead. John would have children. There would be more pasture and less corn. Pa said so. Pa would be dead. And Richard? He would never come here with her. Richard would have grandchildren.

They saw her flying down the hill, scattering sheep, her hair loose under the straw hat streaming behind her. They could hear her voice calling, but not what she was saying.

'What is it, Ma? Are you all right?'

She looked all right, her cheeks a delicate, unusual pink.   'I found it, the poem, and I've learned some, or I think I have.' She was out of breath, panting.

'Why did you run, love? We was worried, John and me.'

'I didn't know how long I'd been, and I thought you'd want your tea.' She got the bottle of cold tea and the special cakes. 'You see, George? Three nought. It's a moulded rice with candied peel, the three, and your favourite, a spicy bread pudding, is the nought.'

'Mary, that's the best birthday cake . . . this is the finest birthday anybody could . . . well, I'm not a one for words.' He held her close, smoothing her hair, till she released herself and looked at him tenderly. In nineteen hundred and forty, George would be eighty.

'We'd all best get down here. Mary, John, are you awake?'

'Yes, Pa.'

'Only half awake,' Mary said. 'Like me.' Polly the pony was trotting on valiantly.

'It's not much of a hill but Polly has done us proud and we don't want to take advantage of her.'

The warm glow of the gas street-lamps had replaced the light of the setting sun as they had rattled through a quiet Wellsbury, populated only by little knots of young men outside the public houses, and now on the outskirts of Findlesham, there was the first evening star. The pony knew they were on the last leg of the journey home and trotted briskly up the hill led by George, her reins lying loosely in his hand, and followed by a sleepy John and Mary.

'That place just grows and grows.' Mary pointed to the cluster of new houses, small and square with tiled roofs, surrounding what the owner called the Model Farm, but which was locally known simply as New Farm. 'It'll soon be bigger than Findlesham proper.'

'Never.' George was quite sure that no new landowner would have the cheek to compete with the real village. 'It'd be like setting himself against the Fiennders'.'

'What does it matter if it's bringing in trade?'

'True, my love.'

She could see in the dark that he was smiling.

'You're your mother's daughter, all right, Mary.'
Laughing, he recoiled from her blow. 'I was meaning the
colour of your hair, woman!'

That little exchange took them into the village and
past Sally's cottage. He hadn't loosened the reins, given a
quick glance or seemed aware. She had noticed the curtains were drawn already. They had been drawn that
morning, too. Monday. That was when she would know
if all was well again, Monday evening. She hugged John,
waking him up. 'Safely home.'

But it wasn't till Tuesday that anybody noticed that
the Webbs' curtains had been drawn all weekend.

'Stay here.'

The girl's pinched little face split into a huge grin. 'I
couldn't, could I?'

Caroline shrugged. She had lost interest now that she
knew the whole story, or what she thought was the whole
story. 'Why not? Look, I've got to get home, help with,
oh, you know, last-minute things. Have a fitting for my
dress. It's quite clear, Maud, that you hate your mother
and that she simply isn't interested in you. Can't blame
her, you know. You *are* the third daughter and she's got
the two necessary sons. I expect she has her own life
now.'

'What do you mean?' Maud said sharply. Had she
given a hint, given something away?

'Heavens, Maud. She was married, had five children,
lady of the manor, did her duty, all that. She might like
to do other things now, hunt, go to London, do the

season without you girls, travel, I don't know, and a bad-tempered little girl could get in the way.'

Maud knew she was teasing, didn't mean it . . . but . . . 'Caroline, thank you. I would love to stay.'

'Not for ever, you know.' She pinned the feather-trimmed green straw hat on her piled red curls without looking and picked up her light, cream-linen travelling coat. 'I don't want a bad-tempered spinster sister-in-law at my dining-table every night.'

'I wouldn't.'

'Or making me feel guilty.' This time Maud wisely sensed she *did* mean it. 'Take Issy and Jess's old rooms, then you'll have your own sitting-room – paint them black if you like, I don't care.'

'What about Richard?'

'Richard? He won't mind. Why should he? You're his favourite.' She turned at the door. 'They're yours till *my* first two are born, all right?'

Maud leaned out of the window, waving gaily as Caroline's carriage pulled away from the courtyard. This was amazing luck. She wouldn't have to live with that horrible, selfish old woman. This forthcoming marriage altogether seemed, so far, to be lucky. Far from being the aloof, cold figure she had imagined, Caroline was jolly and practical and didn't mind how much time Richard spent with her. And funny too. This morning, early, before he set off for London, Richard had asked her what her dress was like. 'Like? White, of course,' she'd said. 'With a train as long as a train and the family veil and tiara. What else?' She had been here organizing gifts, including coal and yards of cloth for all the tenants and employees. Something, Maud felt, her mother should have done. Brushing aside thank-yous, she raced through all her tasks, got all her 'good deeds' and 'must dos' done, and then carried on with her own pursuits. These mainly involved horses and hunting and, out of season, taking an interest in working the hounds and their well-being. She should be the MFH, not Richard. He preferred to hunt from local meets once a week only. *That* was what made it a good marriage, Maud thought, recalling her mother's distasteful references to Caroline's health and hips. She wasn't interested in music but . . . what a wonderful idea! She would act on it now. She flew out of the morning room, across the hall – her shoes clattering on the stone floor – banged the front door and ran down the drive, through the rose garden towards the dower house. She would exact a piano from her mother as payment for not living with her. Perhaps not a piano – might make too much noise. A harpsichord, that's the thing. She mustn't annoy Caroline, her benefactor. There she was, her mother, walking in the newly planted little knot-garden. With *him.* What with Tommy at Eton and her in the Abbey, her mother would probably do everything she could to ensure she went to hell when she died, and that couldn't be far off. She might not look it but she was an old woman. 'Old enough to know better' applies to her as well as to me, Maud thought.

They heard her coming and turned. Ann let out a little gasp of exasperation. There she was, the fly in the ointment, spoiling what would otherwise be a lovely day, free of duties and responsibilities. She forced a smile. 'Well, there you are, dear, at last. Have you come to your senses yet? Just because the room is at the back doesn't mean you can't—'

'No.' Maud stood facing them, her hands on her hips. 'I won't have it, that room.'

'Then you will have to sleep in the old sewing-room.'

Sam backed away a little. He was on the young girl's side in this, but his position as a servant meant he shouldn't have opinions.

'Not at all, Mamma, that won't be necessary. Caroline has kindly asked me to stay with them.' She spoke with worldly disdain. 'She has offered me Issy and Jess's old rooms. They're to be decorated for me. So you see, you don't have to worry about me, dear.' She knew the word 'dear' was absolutely awful; guaranteed to enrage Mamma, which it did.

'You insolent, bad-mannered, nasty . . .' Ann paused briefly, seeking a word that would hurt, 'hideous little creature. How dare you?'

But the word had worked too well and the 'hideous creature' launched herself like a cannon-ball at her mother, nearly knocking her down, and flailing at her with her fists.

Servant or no, Sam stepped in, grabbed the girl around her waist and pulled her away. He held her as she struggled and shouted with impotent fury. 'Now then, madam, Miss Maud,' he panted. 'It's not for me to say, I know, in my position, but you are both in the wrong. It's cruel and a lie to call Miss Maud hideous, or a little creature. She is a young woman and pretty, and you, Miss Maud,' he was having trouble holding the squirming body, 'have no right to address your mother like that.'

Ann felt a little shamed. After all, it was good news; no tiresome little beast in the house. She muttered quickly, anxious to get the ghastly scene over with, 'Yes, Mr Reade, you are right. Maud, I apologize. I'm sorry.'

Maud remembered the harpsichord. 'Very well, then, Mamma. I, too, apologize.' She decided to qualify the apology. 'I will never address you as "dear" again.'

Sam released her, but not before she had aimed a judicious kick at his bad leg. 'Oh, Mr Reade, I apologize for that too.'

He turned his face to the wall, as bidden. Over the years the tenor of their relationship had changed. There was less instantly gratified lust, but when they did make love, it was still with passion and deeply satisfying. And neither questioned the other's love. But Ann was made increasingly insecure by her ageing body. She rarely removed all her clothes now and preferred to make love in the dark. Didn't she realize, Sam thought, that he could see her body with his hands. He sat up, stretching his arms above his head and laughed.

Ann started buttoning her bodice quickly. 'I hope you're not laughing at me?'

He shook his head, smiling gently. 'Not at you. Maud.'

She joined in his laughter. 'When the time comes, I'll have to pay someone to marry her.'

'She, most like, will have calmed down by the time she has had her coming-out.'

'I hope so.' She tidied her hair in the looking glass. The black stuff that old Davis put on her hair at the front where the grey was showing looked wrong. It made her look older, not younger. 'If not, I shall encourage an elopement.'

He wished she didn't colour her hair, but if he said anything she would know that it showed. 'Even with somebody un*suit*able?' He leapt out of bed, unselfconscious of his naked body, and finished the buttons on her bodice, touching her breasts lightly.

'Nobody who would take Maud off my hands would be unsuitable.'

The huge cart-horse buried his head in the nose-bag, steadily munching the hay. It made a change in his diet, for this time of year there was grass enough to feed from. The driver knew, though, from past experience that, after an occasion such as today's and the distance travelled, everybody, men and women, would need a stop or two and the usual custom was to halt between two high hedges. The men would use the left side and the women the right, and it wouldn't do to have his horse grazing on either verge for nobody liked to be observed doing their business, unless, as in this case, your fellow traveller was doing it, too. Above the hedge on the left side the men's heads were visible. They were looking out across the fields and pasture, discussing and appraising their condition and the level of good husbandry. From the right side came shrieks of raucous laughter and a voice was heard shouting, 'You'll need a dock leaf for your bum, Edith.' The driver chuckled sympathetically. There were nettles galore on both sides of the lane, but the men had an easier time of it. Some of the older women were wearing straw hats trimmed with feathers; osprey being too expensive, they had used the long brilliantly coloured pheasant's plumage. A few had small stuffed birds added to the trimming and from where the driver stood stretching his legs, it looked like fledglings twittering on the hedge. Gradually, they all clambered on the bus again, the men with pipes and the young and agile to the top, and by common consent, the aged and women with young children on the lower deck. The singing started up again as the horse settled into its shafts and the bus moved. Three different songs were being sung at the same time. On the top deck, 'Two Lovely Black Eyes' was being hollered with great energy but less melody, while on the lower deck, two hymns were overlapping, the tunes being similar enough for nobody to notice. 'For Those In Peril On The Sea' wove its way between lines of 'Eternal Father', and it seemed quite correct, because of the watery connection, that,

> *Time, like an ever-rolling stream,*
> *Bears all its sons away;*
> *They fly forgotten, as a dream*
> *Dies at the opening day*

from 'Eternal Father', should be followed by,

> *O hear us when we cry to thee*
> *For those in peril on the sea.*

All this was interspersed with good-natured chatter about the wedding. It was, most agreed, the best do, the best bit of merry-making since the Jubilee, and some went so far as to say better, though they were hushed, those sentiments seeming more appropriate to the French Revolution. They had been treated royally: the bus provided, fair shares with the Colcroft servants and tenants as to positions outside the church. The Findlesham lot put up a good cheer when Master Richard, as was, arrived. And he, all natural, had smiled and waved at them, picking out one or two with a 'Got me at last, Seb, eh?' and 'You'll be next, young Jim,' but the biggest cheer was for the bride. All you could want in a squire's wife. Handsome-looking, healthy, high-spirited, friendly, and didn't keep her purse in her pocket. Each in Findlesham had reason to know that, for hadn't she sent coal and a quartern of beer for them to mark the occasion? Aunt Biddy Jackson had been heard to say that coal was cheap in summer, but as old Jack, the tinker, said, 'There's naught so cheap as free.' And that Lady Caroline was an earl's daughter reflected credit on the whole parish.

The smell of an ox roasting had drifted across the park on the still summer's day and appetites were well whetted, but walking to the long barn through the park, dotted with centuries-old oak trees sheltering cattle, not one but three oxen were to be seen turning on spits. It was to be a right feast. Boiled hams were served, plum puddings, huge bowls of steaming potatoes, cream, butter and cheese from the dairy, and no stinting on anything. It was felt that Lady Caroline – *their* Lady Fiennders now – had had a hand in the victuals too, for wasn't she motherless, and all knew her capable?

It was a sit-down do with people seated either in the open long barn or on benches at trestle tables set in the shade of the old chestnut tree. Those in the long barn were the important servants from the great house and the estate, with their counterparts. Butlers at the head of the table; their Mr Caird and our Mr Bulbeck, him being a rare one, no mixer, too grand – too grand for the Fiennders' themselves, he'd have you believe. Old Mrs

Bunn and Mesewer Pepin, the Frenchie cook. Young Sam Reade was up there with his missus, taking his father's place. Old Sam's leg playing him up, shouldn't wonder. Head grooms, George Nichols' Dorcas expecting again, carpenters were there, the Colcroft farrier; they had the smithy on the estate. No Jacksons. Seemed a mite unfair, not tenants nor, strictly speaking, working for the Fiennders. There, it showed, proof positive, it didn't always do to better yourself. Keeper Bowden up there, and Emma. Most knew her well from the days when she wasn't above joining them in the fields gleaning. They had travelled separate, like some others, in their own carts and traps. Not that folk on the bus envied them, for weren't they comfortable and merry together, naught to pay, and no horse to feed, water and care for when they got home?

The bus could be heard but not seen. It was there ahead, hidden by the swirls of dust kicked up in what had so far been an almost waterless summer. Young Sam reined in the pony and slowed the trap to a halt. 'What do you think, let that get ahead, eh, Hanny? And here's where your ma and pa turn off for home, isn't it? It's where we met this morning, anyway.' He steered the smart little pony and trap into the rough track of an old green lane.

'Good. Thanks, Sammy. I certainly don't want dust in my face the whole way back. Why have you pulled off the road, love?'

'Well, say good-night to your folks, you know . . . and . . .' He put his arm round her, tilted her hat off her face, lifted the veil and kissed her.

She responded, leaning back in her seat. 'And . . . I can't get in the family way.'

'Because you're already in the family way.' He touched her breasts through the light silky material. 'I love the children, Hanny, but it's grand having the whole day to ourselves.'

She laughed. 'Hardly by ourselves, biggest wedding of the year, hereabouts anyhow. And us sat at the main table. What with Pa being singled out by his lordship, and your dad's trap, I feel quite the lady.'

'You might not be a lady, Hanny, but—'

She pushed his hand away from her knee. 'I don't get much of a chance to be ladylike what with you and your hand up my skirt for all the world as if we were fourteen-year-olds and it were nightfall.'

'I was saying, or about to say, but as you was the best-looking woman there, including the bride and even . . .'

She pushed away his hand again. 'And even? What do you mean, "and even", Samuel Reede?'

'Even that lovely little parlour-maid with the red hair.'

Hearing the clatter of wheels they stopped their tussle. Hannah straightened her dress as Sammy jumped up and waved, 'We waited to let that bus be gone, with all the dirt it was kicking up,' he shouted.

'Is that so?' John Bowden waved back.

'Don't wait too long,' Emma called. 'Mary will be waiting and the children will be tired.'

'No, Ma.'

The traption bounced along the rough track, skirting a heavy old cart sunk deep in the hardened mud, unmovable since the November rain and now disintegrating.

'It'll be a time before those love-birds get going again.'

'Yes, most likely, and no harm done.' Emma laid her hand on her husband's arm, remembering their own

courting on warm summer nights. Softly she added,
'Makes up for . . .'

'For a lot of things.'

The forge had been busy in the morning. Those who
hadn't planned ahead called in for last-minute help with
equipment, horse and harness. George had dealt with
every equipage from dog-carts to pony-and-traps, pair-
in-hands, coach-and-fours, even the horse-bus had used
him as a wheelwright. Just as well Mary hadn't a mind
to go to the wedding. The shop, too, had been busy all
day. Those few who hadn't gone to Gadstone Park to
see young Mr Fiennders married moved back and forth
between the Bull and Butcher and the shop, gossiping,
mainly about the get-ups of the Findlesham women. Too
elaborate, and the disapproval voiced was 'Airs and graces.
Who do she think she is? Won't look so fancy after
a dusty cart ride.' But the opposite drew as strong a
condemnation. 'Same old Sunday best. Might have put
on a bit of a show. Lets the village down. Grey, I ask
you!' The older women gathered by the well in the shade
of the ornate roof built to commemorate Queen Victoria's
fifty glorious years. Toddlers chased the ducks, who were
pecking in the dust, driving them into the middle of the
half-empty stagnant pond.

Agnes Quinn had come into the shop with her three
youngest. A nuisance they were, playing with the feather
dusters and pulling over a sack of split peas. She'd swept
them up, though, putting them back into the sack. 'Don't
worry, then, Mary. Though it's me that's sorry. Your
floor's cleaner than my kitchen table.' Which wasn't true.

For all that she had a large family, they and the cottage were immaculate. Untidy maybe, but clean. Mary had detained her, talking about the Jacksons' plans for buying a good little trap to use for hire, but both knew there was something else on her mind.

The little ones squealed with pleasure when given a large slice of apricot pie each. 'Those apricots are from the greenhouses at the big house. Sam Reade brought them over.'

Aggy shooed the children outside, ordering them, 'Don't you wander, now. Keep your pinafores clean. Stay in the shade and don't tease the ducks.' None of which commands would be obeyed. She, too, wanted to talk about Sally but it was not an easy thing. She couldn't in all conscience say, Have you heard aught of your husband's woman?

Mary wrapped the slices of cooked gammon and handed it over. 'I'll charge you end-of-the-day prices for that, Aggy, it being a special occasion.'

Aggy nodded her thanks. The Jacksons could afford it, only one child, no rent, fruit given by Sam Reade, the head gardener, father-in-law just about, rabbits all the year and game in season from her old dad. Not that she was jealous. Mary Jackson was a sad woman.

'Have they done anything . . .' Mary busied herself wiping down the marble slab where the large wire cheese-cutter sat, ' . . . anything about that empty cottage? Old Webb's cottage.'

'I don't think they'll let anyone else have it till they hear back.'

'Hear back, Aggy? Who from?' She could hear little Maggie screaming nearby. No surprise.

'I'd best go sort that out. They wrote off to a sister in Somerset.'

'That would be Rose.'

'And one of the others in London, and they're waiting on a reply.'

A very dirty little girl ran into the shop sobbing, her pinafore covered in green slime from the pond and a deep, bloody scratch on her arm. But the main reason for her tears came out between sobs. 'He took . . . he took . . .'

Her mother rubbed the child's back calming and soothing her. 'He took my applecot pie.'

The two women removed the dirty pinafore, bathed and bandaged her arm and Mary gave her another slice of pie, which she held in both hands, concealing it from any sudden marauder.

'So . . . er . . . nothing was said to you, then, Aggy?'

'Not really.' It would be a lie to say *nothing*, for when Sal had come to collect the girls she'd been all pale and trembling, and Aggy had driven all the children out so they could talk. But they'd never talked proper about the goings-on, and best not, Patrick had always said. So she had had to put two and two together. From Mary's questions it was likely she didn't even have two and two. She had suggested, careful-like, that Sal should talk to her priest, but anything Popish was frowned on in Findlesham, and that vicar at St Michael's wouldn't be as comfortable as Father Conlan to make a confession to. All she'd hoped was she'd gone to a sister; that would be best all round. When the curtains were still closed on the Tuesday she'd got Patrick to get into the cottage, and thank God, the woman hadn't killed herself for that was a worse sin than adultery.

After the midday meal, Aunt Biddy had gone upstairs for a lie-down, and the furious argument that had been going on for weeks continued in a whisper. Mary followed George from room to room and then out to the field where Little Dancer was waiting, although it was too hot for her usual training between the shafts. He ignored his wife's persistent questioning and rubbed his face against the pony's silky neck, whispering, 'My little girl, my little beauty.' He inhaled deeply the sweet hay-scented breath. 'You know, I think this young lady is too good for a working horse. I might just keep her for us to ride, and breed from her.'

'Answer me, George, please. I can't think straight. I'm worried, scared, what did you—'

'For the love of God, Mary. Leave it be, woman. You've no sense.'

'Why, George? Why won't you say?'

'You have a brain, Mary, for figures and the Latin and all kinds, but you have no brain for everyday. You don't . . . Oh, hell.'

'Please. Tell me. What happened?' She touched his arm.

The horse, startled, reared and whinnied as he flung her off. 'There, there, girl.' He patted the glossy, sweating flanks, ignoring Mary who had fallen.

She was shaken, but not deflected from her purpose. 'Don't you care about your children, man? She's gone, God knows where, and they've gone too.'

He released the pony, who trotted away up to the end of the field and the shade of a laden crab-apple tree. He glanced up to his aunt's bedroom window, which was wide open. He could see Biddy's hand holding the curtain back. Their voices had been raised. 'Come over to the barn.' He pushed her inside ahead of him and banged the doors shut behind them. 'What do you want, Mary? I do my best for us, you and me, and the way we are. I do my best for John and the family. It isn't natural you fretting and caring about my fancy woman and my bastards. I'll see to that side of my life in my own way. You have no right to know about it, see?'

She didn't reply, shocked by his choice of words. Sally, a fancy woman? Little Gwen and Cora, bastards?

'I don't know where she is. I told her it was over – no,' he shouted, 'don't ask why. And she's done the right thing, gone. Now, unless you want to take her place,' he grabbed her roughly, feeling her flat, undesirable breasts, 'let well alone.'

She walked back to the house, smoothing her hair with a trembling hand. That was that, then. Nothing she could do. One day, when John was grown, she would go: home to Keepers Cottage maybe, or Wellsbury, or Oxford, even London. Meanwhile, she would work, save, like her mother she would squirrel away money. For her future, for safety.

Maud shrank back from the funny red crumpled thing that Nanny held out to her.

'No, thank you. I'd rather not.' Even that usually stern and bossy woman laughed.

'Honestly, Maud. You're quite absurd. Give her to me, Nanny.'

'Yes, m'lady. She wants feeding.'

'You look at her as if she was an unpleasant piece of chicken you didn't want sitting on a dish.' After draping a large lace-trimmed huck-a-buck towel across her mistress's stomach, Nanny handed over the baby who was now screaming, as if she understood her aunt's disapproval.

'You can go, Nanny. Have your tea.'

Maud sat on the low stool by the bed, hugging her knees. 'So, it's a girl.'

'Well, it certainly isn't a chicken.' Caroline shifted the baby to her other breast. 'The first, I suppose, of three, or four, even, if I'm unlucky.'

'Unlucky?' Maud wasn't really interested. She was more concerned with her own future.

'Both of our families tend to have two or three girls before the first boy arrives, if he ever does.'

'Was it because you hunted till the last weeks, Caro? That's what they say in the kitchen, what the servants say – well, Bunny and Violet.'

'Violet?'

'The tweeny.'

'That it's a girl because I hunted? Maud, what are you talking about?'

'No, silly. Was she born early because—'

'Heavens above, girl, don't *you* be such a silly.' She settled the baby on the linen cloth and buttoned her nightdress. 'She wasn't born early.' This was said with the tiniest of smiles. 'And stop brooding. The answer to your question is no.'

For the first time since the baby's birth Maud forgot

about herself and the awful possibility of what was to come. Wide-eyed, she jumped up and down laughing. 'You and Richard – before you were married?'

'Be quiet, you'll wake her. Yes, why not?'

'I don't know. What fun. You are the most wonderful person, Caro.' She paused. 'And what do you mean, "The answer is no"? I didn't ask a question.'

'It has been in your face for days, Maud. The question is, do I want you to go to the dower house now that Elizabeth is here?' She gestured to the sleeping baby. 'And the answer is no.'

'Thank you, Caroline. Seriously, I'm truly grateful. I feel years younger.' This was said with all the weariness of a woman of fifteen.

'If you were years younger, I wouldn't have you here, although I like you – being here. You entertain Richard.'

Maud had hoped she would stop at, 'I like you'.

'May I come in?' Issy's head appeared just inside the door. 'Oh, what an angel. Is that her?'

'Well, it's certainly not a chicken.'

'Maud!'

'I'm going,' she said. Having borrowed Caroline's remark, she decided to leave before being reproved and losing her dignity. 'I'll come up and join you for sherry before dinner.'

Better not let the little minx get away with too much, Caroline thought, and shouted through the closing door, 'Don't forget what I said about the horse.'

Maud clattered happily down the stairs passing a parlour-maid dressed in her afternoon black with white collar, who managed to shrink out of her way although she was carrying a table with fold-away legs, bearing a teapot, hot-water jug, cups, saucers and plates, a china what-not stacked with fruit-cake, pastries and biscuits, and a covered silver dish of hot muffins. Just a second of venom entered the maid's mind as she observed the small brown stain spreading on the pristine white cloth.

She would make a good mother, Caroline. Anybody who could get you to do what you know you should do without making you hate her ... The horse had been a Christmas present from her, Richard, too. 'You can't ride everybody's leavings now your pony is too old and too small.' She was a chestnut, huge, sixteen hands. Maud was using her father's old saddle, except for hunting when she rode, properly, side-saddle. The groom, George, had said, 'A good horse teaches you how to ride,' and Marron had done that. She was less reckless, more in control and just as fast as some of the other horses. But last week after a long cross-country ride over wet ground to visit the Bexley-Wrights, Caroline had visited the stables and seen Marron in one of the stalls where Maud had left her. 'If nobody is here to groom her, do it yourself. Never, never leave a horse like that, dirty, uncared-for. You may be tired but so is she. You should look after her from time to time anyway. That is how she becomes yours. Come on, I'll help you.' Even with her huge belly she had started to brush her down. 'Go on, Maud. Get another brush and the curry-comb.' They had worked together removing the dried mud and turning the dull dusty coat into its usual glowing copper-coloured sheen. Caroline had been lively, full of stories, describing the attributes of the various horses she'd had and finally, handing her the pick, she'd said, 'Here, you do her hoofs.' She went back to the house calling over her shoulder, 'You need a friend, Maud.' Huh, she knew that.

The coat cupboard was full of old, smelly rubber coats, tweed hats and caps, umbrellas, boots, overshoes, scarves, boot-pulls, knitted and leather gloves and mittens, muffs, walking sticks and shooting sticks. There were three hours to pass before dinner. Playing the piano would be considered 'making a noise,' and Nanny Colcroft would no doubt bang into the drawing room and whisper, 'Hush,' in important tones and point to the ceiling, mouthing, 'Baby.' It was raining still but only a light April shower. A long coat would be needed. One of Richard's, probably, and a tweed hat, Richard's definitely, rubber overshoes, her own, and a stick, walking not shooting. Not the weather to use the little fold-out seat. She found a good sturdy one with a wide, solid silver knob. Caroline's, it must be. A swirling 'CC' engraved on it. She would walk through the ash plantation and up Sparrows' Dice Hill – that was what Richard called it – and across the ridge that looked down on Home Farm. That was where she had seen the boy before, or man, was he? As much a man as she was a woman. So boy, then. He had been startled, almost frightened. That had been fun until he looked as if he would cry. She hadn't spoken till he said, 'Go away.'

'*I* don't have to go away. This is part of our estate and *you* are here by our leave.' He was really frightened then and ran off. She'd called after him but he'd gone. Pity, she would like a slave, like Caroline. Richard always said that two of her friends, Matthew and Cathal, were her slaves. They would do anything for her and expected nothing. It had been raining that day, too.

'Hello! You there! Hello.' The boy was there again.

In the shelter of two trees. Somebody, him, perhaps, had woven branches and twigs from the two young beeches together and made a canopy. He could be a bodger. They did things like that. She had seen them over in the woods, making chair and table legs.

'Come in out of the rain.' He beckoned, smiling. 'I won't eat you. I've had my tea.' She stood hesitating at the opening, but he took her arm firmly and pulled her in, gesturing to the straw bales arranged like a sofa. 'Sit down.' She clasped the silver-topped walking stick tightly and didn't move.

'Why do you wear your brother's clothes? Are you one of these new women, after the vote?'

He was rather good-looking when he smiled; his dark hair, slicked back with water, kept falling over his forehead to be pushed back automatically. Difficult to guess how old he was. Could be thirteen or as old as eighteen.

'Come here, then.' She let herself be guided and sat primly on the straw. 'Give us that.' He took the stick. 'I won't rob you of it.'

He seemed to have taken the initiative, which wasn't what she had in mind for a slave.

Miss Crewe had fallen asleep. Mary put down the paper on English grammar that she had been reading aloud. The schoolmistress's comments had been punctuated by little snorts and snuffles as her head dropped forward and jerked back waking her. But now she was fast asleep. Mary blew out the candles and turned the oil lamp down carefully. She didn't want it to smoke. The room shrank now in the low light. The three or four tables covered in books receded into the dark. Those were the books Miss Crewe was using now to help any child in need of extra work, or who wanted it, but they were few. Shelves were filled with books, stacked with them. They were piled by her bed, heaped in what was supposed to be the dining room. 'Books are my companions,' she was fond of saying. Just as well, for she had few others. As a gentlewoman, the villagers were uneasy in her company. She could hardly gossip with them at the village pump or join them for a pint of ale at the Bull and Butcher. Equally the Fiennders' wouldn't be comfortable with her at their dining table. In solitude, she had lost the art of conversation. She made statements or interrogated, the result of being the schoolmistress. This whole house was hers, though, and Mary envied her the privacy. The books that weren't hers she left on the table. The others she gathered up and put in her large bag, including the Latin primer, which she always took to a lesson. It was a talisman.

His name was fading now on the fly-leaf. RICHARD OLIVER ORMEROD FIENNDERS – R.O.O.F. His face was fading, too. She could remember him better as an exuberant little boy, sharing his broad-backed pony, sledding down a snow-covered hill, scrambling to the top of hayricks. And the gazebo and the manicure set. No time to think of things like that now. She was busy. So much work to do for her tests. Miss Crewe thought her knowledge was erratic, inconsistent. That Latin was her best subject was useless for Findlesham School – even the boys didn't have it. But working in and running the shop had improved her mental arithmetic – as well as her pocket.

She let herself quietly out of the school-house, put

the heavy bag in the basket on the front of her bicycle and running alongside she mounted, thankful there was no one to see her. Why should it be easier to get on a horse than a bicycle? She patted the handle-bars and nearly fell off. This was one of her triumphs. George had forbidden it. Her father had begged her not to, but more out of fear for her safety than propriety. Even Aunt Biddy had been doubtful. Only the young ones had encouraged her, John and Bertie, mainly because they wanted to use it themselves. Ma had been the surprise, giving her half towards it for her birthday. Since she'd confided in Emma about the savings, her mother had been pathetically anxious to help. The money was going to a proper bank place where it would grow. It was Mrs Fiennders who arranged it, though Ma said that should be kept secret. What would happen to some or even all of it was a secret too – from Ma. She took her feet off the pedals, slowing down just before the forge and braking close up to the hedge so that she could balance the bicycle against it as she got off. One day they might invent one that wasn't so high.

George was home when she got in. Sitting by the boiler in the kitchen with Billy and Aunt Biddy, he neither looked up nor greeted her. They no longer fought but the peace was a cold one. They slept in the same bedroom but Mary used John's truckle bed now. She would have preferred their old friendliness but after the business about Sally he was distant, avoiding her in look, touch and conversation.

'Something to eat, love? Cup of cocoa?' Biddy got up slowly with a hand on the small of her back and groaned. 'It's still cold. May's starting slowly.'

'I'll get it, sit down. Anybody else? Ham and pickles?'

'A bit late, isn't it, for dinner or supper or whatever you call it?' George still didn't look at her.

'Is it? Well, I'm not hungry, anyway. Goodnight, Billy, Biddy.' She smiled wanly. No point in staying downstairs in an atmosphere. She had no appetite for that or food. She left the room in quietness and went up to their bedroom. George's nights out were rare now. Once a month, that was the average. He took Little Dancer, or the trap with the tough little Welsh cob, and nobody knew, or nobody said, where he went. She had hoped he visited Sal, that her leaving had been planned between them – for 'decency's' sake. If so, why did he return so mean-tempered?

Again, that wonderful smell, he took a deep breath. Aniseed, smoked hams, the mustardy piccalilli, beeswax, lavender bags, and more that had merged with the others and was unidentifiable. Her ivory-white head was just visible above the counter on which was propped a book. She was mouthing words with her eyes closed. He didn't want to disturb her for his own sake, for the pleasure of looking at the beautiful face. Not ageless, but maturing into an eternal age which lines could never diminish. His little laugh at such flowery extravagance did disturb her.

'Mr Grant-Ingram! We haven't seen you for years!'

'Months, I think. I'm happy to find you've missed me so much that months turn into years.'

'What can I get you? How are you?' She ran from behind the counter. His fondness was visibly returned. Her natural instinct would have been to embrace him, had not servility been so deeply ingrained. Instead, they shook hands formally. It wouldn't be wise to tell her why he hadn't called in for so long. He wasn't sure how much she might know or suspect and, although lying when it was expedient didn't distress him, lying to her would.

'I was passing and couldn't resist, well, lots of things – peppermint creams, your cheese, bacon, your mother's pickles, in fact as much as I can get into my bicycle bag.'

'Passing? Oh, yes. You've been to see the baby. *Bicycle* bag?'

He nodded.

'*You* have a bicycle?'

'Yes. It would be odd, don't you think, to have a bicycle bag without one?'

Laughing, she ran to the back of the shop and wheeled out her own. 'Me too. See? Er . . . I also. But is it allowed, a vicar? May I see it? Is it the same?' It was nearly the same, a bit bigger, older, less cared-for than hers, which was cleaned – groomed, she called it – after every use. She examined the size of the stiff leather bag propped inside the basket. 'Come back in, sir, and we'll see.' Once inside she whispered, 'I wear a divided skirt when I use mine.'

'So do I.' He lifted his cassock to reveal trousers tucked into gaiters.

'And,' she added, 'I'm thinking of getting bloomers!'

'Well, I won't be doing that!'

'I'll start with the heavy things.' She studied his list. 'A jar of beetroot, one of piccalilli, one quince cheese, one medlar jelly, half a smoked gammon, one pound peppermint creams and a large jar of spiced apricots. I made those.'

Algernon looked at the book she had been reading.

The Monarchs of England. Some ghastly dry history lesson, requiring only the memorizing of dates. 'Why are you reading this?'

'For my examinations. I'm trying to become a real teacher, then I'll get paid properly.'

'When and where does this take place?'

She grimaced. 'A fortnight, in Oxford.'

Well, well, well. What a coincidence. It was dangerous, but he remembered Mary's tact in the past and this was too good an opportunity to miss. 'I believe I can help you. I have a friend, a good friend. He's a retired schoolmaster. Still works as a private tutor and an adjudicator. He might even be adjudicating, judging, the examinations you are sitting.' He interpreted her doubtful frown correctly. 'I am not suggesting cheating, Mary.'

'No, sir, of course not.'

'But he could help you. Knowing how to pass is as important sometimes as knowledge itself.'

They arranged that she would come early and stay for tea on Saturday. Bicycling to Wellsbury was easy, they both knew, and he would make sure that she was home before dark.

'George won't mind,' she'd said. He might well, though, if he knew the circumstances.

She could hardly tell the woman outright that, although Sam liked her to wear fine silk underpinnings, as he called them, the silk dresses, even cambric and Sea Island cotton annoyed him on the boat. 'I don't see you wearing this in London.' Emma pinned the sleeve of the simple thick cotton dress to the armhole and stood back. She was a big woman now, Ann Fiennders. Still fairly shapely, but for how long? And Sam Reade was a very attractive man.

'It's the new fashion now, simple. Aesthetic, I believe it's called. Like Marie Antoinette dressing as a milkmaid.'

'Let's hope you don't get your head chopped off.'

Ann smiled a little vaguely. She was preoccupied with the news that the first post had brought this morning.

'For the purpose you want these *fashionable* dresses, I would suggest an apron in brown holland or a shepherd's-style smock, for wearing over them.'

Ann didn't notice the irony but was taken with the idea of the smock. 'Cream? Tucking at the shoulders? What a good idea, very flattering. Could you make me one and make it look old? Well, *used* say.'

'Yes, I could do that, madam.' What she would do was get an old one – most of the older farm-workers still had them – and make it look new. All this was for the boat, must be. Her Mary had seen them last year. They had been going through a flash lock over near Shillingford somewhere. She could only hint not say, for, regretting the telling, Mary had sworn her to secrecy.

'By Saturday?'

'I'll do my best, but all that smocking's not easy.' In truth she would have it by Friday. The dress was almost done, and she'd drop into old Seb or Adam Corrigan for the smock. All she need do was boil it, give it a good hot iron and add a little fancy stitching.

Ann watched her go reluctantly. She would have liked to talk to her, tell her about Edmund. She supposed he must be dead. Nothing other than his death would have stopped the money. She was clever, Emma Bowden. Trustworthy. She received gossip from the servants but never gave any back, she was sure, but this the servants didn't notice. Not a good idea to tell Sam. It was one of the less appealing episodes in her history. Impossible to talk to Richard, any of the children, and certainly none of her friends. Nobody there she could trust. It was too good a story. She read the letter again and sighed. Secrets made one lonely.

'It's good of you, Hannah, to help out on a Saturday.' Biddy took the baby from her mother's arms. 'And bring my little dumpling.'

'Lovely, isn't she, Aunt Biddy?' Mary steadied the bicycle against the wall and put her book and a box of fudge in the basket. 'She's put on weight since I last saw her, Hanny. She's a double dumpling!'

'Wish I could say the same for you, Mary. I wish you well, love. Don't you be nervous now, and don't worry about us. We'll manage, won't we, Aunt Biddy?'

'We will, and I'd rather have my goddaughter any day of the week than your auntie, wouldn't I, Bridget?' She tickled one of the many folds under the baby's chin. 'Funny to think that one day *she* will be an Aunt Biddy too.'

'Off you go, Mary. Don't look so feared, this isn't the real examinations.'

They saw her off, laughing at her run-and-leap method of getting on the bicycle.

'Why didn't George come out, wish her good luck? That's not right, Aunt Biddy.'

'There is "not right" on both sides, Hannah.'

'I know well enough there are bits of the marriage

where she and he . . . but nobody can say, no one, that Mary doesn't look after the house, that she doesn't work harder nor than most and if he cannot bring hisself to the hand of friendship, it's a poor—'

'Don't get heated, girl, hush.' Biddy nodded to the forge.

Mr Grant-Ingram had told her not to bother about books. His friend Mr Clarke had all that was needed, a library. He might have as many books as Miss Crewe. But she had brought the Latin, as usual, just for luck. She would leave it with her coat, like she would at the real examination, for to take it in would be cheating and she, Mary Bowden, wouldn't need to do that! She pedalled fast, happy, singing, 'Ride on, ride on in majesty! In lowly pomp ride on to die.' That wasn't right. Comparing her ride to Wellsbury with Jesus's ride on Palm Sunday wouldn't do. She bravely took one hand off the handlebar to wave, quickly, to men in the fields and women in their front gardens. The March winds and April showers *had* brought forth May flowers. They studded the meadows, gardens and hedges. There by a shallow pond, not much more than a puddle, were the pinky-mauve flowers of the butterbur plant, the leaves of which her mother once used for wrapping butter. Clumps of yellow groundsel grew at the edges of fields – swallowing the ground, the bane of farmers – and short white daisies fought for room with ground elder and fool's parsley. Two different scents, vanilla and onion, mingled, telling her that woodruff and allium were nearby. And there, almost indistinguishable from ordinary nettle, was the white dead nettle which didn't sting. Her father had taught her to make whistles from the hollow stems. She had only once mistaken the common nettle for the dead nettle, and that experience had been so painful, she wasn't likely to repeat it.

Nearing Wellsbury, she dismounted at the foot of a steep hill and started pushing what now felt like a very heavy piece of machinery, reminding herself that there was a decline to every incline and hoping that was not true about life itself. She felt elated, on top of the world not at the foot of a hill. Children paused briefly in their intricate games to shout rudely. They were playing in the street: the houses here were terraced with tiny patches of garden; no room for pigs or chickens, vegetables – or children. They had been built to accommodate workers at the gradually expanding furniture factories. At the top of the hill she remounted, trying to ignore the screams of derision at her clumsiness, but once on, she free-wheeled down the badly rutted hill, holding onto her hat and careering round the many pot-holes. As she neared the bottom, braking but still going faster than was safe and almost out of control, she saved herself from an ignominious tumble into a steaming pile of horse manure by dint of aiming her machine at a gaggle of taunting ragamuffins who scattered as she sped past. The 'thank you' she called was lost in a collective chanting of, 'Horse dung, horse dung, tell a lie it's on your tongue.'

It was what Mary called a 'serious' house: plain, square, pale rose brick and no ornate stonework. Definitely not Victorian. The door was opened, not by a servant, surprisingly, but by the Reverend Mr Grant-Ingram. He hurried her in, took her coat, thanked her quickly for the fudge, and showed her into a parlour where his friend Mr Clarke was waiting, and left them together.

'Sit down, Mrs Jackson. Don't look so nervous. I'm here to help you.'

She looked anxiously towards the door. 'Am I late?'

'No, no. The Reverend is always in a hurry.' He sat and examined her closely. Algernon had spoken about her with sympathy, which was understandable considering her strange little life, but less understandable and more worrying was his frequently voiced admiration for her appearance. He had been eulogistic, poetic, in his praise. It was the jealousy, the nagging doubt, that had persuaded him to agree to coach her. He had never doubted his friend's love and fidelity – they were both old and wise enough to be circumspect about their relationship and to enjoy the peace of trust after youthful indiscretions – but this had been different. And now he could see why. He smiled broadly at her. It was simple, like a painting, a perfect jewel, a piece of sculpture. She was an object of beauty.

The interview had gone well. Mary was amazed when Mr Clarke had said, 'That's enough for today. I don't want to tire you and put you off. Tea, I think.' He had warned her at the beginning that he would treat her as he treated his other pupils – all men. He had never taught females and wouldn't know how to alter his ways. The questioning had been fast, correction immediate, and he was abrupt when changing subjects. The groans at her foolish mistakes were balanced by nods of approval and a quick, 'Good, good.' She joined in his laughter at her mispronunciations of French. 'Hmm, your Miss Crewe is right about your Latin. It's excellent, but useless for this examination. And your French will be all right when you hear it spoken. A *sou* is a coin. You make it sound as if a loaf of bread costs two pigs!'

'I thought that was rather expensive!'

'I am giving you the examination papers for last term, with the answers, that will be a guide. Don't expand on the questions given beyond the subject matter. Some of the judges wouldn't care for a mere girl knowing more Latin than they.'

Algernon knocked on the door and entered. Mary could hear the chink of china as he closed the door behind him. 'Well, Francis, what do you think?' He patted Mary's shoulder lightly.

'As long as she keeps her nerve she'll pass easily. She should really have tried for a scholarship to a grammar school years ago. Wantford has a good one and that's not too far.'

'Mr Clarke, thank you for all that.' She spoke quietly, suppressing her excitement. 'But I was married you see. I had my son John when I was fourteen.'

'Good, Francis, that's wonderful.' Algernon took Mary's hand. 'I have an odd request to make. I need you to trust me, Mary.'

'I do, sir. And you ask away.'

'Well, I need a promise from you, but without giving you . . . let's see . . . without giving you any reason. Do you understand?'

'No.'

Francis took over, exasperated with his friend's dithering. 'Algy means, Mary, that he wants you to promise that what happens between now and your leaving will not be repeated without a certain person's permission.'

'I still don't understand, but I will trust you and I give you my solemn oath.' She felt fairly comfortable about that, for no harm could come as far as she could see, given that the two gentlemen were as they were, whatever that was, and whatever it was it wasn't likely they would want to – whatever. And, anyway, she had crossed her fingers for safety, just in case.

The two men smiled across the table. 'Don't be so fretful, Algy. You did the correct thing. You had to help her. Very interesting, you know, trying to understand how something like that happens. A poor farm-girl, working as a labourer from dawn to dusk, has a natural desire for learning. It isn't just the job she wants or the money. She reads and studies for its own sake. Not a genius, just bright. You should have heard her talking about the Eclogues and *Villette*, the Brontë book, such excitement.'

Algernon looked swiftly around the tea-shop and brushed aside the limp mousy hair framing the animated elfin face. 'Yes, she has responded to the occasional good influence. The Fiennders boy first, then her schoolmistress and there's an aunt Biddy, who is quite a free thinker. In some respects she has been lucky. I too, Francis. You are a good influence.' He gently squeezed his friend's hand, smiling with just a hint of malice. 'You rescued me from the shallow pleasures of provincial gossip.'

'Rubbish! You may read now but you still adore gossip, as do I.'

She had heard the front door close and their voices in the street. Now Mary was alone, sitting here in this room, not knowing why they had left the house. The relief, the excitement had gone. All that had happened, the joyous bicycle ride and their comments, 'clever – quick – pass easily', led up to this unease. And the promise of secrecy, about what? It couldn't be good. There were sounds in the house. Probably coming from the kitchen. Maybe there would be a visitor, someone to do with examinations. Yes! That was it, most like. An inspector. Another friend to help, perhaps, one who shouldn't. At least her tea was here. There was a rattle of dishes on a tray at the door. How ridiculous of her! She was just a little bit scared. She rose and opened the door slowly.

'Sally! You! Oh, I can't believe it. Is that why I had to . . . Oh dear . . .' She sat down, her heart beating so rapidly she felt faint.

'Oh, love. Oh, Mary love. You're not going to pass out, are you?' Sally dropped the tray on a table and rushed to the door. 'I'll get you some smelling-salts.'

'No, no, don't go. I'll be all right. Don't go, please. I was that wrought up, what with all the excitement and nerves. Him, Mr Clarke, testing me, and then the promise, so peculiar. I was frightened, tell the truth. Oh, Sally. You're alive, and well to look at you. Come here.' They embraced and kissed. Something they had never done before. 'I'm so angry with you, Sal. Oh, so happy to see you – and the girls? Are they here? Oh, my Lord, I do feel faint.'

'Put your head between your knees and I'll pour you a good cup of tea, plenty of sugar.'

'How did it happen?' Mary said weakly. 'I see now, the promise, it was from you, wasn't it? Not to tell *him*, George. You needn't have worried. We hardly speak these days.'

'Here you are, drink this down.'

'That's enough, Sal. Thank you. I'm better now. Why are you here? Do you live in Wellsbury? Have you got work? Oh, why didn't you tell us? Pat Quinn broke into your cottage, you know. Everybody feared the worst.'

'But you see, Mary, for me the worst had *happened*. George, he just gave me my notice, like a housemaid no longer needed. "Money to come regular," he said, till Gwennie was fourteen, all cut and dried.'

'He can be a cold man. Very set. Doesn't brook argument, I know.' Mary trembled a little, remembering the first year of her marriage. 'I know.'

'I want you to have another cup of tea, and eat this.' Sally passed her a plate of bread and butter and potted meat. 'I made it.'

'And brought it here for my tea? Or their tea?'

'I never brung it, and it's for our tea, and theirs if they want.' Sally tried to be casual but her pleasure and pride took over. 'I'm housekeeper here, Mary, and live in, and the girls are with me.'

'But how, Sal? Did you come straight away after, well, you know, from Findlesham?'

'It were something Agnes Quinn mentioned. I was in a right state that night, nothing said, mind. She said,

"How about confession?" and I said – well, I didn't say, of course, but I thought, I don't want nothing to do with her popery, devil-dodging they say, not but what it isn't her business and her as good a soul as I know, but it put me on to thinking of Little Bewdley and how decent the vicar had been previous. So.' She paused, partly for breath, but it was rare that she had someone hanging on her every word and she wanted to savour it.

'So?'

'So I went over early on the Saturday, long afore you was off to the river. I knew the cart would be collecting all the milk churns from the farms to take them off to the station and I got a ride as far as Bewdley Magna, and do you know, Mary, that great idiot, Gaby Shippon, tried to get me into the hedge? Him married and it only four in the morning.'

'For goodness sake, Sally.' Mary pushed her friend into a chair. 'Get on with it, they might be back soon.'

'Not them. Anyways, I just sort of collapsed when I saw him – Mr Grant-Ingram. On top of all else I remembered my little baby. And he said could I start straight away.'

'What?'

'Here, of course. The old housekeeper as was had gone sudden after a spot of unpleasantness. Didn't like two gentlemen, and all that. We've got – the girls and me – a big room at the top and use of sink *and* our own water closet!'

'Couldn't you have let me know, Sally?'

'No. I was frightened of telling in case I gave in and stayed in Findlesham. When you love a man, and I loved George, very truly, Mary, there's something in you that puts up with all the pain just to see his face. And that's natural.'

The ride back had been even better, cycling through tiny hamlets and settlements, along narrow lanes with may blossom almost meeting over her head. She had wanted to delay the arrival home, to enjoy peace that she hadn't known for months. Sally was safe. And she wanted to sing and shout for joy at Francis Clarke's words, 'She'll pass easily.' *She will pass easily!* He had said, 'Call me Francis'. As if she could, any more than she would address Mr Grant-Ingram as Algernon. But she knew why. He was clever and looked right, but had in his voice, almost hidden, what Miss Crewe called dirty vowels. Unlike his friend, he wasn't a cousin of Ann Fiennders of Fiennders Abbey. He was more likely to be a cousin of a mill-hand in Manchester or a factory worker in London, and that was why he admired her, for it was clear that he did. They would be pleased at home but it wouldn't do to boast or brag, especially with George. And then her promise. She had to keep that for Sally's sake. Not that George would pursue her. That, Mary knew. George had rid himself of that part of his life, children and all.

George stood on the mounting block, shading his eyes. She was late. That bicycle, that was what had done it. He had been worried all afternoon, angry with himself for letting her go on her own, angry for not seeing her off. That was the trouble these days, always angry, and no sense to it, and her frightened now, avoiding him. He squinted against the sun. There was a little cloud of powdery grey dust bowling along, preceding something. Too big for her bicycle, was it? Yes, it pulled up at the inn. Just a small trap. At least the sun wouldn't be setting for a good hour or so.

He crossed the lane to the village pump. They had running water at the forge but he'd always thought the spring water from the well sweeter, fresher. He pumped a little into his hands, splashed his face and brushed the hair out of his eyes. It was the shame that had turned him from her. Even at twenty-six and with a child she still had that look of purity. He pumped more water, after looking round to make sure no busybody was watching – there were signs, unusual in May, of a drought and it wouldn't do to be seen wasting water when he had his own – and drank from his cupped hands. Who would have thought . . .? He shook his head in disbelief. Who would have thought a whore for an hour, less, would cost as much as Sal and two children? The women he chose – for he never had the same twice, didn't want any sentimental developments – were older, comfortable types. You'd never know to look at them they were streetwalkers. One of them had been a widow, another married. They cost more than the youngsters but he felt easier with them.

If she wasn't back in a half-hour he'd saddle Little Dancer and go and look for her. No. He wouldn't wait. He'd go now, show her he cared. Show Hannah and Aunt Biddy, too, but show *her*. They most like would be married, be together, for another fifty years. That thought pleased him. There would be grandchildren.

They met at the corner of the new lane leading down

to Coddlestone Halt and the old Oxford Road. It was lucky he'd stopped for a word with Joe Hogg who'd taken on old Coddlestone Farm. Full of himself he was, like a pig in clover. He and the family had been farming up on the downs at the rightly named Starveall. This was a holiday after that. She was pushing her bicycle and looked tired and dusty.

'Mary! Mary!'

She hadn't noticed him: other riders had passed her and greeted her, some laughing and shouting, 'Get yourself a horse', or some such thing.

'George? Of course it's you. That's Little Dancer.'

'That's a fine thing.' He swung out of the saddle and soothed the startled horse. 'My wife recognizes a horse before a husband.'

She smiled, a little shy. They were rarely alone now. 'It was the surprise.'

'I were worried, Mary. You were later than expected, see. Right, now, what's happened there? You've got yourself a flat tyre.'

'There was some broken glass. I didn't see it. I fell off.'

'Oh, love. Are you safe?' He held her briefly. 'Not hurt?'

'No, I promise.'

'Not cut?'

'No, nothing.'

'Well, then, you get up on Little Dancer and I'll walk this here bicycle home, and no argument, Mary. Oh, my Lord. I forgot, what with the look of you. How went it?'

'They said . . .' She was choosing her words carefully,

controlling her excitement, when she saw the pride and expectation on his face.

'They said? Go on, love.'

Encouraged, she spilt out the praise and approval she had received.

'So the gentleman said you'll pass easily?'

'Easily.'

'No surprise to me, Mary.'

They set off home, both walking, leading the horse and pushing the bicycle.

'It was only a walking stick, Caroline. I know where it is. I haven't lost it.'

'Only a stick that wasn't yours. Taken without permission, miss.'

Maud slid her eyes, mutely pleading, round to Richard, who was lounging in a chair, pretending to read the newspaper. So far he hadn't said anything.

'Nobody has ever said I couldn't take a stick or a parasol or umbrella from that cupboard. We keep favourite things and new ones in our rooms.'

'Listen to me, young lady. There is no *we* about it. This is *my* house, our house.' She pointed to Richard, grudgingly including him, and raised her voice even further. 'Any fool should know that a walking stick with a silver top isn't to be taken by little girls.'

Her colour was very high, thought Richard, surprised. No wonder poor Maud seemed scared. This was not like Caroline's usual reaction to such a small transgression.

'What did you want it for, eh?' She was shouting now.

'The nettles, that's all. Beat back the nettles.' She

couldn't look at her sister-in-law and added lamely, 'I liked the feel, the weight.'

'That is precisely why *I* like it. It is mine. *I'm* not allowed to ride for another month. *I* would like to walk and beat back the nettles.'

'How could I know it would annoy you so?'

'Annoy me?' Caroline screamed.

'It's so unfair.' Maud was near to tears. 'I've hardly done anything and you are – you are vile.'

Caroline lunged forward to strike her but Richard jumped up and put out a restraining hand. 'Now then, you two. Stop this. Maud, go and get the blessed walking stick – you really do know where it is?'

'Yes.'

'All right then, run along like a good girl.'

Caroline was a little calmer now but before Maud could leave the room she snapped, 'You had better stay at the dower house tonight.'

'Why, Caro? What for?' He kicked the door shut to stop his wife leaving. 'She adores you and you have been so wonderful to her. Is that what you do? Enslave people and then discard them, torture them?'

He said this lightly but her behaviour had shocked him, she knew. 'She had been getting very out of hand, you know that, Richard. It isn't good for her to be allowed so much licence. I'm going to the nursery to see Elizabeth.' He followed her upstairs to her bedroom without speaking. 'Oh dear. Are you trotting behind me like a little dog?'

Sitting her firmly on the bed, he held her shoulders and then pushed her back. 'Don't ever make a mistake about *me*, Caroline. *I* am not your slave.'

She lay submissively as he undressed her. They made love for the first time since the birth of their child. He did it with care as always but silently, with no endearments. He only spoke as he stood by her bed, putting on his trousers. 'It must be a very special walking stick.'

Running through the long grass, Maud still felt trembly at the horrible scene. And those hateful words, 'miss', 'little girl', 'any fool', '*my* house'. Even Richard's hurtful, 'Run along like a good girl.' *Good girl?* She would damn well show them. Damn them. Double damn. He was there, thank goodness. Breathless, she demanded, 'The walking stick please, immediately.'

'No need to talk like that. It's here.' He handed it over. 'I even polished the silver top.' He didn't tell her what he'd discovered there whilst doing so. 'Gave it a rub.'

'Very well. Thank you. Good day.'

'Something wrong? Get into trouble about it, did you? I wouldn't have stole it. You left it here, forgot it. I took care of it. Come on, sit down.'

She sat down on the straw bale, primly, just as she had the last time, the stick held firmly.

'Go on, tell. You're right upset, aren't you?'

She hesitated, then tried to explain, but as she was talking her bewilderment increased. 'It's all so peculiar, and to add to all that, she's ordered me out of the house. I'm to stay with my mother. Yes. That's almost the worst bit. She, my mother, was so relieved I didn't have to live with her, so was I, that it will be horrible asking to go back, even if it's only for a night or so.'

'Don't ask. Do what I do.'

'What's that?'

'Not for the same reason, you know. No silver knobs in my family.'

This was interesting. He hadn't talked about this before. A family, though. That was disappointing. She had rather hoped he was a changeling, or a gypsy. Even a bastard would have done.

'They don't always know where I sleep. One lot thinks I'm with t'other.'

'And where *do* you sleep?'

'Here, in fine weather.'

'And in foul weather?'

Ah, he had her all interested now. An adventure was what she was after. 'In foul weather, I sleep in the attics of your farm. Home Farm.'

'Get away!'

The shout, which had come after so many grunts and growls that she hardly bothered to look, brought Biddy to the window. She knew the reason for the trouble. It had been going on all day. Mary was due in Oxford at three o'clock for her examination and George was taking her to Wellsbury station for the one o'clock train. The anxiety about what to wear, and her constant recitation of facts to anybody available to read and check them, had also been unceasing. More than all day, all week. She had settled on her dove-grey cambric, and had finally accepted Hannah's opinion that if she didn't know it now it was too late. But poor George was having trouble catching the pony for the trap. He had tried this morning, hoping to groom and have her ready but what he hadn't allowed for was the fact that she was in season, and in the next field, usually occupied by a couple of geldings, was an interested stallion.

'Curse the man. I'll have a word or two with Jack Rigger about that there horse. Our agreement was mares or geldings, and he gets that field for less than nothing, for isn't he supposed to be the mole-catcher, and *if* he's catching them, he must be hatching them too!' Little Dancer was so skittish that she had been impossible to approach even with all his usual bribes: sugar, oats and carrots. He had tried peppermints, too, but the scent of the stallion had overwhelmed the pungent oil.

The 'Get away' had been shouted to Mary, out in the field trying to help, nervous about the time. She ran into the house and called up the stairs, 'I'm going to read through one chapter of my grammar – *one* – and then I'm getting my bicycle out.' Biddy prayed that he would catch the pony. It gave him pride, his way with horses, and he wanted to be seen taking his clever pretty wife to the railway station. And with them having one of their good patches too.

Biddy's screaming, as she helter-skeltered down the stairs, 'Get your bicycle, she's got him', was confusing. Especially after studying her English grammar. It should have been either, 'Get your bicycle, he can't get her', or 'Don't get your bicycle, he's got her.'

'Get the doctor. Quick now, Mary.'

'Doctor?'

'George was kicked. I'm going out to him. Fetch Dr Henders, that new house out along the spur road.'

'What's happened, Aunt Biddy?'

'Don't wait, child. Just go,' she cried as she sped out to the garden.

Mary was ashamed later, remembering her anger, 'All his own fault, insisting. I could have been at the station by now.' Her first time on a train, too. She had wanted to be there early, savour it; the sharp tarry smell of the steam, people standing uneasily next to porters, guarding piles of heavy leather suitcases and trunks, not knowing how much to tip them. The important voices announcing arrivals and departures from and to places she had heard of but not seen. Towns that existed only on maps, and villages known to her only as signposts passed in the trap. And she had longed to be alone. 'She will pass easily' was becoming a memory not to be trusted.

Doctor Henders *was* to be trusted. She could tell that immediately. He looked cosy, his rosy complexion almost concealed by tufts of tobacco-brown hair, beard, mutton-chop whiskers, moustache, and eyebrows that looked in need of a comb, but his eyes were bright and intelligent. He ordered his coach round before she had finished speaking and the coachman cantered the horse all the way back to the forge. Hannah was waiting for them outside.

'Oh, Mary. I'm so sorry.' She pointed to the field at the end of the side garden. 'He's out there, Doctor.'

'Thank you, Hanny.' Mary shrugged. 'Well, that's that, then, for this year, anyway. What has he done? Hannah? Did she kick him? Lord, I hope it's not his right arm. That would be hard with the shoeing. Best get Billy, I suppose, or Albert could help him. He's quite handy with the iron, if it's not too bad . . .'

She stopped as Hannah put out her hand to hush her. 'It *is* bad, Mary.'

Everything else was untouched. His body, arms, legs. He lay on his back as if enjoying the sun. They tried to stop her, Aunt Biddy and the doctor, but she had to see, to understand. His face had gone. The skin, bones, teeth, brains, all matted with his yellow hair and the blood, congealed, set, like Chinese lacquer. The impact of the hoof was clear in the scarred grass surrounding the ruined head. She looked over the hedge where the stallion and Little Dancer were now grazing quietly. 'He loved her so.'

Caroline had changed the footmen's livery to incorporate a touch of the Colcroft colours. The man now clearing away from the left, as the butler placed clean plates from the right, was wearing a discreet navy blue, the jacket trimmed with a dark red braid. Ann had to admit that as the man probably weighed at least fifteen stone, this certainly suited him better than the rose and silver of the Fiennders' livery. The salmon dariole, delicious in its aspic-stiffened mayonnaise, with the first tarragon of the season from Sam's sheltering cloches in the herb garden, was replaced by lamb's sweetbreads cooked in béchamel sauce and baked in puff pastry cases. Mrs Bunn had risen to the challenge of her new mistress.

The almost dry, flowery, apple-scented Riesling was removed and decanters of claret were being poured by Bulbeck. Good of Caroline to keep him on. With his taste for claret, let alone Burgundy, hock, port, sherry, Madeira, brandy, whisky, it would be cheaper to give him a cottage and pension him off. The wine was no doubt one of Thomas's best, if not *the* best. Quite right of her to serve and drink from the best of the cellar. She must make sure, though, that Richard was re-stocking it. He must lay down, as his father and his grandfather had, wine for future Fiennders' consumption as well as his own.

Richard, at the head of the table, nodded to his mother. 'Would you like to come with me later, Mamma? I'm deciding on the extension to the kitchen garden with Mr Reade. We're going ahead with my – *our* plans for the market garden, you know.'

'Yes, I'd love to, darling. That is kind of you to include me.'

'It was always your domain and it doesn't really interest Caroline, or not as much as the stables.' He looked at his wife entertaining Dr Henders. He was a useful addition to their world, not only for medical reasons, though he had been helpful with Caroline. 'Many women have extreme changes of behaviour after childbirth. Some become almost suicidal. Just be patient,' he'd said. He also liked music and played the violin. They could have duets or even trios, quartets! Maud was doing so well with her harpsichord. He exchanged a warm smile with his sister. This friend of Algernon's played the flute and sang. That had been so good of Caroline. She had dismissed any suggestion of kindness about inviting a 'friend' of Algernon's to the house. 'Nonsense, an extra man is always useful.'

He had responded facetiously. 'Even if he isn't useful in all ways?'

Algernon was talking across the table to Frederick about their respective morning sermons. As usual the hint of rivalry lay just below the surface, for Frederick was sighing and boasting about too much work. 'No sooner have we finished with Easter than the whole world starts marrying!'

On his hostess's right, Robert Henders, having exhausted his knowledge of the treatment of horses' ailments – why did people think he was an expert on animals as well as humans? – joined in. 'Well, your work will be increased next week, Vicar. You'll have a funeral.'

'Indeed? I've not heard about that,' the Honourable Frederick Baring-Kimball said petulantly. 'But then *you*, I suppose, would be the first to know,' he added magnanimously. 'Who is it? Some old character from Findlesham?'

'No, not old. A sad – a tragic death.'

'Oh, yes, tragic,' his wife Grace added. 'Only yesterday, just as luncheon was ready, the blacksmith's wife . . .'

The desultory to and fro of pleasantries, the superficial conversation, the niceties about the food and wine, the weather, the new baby, faded away. Robert Henders was aware of an ice-like feeling invading the party. He rapidly corrected his wife's false impression. 'The smith's wife arrived on her bicycle, asking for me. Her husband had suffered an accident.'

'Dead, is he? What kind of accident?' Frederick asked with indifference.

'He was kicked by a horse. Yes, he is dead.'

Caroline put her claret glass down firmly with a little bang, indicating that it should be refilled. 'The blacksmith? Jackson? Very good farrier. How frightful. How did it happen? Where was he kicked?'

Around the table Henders surveyed the guests. The reaction to his announcement was unexpected: news of the death of the village smith shouldn't have disturbed so many people. He felt isolated in a group that included the Vicar of Findlesham and his wife, Grace his own wife, and his hostess, Lady Caroline, all of whose reception of the news was, well, normal. He hesitated describing the ugliness of the accident.

'He fell, you see, and the horse, a mare, high-spirited,' he used the euphemism hoping they would work it out for themselves, 'was disturbed by a stallion in the next field and kicked the poor man when he was down.'

Caroline helped him out. 'Never a good idea, this time of year, mares and stallions in the same field or near by. The mare could be in season.'

They resumed their previous conversation, expanding the subject to include dogs and bitches, and specifically bitches on heat.

Algernon and Francis, however, perceiving the degree of dismay shown by their fellow diners, were agitated after the initial shock and clearly longing to talk about it. Ann was flushed and ill at ease. Maud looked as if she could fly from the table, and Richard was pale, incapable of responding to Mrs Henders who, seated on his right, was good-naturedly attempting small talk whilst her husband listened, puzzled, and tried to understand all the sub-texts of conversation.

When the party withdrew from the dining room to the drawing room, leaving the ratafia trifle almost untouched, drawing comments later on in the kitchen with special reference to the waste of the bottle of good sherry that went in it – although all knew it wouldn't be wasted. Maud had disappeared and Ann excused herself with a migraine. Richard had recovered sufficiently to sit with Algernon and Francis, hoping to be distracted by discussing their mutual admiration for the music of

Brahms. But they now felt free and able to talk with him about the shock of George Jackson's death and the effect it would have on Mary. Obviously she had been prevented from taking the trip to Oxford for her examination. They had intended visiting the forge to see how she had done.

'Poor, sad creature,' Algernon said, and Richard sensed he was referring to Mary and not to her dead husband.

Maud, astride a hot and sweating Marron, concealed herself under the large, flourishing chestnut tree. She could see the forge easily from here. Leaning over the horse's neck, she whispered, 'You'll cool down now. Good girl, see, you're under your own tree, two chestnuts together.' The huge doors of the smithy were closed. She'd never seen that before. Keeper Bowden's carriage was outside. Very gay, with its blue and yellow paint, a funny-looking thing, half haycart, half trap. The garden at the side of the forge was gay, too, with the endings of primroses, the beginnings of tulips and the promise of sunflowers, hollyhocks, delphiniums, lupins and poppies, grading down in height. The field was through there. She shuddered. Through the half-open windows she could see into the front parlour where people passed back and forth. That must be Mrs Bowden or the other sister, not Mary. The figure was too big to be Mary. One of the upper windows was closed. That might be where the dead man was laid out. Albert wasn't there, she knew that. He wouldn't have stayed inside with the others, the aunt, the man's brother, his parents. He would be sitting outside, alone, on one of the staddle stones or the mounting block. Marron responded to the gentle pressure of her left heel and turned away from the house, walking slowly under her constraint till they were out of eyeshot and earshot. Then she released him and they cantered down the fields parallel to the lane, jumping two hedges and a ditch before wheeling left into Drover's Lane. He was there, outside Keepers Cottage, leaning on the gate, looking in her direction.

'Funny that, Maud. It's such a still day, I heard you a mile away.'

'I thought I should come. You'll need to be with somebody. We heard today, at luncheon, from the doctor. I went first to the forge.' She swung out of her saddle and jumped to the ground. 'May I hitch him here to the gatepost?'

'Give it here, yes. I did go to the forge but nobody knew I was there. She's sitting with her John, you see.'

'Oh, of course.'

'My nephew,' he added.

'I always forget, seeing him with your father . . .'

She hesitated, but he nodded and finished her sentence without resentment. 'You think of him as Dad's son and me . . . as Mary's – right? Come in. Would you like some lemon barley? My ma's famous for it.'

She followed him into what the Bowdens called 'the room'. She liked it immediately. The stone-flagged floor scattered with bright rag rugs, the plain furniture, either scrubbed ash and pine or waxed oak, the geraniums on the window-sills, their brilliant crimson flowers making the sun even brighter. Candlesticks everywhere, short and tall, dull pewter, brightly polished brass and copper, and white china. He returned from the larder carrying the barley water. 'Thank you.' She sipped. 'It *is* good.' She examined a spit hanging on the hook above the fire.

'Does your mother still cook with this?' He nodded, pleased with her approval.

'I could cook then, at the farm one day, using that spit, a picnic.'

'Yes, you could, if I give you a hand.'

'I suppose that would be necessary.' She started to laugh but composed herself, thinking of the reason for her visit. 'Is she all right, Albert? I'm so sorry.' Her offer of sympathy, the dignified but awkward attempt at being grown-up, reminded him of the one night she had spent at the farm. She had graciously accepted that she would sleep in a separate attic room, the best one, but he'd expected her to join him, scared, at the first sound of rustlings and scuttlings. She had appeared at the first light of dawn, however, dressed and ready to leave as planned, to avoid the men bringing in the cows for milking. She had referred bravely to the noises of mice, and in case she ever wanted to stay again he didn't tell her that the mice were rats and bats.

'It were because of him, George, I went to the lock-up that time and it were after that I didn't see her so much. No, she isn't all right.'

'I think love and friendship, once given, should be there for ever, whatever one does.'

'Doesn't work out like that.'

'I like this room, Albert — *our* house is so full of stuff, hot velvets, slippery satin and small tables . . . Well, of course I know it doesn't. Look at Nanny — not Nanny Colcroft who's with Elizabeth, but Nanny Fiennders. She was my absolute biggest friend, but when Mamma let her go after Tommy went to Eton, she took the money, kissed me goodbye, joined her sister in Kent and that was that.

I know I behaved atrociously sometimes, but she knew I loved her.'

'Can't blame her. Bit of money and a bit of peace from you.'

She ignored this. 'Anyway, that's what I came to say, Albert. I *was* disappointed that you weren't a gypsy or a ne'er-do-well, it's true, but that's childish for a person of my age. I'm your friend, even though you are an ex-convict.' They shook hands solemnly.

'And I'm your friend, atrocious or not.'

She pretended to be asleep until the door of his dressing-room closed. It was necessary, with the baby being brought in for her feeds, to sleep separately, but it meant they didn't have their usual talks, discussing tomorrow and reviewing the day. Not that she wanted to review this day, or the awkwardness that started at luncheon and continued through the afternoon and supper. Algernon's friend had returned to Wellsbury but Richard had insisted that Algernon stay, though it was obvious he didn't want to. He had accompanied her on a walk while Richard was with the gardener discussing his new plans. *That* was causing quite a little difference between them: the idea of extending the greenhouses for marketing was a little too much like trade, she thought.

Then Algernon had asked Richard to play the piano before supper. He had started on one of those gloomy pieces that always seemed to be written by a German whose name began with a B and, God knows, there were enough of them. After the first few bars, she had interrupted, asking for that jolly little thing, 'Oh, Sir, A

Maiden Sighs'. He had glared and then slammed down
the lid. Then at supper, from far away in Maud's room,
one could just hear the faint sound of her harpsichord
playing the same old piece that Richard had started, and
he and Algernon exchanged small smiles, excluding her
as she had been excluded at luncheon. Restlessly pushing
off the delicate tea-coloured crocheted blanket and throwing one of the large goose-feather pillows accurately onto
the pink armchair, she decided to speak to Nanny in the
morning. There must be a wet-nurse in one of the villages, then she could let her milk dry up and be free of
all this routine and care: 'Must be home for Elizabeth's
feed', 'Mustn't drink too much wine', 'Pickles make your
milk curdle', 'You must have a rest in the afternoon'.
Richard was almost as bad as Nanny; to be expected with
the first-born, she supposed. He had whispered a little,
'Sorry, Caro', as he made love to her, but in the darkness
of the room she couldn't tell whether his face was damp
from perspiration or tears.

The quiet in the little room behind the shop was total
except for the tiny dry cough, which Biddy had only
noticed today. All through the time of harvest, when few
people used the shop – for all were out either in the
fields or driving the carts – Mary had sat with her books,
usually one open on the table and one held in her lap. If
she was studying, it wasn't apparent. When Biddy had
silently peeped in, she was staring into the distance,
unmoving. She had ignored the activity in the lanes and
fields; the dawn-to-dusk-and-beyond yearly work of
bringing in the corn had passed unnoticed. The noise

of Billy in the forge, hammering at the anvil and shoeing the great cart-horses that pulled the farm wagons, the sound of the wagons laden high with the corn, forcing the horses into a slow, plodding gait on their way to the farm and the swifter trotting back after shedding their loads, all unnoticed. Through the boisterous voices of the farm-hands, increasing in volume during the day as they drank the free strong ale, Mary sat, only moving to serve the occasional villager, either too young or too old to help in the fields. She had been still, apart, only responding when spoken to throughout the months – was it three already? – since George's death. It was a painful grief, Biddy knew, worsened by guilt and without the release of tears.

But today it was the little cough that worried her. The doctor had said it was one of the signs. He had wanted to speak to Mary herself but Biddy had dissuaded him. 'I'll give eye to her, I know her, I will notice aught wrong.'

'If you notice,' he'd said. 'When you do it might be too late.'

The shop door-bell clanged and the door banged as it shut automatically, an old iron horse-shoe serving as a counter-balance.

It was the bright little Quinn girl. 'Me mam says, if the ham's finished, can I be having the bone, miss?'

Aggy Quinn had infallible timing, judging perfectly when the meat from the boiled ham would all be sold and the bone available for the usual halfpenny towards the end of the day. Mary wrapped the bone and opened the heavy door for the child, pausing only to return a good-humoured shouted greeting from one of the Corrigan men seated atop a precariously high load of corn being pulled at a snail's pace by the two heavy shire-horses, now worn out after a long day. Closing the door, she put a little fist – one finger of which was marked by a sore – to her chest as she coughed.

'What is it, Aunt Biddy?' The woman stood waiting for her at the entrance to the little back room. 'You've been looking in on me all day.'

'Sorry, Mary. I didn't mean to disturb.'

'I'm all right, you know. I'm working.'

'It doesn't look like it, love. That book.' Biddy pointed to the French grammar opened on the table. 'It hasn't moved.'

'I'm conjugating my verbs, repeating them to myself.' She sat, dismissing the old woman.

Uneasily, Biddy lingered. 'This is so hard, Mary, but I have to speak. It's because I'm more than worried for you.'

'I've told you not to. Leave me be. If I worry you perhaps I should go home.'

'That does make me sad that you should speak so, love. You came here over twelve years ago. No, anyway that isn't it. You grieve your own way, Mary. You get through it as best you can.'

'What is it, then?'

'I don't know that this is the right place.' But she didn't know where else to suggest. To go for a walk with every man and his wife out, cutting, stooking, binding, loading, driving, making the most of what could be the last day of the good weather, according to John Bowden, who was reliable to do with the forecasting – his birds told him, he always said. Her bedroom wouldn't do: it looked onto the field where Little Dancer, now in foal, grazed. In the kitchen or the parlour they would likely be interrupted by Billy. Another little cough from Mary gave her the courage. She changed the sign on the shop door to CLOSED, shut the door between the two rooms and stood, barring the way into the house.

Mary waited, her hands clasped in her lap. 'What is it, Aunt?'

'I have to ask you the most private questions, dear, and it doesn't come easy. In all the time of your marriage, I've known most, guessed some, and loved you both equally. Tried not to judge . . . Oh, Lord!'

'What is it? Don't fret, Aunt Biddy. I will listen.'

The old woman's face was scarlet with shame, her hands twitched nervously. 'A time ago, Dr Henders asked for a word with me. He was, well, anxious about you.'

'You should have told him nothing was wrong. I've always been a bit scrawny and I don't need a tonic.'

'You're a beautiful young woman, Mary, rare, but it wasn't that you see. It was the future he was concerned with, and . . .'

'And what?'

How could she? Biddy thought. How could she ask and tell such intimate, horrible, sad things?

'Biddy.' Mary stood. 'I'm frightened now. Just say.'

Yes, she would just say. There was no way of disguising it. 'Dr Henders asked to see me because he examined George . . . George's body. He told me he discovered a chancre on his . . . body.' She gestured to the lower part of her own body. 'And a chancre,' she said, in answer to Mary's look of bewilderment, 'is a – venereal ulcer.'

The livid sore on the finger was evident as Mary put her hand to her mouth.

'He, the doctor, told me to look for signs.'

'In me?' Mary whispered.

Biddy nodded. 'He wanted to see you but I didn't think you were up to it, and I explained – you know.'

'Yes,' she shouted. 'I know and you know and now he knows. I wasn't George's wife after young John was born. Oh, God. Oh, Biddy. I don't think I can bear it. He must have gone with street women after he and Sally—' She choked, catching her breath on a cough as she sobbed, 'I drove him there. I as good as gave him it. Syphilis. Oh, George. Oh, my poor George.'

'But, Mary, I have to ask you. When you and he were getting on a bit better, did you sleep with him again as man and wife? For you have two of the signs that the doctor told me to look out for.' Even at George's death, Biddy had never felt so utterly wretched.

'Signs? What signs? What does it matter?' she screamed.

' "A cough, a dry throat," he said. "And a sore." ' She pointed to Mary's finger. The cough was now evident, punctuating the sobs.

'My cough? You've forgotten, I always get a cough at harvest time.' She nodded towards the lane from where the sounds of the end of the day, the end of the hard work, could just be heard, the men and boys singing, 'Praise him for our harvest-store, he hath filled the garner-floor', and cottagers echoing all the way through the village, 'Merry, merry, harvest home'.

'It's the dust from the corn.' She was laughing now through her tears. 'And my finger, the sore on my finger?'

The picture of Caroline Fiennders, her face glowing, radiant, under the mass of coppery brown hair visible beneath the green velvet hat, the full bosom encased in a high-necked, tightly buttoned jacket, easing herself off the lame horse. The swollen stomach, the obvious early pregnancy, returned to her. What love must be there in that marriage, two babies conceived in one year. 'This?' She held up her damaged red forefinger. 'This is an old wound.'

1899

'And you so good with your brain, Mary. I can't believe it. Must be because you're a woman.'

It was Biddy who responded to this insult, on behalf of Mary, Hannah, herself and all women who weren't present at their midday meal. 'It is because, Billy my lad, you can't explain it. It's my betting you can't even spell it.'

He reddened a little and helped himself to a big spoonful of rhubarb crumble. This wasn't a fight but an argument, and if he could win it, and he knew it might take months, he would feel in charge, the man of the house, it would finally be *his* business. 'I can too, Aunt. Enough as is necessary. Combustion! C-O-M, maybe another M.'

'Maybe not,' Mary murmured.

'After that there's, B-U-S-T-E-O-N, and then, E-N-G-I-N.' He plopped some clotted cream onto the crumble, pleased with himself.

Mary smiled gently. She didn't want to discourage him. 'Nearly there, Billy. Change the first E to I then add an E on the end of "engin", and don't bother about the extra M.'

'I'll do that, Mary. Ta.'

'What I don't understand is why, Billy. What's the

point of a horseless carriage, when we've got horses?' Hannah started clearing away. 'There's enough, to my way of thinking, with the steam train and bicycles. What more do you want? I've got to open up the shop.' Hannah ruffled his hair lightly as she left the kitchen.

He didn't need to win her round but he wanted everybody on his side. 'Progress,' he called after her. 'You'd have settled for tallow instead of gas, you'd have made do with the penny post and not the telegraph.'

'Are you going to Miss Crewe's, Mary? There's a bowl of soup ready for you and the calf's foot jelly.' Biddy pointed to the still-room. 'It's cool, I left it on the slate shelf.'

'You're not going because of me, Mary, are you?' Billy was dismayed. The comfortable meal-time was over and he didn't seem to have made his point.

'No, course not, and I'll think on it, Billy. I promise.'

'What are you sitting there for, like "Jack all alone"? You get back to the anvil and I'll get on with the washing up.'

'I was thinking.'

'It will all come in good time, Billy. Mary doesn't want you to waste your money. She's wise, you know.'

'She is that, though what good half her learning does beats me. Speaking the foreign tongues when she isn't going to meet no Frenchies or Latins.' He rose and stretched his arms above his head. 'Ooh, my back. 'Tis always the same in the hunting season, bent over a hoof with a horse behind pushing me.' He sighed. 'I wish . . .'

'And what is it you wish?'

The reply was unexpected.

'I wish John and Emma Bowden had had one more girl – one for me.'

Biddy put the dishes to soak in hot water. 'Do you still hanker after her, then, Billy? After all this time? And her with three children?'

'Not just Hanny, I care for Mary, too. I want to take care of her.'

'I'll tell you something, lad. You're too comfortable here with two women – three when Hannah's here – to look after you. You're all settled in like a rooster with three hens. It's about time you had your own woman to take care of, started a family. You're getting on you know, Billy. Thirty. What's the matter with young Kathleen Quinn? You've been walking her out a bit.'

'Nothing, Aunt. Nothing the matter with Flora Nichols either.'

'The groom's daughter? You been seeing her?'

'Yes, on and off. Nothing the matter with Mary Sharp, from the inn.'

'That's enough, now.' She shook a dish-mop at him laughing.

'Nothing the matter with wild Violet up at the big house.'

She chased him into the forge, panting. 'I'm too old for all this and there's plenty the matter with *her*, as well you know. She's, well, she's talked about. All that she gets up to and who with, and more. She's lucky that she's never . . . you know what.'

★

Mary supported the old woman's body with one arm as she rearranged the stiff horse-hair bolster with the other and then placed the softer pillows behind her back. 'You should sit up, Miss Crewe. That's what they say about pneumonia, you know, then it cannot get a hold.'

'They also say, Mary, it is the old man's friend, so it is probably the old woman's friend as well.'

Mary ignored this and placed the tray on the bed. 'I've spoken to Biddy and she agrees it's a good idea. If they do get the new schoolmistress and give her your cottage, you will come to us.'

'This all comes of you being so stubborn, Mary.'

'Looking back and looking at it from outside, I was wrong but it was all I could do. It would have been unloving, the examinations always being around the time he died. And I couldn't talk about it then. I had a hurt.'

'A pain,' the teacher corrected automatically. 'That's rubbish. He was proud of you.' She turned her head and put a handkerchief to her mouth to conceal the extent of her coughing. 'That is all sentimental superstition.'

Mary didn't argue. Miss Crewe was a spinster, she couldn't understand. 'I'm busy enough, anyway, what with the shop and the house, and I like helping the young ones you send me. Those that got their scholarships, well, it's like . . . it's as if I'm a part of it. I'm off to school with them, on the train.' She took the tray off the bed. Miss Crewe wasn't going to eat any more. 'Aunt Biddy's eager for you to come, soon. She says she's in need of a good argument, and now that young John is over at Keepers Cottage permanently, there's an empty room.'

'Under-keeper, is he?'

'*Head* under-keeper.'

Sarah Crewe patted her hand. 'Very kind.' This woman, with all her energy, managing such a difficult life – *lives*, really, for it had changed more than once – wouldn't be able to understand. The illness itself had tired her, but losing her profession and her home together had taken away her will. Ten years ago, to live at the forge with this brightest of girls and the opinionated aunt would have been welcome, stimulating, but now her world had narrowed to books, previously read, that she was too weak to hold.

'I'm going to bring up another hot brick. There's one warming in the hearth.'

Mary returned with the brick wrapped in flannel. Miss Crewe was lying down again. 'Your aunt knows she won't get any argument from me about the Boers, that is not a war I could approve of, but she cannot think that her "new party",' Mary was pleased that the old woman was sufficiently animated to say 'new party' with an explosive 'p', indicative of contempt, 'is the only repository of global morals. The Independent Labour Party – nothing independent about it. What does she know of Tory radicalism?'

Mary put the back of her hand on Miss Crewe's forehead. It was hot again. 'I'm not too sure Aunt Biddy should be allowed to see you until you're better. She's bad for your temperature.'

In spite of the lined yellow skin and the wispy grey hair, Sarah Crewe's smile was bright and warm. 'I've got to teach her the difference between ideas and ideology before I die.'

Mary pedalled fast on her way back to the forge, partly to keep warm. Her new bicycle was comfortable even on this deeply rutted lane, a big improvement on the old bone-shaker which she had given to her John. She was also pedalling fast because she was anxious to speak to Billy. Miss Crewe had been very interesting about the motor car and its possible future. 'It will never supersede the horse, no doubt, but it will have its place, however small, and Billy is right to take it on. A new invention, my dear, a new century.'

Across the fields, through the far distant copse, she could see a faint flash of pink and then the sweet melancholy sound of the huntsman could be heard blowing 'going home' on his horn, indicating the end of the day.

Caroline joined the crowded tea-table. She was still wearing the over-skirt of her riding habit but had changed the shirt, stock and jacket and removed the top hat and veil. She always disliked changing fully after a day's hunting, knowing that she looked her best in the formal side-saddle riding habit; the severity of the white cotton stock knotted just under her chin, the curve of the fitted jacket flattering her waist, the black veil adding a little mystery to her otherwise open, healthy face, but most of all, the exquisite black kid boots showing her ankles and calves to advantage. Men were enchanted by her acceptance of help dismounting, quite willing to have their hands sullied by her slightly muddy boots as she placed a foot in their clasped hands. Her 'thank you' as she touched the ground was a glance through her veil that lasted just a few seconds longer than necessary.

'How was poor Adam?' Richard called across the table. 'I'm passing down the decanter.'

'He was fine – forgotten all about it.'

'What a fearless lad, though, like his mother.' Cathal Watson, typical of one of Caroline's 'slaves', tipped his chair back, roaring with laughter, watched discreetly by an anxious butler.

'Hardly the sort of thing I do, Cathal. When did you last see me standing on my saddle screaming, "Me, me!"?'

'I believe if young Nichols hadn't been there as well as Nanny, holding the reins, he would have followed us for as long as little Shetty could keep up.'

'Silly, Papa. He's only a baby.' Oliver spoke with all the wisdom of a five-year-old.

'So are you, small beast. You only kept up for an hour and you were on a proper pony, not a fat little Shetland.'

Caroline poured whisky from the decanter into her tea and sipped. 'Ah, I've earned this. Be quiet, both of you. If you're going to be tiresome, do it in the nursery.' At the tiny signal of her raised finger, a footman stepped forward and deftly removed the top of her boiled egg with a sharp tap of a silver knife.

'Mamma is quite right. It is generous of her to have you children at the dining table.' Then Richard choked on his tea, drowning the mutter of 'teaing table' from Oliver, and was patted on the back by his mother.

'How old are *you*, Elizabeth?' Algernon, of course, knew.

'She's a very old eight, aren't you, my darling?' Richard leaned across Millie Watson and blew his daughter a little kiss.

Poor little monster, Algernon thought. Flirting with her father, amusing him with her self-conscious precocity.

It was the only attention she got in this family, over-whelmed as it was with an embarrassment of riches, three sons. Fiennders Abbey secured for this generation. 'This is very good, Richard.' He raised his tumbler of whisky. 'Far too good to put in your tea, Caroline.'

'Well, you see, I don't really drink any more.'

Or any less either, he thought.

Even Richard was surprised. 'You don't?' he said. 'I hadn't noticed.'

Caroline shrugged. 'Wine at dinner, of course. The whisky is sent to us from the distillery in Inverness, Algy. Jessica's husband arranges it. We were there the year before last for the Twelfth. It was always sent out with the shooting lunch, *Richard* rather took to it.'

'I can understand why.' He drained his glass, as she finished her tea.

'Then, Algy dear, you will take a couple of bottles home with you. Francis must try it too.'

Ann watched her daughter-in-law at the end of the table. She was extraordinary, perfect. How well she dealt with everything. She had stopped the children's nonsense immediately, for instance, and without noisy tears. Every-body's affection was won so easily. Algy was an example. Only two bottles of whisky, but just the right thing to do. She accumulated friends who were happy to be used by her; even her 'slaves', as Richard called them, were retained after their marriages, their wives happily absorbed into her circle. What was so charming about her was that in spite of all her dutiful behaviour, to the children, to the servants, tenants, villagers, and Richard, she obviously had such a good time. She had enjoyed her day's hunting, kept up with the hounds, always in control and never riding ahead of the master or the huntsman, another display of good manners. The servants were managed cleverly, too. A little word of apology after they had all tramped through the hall. 'Oh dear. Sorry about the mud,' meant that the mud had better be gone by the time they had finished tea, and it would be, and all the mud brushed from the coats and jackets.

Ann basked in the luxury of her retirement from the duties of chatelaine of Fiennders Abbey, all her responsibilities assumed so naturally by Caroline. All but one – or maybe two. Tommy would be easier to cope with at Cambridge. So much better for him than Oxford, where he would be competing against Richard's reputation, and it was too far to visit unexpectedly. These were only wild oats he was sowing. Thank heavens he was sowing them somewhere else at the moment. Italy – or was it France? She would know when he wired for more money. So hard for him, poor darling, younger son and even then the usefulness of being 'the spare' swamped by the birth of three healthy boys in a row. But it was Maud, as ever, who was causing the biggest problem. Richard would be sorting that out, she hoped. He had promised to visit her in London, if he could find her. Only the music teacher had news of her with any regularity. What the Ormerods and the Bexley-Wrights had discovered was the same situation that had been going on here, for Lord knew how long. Maud would tell each family she was with the other. It was only when Caroline had spoken to her after the birth of little Adam, saying that Maud must move into the dower house permanently now, and how happy she was that Maud had stayed there occasionally, that the deceit had been discovered. Sly little thing. She had refused an explanation. It was serious enough here, but for that to happen in London was appalling. Maud was endangering herself and the family name. She didn't want to think about it. She wouldn't. Catching Caroline's eye, she gestured her intention to leave. 'I don't want to break up the party, dear, but at my age . . .'

'You're quite right at any age. We're all tired.' Murmurs of assent, except from the children, circled the table. 'Would you like a carriage? No? Then Richard must walk you home.'

'Nonsense, Caroline. Well, if I must have an escort, I will choose Algy. We've hardly spoken. What do you say, Algy? See this old woman home?'

They walked arm in arm through the rose garden, taking the new brick path at the edge of the kitchen garden and cutting across the corner of the park, both carrying lanterns. He knew why she had made this request. It was safer to walk so near to the gardener's cottage with him rather than with her son. Although not to be spoken of, there was an acceptance of his knowledge of the affair. Except for his one blunder many years ago, he had proven worthy of her trust. The rough track forked here; down the right-hand side strong lights were visible from the dower house, while on the left, through the trees, only a faint, flickering candlelight could be seen from the gardener's cottage.

'I can see my way from here, Algy. I'm quite safe now.' She put up her cheek to be kissed.

'If you're sure. Good-night, Ann. You look lovely.' He made his way back to the house, pausing only briefly and shielding the lantern, to look over his shoulder where, as he expected, a faint light bobbed down the left-hand path.

Her face was becoming florid, the broken veins around her nose spreading across her cheeks: he hadn't noticed it before. She was still a good-looking woman and he was erect, but . . . he turned her onto her stomach gently, holding the full breast and large distended nipple, thinking of his first mistress of years ago and all she had so gently and thoroughly taught him. He was careful not to put too much weight on her as he stroked her thighs and touched between her legs where she reacted so strongly. He was about to enter her from behind as he kissed the nape of her neck, when she sighed. 'Oh, God, Richard, do we have to go through the whole thing every time we do it?'

'What!' He raised himself on his elbows. 'What do you mean?'

'Well, now you've started you might as well finish.'

His erection gone, he rolled onto his back.

'It's only that – do we have to do everything each time we do it? I mean, it's jolly nice, of course, but do we have to do, well, one to ten every time? I was up early, you know, having the hunt meet here.'

He felt years of vanity, years of complacency in knowing he was a good lover, fade away.

'Don't sulk, darling. It's only a suggestion. Go on.' She pushed herself at him, waiting.

He tried to think of someone, a body, that would make him erect again. Madeleine? That was no good. He had seen her recently in London. She had aged appropriately, still touching and lovely, but no, her present looks erased the erotic memory.

'You're not hurt, are you?' Caroline spoke with a yawn. Clearly she wasn't interested in a reply. Pulling down her nightdress she was soon asleep. He waited for the little snore that meant little would wake her and, easing himself out of the four-poster, he padded silently out of the room. Sitting on the edge of the bed in his dressing room, he buried his head in his hands, shaking. One of the clocks in the house chimed twelve – the last time it would chime until seven in the morning. Hearing the footstep of a servant on the back stairs, he tried to control himself, stuffing a piece of the counterpane in his mouth to stop the laughter.

She joined him as usual in the morning room for coffee after his breakfast. They kissed briefly. She helped herself to coffee from the sideboard, pouring it into a large teacup, ignoring the display of poached eggs, boiled ham, cold grouse and kippers, added neither cream nor sugar and drank it standing up. Refilling the cup, and this time adding a little sugar, she took it to the table. 'What are you reading?' She looked at her own letters, playing with them like a pack of cards, deciding which to open first.

'Just some information about farm machinery. I think we'll get one of those things that "reaps as it bales as it flails". Got that wrong, I think. It will pay for itself in two or three years.'

'How?'

'Hiring it out.'

'Oh, good, I suppose.'

He examined her covertly, holding her coffee with both hands, looking over the cup at him. Not *at* exactly, through. 'How do you feel, Caro?'

'Fine. Why? Shouldn't I?'

'Well, you were so tired last night, weren't you?' His laughter unexpectedly returned. 'Weren't you?' He hoped his tone showed he wasn't angry, just amused.

'Was I? I don't remember. Get me another cup of coffee, will you?'

He fetched the silver pot to the table and filled her cup. Didn't remember. Was that better or worse? Was it, *in* whisky *veritas*?

Irritably, she drank the coffee. 'What are you laughing at? Is it me?' She looked down, pulling at her loose robe.

He looked at her too. She wasn't wearing her corsets yet, which suited her. The full breasts and hips and the slightly protuberant stomach, when encased in stiff cotton and whalebone, made her look like an egg-timer. That was, to be fair, true about most women. The robe gaped a little. He could slip a hand inside and fondle a breast. He could run a finger down her spine reaching the crevice of her buttocks. He could brush away some of the wavy, springy hair and kiss her ear – he could have – he could – but the laughter returned and he sat down. What would she like? Something fast, brutal? To be taken in her sleep, through her snores? It would save time, if she were tired, if he did it while she was brushing her hair. Would she prefer to delegate her wifely duties to a parlour-maid – Tommy's pretty little piece, Violet, would surely oblige. Oh, the chagrin! He mocked himself. But these were dangerous thoughts. Their physical relationship had always been important, a strong part of the marriage. He mustn't let it go. One to ten? A to Z? Tonight he could try one to three.

'*Now* why are you laughing?'

'I'm sorry, Caro. I'm just being childish, it's too difficult to explain.'

'How old are you, Aunt Biddy?'

'No, no, no, no, no, Bertie. I am not so old that I can't see through *you*.'

'Your eyes are good for whatever age you are.'

'Stop it, now. I want this sorted out before Mary gets back. I want an answer even if it isn't true. I want an answer I can get along with.'

Albert smiled. He was impressed. Biddy was a wise woman, he had always known that, but this was extra proof. 'Help me, then,' he said obligingly. 'Where can I say I've been, that I go, for Mary not to fret about it?'

'I don't know. She thinks you're a tinker, a cheap-jack, knife-grinder, chair-mender. That was after you helped the man recane that rocking-chair so beautiful.'

'Right. What about — I got a job with one of the furniture places in High Wycombe?'

'Yes! There's something. Have you? Oh, Albert. That *is* good news.'

'I'm not saying I have but if you believe it she might.'

'And you could get back from there every so often, change coaches in Thame but not every night — that's very suitable.'

'Thank you, Aunt Biddy.'

She gave him a sharp push. 'I must be a crazed thing,

talking to you like this. And I'm sixty-four years of age, since you ask.'

'Well, I reckon you're doing fine for an old hen. Wait on, that's her, isn't it?'

Pulling aside the curtain they leaned out of the window and peered down the lane to where a figure on a bicycle was wobbling towards them.

'It looks like her, Bertie, but she's been in Wellsbury, so by rights she'd be coming from the opposite . . . No, it's her, right enough. Why is the bicycle so—?'

But he had gone, tearing out of the front door and down the lane to his sister, followed by a slower Biddy. 'What is it, Mary?' Albert called. 'The bicycle was weaving away so, I thought you'd fall off.'

She dismounted and handed it to him silently.

'Tears? What is it?'

'Leave her be, Bertie. It's Miss Crewe, isn't it? You've come from her place.'

Mary nodded.

'Now then, love. She was getting on. Not well for a long time and what with the cottage and the school took from her . . .'

'Taken. Yes, I know. She wanted to go.'

'Mary, that's all too much, too tiring. Why did you cycle all the way to Wellsbury too?'

Hesitating, it wouldn't do to tell Bertie about Sally's Cora, she thought of the envelope. 'Miss Crewe had asked me to call on someone. Someone legal.'

'I wish I'd been there. I would have gone for you.'

'If wishes were horses. Or bicycles,' Mary said, wearily. 'Now I must get up to Dr Henders. Miss Crewe isn't dead just on *my* say-so.'

'Biddy, sit her down, give her tea with something strong in it. I'm to Dr Henders,' said Albert.

'It wasn't just that she died, Biddy, it was for it to happen when she was alone.'

'Pneumonia?'

'Oh, yes. Definitely.'

Biddy had nursed enough through that to understand Mary's painful feelings. 'Poor little love.'

'Poor Miss Crewe.'

'Yes, her too.' She fetched the tea with a drop of brandy in it.

'Funny day I've had, Biddy. A bad ending for Miss Crewe, but a good beginning for Cora. She's so happy – Sally – seeing Cora settled so well. He's a good young man it seems, steady employment in the brewery, for whatever else happens in the world, a brewery will always be needed. And the house, too. It's a brand new estate barely a mile from the centre of Wellsbury. Villas, they're called. All two by two in a long row.'

Good, thought Biddy, you've discharged your so-called obligations, my girl. Now your hard-earned money is your own. 'Dr Henders will stop his carriage here for you, won't he? Would you like me to come and help you lay her out, Mary?'

'Would you? I don't like leaving her there, but we can't bring her here with Bertie back. I suppose he's staying over.'

It didn't appear to be a question so Biddy didn't respond. 'What about taking her to Keepers Cottage, love? They hardly ever use that new parlour and the funeral could go from there too.'

'That's the very thing, Biddy. We'll go to the schoolhouse, do the laying-out and send Bertie on to Ma and Pa's to warn them and bring back the traption, then we'll all go to Keepers and return here in it.'

'I'll leave a note for Billy. What was that legal note for Miss Crewe? Was that just so as you didn't mention Sal?'

'It was a white lie. There was an envelope for me to take. I've got it here.' She patted the deep pocket of her long hessian jacket. 'I can guess what it is. She had no folks, or if she did, none that kept in touch. This will be to say I should have her books and maybe her things – furniture and such. She's been saying that for years now.'

Mary thought she had done with the crying part, alone in her room at night. She had been so busy, helping the new schoolmistress, who had arrived just in time after the Easter holidays, and encouraging the two new twelve-year-old pupil monitors; starting the day at five o'clock, cleaning and preparing the shop to make up to Hanny for being there all day and organizing everything to do with the funeral. The sight, however, of six schoolboys – normally seen with hair on end, dirty knees and ink in unlikely places – well scrubbed with their hair plastered down with water, carrying the coffin down the aisle of St Michael's made her catch her breath. She missed attending service here, the beauty, the ritual. Quickly she returned to her hymn book and joined in, singing out with the rest of the congregation:

> '. . . and tears no bitterness,
> Where is death's sting? Where grave thy victory?
> I triumph still, if thou abide with me.'

She had chosen well-known hymns to ensure everybody joining in; none of that half-hearted, embarrassed chiming in off-key. The Vicar – Miss Isabel's husband – spoke very well and all truthful too, about not only Sarah Crewe's sense of duty ('Sarah'? 'Sarah Crewe' surprised everybody by its over-familiarity; *Miss* Crewe to you!) but her enjoyment in passing on learning and, at that, he looked straight at Mary. The church was full. The children had been given the morning off as a mark of respect *only* if they went to the funeral, and cottagers who hadn't planned to attend had seen the hearse pass by, drawn by two black horses with plumes in their head-bands, and slipped out to follow it. Mrs Fiennders was there in her pew with Lady Caroline. *He* was away – in London they said – thank goodness. It was kind of Mrs Fiennders to pay for it. Mr Baring-Kimball had refused her own offer. The family wish to take care of it, he'd said, but she knew he meant Mrs Fiennders. Ma had said it was a compliment to her. Maybe in some way she couldn't work out, this was so.

When the last ham sandwich was eaten, the barrel of home-brew finished and the cottagers had drifted away, Sam Reade gave Mary his usual hug that lifted her off the floor. 'You've done real well by her, love, a good send-off. Now I'm taking Hannah and these here grand-children of mine off home, and you two should have a rest.' He included Biddy in this.

'Oh yes, yes, we will.'

'Sure now we can't help, Mary? You look tired.' Her mother started stacking plates.

'No, Ma, Pa, all of you, just leave it be. It's easier with just us, Biddy and I have a method.'

'And when I'm not in the forge, *I*'m the method.'

'Just you take yourself off there, Billy, and don't you take credit where credit isn't due.'

Mary walked back into the kitchen after waving them all off. 'Biddy, come here.' She held her arms wide to embrace the old woman. 'I care for you so much, you are a true friend and more, yes, more.'

'That's a strange thing then, Mary love, for I was just thinking such a foolish thought for a woman of my age.'

'Yes?'

'I was thinking that, in death, I was a little bit jealous of your Miss Crewe – the strange part being I wasn't jealous in life – and now you say such a beautiful thing.'

'Ah, I must be one of these psychical people! Now, this is my plan. To be obeyed! All dishes scraped and rinsed and left to soak, then, you go and put your feet up, and I'm going—'

'Please God, *not* to open up the shop?'

'No.' She laughed. 'No, I'm going for a good long walk and a think. When I get back, I'll wash up, you'll dry, and I'll put away. I know you *will* obey, because I can tell from your face that your feet are aching.'

'No, you're right, Mary. I'm going up. Have a good think, love, but don't be hasty.'

The weather was perfect for a walk. A clear cold day with a sun so pale it could hardly be seen. The ground dry but not dusty, and trees coming into blossom with their leaves too sparse to overshadow. Away from the lane and inquisitive eyes, she skipped and leaped and sang snatches of the morning's hymns. Miss Crewe, Sarah Crewe, had been buried but, like the Vicar had said, she still existed because her work lived on in her pupils.

'Me!' She ran and vaulted over a broken stile. 'Teresa Quinn, the monitor.' She copied the sudden little jumps of the tiny new spring lambs. Arthur, Betsy, Laura, Maria, Jack and the others, all the successful scholarship children, all would remember Miss Crewe and pass it on. And then she brought to mind what the legal man had said, 'I herewith bequeath all my books to Findlesham School for the use of children and teachers, to be used as a library, with hopes that others will add to it.' Smiling at her show of surprise and disappointment, he'd added, 'And everything else to you.'

'Tables, chairs, lamps?'

'Yes. All household effects, small items of jewellery, very small — an agate brooch, a gold fob watch and a cameo set in seed pearls. Her entire estate.'

She frowned. 'All the books to the school? Even the illustrated edition of—'

'All the books.' His manner, which had been so jolly, now seemed cold and business-like.

'Yes, sir, I see. Thank you, Mr Roper.'

'There is a proviso attached to that part of the will pertaining to the rest of the estate, which is, to wit, that it is for your use only, for your ease and comfort. Do you understand?'

'Oh, I think so, Mr Roper. The tables and the easy-chair are not to be given away. It is for me to *wear* the cameo, for instance, not sell it.'

He leaned back in his chair behind the large mahogany desk and rearranged the heavy onyx ink-stand, the pen wipers and blotting sand, then, shuffling the pile of papers in front of him, he removed one and handed it across to her. 'Not the furniture,' he said. 'The money.'

She lifted her eyes from the paper to see his hugely smiling face. Fearfully she said, 'Two hundred and fifty guineas?'

Suddenly he pushed back his chair, stood and made a little jump – which, in fact, was a big jump for someone of his small height and considerable weight. 'Yes, indeed! Oh, this gives such pleasure, such pleasure!'

It wasn't an idle walk, she was looking for the cottages at the edge of Long Pightle and Withey Piece. They had been abandoned when work stopped in the wood a few years ago. The Elkins family had occupied the cottages for as long as Mary could remember. All of them, fathers, sons, cousins, working with timber. They were sawyers, coopers, making barrel staves and hurdles. The wood had been replanted after the Napoleonic wars because so much had been cut down for the ships, but now ships were no longer made solely of wood. The oak, hornbeam, sweet chestnut were left to grow and only coppiced every five or ten years. Healthy for the woods, not so healthy for the likes of the Elkins'. The old track to the cottages had almost vanished from lack of use and the footpaths had been diverted by regular walkers to a more convenient route. She was guessing her way, but the strong scent of balsam proved her final guide – a light gust of wind had blown it her way – and there they were, set away from the wood, on a slight rise.

The hedge that enclosed the large, ragged garden was patched with hurdles made from withies of hazel cut from the woods behind. The holly and quick-thorn of the hedges were flourishing but the interwoven wattle of the hurdles had nearly disintegrated. The sun was stronger now, warming her back. That meant the cottages faced south. Perfect. It must have been hard leaving this, specially for old Rosina Elkins – Granny Elkins – the last to go, for she had been a pauper and was taken to the workhouse. Like Ma's grandparents, only they had been separated. The workhouses then were for men or women only.

It was Ma who had understood – 'You will be safe then, always' – when she had told them yesterday about the money and her plans.

Pa had worried. 'Why? You'll be so lonely. Come back to Keepers Cottage if there's not room enough for you at the forge.' He didn't like her spending so much of the money either.

There had been no choice. The little lie had been forced on her. Not only was the money not to be given but no one must know how much. Mr Roper said he understood she *could* tell, *could* give, but her conscience, he hoped, would bow to Miss Crewe's wishes, with which, he said – with all the dignity he could muster, which wasn't much, considering his height, rotundity and the excited little jump – he agreed, having heard satisfactory explanations and reasons, whys and wherefores.

Forty guineas for the two cottages and two acres. Without the Elkins' shabby carts, traps and horses, the tools of their various trades, without tree trunks, bark, branches and twigs scattered about, the cottages were larger than she had remembered, not quite as tumbledown as she had expected. Tiled roofs, not thatch, good-sized windows; well built, probably at the beginning of the century. Sturdier than the old farm-hands' cottages, they had survived their neglect quite well.

The answer to Pa's question was simple. She should

never have gone to the forge. She was giving it back to Billy, to the Jacksons. She would help run the shop for as long as need be. The income was partly hers and she *would* be too solitary sometimes without that and Biddy. The cottages would be not only her home but somewhere for Bertie, too, if he wanted. She had carefully climbed through a glassless window of what she thought of as Pightle One and discovered the back door swinging unlatched, when she heard the sound of voices and bodies forcing their way through the dry undergrowth. It sounded like her parents and John. She would stand at the front door, welcoming them! Using her shoulder she forced it open but the heavy planked door came off its rusty hinges so that when they arrived, running in response to her shouts, they saw the slender figure of their daughter supporting the thick oak door on her back.

'Mother, wait!' John called. 'Don't move.' He could see the white face peering up, startled.

'How did you know I was here?'

'Be quiet!' John lifted the door off, dropping it to the ground. 'Are you all right?'

He brushed dust off the pale hair and pressed his cheek against hers briefly and, though wanting to hold her, stepped back awkwardly.

'Yes. I think so, thank you, John, my love.'

'We went back to the forge, see,' Emma said. 'Thought it might cheer you to come in the traption, see the cottages.'

'You didn't wake Biddy?'

'No. Billy said as how he'd seen you stepping out, no bicycle, and we thought it out.'

'Where's the traption?'

'We followed the wrong track,' her father said. 'And when it ran out, young John said it were a deer track.'

'It *were*, Grandpa.'

'We tethered the horse and came on foot.'

'So then, Pa, who do I have to see if it's nothing to do with . . . Mr Fiennders?'

'You've decided, then?'

'Of course she has. It's just right. All will help you, Mary. You'll have your father and young John here, Bertie – where is he by the way? – Sam Reade, young Sam, Billy . . .'

'Uncle Billy?' John interrupted.

'And Billy the brick-layer, staying at the Bull and Butcher, nice helpful young man, did our wall for naught but a couple of brace of pheasant. There's the carpenter up at the house. And I'll help with a few shillings to getting the water on. You'll need a glazier—'

'Well, Emma, put like that, she can buy and move in by Whitsun!'

'You'll see, John Bowden. "Where there's a will there's a way." '

'There certainly *was* a will.' Mary smiled.

'And, Mary, what you want to do is let one of these for two or three shillings a week, maybe more. There's plenty looking.'

'No! Ma, stop!'

'Sorry, love. I'm so excited.'

'Of course, but I'm not letting one of them. I'm going to put the two together.'

'Six rooms, you'll have, only downstairs, what for? And the few extra shillings will come in handy.'

'No. I want to make it – different. Not little rooms, six little rooms. Three big ones, with plenty of light. Kitchen, parlour and one for books and things, and upstairs, bigger bedrooms and a whole room for a bath and maybe even—'

'You'll never warm it, girl. It'll cost you.'

Mary could see that her mother's old habits were dying hard, but it was young John who came to her rescue.

'Not so, Gran. Look where she is, all the wood for the taking. From what's fallen and lying about there's a sufficiency for fires and a boiler for a lifetime. Now, about the water. There's sure to be a spring here somewhere – look at all the hazel there is. You know what they say about hazel?' He looked at them expectantly.

'No, I don't think I do,' Mary said.

'Oh, well, neither do I. Not exactly that is, but it's something like "Where be hazel, there be water." '

'And nuts,' his grandfather added, with a laugh. 'As to who you see, Mary, from the wood, including this, all over to New Farm and beyond was bought up when the Berrefords needed the money.'

'Gambling debt,' Emma said, her mouth pursed with disdain. 'They used to own half this county and more.'

'And that's the truth. I seen papers, beautiful things, old Mr Fiennders showed me in his monument – no – muniment room. When they, the De Fins, as they were, got given the Abbey, the Beurreforts, as *they* were then, got given a great deal more, thereabouts of five hundred hides they had.'

'Hides, Pa?'

'A lot of acres in modern terms, a hide.'

'But who do I see?'

'Right. Joe Hogg, him at Coddlestone, who told me of it, wanted the land not the cottages but they wouldn't separate them, he had to see a land agent. You'd need someone to see to it, all nice and legal.'

'Yes, that's right. Be careful who you trust, child.'

'I will. I have a solicitor, you know.'

'Yes, yes, I *do* approve, Mrs Jackson, and I approve of you consulting me, for this is a complicated transaction with hidden pitfalls, more so than usual, in so far as—'

'Should I not, then, be too confident, Mr Roper?'

He regarded her face, which was saddened by his words. 'It is always as well to save celebrating till the ink is dry, but – with a certain amount of give and take, negotiation, adjustment, a little risk-taking on your part, a compromise from all parties—'

'Risk? All parties? I thought it was owned by Mr Coffield.'

'The cottages and six acres are owned by the son, the wood is owned by the father, the land abutting it is owned on two sides by the Fiennders' and on the other by the father on a long leasehold to Mr Joseph Hogg, the farmer. The cottages and their land have no right of access, no legal right of way.'

'Wouldn't the father just give his son – ?'

'No. And more is involved than that. You will have to try to understand these confusions and complexities, Mrs Jackson. Mr Hogg would have to give permission for access across the land he leases and he has intimated that he would require a large easement in rent for the privilege. It is out of the question that the Fiennders' would for any price establish a legal right of way through their land – oh, no. That would be foolish. That is why the property is a considerable bargain.'

'Not if I can't get to it,' she said mournfully. 'Why does the son own it? An odd arrangement in a family, isn't it?'

'Oh, Mrs Jackson! Families! Do not speak to me of families! Odd arrangements are not odd in families. Blood may be thicker than water, but money seems to dilute it remarkably quickly.'

Mary laughed. 'I think you enjoy this, Mr Roper.'

'I do, I do.' He jumped up from behind his desk. She wondered if he was going to execute one of his little leaps. 'To answer your question. When the Duke of Berreford needed money, he needed it quickly. Cash, a great deal. Young Mr Coffield was apprised of this by his friend, Lord Wittenham.'

'Like the Clumps.'

'I don't believe I know the Clumps.'

Mary let that go. This was not a time to be facetious.

'Lord Wittenham knew of his friend's father's search for an estate, not too far from London, Mr Coffield being in the City as well as a tea planter. The young men effected the introduction of their fathers and more or less brokered the sale. Naturally, they both exacted a fee – well, not *naturally* because they did it *sub rosa*.' Smiling benevolently, he explained, 'Secretly.'

'I know what *sub rosa* means, Mr Roper.'

'Er . . . yes, I apologize, of course. Most unusual, you see, in a young lady or, indeed, any lady.'

'Or man, wouldn't you say? And the fee was?' She knew the answer to that too.

'Two awkward parcels of Berreford's land for young Coffield and a stretch of good fishing for Lord Wittenham.'

'I do see what you mean now, Mr Roper. It *is* very complicated. I suppose old Mr Coffield could not have been pleased with his son's slyness. Oh dear . . .' She sighed. 'Why does he want to sell?'

'Another bone of contention, I'm afraid. James Coffield senior has his heart, soul and money invested in the Model Farm, though he has been influenced by the young James to the extent that he is introducing new machinery, slowly and with caution. But the son is interested in the new world. He wishes to invest in the motor car, of all things!'

She looked around the office as if seeking a solution. 'How does Mr Coffield get access to the wood?' She answered her own question. 'Off the old Oxford road, a long way round.'

'Yeees.' He nodded, encouraging her thoughts.

'Mr Hogg wants those fields for his sheep.'

'Yeees – go on.'

'If – I let Joe Hogg use those fields for nothing—'

'No, no. A peppercorn rent would be safer.'

'If I let those fields for a peppercorn in exchange for him giving me access *and* let Mr Coffield have right of way to the wood, all would be satisfied, wouldn't they?'

His look of approval for her deduction was spoilt by the accompanying shake of his head. 'That is excellent,

Mrs Jackson, your theorizing, but you have left one element out of the equation.'

'No, don't tell me, Mr Roper. I think I understand why you enjoy this.' She got up and paced the room. 'There *is* something wrong, I can see that. My reasonings are not so clever that you wouldn't have reached the same conclusion earlier.' He accepted her compliment graciously, bowing from his waist or, to be accurate, from the fourth button on his waistcoat. She stopped her pacing at his desk and noticed the silver-and-velvet-framed photograph of Mr Roper himself and a stout woman, even shorter than her husband, posing on either side of an eager-eyed young man, their hands resting on his shoulders with an attitude both loving and proprietorial, all of them overshadowed by a large aspidistra sitting on a high mahogany stand. 'Oh, I see. How stupid of me. You said *risk*. It would be a *risk*. Why doesn't the father buy the property and put the land, cottages and wood together? That's the sensible thing.'

'Exactly! The answer is, the young man offered the other parcel of land to his father, who accepted but put the money in the young man's trust which doesn't mature until he is thirty. A very wise decision, I would say.'

'If I buy, I can easily – anybody can – get to the Pightle on foot, but by horse and specially by trap, it's almost impossible. If I make a track---'

'You would be breaking the law, and perhaps making an enemy – at the very least a bad neighbour, if you present him with a *fait accompli*.'

'Accomplished fact,' they said, in unison.

'And one day, who knows, I might need a proper surfaced path for a motor car.'

'That is not very likely, Mrs Jackson.'

'You're laughing, Mr Roper, but people as different as Miss Crewe and my brother-in-law, Billy—'

'The smith?'

'Yes, they both thought motor cars could be a part of things to come. Billy wants to try working on one at the forge, and you can see the usefulness, if they ever work properly – smaller and quieter than a carriage with huge wheels and two horses, and cleaner too.' She sat down in the large leather chair and gazed at the solicitor, her elbows on his desk, her face cupped in her hands. 'What shall we do?'

'You ask my advice and I will give it. You buy the property from young Coffield, you have no dealings with the old man, he is not your concern, not legally anyway. You wait until winter, when the fields are bare and crops won't be ruined, to repair the cottages.'

In her bewilderment she looked twenty years younger than the thirty-four he knew her to be. 'You understand, Mary – oh, I do beg your pardon, Mrs Jackson.' She shrugged, forgiving him. 'This is a compromise, remembering that when the old man dies, young James will inherit, and it is always possible that filial and paternal feelings' he glanced briefly at the photograph on his desk, 'will effect a healing of the breach.'

'What has winter got to do with it?'

'Oh, yes, I stopped in mid-air, so to speak. Well, you are in a very advantageous position through your father's employment and good relationship with the Fiennders family. I suggest he approaches Mr Richard Fiennders requesting temporary access only, while the building work is being carried out.' He was surprised at her violent reaction.

Taking her elbows off the desk she stood up, shaking her head in agitation. 'No. No, not possibly. It wouldn't be right, he couldn't, no.' She collected her short cape from the antlered coat-stand and picked up her gloves and bag. 'Thank you, yes, thank you very much, Mr Roper, but I have decided to be absolutely open and straightforward about the whole thing. I'm going to try blackmail. If it works, we will all start with a . . . ' she eyed him with a hint of mischief ' . . . with a *tabula rasa*.'

Richard worked his way through the farmhouse, weighing its possibilities. Whether she wanted it or not, something must be done. It had been neglected by tenants, unable to do more than scrape a living, and it was too good a house to be abandoned. He made his way at last to the dairy, drawn by the sweet-sour smell of milk and its by-products. Looking out of the window he could see his horse beyond the low brick wall of the yard, cropping grass still wet with dew. All the outhouses, barns, cow-byres were in good order and everything here in the dairy was clean and well-kept. All the churns, sinks, ladles, wooden butter-pats, crocks, all scrubbed, immaculate, just like . . . just like the old days. That nobody had spent money on the house had its advantages. Nobody had altered, rebuilt, spoilt it. But Maud was right. It would not do for her – too near the house, too near the village, prying eyes, knowing eyes. Shrewd peasantry and malicious gentry. Anonymity was what she had in London and what she needed. Avoiding the sun shafting indirectly through the window, he leaned against the wall, spreading his hands and laying his cheek on the cool plaster-covered brick. Slowly he pressed his whole body to the wall as if embracing it, grateful that there was no response, no hot body reacting, no eager hand reaching out.

From maybe a mile away, he heard a dog bark. It must be about five o'clock; that bark heralded the arrival of the men bringing in the cows for milking. He yawned. His days now were long, going to bed late and rising early, sleeping in his dressing room, trying to avoid Caroline awake. It would be as well not to trust her with the news about Maud. Last night at dinner she had been suspicious about his trip to London and hadn't fully accepted his explanation until distracted by the need to send Bulbeck down to the cellar for yet another bottle of the La Tâche. He smiled, remembering his mother's consternation when he mentioned he might do something about the farm, enlarge it, perhaps, give it to someone in the family.

'Oh, Richard. Leave well alone,' she'd said. 'Let Tommy travel for now. He'll settle down when he's ready.'

He was more than willing to accept that advice, but he would do something about the farm. Somebody in the village? Give a good man a chance to better himself, a man with ambition and a wife who'd back him. Lease it again at a reasonable rent so he could make it pay, not just fill the Fiennders' larder. He would ask Bowden: he knew everybody, he was a good judge.

'This is blackmail!'

'Yes, exactly.' She was glad he had understood so quickly.

'I have no choice!' The young man was truly flabbergasted, she could see, but at the same time there was a sense of relief. He was in a mess and had been floundering. Now somebody had appeared to take charge and organize a rescue.

'Let me see.' He tugged at his moustache as if it were a bell-pull that connected to his brain. His eyes narrowed. She hoped it was with thought. 'I must sell you the property.'

'Yes.'

'Or you will go to my father and tell him my plans.'

'Yes.'

'But, having sold you the property, we must *both* go to my father and tell him my plans.'

'Yes.'

His frown showed that the process of thought wasn't working too well. He stroked the other side of his moustache. This time his eyes widened. 'I think I see.'

'Go on,' she encouraged, feeling quite maternal, though the young man was six inches taller and three times as broad.

'We sign the contract now, you give me the money *now.*' His eyes slid to the pile of large white notes, weighted down by a glass case containing a twig on which perched two stuffed birds, magpies, looking more benign in death than they ever did in life. 'Then we visit my father and I tell him the truth, if I can remember it, and beg for his forgiveness and . . . '

'And I beg for a right of way. And, Mr Coffield, I, too, will ask for your pardon.'

Briskly she rang the little silver bell on the desk,

summoning Mr Roper. 'We had better get on with it, see your father before luncheon.'

'Oh, Lord! Now? Today? Oh, I don't think so.'

She smiled up at his anxious face, lightly patting his arm as if to brace him, a soldier going to war with an enemy known and feared. 'Come now, there is no time like the present.'

'I've never believed that, Mrs Jackson,' he said miserably. 'I think there is no time like tomorrow.'

'I think Mr Coffield would rather speak to Mr Coffield, that is, his father, before Mr Coffield, and Mr Coffield, his son, speak to me.' Mary said this with a feigned composure.

'Yes, madam.' The 'madam' was articulated with a little too much emphasis.

Understandable, she thought. It wasn't usual for Crumthorne the butler to receive the likes of the keeper's daughter at the front door. Once they had arrived, she had realized that he would recognize her, but bowling along in a fly they had hired at the station, with her bicycle on the roof, she hadn't thought about it. Only that so far everything was going rather well. As planned. But then, the front door – that she hadn't planned. Of course, the son of the house would go to the front door, but she had never, ever, gone to the front door at a house of the gentry.

'Would madam like to wait in the hall?'

'Of course she wouldn't.' James was surprised. 'Show Mrs Jackson into the drawing room, Crumthorne, and tell my father I'm in the library.'

'Yes, sir. Certainly, sir.' Never had the word 'certainly' been said with such lack of conviction.

'Well, if there is a choice, *I* would rather wait in the library and *you* can have the drawing room.'

'Ha ha, ha ha, that's very good. Oh, God! What am I laughing about?' He looked stricken.

'I wish you luck.' Her huge, lovely smile heartened him and, bowing a temporary farewell, he slunk into the library.

Below stairs in the hot, steamy kitchen, Crumthorne and the cook exchanged a low conversation, hissing in tune with the pig's fry for the servants' lunch. 'She's thirty-five if she's a day, Mr Crumthorne. The master will never stand for it.'

'He may have no choice, Mrs Point. She seems quite in control.'

'I'd never have believed it. Butter wouldn't melt in her mouth.'

'The front door, Mrs P. – the smith's widow!'

'The keeper's daughter!'

'I blame the mother.'

'I blame the post office.'

'The post office?'

'Broadening people's horizons.'

'Oh, I see.'

Taking a spatula she quickly moved the swiftly browning pieces of pig's innards – heart, lung, liver and other unrecognizable bits.

Crumthorne pointed to a large steamer on the stove. 'Is that asparagus, Mrs P.? Must be the first of the season.'

'It is. Lovely time of year for food, what with salmon and all. Not for us,' she added, casting her eyes to the ceiling. 'For them.'

'I think she's a mite too thin to get above herself so.'

'Not that she hasn't had her share of woes.'

'True indeed, but we don't want her bringing them here. And I would never live down the shame, Mrs Point. What would Mr Caird say, him from Colcroft, *me* buttling for someone little better than a cottager?'

'There isn't a post office in Findlesham.'

In its stark simplicity, the drawing room rather cowed her. It was even more intimidating than Fiennders Abbey, each piece of furniture set in position as if to be admired but not used, and the chairs placed to be seen to advantage but not sat on. No photographs, no little pieces of porcelain, no tassels, no clutter. Nothing extraneous. The cold, clean, pale colours, the yards of unused space gave her the uncomfortable feeling of having dirty shoes, even dirty feet. She felt marooned in the large room, unable to sit and unable to stand naturally.

'Follow me, Mrs Jackson, please.' Again the heavy emphasis, this time on her name. He was warning her, she knew, that he disapproved of her presumption in putting herself in a position of superiority to him, the butler, who superseded all others, apart from the family. There was another glint of distaste in his manner, but to what she couldn't ascribe. 'Mrs Jackson, sir.' The library door clicked firmly shut behind her. Even the click sounded reproving.

'Oh, it's you! The girl on the bicycle. I've seen you,

wondered who you were.' The library was more welcoming, a smaller room, warmer colours, chairs for sitting in, an untidy desk, her shoes felt clean again. Not that his manner was welcoming. 'Come *in*, for goodness sake. You're not stuck to the door, are you? Are you frightened of me? Did my son tell you I was a beast, a bully?'

'No, sir.'

'He didn't?' The son laughed, timidly. 'He should have.'

'Well, he did warn me that—'

'That I could be?'

'Rather ... stern.' He was more than that, she thought. That was an understatement. 'But he also said, sir, that you were fair and honest, which,' she said boldly, 'is more than he has been.'

'Yes, Mrs Jackson. Much more.' He advanced towards her. His height and weight were similar to his son's and her instinct was to shrink from him but, although he might be a bully, he would hardly strike her, so she stood her ground and was pleased she had when he stuck out a large hand and said, 'I give you my blessing.' Behind him, the young man gave her a pathetic smile of relief. 'Not that I have any choice, it seems.'

'You do, Mr Coffield. You could make my purchase worthless by refusing the right of way.'

'No. The boy has apologized fully, admitted his behaviour was despicable, quite appalling. Not easy for a young man to admit he was wrong.' The young man in question nodded eagerly, agreeing to his appalling behaviour and his nobility in apologizing. 'And I'm sure Wittenham led James astray.' He gestured weakly to his tall heavily built son. 'My son is not strong. Nevertheless, both Berreford and I got what we wanted. Sit down,' he said abruptly, lowering himself into a large armchair and gesturing for his son to do the same. 'What do you think about this motor car business? You're a shrewd woman.'

Mary perched uncomfortably on the edge of another huge armchair, feeling far from shrewd. 'I do not know enough about the combustion engine to speak with authority,' she began, choosing her words with care, 'but my brother-in-law does, and he says they're making advances in America and we should support our own, like Edward Butler, son of a farmer he says, a genius. I think that it is worth investing a little time and money, if only to oil the wheels.' Delighted with her pun, she laughed, and slipped back into the depths of her armchair. Like a naughty child, James Coffield thought, as he joined in her laughter.

It was when young Mr James also joined in that Crumthorne left the door and slipped quietly down to the kitchen. 'I don't like it, Mrs Point. "I give you my blessing," he said, and I left them having a good laugh all round.'

'That's not right,' the cook said, folding flaked smoked haddock into the soufflé mixture. 'Laughing with your betters shouldn't be encouraged.'

'Quite so, Mrs P. There's laughter and there's laughter. Take me for an instance, the master says he thinks I'm pompous.'

'That's nice, Mr Crumthorne.' Deftly she spooned the fish mixture into small buttered ramekins.

'*And* he says I make him laugh, *but* it's respectable, you see, because he's laughing *at* me.'

'Just as it should be.' She placed the ramekins in a *bain-marie* and put it in the oven. 'These soufflés will have risen in a quarter-hour, so it's for you to ring the luncheon bell, Mr C., and let's hope we hear her bicycle bell too. And no more about wedding bells.'

It was wonderful! A freedom Richard had never known – his house to himself, except for the servants. The children with Nanny, the nursemaids and Anthony Willson – the boys' tutor – up in Inverness with Jessica and her husband, and Caroline staying in London with her Colcroft aunt. Even his mother was away somewhere. The pleasure was marred a little by the memory of Caroline's explosion of rage at the news that he wouldn't be accompanying her. He had wanted to go to London alone and be with Maud, but to stay in Kensington with the Colcrofts, miles from his sister, and be dogged by Caroline was a waste of time. At least Maud didn't mind, was pleased, if her telegraph was anything to go by.

> I AM ALL RIGHT STOP EVERYTHING IS ALL RIGHT
> STOP DON'T COME TILL ASKED STOP THANK YOU FOR
> PIANO STOP AFFECTIONATELY MAUD STOP

The freedom from people had freed him from habits, too. He had taken his horse out early, forgetting it was Sunday, intending to ride over to Hemsdutton to see how the farm was faring after the fire in the thatched roof. Then he had been attacked by a pang of guilt on seeing carriages, carts, traps, people on horseback, one or two on bicycles and many on foot arriving at the church in Little Bewdley, so he had joined the congregation. The sermon was good, short and to the point, making an analogy between farming and friendship: 'Take care of your friends as you would your crops. Everything needs watering and fertilizing.' Algernon had turned the subdued titter into a full-blown laugh, adding, 'That does not mean I am advising the throwing of manure on to your neighbour.' Algy had been extremely pleased to see him but worried that Freddie Baring-Kimball would get to hear. 'Very naughty of you, Richard, but flattering, of course.' He spoke with undue modesty. 'It's the sermon, isn't it? That's what they all come for, not the content but the length. I have members of the congregation coming from as far away as Gadstone Magna. They say the travelling time is more than made up for by my brevity.'

'Algernon, that's nonsense. There are short boring sermons as well as long boring sermons.'

After the service he had ridden on to Hemsdutton where the thatcher was already working on the roof and the family was happily camping out in one of the barns. The mother was cooking their Sunday roast in a haybox, started the night before. Feeling a responsibility to his own Sunday joint, no doubt being tended by a kitchen maid under the direction of old Bunny, he had rounded up the doctor and his wife, having coerced them into sharing what turned out to be a light luncheon of poached turbot preceded by asparagus from the garden with hollandaise sauce. More to his taste than some of the more elaborate menus ordered by his wife. Now that he was aware of her problem, it was easy to see the advantage of a menu including many courses. It would also include many wines.

Grace Henders settled in the garden after luncheon with her water colours while he and Robert played some duets, very badly. They both needed to practise. Trying to struggle through Beethoven's opus ninety-seven – the Archduke – Robert, scraping his bow hideously across the strings, started to laugh. Richard threw back his head dramatically and swung round on the piano stool. 'Why are you laughing?'

'Firstly, we need the other string – it is, after all, a trio – if only to drown my playing and secondly, well, it's you. You look exactly like Delacroix's painting of Chopin. You really are the romantic hero as pianist.'

Richard had been amused by this and joined Robert's laughter but now, sitting alone in the new conservatory, enjoying his solitude and freedom, he was conscious of a truth behind the teasing. He was always *playing* the hero but never being one. He was a dilettante, an amateur in most things. He ran the estate, yes, in a way, but dele-gated most of the responsibility. He loved his music, but didn't practise regularly, and he had played at being a husband and lover, but his wife had been aware and pricked his conceit. He reached for the decanter and poured the last of the claret. These things could be changed, surely? More time for the estate management, two hours a day practising the piano. And his marriage? He sipped his wine. Lowering the glass he saw his reflec-tion in the arched windows that looked onto the blackness of the gardens. Beyond his one-dimensional silhouette he could see the pinprick of two lights a long way off and suddenly what he'd thought of as solitude and freedom became loneliness and isolation.

She stood inside in a shaft of sunlight at the open door. The man, Roper, could be heard shouting at her to keep still; she could be heard laughing. An occasional flash of light accompanied by a loud pop was followed by exasperated screeches from the photographer.

'Still, *please!*'

She peeped over her shoulder at them, smiling, her pale hair escaping untidily from the old-fashioned cotton bonnet.

'*No!*' A roar like an animal in pain, a groan, and a yell of 'Impossible! You are *impossible!* I am wasting my time,' signalled that the photographic sitting was over. The two men observing this scene from the garden were delighted. They had been waiting to see the house and its mistress, and for the picnic luncheon.

'Mr Roper, you are a saint.' Algernon and Francis grasped the brass handles of the large wooden box and helped him load it onto his trap. 'And in my calling I can recognize one, you know. Is this all?' All, it would have to be; the little trap was piled high with other equipment.

Herbert Roper beamed down at them from his seat behind the pony. 'I am an artist, you see, outside my office, and therefore temperamental. I have, in fact, an artistic temperament.'

'You do, you do.'

Mary was a little ashamed, giggling like some silly girl. 'When you come to photograph it finished, I promise you I will be good. And still!'

He inclined his head. '*If* I come again, to attempt my photographs, *if*, I will get Mr Algernon and Mr Francis to hold you down.' He had rattled through the bushes on the makeshift path and disappeared before they released their laughter.

'Such a little bouncing ball of a man until he set to work.' Francis stood in what was once Pightle One's front room, looking through to the far window, which was almost covered in ivy. 'Are you sure, Mary, this is safe without the old wall?'

'Oh, yes. It is all being done properly. A lot of friends and relations are helping but there is a man in charge of, well, strains and stresses.'

'You mean in the house, I hope, not in people like poor Mr Roper.'

'Isn't he a joy? He even bounces in the office, but he is very good. *I* would never have known about all the complications in the Coffield family.'

Algernon coughed. 'This is dust from the plaster. May we go outside?'

'Yes, of course. Let's have our picnic – I'm famed for my picnics.' She had laid out the food on a plank stretched across two carpenters' trestles and they sat on old bodgers' benches rescued from the wood.

'I don't know whether to have three goats or one cow . . . Wait a minute, let me give you a little more chicken, Mr Clarke.'

'Yes, thank you. I thought it was agreed that we would

be Algernon and Francis from now on. What is it stuffed with?'

'Mushrooms from the wood and grated lemon peel bound with egg and breadcrumbs. It is difficult ... Francis, after a life-time of respect ... '

'That is all very well, but you are a woman of property now.' Algernon spoke while attacking the boned and stuffed chicken leg. 'And respect can become subservience.' Mary reddened. 'Not in your case, my dear,' he added hastily. 'Or, for instance, your father. He was truly one of Tom Fiennders' best friends, and the gardener, Reade, he, too, has his own dignity. What's this green stuff on the potato salad?'

'Mint.'

'No, there's something else as well.'

'Oh, yes, that's young nettle.'

'Stinging nettle?'

'Haven't you ever had nettles before? Nettle soup?'

'Never.'

'Don't look so worried. They haven't stung you. They don't, once they're blanched.'

'How extraordinary. Well, until I knew what they were I liked them, so I will just go on eating them. I had always thought they were one of the many things to dislike about the English countryside.'

'They are not English, though. Of course you knew that?' She asked this innocently enough, knowing full well he didn't. Algernon continued to eat the nettle-strewn potatoes, ignoring her guile. 'They were brought here, of course, by the Romans. Knowing ours to be a cold and damp climate, they thrashed themselves with nettles to heat their blood,' she said, triumphantly.

'If you don't cease this awful smugness, Mrs Jackson, I will be forced to thrash you.'

'Sorry, Algernon.'

'That's better. Don't forget you were being seriously considered as a daughter-in-law to the Coffields.'

'Only by the servants.' She laughed. 'Wasn't that quite startling? Billy came home from the Bull and Butcher really angry with me! Said I was old enough to be the young man's mother and how could I carry on behind his back. The cook, Mrs Point, had sent Crumthorne to the ale-house to talk and listen, see if anybody said anything about me. She even gave him beer money!'

'The inn?' Algernon was amused. 'Hotbed of gossip.'

'Here.' Mary pushed a raspberry tart towards him. 'And there is cream, keeping cool by the stream.' She sprang up to fetch it.

'And bring back the Moselle, Mary.'

'It's only the centre of gossip, the Bull and Butcher, for the men, you know. Too thick to pour, this cream. Use a spoon.'

'And for women? Oh, Mary, delicious – delicious the whole thing.'

'For women it's the well, of course, Mr Clarke – oh, it's so difficult . . . Francis. It's all so difficult, like being with friends separately and not knowing quite why.' She sipped the greeny-yellowy wine. 'I like this very much. Sally, for instance. *She* can be with you. *I* can be with you. But we can't both be with you together. And although I can be with you, I couldn't be with you and the—' She faltered.

'The Fiennders',' Algernon finished.

'Not quite true.' Francis frowned. 'You could if you

hadn't been born here and you married young Coffield.'
They laughed.

'No, I'm serious. And that shows how silly the whole thing is.'

'Have you thought, Mary, how much easier it would be, given the nature of the beast,' Algernon loosened his stiff collar and helped himself to another slice of raspberry tart, dropping a large spoonful of thick yellow cream on it, 'to have *three* cows and *one* goat?'

Mary watched the figure of the young woman swinging confidently down the lane and turned back into the house. 'Billy, what was she *really* doing here?'

'I don't know as how what you mean by *really*, Mary. It seems to me she dropped in to discuss mechanically propelled vehicles.'

'At lunch-time? In the middle of a working day?' Mary snorted. 'There's something more to it, I know. This is the second time in a week she's dropped in, "Just passing," she said. Passing to where?' She looked out of the window. 'See? She wasn't passing. She's gone back down the lane. Gone home.'

'She's quite a modern gal, is Dot Sharp. She gets to hear menfolk talking about the motor car in the bar.'

'She's not allowed in the bar, her parents are good and strict. You ought to know that.' Biddy shot him a warning glance.

'The snug, then. She's often expressed an interest in the British Motor Syndicate.'

'Are you walking out with her? And you'd best be satisfied with the Findlesham Motor Syndicate.'

'No, Mary. Course I'm not walking out with her. She's a friend, that's all.'

Mary sensed that this, at least, was true. Biddy was amused. It wasn't usual for Mary to be behindhand with family or village affairs. 'If you've finished that cup of tea, lad, you'd better be getting on with repairing all those hoes and rakes and things out there so I can get on with the clearing away.' He nodded but didn't move, handing her the empty cup and passing plates for stacking.

'You know, Mary, Dorothy Sharp is just being neighbourly. She often drops in to see me to discuss the ILP – the Independent La—'

'Yes, yes. I know what that means.'

'We've talked of distributing leaflets together, rallying the workers.'

'Now that, I know, isn't true. The Sharps are true Tories, and if they can get away with it they even give the Liberals short measure.'

'Ah, very like, dear, and that's why she has to come here!' Mary knew she was being teased but couldn't understand why. 'Makes a habit of calling by, she does. You wouldn't know, see, 'cause of your being over at the Pightle, chivvying the workmen along, seeing to things.'

'Nearly finished it is, and then you won't have me around to torment like this.'

Billy ignored this, just nodding with a grin.

'Quite a range of interests Miss Sharp has, according to you two. Has she got any opinions about the best phonograph? Does she approve of our having the post office here? What does she think about the Prince of Wales?' They smiled. Mary would find out in time enough.

'Is Hannah coming in this afternoon or will you stay, Mary?' Biddy asked, the smile gone, replaced by anxiety.

'No, I'll stay. Little Biddy's getting better but she's still sick and Hanny thinks of young Liam Quinn. It was the scarlet fever that took him.'

'Now then, you two women, little Biddy isn't that bad. When I popped over yesternight, she was all eager for the big new year, the bonfires and fireworks.'

'You didn't get too close, I hope. You've never had it, Billy.'

'I didn't even go in. I leaned a ladder up against the wall and talked to her through the bedroom window.'

'Oh, she must have liked that. It's just the sort of thing Albert would do. Oh my Lord, if it isn't you, is it him? Is it Bertie Dot Sharp's looking for?'

'Maybe she is and maybe she isn't.'

'Anyway, it's about time, Billy Jackson, that you did take a wife. If you don't do it soon, you won't know what to do when you do get one and what with the post office coming, we'll need some help, Hannah and I and Biddy here.' She pointed to the spry old woman. 'Biddy's getting on and it's beginning to show.' Satisfied with the effect of her barbs she added, 'And now, you two may be concerned with the ILP and the BMS, but I have to run the FVS.' To their blank faces she said, 'The Findlesham Village Shop!'

It was freezing. Ann stretched out her feet to the fire. Although she was tired, it wasn't the fatigue of sleep and the thought of climbing into the big soft bed alone that saddened her. This time of year, had she always disliked it? No. There were hunting and shooting and the parties. Hunting especially. Like Caroline, she had always loved that part of country life, being with horses. Oh, she didn't want to think about Caroline. Too worrying. Wasn't it enough having the two monstrous younger children to worry about? Whatever had gone wrong there it must be Richard's fault. Caroline was an angel. Everybody adored her.

She took her legs away from the fire – that was how you got those awful marks – and tried to tuck them under her. Too stiff – no, too *old*. She got up and fetched another soft vicuna blanket, then settled back in the deep chair again. There was no doubt that Caroline had hit Richard. The red mark was still clear on his face when Ann had gone into the morning room to say goodbye. Luncheon, too. That hadn't been right. Uncomfortable. Caroline over-bright, talking, talking, but in her few silences nobody else contributing anything. A bad day altogether. Foul. Sam, morose, silent, obviously pleased to be rid of her when she went off to church. And she had risen early, not breakfasted, just to go over to see him. It had been the shock about Biddy – the little girl's death hadn't been expected – but he wouldn't be comforted, shrugging off her touch. 'Sorry, Ann. I'll be best alone.' Then this evening when she left, he had been angry. 'You have to go? What am I asking? Of course you must go. You must go *home*.' It was only on the boat they stayed together at night and that wasn't possible in the winter. That spring would come early and be warm was all she wished in this damp, wet-leaved, uninviting month. Not sleeping together wouldn't have mattered in the days of their . . . not youthful, *middle-aged* passion. Now, though still lovers, it was the other part of love that sustained them. Companionship, familiarity, memory. But that needed the continuity of everyday life, mealtimes, sleep, the waking together in the morning.

A little smile, as of old, curled her mouth. It was in the mornings usually that, half awake, their bodies shaped together in the narrow bed, they made love with the expertise of mutual knowledge compensating for the heat of early passion. Her bed at the dower house seemed even less inviting. The stone bottle there would be nearly cold. Only Thomas had slept with her in it and that rarely. For years his visits to her bedroom had been almost formal occasions, for the purpose of procreation, and when the process was complete, he had left and slept in his own small bedroom. She put a piece of coal and a log onto the fire and pulled out a low stool for her feet.

Anthony Willson had asked him to speak to the boys about bullying Elizabeth. They stood in front of him, side by side, in their white nightshirts, looking like innocent angels, listening patiently as he explained the duty of a gentleman to a lady. 'They are weaker than us, therefore we should protect them, not take advantage of that weakness. It would be possible for a man to pick up a woman and throw her out of the window, but . . . ' There was a gleam in Charles's eye that made him wish he had phrased it differently. Quickly he went on, 'But that would not reflect the strength of the man, only the frailty of the woman.'

Silently, young Oliver pushed back his sleeve to reveal

a livid purple bruise on his arm. 'I'm not the average man yet, Papa, but Lizzie did this.'

'She was holding him down on the floor when she did it, with a foot on his chest.' Charles produced this piece of information with ill-disguised relish.

'Yes, well, she probably had a reason,' he said, lamely, touching his still sore cheek. 'Goaded beyond endurance, I expect. Yes, yes. Naturally I intend to speak to Elizabeth about this as well.'

'Yes, Papa.'

'As a general rule, though,' he rose to go as Nanny Colcroft's heavy tread could be heard on the servants' stairs, 'it is as well to remember that gentlemen never strike ladies, however provoked. Do you understand?'

'Yes, Papa.'

'Goodnight, then. You're late to bed.'

As he descended the stairs, he heard the shrill voice of Oliver. 'When I'm a man, I'll be able to throw you out of the window, Nanny. Papa said so.'

Had he goaded Caroline beyond endurance? They hadn't been alone since his mother had walked in on their – what? Row? Argument? Discussion? *She* had been the guilty party, admitting to a romance, and *he* had been the one to be struck. There was a line of light showing under her bedroom door. Should he speak to her now, or would she think his appearance in her bedroom meant something else? But he had no choice. She had heard his footsteps and called him.

'Do you agree?' she said impatiently. 'It would be foolish to do anything here in the park and have hordes of villagers and tenants from miles around trampling all over the place in the dark, wouldn't it?'

'Oh, yes. I do agree. There'll be a bonfire on Beacon Hill anyway and if we organize fireworks . . . '

'And beer and that band that plays in the park in Wellsbury.'

'A good idea.' He moved from the foot of her bed to the fire, pushing a log with his foot so that little sparks spat out.

'There is no need to walk away from me, Richard. I'm not going to hit you again.' Her speech was just a little slurred from the wine at lunch-time, followed by quite a lot of brandy at dinner.

'Why did you hit me the first time?'

'When your wife tells you she is sleeping with another man—'

'Oh, you are, actually—'

'Yes, I am, actually – she doesn't expect you to smile with pleasure. It is very bad manners. Rude.'

When he had questioned Caroline about her excessive high spirits, the suggestion that she had a lover had been just a little joke. His involuntary smile had been of relief not pleasure, although it shouldn't be pleasurable to think that someone he didn't know had made love to his wife. Childish masculine possessiveness, that's all it was. Did he want his wife to wear a chastity belt? *His* wife. He turned back to the fire and kicked the log again. One of the sparks landed on the rug. There was a brief smell of burning before he stamped on it.

'It isn't worth setting the house on fire for, Richard.'

Was she crying? Surely not, not Caroline. Even so, he wouldn't look at her, just in case. Picking up the heavy brass fire-guard, he placed it in front of the now dying fire. 'Who was it, Caroline?'

'Who *is* it. You have no right to know. I suppose *you* have a mistress.'

Surprised, he turned round. 'No, I don't.'

'Well, why, then, oh . . . what's the point?' She slumped down in the bed. 'I'm going to sleep. Good-night.'

He looked back at her from the door. Her eyes were open, staring at him. It wasn't the first time he had noticed how intense the green was when they were a little bloodshot. 'Good-night, Caroline.'

Reluctantly he responded to the outstretched hand. 'Just a second, darling.' She pulled him to the bed. Her breath was still sour from the alcohol. 'It's Andrew.'

'Andrew?'

'My lover. It's Andrew Osmund.'

He snatched away his hand. 'Andrew Osmund? He's my friend. They are our neighbours. How could you, Caroline. A friend of mine.'

'That is who I meet, friends of yours. Would you rather I slept with an enemy? God! Men are so stupid! Who *are* wives supposed to sleep with?'

'I can't believe it. We were at Eton together!' He laughed at the ludicrous pomposity of this statement and, once again, she slapped his face. Laughing was not the reaction she had expected or wanted.

Positioning the trap on a little knoll facing Beacon Hill, quite a long way back from the crowds who had lit small fires that appeared like sparks blown from the great bonfire on top of the hill, Mary stood with the little pony until she was sure he wasn't frightened and then gave him a nosebag of oats to keep him happy. Slinging the field-glasses, borrowed from her father, around her neck, she climbed on to the driver's seat and wrapped herself in a shawl. From here she could see everything, figures moving in the light of the fire, some of them children hurling pieces of wood as big as themselves. She hoped that in the excitement they wouldn't hurl themselves onto the fire with the wood. There were a few curious glances at her perched on the strange contraption and some people followed her example clambering on the tops of their own conveyances. Through the field-glasses, she could just make out the shapes of Dot and John, one shape, really, with two heads, so close were they sitting together, a rug enveloping both shoulders. What a fool she had been! Blurting out at Keepers Cottage, 'Oh, I see! It's you she's been—' stopping short of 'after' just in time. The girl had been anxious to please her – her future mother-in-law, she hoped. All part of a strategy to catch her John. Which, it seemed, she'd done. Ma had invited her to tea, or asked her to stay because they were about to have it, more like. Another example of Miss Sharp's 'just passing'.

Later, when young John had offered to walk the girl home, Mother had defended her. 'Dorothy Sharp is a good girl. John couldn't do better. Of course she chased him, Mary. What's a girl supposed to do? If you waited for a man to speak you'd wait for ever.'

'And I thought it had all been my idea, our courting.' John Bowden chuckled as he refilled his pipe. 'What do you reckon, Mary?'

'Well, if Ma set her bonnet at you, I reckon you had no choice. As for Dot, I don't know. She *is* a good girl, head screwed on, but our John is a mite young...' Her voice trailed away. *She* had been six years younger.

'Ah, but, Mary, he's a settled type. It wouldn't suit him being a bachelor, and the Sharps have a very good tenancy from Brakspeare's the brewers, and that little cottage and barn out back, they own that.'

'A woman of substance,' Mary had whispered to her father.

It was colder now. The wind was getting up quite a southerly. It was carrying the sound of the bells of St Michael's starting to ring in the new year, the new century. But they were drowned, first by the thunderous clap of the first firework and then the concerted 'Aaaaah' as it exploded into trails of white and blue fire, lighting the sky for seconds before the trail became vapour and vanished when the 'Aaaaah' turned into a sad 'Ooooh'. She hoped Hanny and Sam couldn't hear the fireworks, that the wind wouldn't carry the sound back to the cottage where they both still grieved for poor little Biddy. It would drive the children wild to hear the fireworks they were forbidden to see. More and more explosions. Some like rumbles of distant thunder, others just a sharp pop, but all with their attendant flares and cascades of light and stars, silver and red, blue and green. It was so windy now; the pony leaned against the trap for shelter, shaking it. She was cold now, too. Another series of fireworks was let off, a giant rocket showering gold rain and a Catherine wheel throwing out its circular spokes of multicoloured flame. This was popular with the children whose 'Aaahs' had turned to shrieks of pleasure.

Just as well they didn't know it commemorated the death of a young woman burned on the wheel. In the last rays of the glitter of gold from the rocket, she saw the Fiennders' carriage. By common consent, an unspoken rule, the gentry parked their carriages together in the most advantageous position. Lady Caroline was drinking from a tiny silver cup and leaning on a stick. But then, how odd, she screwed the cup onto the end of the stick. And now Richard was helping her into the carriage out of the cold. He had changed. Of course he had. Twenty years. He was bigger, heavier. Quickly she jumped down from the roof. It was too cold. Time to go. Time to return to her house, her beautiful home. Put another log on the fire, eat her supper, drink the delicious wine – Moselle that Algernon had sent her. He was staying at home with Francis. That wasn't by choice, though. He had his bronchitis again.

She led the pony off the knoll and turned towards home. As she shivered in the dark and cold, she thought with longing of the warmth and brightness of the Pightle and shouted aloud, 'Thank you, Miss Crewe.' The pony thought it was a shout of encouragement and trotted faster over the frost-hardened ground, slowing only when they passed through the edge of the wood on an old Roman way; just a track now but, hundreds of years ago, a major route for tradesmen. The pony picked his way with care, wary of fallen branches. Behind them, Mary could hear the snap and crack of twigs. He knew his way home already, even when pulling the unfamiliar trap. Skirting the edge of her fields, soon to be planted by old Joe with wheat, a tithe of which she had exacted from him as part of the rent, the path opened out to reveal the cottage sitting waiting for her, the downstairs windows lit by a flickering light, the remnants of a well-banked fire. That was the first thing to see to.

She laid two large logs across the fire-irons and piled coal around them, then lit the oil lamps and turned up the wicks for brightness. There was a large brass one with a milky opaque glass shade and one in a pale pink china with a tall chimney-shaped shade in a paler pink that cast a soft warm glow. Clustered together on the long serving table made from four big logs and a plank of scrubbed pine, were six white china nursery candlesticks of different shapes and sizes. The chairs at the polished elm dining table had straight backs and newly woven rush seats. These she had found, shabby and broken, in the store-room at the back of Billy's forge. The undersides had been signed 'JT'. They had been made by Jim Turner's grandfather, Jeremiah, an apprentice carpenter on the estate in 1790. Her small lectern was ready on the table holding the book she was reading – *Deerbrook* by Harriet Martineau. It had been purchased to please Biddy, who admired Miss Martineau for her knowledge of economics and politics, and her atheism. But the novel was more than ideas, it was extremely entertaining.

Outside, the wind changed direction. It made the fire roar, and a tree near the side window creaked, making her jump. She closed all the heavy chenille curtains, shutting out the sounds of the night. Over and over people had said, 'Won't you be frightened, living all alone?' 'What would you do if someone bad came along? Someone mad? Aren't you scared of something out there coming after you and you all on your own?' The some-*thing* was more alarming than a some*one*; its vagueness was disquieting. Like the Green Man, half woodland creature, half human. No. She was not frightened. If there *was* a Green Man, why shouldn't he be friendly? But she jumped again when the wind rattled the front door.

Her supper was ready, the potatoes boiled and dressed with butter, the cold chicken carved and the mayonnaise in its simple white bowl placed on the table. One knife, one fork, one glass, one napkin. A bottle of Moselle. The first from Algernon's case. The mayonnaise was a tremendous treat, a luxury. She had made it from her own eggs. The chickens and geese were shut up for the night, but there must be a fox prowling. There had been the occasional honk from the geese. The old carriage clock that Biddy had given her struck eleven o'clock, with its slightly muffled chime. It was five minutes fast. She always kept clocks fast. It gave her time put aside, like money in the bank.

She gasped as the door rattled again. It would be more secure if she locked it. The heavy iron key with its thick tassel was in the lock. All she had to do was turn it, but she felt magnetized by the lock, by the whole door, unable to move, like a rabbit transfixed by the gaze of a stoat. Yet still she wasn't afraid. The door wasn't rattled by the wind. She could tell that now. It hadn't been a tree bending that she had heard at the side window. It wasn't a fox disturbing the geese. And on the journey home through the wood, the snapping of twigs behind them hadn't been caused by the trap. She had been followed home.

He closed the door behind him and locked it. The wind had whipped his hair around his face and his cheeks to a quickly fading red. He stood hesitating at the door, then shyly offered his right hand. 'I shouldn't have come. I don't know why I did. I followed you, like a magnet.'

She put out her left hand, unsmiling, and touched his palm; the touch was intimate.

'Did I frighten you? Did you hear the geese?'

'Yes, I heard the geese. I wasn't frightened.'

He took her hand and placed it over his eyes. 'This is so painful, Mary. I can't look at you. I can't breathe.'

She lifted her other hand and parted his lips, something she had done as a child when he wouldn't talk to her. 'Why don't we do something ordinary, Richard?' she whispered. 'Stay and have supper with me.'

He nodded. Taking her hand away from his eyes, he examined it, smiling. 'Do you still scrub your hands with soda?'

'Of course I don't.' She laughed. 'They have to be worthy of your manicure set. Would you open this?' She handed him the wine and a horn-handled corkscrew. He watched her hands as she laid another place for him. Manicure set. He had forgotten.

'Algy sent me the wine when I moved in last month. A whole case! This is the first time . . . you do drink wine?'

'Yes, I do. I expect it will be delicious.' They sat facing each other, eating awkwardly at first, shy.

'I saw you – I thought I saw you leastways, helping . . . standing by your carriage. It was not you – for you've not changed. He was heavy, older.'

'And I?'

'Only . . . older.'

'The cottage is lovely, Mary, I didn't know it was here.

I remember it as a shack, where the forester and his family lived. Who owns it? Berreford? Or Coffield, is it now?'

'It's mine. I own it.' There was the same pride, the same awe of ownership in her voice as when she had said, 'manicure set'. The clock chimed twelve.

'It's midnight,' he said.

'It's tomorrow.'

'It's the next year.'

'It's the next century.'

'It's Monday.' He leant across the table and kissed her cheek lightly. 'Happy all those things.'

'In truth it's only five to twelve. I keep it fast. I'm going to make the most of last year.' She looked into his eyes. There were many Richards there: the boy, the young man, those she knew, but the grown man, wise, sad, disappointed, cynical, she didn't know him. They held their gaze until it really was 1900. 'Nineteen hundred and nothing,' she said at last.

'No, nineteen hundred and something.'

It was nearly dawn when she took his hand and led him up to her bedroom. They lay together, touching, gently exploring, lit first by the light of a guttering candle and then by the moon, which appeared and disappeared, hidden by clouds which were blown away by the wind, and then by the shadows of the trees. He held her long, fine, pale hair, traced the blue vein that elongated her right eye like an Egyptian princess, pressed his lips against the space between her top lip and nose and let his mouth slide down to meet hers. And when they made love he used no previously gained expertise and had no erotic

memories. They were children together in the secrecy of
the woods. They were young lovers on Paradise Hill and
they were a man and woman turning a friendship into
every kind of love. And for her the memory of a year of
a loveless and unwanted invasion of her body was removed
by his gentle passion.

'Please don't.'

'No.'

They both raised their hands to wave away the
questions.

'It's too soon, Richard.'

'Yes, I know. Foolish of me.'

'No. Or yes, of me too. Foolish to ask. I can't talk
yet about me *then* and I don't want to hear about you.'

'It's too soon,' he agreed. They had risen together,
still sleepy, holding hands. Lit fires and banked up the
boiler. Bathed in the deep copper tub and made love.
Still hot and damp, fed the pony, his horse, the cow and
the goats, let out the geese and chickens, threw them
corn, collected the eggs and were now eating them.
Everything was new, everything had to be learned. Thick
or thin toast, dark or golden; eggs, runny or slightly set,
the top cut off or tapped into pieces and peeled off. Salt
and pepper in the egg or on the plate. The tea, strong or
weak, milk added first or after. And marmalade or honey
or jam. These were safer things to talk and laugh about.
Everything was interesting and surprising about your
lover. It was safer to stay in the present. The past led to
the future. The past included his wife, in his house, with
his children, to whom he must return. The house where

she had blackened the grates, mended his mother's clothes in the sewing room and heard him playing the piano as she hid outside in the shrubbery.

'Just one question?'

Her eyes, large with fear, peered at him over her cup. 'All right. Just one.'

'What time may I return, Mary?'

She sped around the house – her even more beloved home now, where he had been – washing up, cleaning the sink, polishing the table, shaking the rugs, saving the bedroom for last. Reluctantly, she made the bed, straightening rumpled sheets, punching goose-down pillows into shape, tucking in the blankets made of squares of knitting and replacing the counterpane. Had it returned to its usual appearance of white, tidy, innocent maidenhood? Not quite. She could imagine the imprint of his head on the pillow and under the pristine whiteness of the cotton sheet, the shape of her body stretched, legs parted, pressed against him. She reached behind her neck, undoing the hooks and eyes that fastened the warm woollen dress. Stepping out of it she rolled down her stockings, removed her stays and, naked, lay on the bed. Thinking of him, she took the pillow on which he had slept so briefly, and held it like a lover. Only the clock, telling her not just the hour but that it was time she left for Keepers Cottage, kept her from sleep.

As she hitched the pony to the trap, which she had to return to her parents, she smiled at the memory of what she had done in her bedroom. The initials R and M were carved in the oak beam above the bed and MDCCCC. She laid the whip lightly across the pony's flanks and put him to the trot.

'It suits you living out there, love. You look well.' Her father unhitched the trap and put the pony in the lean-to, out of the weather. 'You ought to get yourself one of these, you know. A bicycle is all very well, but in this weather . . .'

'I hope you're not suggesting, Pa, that I get one of *these*.' She pointed to the ungainly contrivance. 'Though I have loved it in its time.'

'You'd be hard put, girl, to find another one. It's a law unto itself!'

'Mary! You're earlier than I thought. And how is Mr Grant-Ingram? And that school-teacher? Have you come from there? What was the band like last night? Did you stay up – see the new year in?' Emma hustled her daughter in out of the cold. 'I'll put the kettle on straight away.'

Fortunately, she didn't wait for answers. How could she say, 'I didn't go to see my good friends who were expecting me because . . . ' She felt the cold and huddled near the fire. This house had always been full of draughts. They whistled down from the attic, crept in under the doors and whispered through ill-fitting casements. But with the chill, they brought a freshness that alleviated the cosy fug of winter.

'Hanny, Sam and the children will be here and young John's gone to fetch his Dot – John said he didn't see you last night. Plenty there, though. No wonder he missed you. Are you all right? Don't you catch a cold or this 'flu thing.' Her mother prattled on, happy. Her children were doing well and all coming to see their parents, as they should, on the first day of the year. 'Biddy stayed the night with us. John slept down here. Nobody managed midnight. I don't know why they fix New Year's Eve near enough to the longest night of the year. It being Monday today, though, is most convenient. Doesn't matter the shop being closed for most will be eating the Sunday roast cold.'

Mary exchanged the usual discreet glance of amusement with her father.

Even George Nichols hadn't noticed. 'Morning, sir. You were up betimes, then,' he'd said, removing Peckwood's saddle. 'Didn't have to sleep it off, not like someone standing not too far from here.' He glared at the pale stable-boy. 'Here, boy, see to him. I suppose even in your state you can tell the difference between his 'ocks and his arse.'

Richard guessed, from the man's unusual display of bad temper, that George himself might be paying for an excess of celebration. The butler had been told not to wait up, just to leave the usual sandwiches and decanter of whisky and two bottles of Bollinger in an ice-bucket. Cathal and Millie would have come back with Caroline. There had been no surprise last night when he had said he was going out. She had been rather triumphant. Imagining her flirting with Andrew had piqued him. But it was boredom that took him away. Her public flirtation with Andrew Osmund was well judged. Nobody would think it was anything other than playful, including Andrew's wife.

It was just after ten o'clock. The house was full of sounds of people behindhand with their work; scurrying housemaids with buckets of coal and dusters, red-eyed footmen with trays and the boot-boy bearing gleaming leather shoes to their owners. He peeped into the study. The whisky and sandwiches had gone although the ice-bucket remained, with one bottle of champagne which he removed and concealed under his long coat. Ridiculous! Stealing from himself.

The morning room was empty. A fire blazed and breakfast was on a hot-plate on the sideboard. The food had been disturbed – there was an indentation in the bowl of kedgeree and at least half of the dish of devilled kidneys had gone. The Watsons must have eaten and gone out, maybe to the meet at Edgecombe. Both of Caroline's hunters were still in the stables, groomed and ready for her, so she wasn't up yet. She would join them, no doubt, over at Great Giddesly. He took a cup, poured coffee into it, swirled it around, poured it back into the silver pot, then pushed a spoonful of scrambled egg around a plate. He would be safe in his bedroom. Nobody came unless he rang.

'What *are* you doing, Richard?' Caroline, immaculate in her dark green well-fitting riding habit and glossy boots, surveyed the room through the fine veil attached to her black bowler. 'If you're going away, ring for someone to pack.' Drawers were pulled out, cupboards open, garments strewn on the couch, on the bed and on the floor.

He looked up, startled. 'What do you want, Caroline?'

'I've forgotten. What do *you* want? Are you running

away?' She lifted some shirts with the toe of her boot and kicked them in the air. 'Oh, yes, are you hunting today?'

'No, but as you obviously are, I suggest you leave me to—'

'To what? Are you sulking about last night? Louise didn't mind us flirting.'

'Neither do I.' He smiled gently at his memory of last night as he continued to rummage through the drawers in his mahogany tallboy. Then he remembered. He had put it in a drawer of his old travelling trunk. 'Louise doesn't know about you two, does she?'

'I don't know.' She shrugged. 'No, I don't think so.'

'That's all right, then.' He started replacing the scattered shirts, socks and handkerchiefs, untidily, and smiled again. 'She doesn't know and I don't mind.' He was kneeling at the bottom drawer when a sturdy leather shoe, with a wooden shoe-tree inserted, hit him on the head.

Mary bent over the pony, avoiding the drooping branches of the leafless trees as she jogged down the uneven track. The occasional splash of rain fell on her but this path was more sheltered than the official right of way granted by James Coffield. It had been nice to be with the family and to see Hannah, pale and thinner, but beginning to recover from her grief. But, oh, it had been hard to join in their chatter. She wanted to be silent with her beautiful memories. Ahead now, soon maybe, were more memories to be made. For now she had erased the bad ones, so that miraculously the ages of fourteen and thirty-four fused together.

He was waiting for her outside the cottage. 'I got here half an hour ago. I heard the horse. You get inside quickly before you get wet.' He felt the dampness of her cloak as he reached up to hold her as she jumped. 'Wetter. I'll stable him. You need a piano.'

She laughed, delighted. 'A pony *and* a piano. What an original idea!'

'Get inside.' But he held her, wiping the rain from her face, kissing her. 'I love you, Mary, love you. And you need a trap,' he said, looking round the room – a perfect square now that the central wall was gone, with windows at both ends.

'Am I to keep the piano in the stables and the trap there against the wall?'

He lifted her, swinging her high in the air. 'I am so entranced by you, I am like the Green Man with a witch girl and have become a foolish boy.'

'Become? I remember you well as a foolish boy – no don't!' He swung her higher. 'I remember you picking blackberries and putting them in my bonnet. It was never white again.'

'Did you use any buttermilk that you could spare from your face?' He lowered her, sliding his hands down her slender body, feeling the bones of her narrow back, pressing her body to him. 'I have lit the fire in your bedroom,' he whispered as he lifted her again – this time like a child in his arms – and carried her upstairs.

'This isn't all we want, is it?' His hand rested lightly on the slight curve of her breast.

She turned her head. Through the tangled silky hair

he could see the brown eyes, changing colour constantly with the light – topaz sometimes, even the glossy speckled brown of a river trout – but now they were alarmed. 'All? It's a lot, Richard. Think of what we had before. Nothing.' Agitated, she slipped out of the bed, pulling her shift over her head quickly, conscious of her nakedness, and crouched by the fire. 'Not "nothing". I don't mean that. You . . . you have your family, your estate, your . . . everything. And I have my lovely cottage, and my . . . son, and friends and work and—'

'Please don't, Mary. You're shaking.' He wrapped a blanket around her, stroking her hair.

'There isn't any more, Richard, than this. Sometimes . . . You will always have to go home.' She tried to banish the thought of Sally, abandoned night after night by George. 'It's the way of the world.'

'It doesn't all have to be a *via dolorosa*.'

'But it can't be a *via matrimonium*.'

'I know. I can't divorce my wife.'

Shocked, she scrambled to her feet. 'No, no, no,' she almost shouted. 'You can't. No, *she* has done nothing wrong.'

'Hush. I can't divorce her because one doesn't, but in fact she has done something wrong. Not that I mind. It means that I can love you without guilt.'

He held her close, smoothing the hair off her brow. 'The tip of your nose still escapes your bonnet – even now, in winter, it's just a little brown. Not like your eyes, for which brown is an utterly inadequate adjective; so many different shades, caramel, hazel – oh, Mary! I forgot. Wait there.'

He took the stairs both down and up in giant leaps.

'Look, I bought this for you in Rome.' Unfolding the yards of shimmering shot silk, he held it up. 'You see? It's some of the colours in your eyes. Twenty years I've had it in my steamer trunk. I wanted to give it to you. I had planned it, in the gazebo. Do you remember the gazebo?'

'Of course I do,' she said softly. 'You thought of me in Rome?' It was strange, wonderful. She had been with him then, in Italy. 'It's very beautiful.' She held the material against her body, admiring it. 'What is it, Richard?'

He had closed his eyes and was trembling. 'You,' he said. 'You outside the church that day.' He touched her stomach, flat now, remembering it swollen with pregnancy.

She held him, the material crushed between them, soothing him, but she was calmed by the memory that after she became pregnant George had never forced himself on her again.

'I think I should take you to the Bull and Butcher, just like that, your hair falling down your back, your little white shift and the silk tied around your shoulders.' The sad moment had passed, the scene outside St Michael's had become a part of their history. 'Now, what are we having for dinner? I brought us a bottle of champagne – and shall I shut up the geese and the chickens before the fox helps himself to *his* dinner?'

'Dinner? You can stay?' She had prepared herself for an evening alone, he would be gone.

'Yes, there is dinner, a big party after the meet, at the Bexley-Wrights. I won't be missed. I'm going to London, anyway, to see Maud tomorrow. People will be told I went today.'

Maud. London. A party. The meet. Twenty years might not have passed. He was still talking of alien experiences that she couldn't share. *Then* it had been Eton, university, grouse-shooting. 'How wonderful that you can stay.' What she thought was, How wonderful that you *want* to stay. She folded the material, wrapping it in its original tissue paper with great care. 'I will make a dress, Hannah will help.' She smiled up at him. 'It will be quite beautiful. But when will I wear it?'

'In France, don't you think?'

'It's not that I think you're wrong, Ann. Putting things off, problems, can mean they solve themselves, but this one's got to be faced now. It has been put off more than once, and hasn't been solved. What are you looking at out there?' Sam joined her at the window. Snow was falling, but not heavily enough to obliterate her tracks. Her neatly booted feet had left an orderly line as far as his eyes could see. 'Do you reckon that goes all the way back to the dower house? If so, my dear, you have lost your reputation and we will have to wed!'

'How long will it take for the snow to settle and cover my tracks?'

'An hour or three.'

'Then I will have to stay for an hour or three.' She smiled for the first time that morning.

'Not altogether so. You could leave now and I could shovel the snow – and the evidence – off.'

'Is that what you want me to do, Sam?'

'No. No, I don't, so come and sit by the fire. What's the bit that bothers you most? The lady-friends, or the money, or the drinking?'

'It all returns to money, doesn't it? Tommy has had more than he should from his trust. That doesn't really become his until the age of twenty-five and then thirty, or marriage. Even then it is an income, not the capital. Lady-friends? Well, they cost money to "tidy up" you know, especially if they *are* ladies. Thank goodness they've been servants and shopgirls so far.' She knew, before she had finished, that she had made a mistake. 'Yes, yes, I'm sorry. That was wrong of me. As for the drinking, that matters both generally and specifically.'

'What do you mean?'

'Drinking makes for bad judgement in a general sense and he doesn't need whisky to make his judgement bad.'

'And specifically?' He fetched a rug and put it across her lap. 'You keep warm now. I've heard of the influenza being bad as near as Oxford – hospital's full.'

'I know, but not as bad as London, so Maud says. Tommy encourages Caroline to drink. It's something that runs in that family. Charlie Colcroft, they say, drinks at least four bottles every day.'

'Whisky?'

'Good gracious, no, wine. And brandy, of course, and whisky as well.'

'Ah, that explains the colour of his face. I seen him at the last shoot. He looks as if he's exploded!'

She laughed. 'What a good description.'

'And his loader all but pulls the trigger for him.'

'I will be glad when Richard returns.'

'Then you're adding a problem, by all accounts.'

She looked worried. 'All accounts, Sam? Who else talks of it?'

'Nobody. No one,' he soothed her. 'I just meant all your accounts.'

She sighed. 'I don't know what went wrong, or when, but they have changed. Never together, cold when they are, or bad-tempered.'

'Married awhile now, Ann. Children. They've got used to each other . . . '

She wasn't listening, just fidgeting with the rug and tapping her toes on the brass fender. 'Sam, I want to ask your advice . . . but . . . ' She held up a hand imperiously. 'Don't interrupt.'

He caught the hand and pulled her to her feet. 'We're in my house, Ann, on equal terms, man to woman, which to some makes you less equal. I will give you advice if I can, but I won't if you "my lady" me. And if you do, you can make another set of tracks with those pretty boots of yours.'

She inclined her head, accepting his rebuke. 'The advice goes with a confession that is hard to make. I want to tell you about something, something long ago and it's very difficult. Nobody knows, I think, except the person involved, and he doesn't because I believe him to be dead.'

He patted her shoulder. 'Then I shouldn't have interrupted. You sit down and we'll join the drinkers in these parts. I'll get you a glass of Canary wine and a beer for myself.'

'You see, I was quite happy with Tommy away, let him behave badly on the Continent, and I sent him enough money – not much – to keep him away.'

'Out of sight, out of mind. And handier for us, Ann. I've thought that, you at the dower house on your own.'

'Exactly.'

'Not much of a confession there.'

'No, but it brings me to it. Before I married Thomas, I think you know there was someone . . . someone I liked.'

Why was she so shifty, not catching his eye? There was no doubt she found this hard. Not like her. He knew about the man, or that there had been a man. 'Someone you loved would be nearer to it, Ann. If you're to tell, tell all. No point in holding back. If it puts you in a bad light, you was young. I know you well enough now to understand you then.'

She got up and returned to the window. There were more tracks in the snow – the claw marks of birds seeking the crumbs from his unfinished breakfast. 'Thank you, Sam. He, the man I loved, was the second son of a second son. Not a good marriage, but a passable one. Our friendship wasn't encouraged but if, say, he had taken orders and his family had given him a reasonably good living . . . '

'Like St Michael's, Findlesham, being given to your Isabel's husband?'

'Yes, like that. The usual choice of younger sons – Army or Church. If that had happened and I had insisted – oh, what is the point of telling you all this? His father thought it possible he wasn't his son. He didn't get a living and I didn't insist. I didn't want to live in rooms in Bath on the income from my money.'

'He lost some of his attraction?'

'Not his attraction, no. Most of the young women

from Shropshire to London were in love with him. That was part of his appeal, but I was the chosen one. He lost any eligibility.'

He wondered if that was it, but she still stared out of the window and there was no note of finality in her voice. 'And then what, Ann?'

'Although I gave up hope of marriage, I didn't like – don't forget I was only seventeen – giving up his company. My parents were carefully promoting an alternative . . . '

'Better catch?'

'Oh, yes, much better. They were talking about a substantial dowry – money, land, investments.'

'Funny, isn't it? They were all right for giving to someone who had, but not to someone who needed. Go on.'

'They reasoned that, with Edmund away, I, a good daughter – and I was – would come round to their choice.'

He didn't like her saying his name. Edmund. It made him flesh and blood, and for the first time, he felt a real pang of jealousy.

'His father wanted him away as well.'

'Ah, well. Natural, that is. Wouldn't want reminding of his wife's carrying on.'

'They sent him to America, paid for him to go and gave him an allowance, yearly, for life, as long as he stayed away.'

'And he took it? Not much love lost there, Ann, if you don't mind me saying.'

'Took it? No, not exactly.' She pressed her hot cheek against the icy pane of the window. Still the snow fell, a frozen crocheted blanket of white. 'He asked me to marry him. I refused. The decision to go to America was made by him, but he wanted to refuse the allowance. I persuaded him . . .' She faltered again, her voice low. 'I persuaded him to accept the money and, if he didn't want it, send it to me, secretly, and he did. When it stopped, I presumed he had died.' She waited for him to speak. Then, attempting to justify herself, she said hotly, 'It was before the Married Woman's Act. Everything that I had would belong to my husband, nothing was legally mine.' She waited again for him to say something and heard his laughter.

'You are a card, woman, and no mistake. Shrewd. I wonder what way you've got me all tied up! Well, your Edmund was a gentleman, the only one to come out of this with his colours.'

Relieved at his reaction, she said, defensively, 'Of course he was a gentleman, all Fiennders men are.'

'Fiennders?'

'Yes. Didn't I say? He was Thomas's younger brother.'

Sam shook his head. 'Too much for me to take in, my lady. Now look,' he pointed to the garden, 'see how your luck stays with you? The snow has covered your tracks.'

'You don't think I'm so wicked, then?' She peeped coyly over her shoulder.

He moved away, embarrassed. She was too old to feign a look of innocence. 'Judge for yourself, Ann. It's a nasty tale, but not a wicked one. Petty is all. What was all that before, about advice? Isn't it a bit late for that?'

She brushed aside his criticism. 'It's about the money.'

'You still have it?'

'Oh, yes, and a life-time of interest too!'

'A pretty penny then, no doubt. I suggest you use it to start a fund for the second sons of second sons.'

'That is precisely what I mean to do. I think.'

'Oh, no! I see what this is all about. Oh, no, Ann. Are you going to buy off your conscience and get rid of your second son at the same time?'

'That is an extremely coarse way of phrasing it but—'

'But it's true. You might as well throw it in the river Thames for all the good it will do. Tommy is no Edmund, from the sound of him. *He* would go to America, take the money, come back, seduce a serving girl, go to Canada, gamble the money away and come back, get a young lady with child, go to Australia, take the money and come back.'

'Thank you, Sam. You have illustrated your opinion of my son very well. Why don't you stop before you run out of colonies?'

'I'm right, you know, and that's why you asked my advice, because you know.' He led her away from the window.

'I'm tired.'

'No surprise, not after telling that tale, all bottled up for years. Lie down here on the couch, put your feet up and I'll take off your boots.' He went to the dresser drawer and fished out his button-hook. Love. Funny that, he loved her in spite of quite a lot!

'Difficult for me to judge Tommy, you know, Sam. I'm no paragon of virtue.'

He unbuttoned the high boots and eased them off, rubbing her feet. 'No, you aren't, and I intend to keep it that way.' Leaving her clothed, he folded her skirts and petticoats back and knelt over her, determined, as he pushed inside her, hard, to erase the memory of Edmund.

The pain had been unbearable, choking her. Behaving well, not crying, not clinging, smiling, had all been possible only because the alternative was out of the question. To say goodbye, so lightly, after nearly three weeks together, alone, unafraid of being recognized, free! They had been sharing the twenty-four hours of every day, walking on the beach and cliff-top, sitting at concerts holding hands, eating strange delicious food in tiny cafés, sleeping every night together in a large four-poster bed festooned with lace-trimmed white linen curtains, waking, limbs entwined, with the faint scent of last night's love. As they stirred in the morning, tumbling together, his mouth automatically sought hers. 'Your breath smells like raspberries,' he said. Thin sticks of chewy bread and dark, dark coffee with warm milk for breakfast. No handle on the coffee cup, a bowl to be held with both hands. After *le petit déjeuner*, there was always love again. He watched her dressing, laughed at the needless corsets. And talking, gentle with each other, slowly piecing together the map of the last twenty years.

But now she was back in the Pightle, with this ache in her chest, in her heart. He had been unable to hide the pleasure of going home, seeing his children, riding round the estate. They had separated at Dover – she to take the steam train and he the coach across country to where he would spend the night with friends and then take the train to Oxford where his carriage would await him. She had chosen an unfamiliar driver at Wellsbury station to bring her home and had given him a circuitous route to follow. The amount of luggage would surprise anybody who thought her time away had been spent in Bath and Oxford, cities she had never visited.

Perhaps this ache would go if she busied herself. Unpack first. There would be nothing to wash, the *femme de chambre* had washed and ironed everything exquisitely. The sight of their clothes drying together hanging on a line, shirts and blouses embracing in the breeze had pleased them both, but her pleasure was increased by the luxury. When she had unpacked and stowed the suitcases in the attic she would . . . what? Teresa Quinn had looked after the cottage perfectly. It was absolutely immaculate. Not just to look at – the smells of lavender oil, beeswax, black-lead, coal-tar soap, all were proof of her industry.

Stop looking out of the window, she commanded herself. It was bleak enough to increase her sadness. A bare garden surrounded by trees bent in the March winds, the grass covered in twigs blown down. They must be collected for kindling. Kindling! That was the answer – *an* answer. Light the fires. She put a match to the grate in her bedroom. The twists of paper, sticks and coal soon caught and she ran downstairs to the parlour. His piano was open as they had left it, the music he had been playing still on the stand. When the fire was lit she sat on the stool and touched the keys, producing not music but an ugly discordant noise. The knock at the door distracted her from tears of self-pity.

'Algy! How good of you to come. What a wonderful surprise. Come in, it's so cold, give me your coat and sit by the fire.' She pulled a chair right up to the fender.

'Not *in* it,' he protested.

'Oh, I'm only just returned and feeling . . . You are a magician to come at such a time.' She fetched a little stool and sat opposite him. He looked drawn and tired. 'You are a kind and thoughtful friend – but so am I. I have brought you a present from France.'

'I'm not a magician, Mary. More of an emissary.'

'From?'

'Richard. He wrote asking me to come.' He turned and put his cold hands to the fire, rubbing them.

'He wrote? But why? He's still in Kent, not coming home, not *going* home until tomorrow.'

'He posted it in Dover. Did you enjoy yourselves? Did you like—'

'What *is* it, Algy? What's in the letter?' She was frightened. Why would he write when he was still with her? The memory of Sally's words still haunted her: 'It was over, he said. He had decided, nothing to do with me.'

He saw her fear, her fluttering hands, the anguish in her eyes. 'He asked me to call on you today, thinking you might be lonely, missing him.'

'Oh, what a relief.' She leant back ecstatically, forgetting she wasn't sitting in an armchair, and fell to the ground.

'Don't you think you're a little old to romp around on the floor? You still look charming, of course, like a rather large cat.' He put out a hand to help her up. 'Did you hurt yourself? You have very little flesh to cushion those bones.'

'I'm too happy to be hurt,' she said, rubbing the base of her spine. 'Did you know, Algy, that in France it is not unusual to have brandy *inside* one's coffee?'

'I have heard tell of it. Do you mention it because you intend introducing me to it?'

'I do.' She called from the kitchen. 'My present from France is a bottle of a sort of brandy, apple-ish brandy. Not unlike cider.'

'Calvados.'

'That's right. That is where we were,' she said, giving him the coffee. 'I am having mine *avec du lait, pas de fine.*'

'You were in Normandy?'

'Yes. It's nearer, you see, than Paris, so we had longer together.'

Love and passion had altered her face, whose beauty had lost its detached, ethereal quality and was now more animated; the mouth was fuller, the eyes livelier and more expressive, the whole had a delicate sensuality.

'Where were you?'

'Er . . .'

'Where?'

'I know, I can't pronounce it. I can pronounce *prestidigitateur* but not "Er".'

'Eu. Place your lips forward,' he encouraged her.

'Oo.'

'Well, my advice to you is, go to Trouville next time.'

'If you tease me you won't get your Calvados.'

'Then I won't tease. Or not till after I get it. So you're happy, Mary, are you, at last?' His voice was gentle, without the usual acerbic tone, the sense that he was waiting to pounce on an error and use it for its comic value.

'I think I am, yes, most of the time. Richard has made a life for us of sorts, you and Francis as friends – that is very important – and we do some ordinary things. It isn't only excitement and secrecy. We eat together, work here sometimes, we talk about everything, the goats, the Boer war, what to do with Home Farm, the new Labour Party, Mr MacDonald, motor cars . . . No, not everything – little is said about Fiennders Abbey, or at least . . .'

'Caroline?'

'Yes.'

The girl – he couldn't yet think of her as a woman – did not look happy now. 'You feel responsibility?'

A nod was the only reply.

'It is excessive, your sense of responsibility, Mary. You assumed a little too much for Sally and your husband and their children.'

'It's Jane Austen's fault,' was her surprising defence. 'I would like to be as good a woman as Fanny Price, but I can't.'

'*Mansfield Park* was written years ago. These are modern times.'

'I know. Sometimes I hate her.'

'She does set improbably high standards. I would forget Fanny Price. An irritating little prig. I prefer Mary Bowden.'

'Algy!'

'I don't know many marriages that were made in heaven. I should not talk to you about the Fiennders', but although it wasn't just a marriage of expedience, it was not a love match and not likely to survive their differences.'

'Hannah and Sam.'

'A love match, yes. That was made in heaven. Young Sam, the son of an excellent man, and Hannah also, the daughter of an excellent man.'

'What about the mothers?'

'I don't know about his mother, but your mother is not an excellent woman, any more than Richard's is.'

'You think that? Are you fair? It isn't because you are . . .' A slight flush touched her cheek.

'Not quite fair, no. And it isn't because I am, to quote the Marquess of Queensbury – what an apt name – a sodomite.' She gasped. 'Have I shocked you?'

'Yes! My word, Algy, you are . . . extraordinary! I love you being so forthright.' She laughed delightedly. 'Nobody has ever . . . I have never in my life heard that word said by anyone.'

'I like women, Mary, but circumstances have worked against them. It is easier for a man to be fine and noble, though many aren't, and easier for a woman to be devious and practical. If not easier, necessary.'

'You do understand. I *try* to understand my mother's parsimony, but it hurts when I hear her spoken of as a lickpenny, and I can't deny it because it's true.'

'Lickpenny. What an exact word.'

'More coffee? More brandy?'

'No, if you are all right, I will go soon.' But he sat looking at the fire, silent.

'Are *you* all right? And Francis?'

'Oh, yes. But, apropos heaven, I am giving it up.'

'Giving up your living? Little Bewdley? Why?'

'When I was ordained, I didn't have a vocation. To me it was a profession, how I earned my living, how I eked out my small income. It has become a vocation now and I don't feel worthy of it. And I am too tired and old to wrestle with my conscience.'

'Now, you *have* shocked me. I consider you to be a

really good man. I know you must have given great help to others because you have to me and I am not special. Have people like me—' Oh dear, this was hard, thinking about the past and pain received and given. 'Have people like me corrupted you? Baptizing illegitimate babies, condoning adultery, causing you to be disloyal to friends – well, to Richard's wife?' She leant forward and took his hands. 'I am – I am very distressed for you, it isn't right. All the care and help you've given, and I haven't returned the care. Don't do anything yet. Talk to me, talk to people.'

'Thank you, Mary, but I have decided, written to the bishop. The help I've given should have come from a layman not a man of the cloth and,' he smiled, at the earnest face, 'I doubt that you could corrupt anyone.'

'I like your Mr Roper, Mary. Not what I expected at first, comical like, then when he got down to business, proper serious he was.'

'That's true, Ma. When he's working he even looks taller, and not so tubby! Now, anything else you want to do in Wellsbury, seeing that I have my trap? Any shopping?'

'It's a pleasure just sitting in it, love. Smell of the leather, all spanking new. Worries me, though, you know, you going through your little bit of cash.'

No little bit of cash would have paid for this trap, but no harm in her mother thinking so. 'I got it for a bargain, Ma – bankruptcy sale and the axle needed fixing.'

Her mother smiled, able to enjoy the comfort at the expense of some unfortunate bankrupt. Mary, irritated by her usual penny-pinching, had to remind herself the insolvent gentleman didn't exist. Richard was hardly that.

'I don't want to spend any money, Mary, but if you've the time I'd like a ride out, go through some of the hill villages, a bit of a detour on the way home. What do you think?'

'I'd like that too.' She squeezed her mother's hand affectionately.

'You've got time then? Don't have to get to the forge?'

'Hanny is there all morning, and she is the best – by far – at the post office, and Dot is there this afternoon with Biddy, so I am a lady of leisure.'

'This is a treat for me, love. We don't see much of you now you're at the Pightle.'

'You've seen plenty of me, what with the wedding, and Bertie too. He's a rarer bird than I am.'

'He only come when I wrote I was making my will.' She laughed – but there had been a half-truth in it. She knew her children well enough.

'I don't want to pry, Ma, but I hope you've seen Bertie right with your little savings. He lost out to my John with the keepering and it was that, knowing he'd be head-keeper, made him feel safe enough to marry Dot. I'm more than all right with my cottage, and Hannah and Sam, well, they're just perfect in their place, perfect all round.'

Emma Bowden smiled, a sly secret smile. 'Bertie's there in the will, you all are.' How needy he was she was beginning to doubt. There was the wedding present. And this morning at the railway station, he wouldn't let them see him off, hadn't got it right neither, about where to change for High Wycombe. They were passing through the tiny hamlet of Up Riddings. On the left was a terrace of ancient cottages all leaning together as if for comfort and protection against the winds that blew in winter, uninterrupted by any barrier, through the valleys. Some cottage women were gathered at the middle gate gossiping, but they stopped to stare at the unusual sight of a smart pony and trap trotting down the rough lane scattering chickens pecking in the dust and idle cats supine in the midday sun. Emma smiled graciously out at the women and raised a gloved hand.

'Stop it, Ma. Anybody would think you were the old Queen herself.'

'I hope as how I don't look like her.'

'Not yet, but if the wind turns you might, so don't act like her. You're no better than any of those women.'

'Well, Mary, I don't know that any of those women have a daughter who owns her own cottage and a new carriage.'

'Trap.'

'Trap, then. And how many of those women have been to a solicitor this morning to make a will, I ask you?'

'A lady wouldn't boast about that.'

'I'm not boasting, I'm telling you.' She gave one last little wave and what she hoped was a dignified but kind smile, and settled back against the leather-padded seat.

'It's beautiful up here, isn't it, Ma? You can see for miles.'

'Yes, I suppose so. Wouldn't want to live here. Did you see their faces?'

She had. The women were lined before their time, skins weather-beaten, their faces thin and pinched in contrast to their bodies, which were sturdy from hard work and fat from an endless diet of bacon and potatoes.

'Why don't you eat breakfast at the dower house?' The sight of Tommy reading *his* newspaper, eating *his* grilled bacon was, as usual, very irritating.

His young brother didn't look up from the newspaper and spoke through a mouthful of toast. 'Mother doesn't keep as good a table as you do, Ruthie, and I am not sure this *is* breakfast. I've been up all night playing cards.'

'Where?'

'In the card-room.'

'Where? Which card-room? Where?'

'Here, old chap, of course.'

'I do not have a card-room, Tommy.'

'We've set up some tables in Father's old study.'

'We?'

'I have – don't lose your temper – with permission and assistance from your lady wife.'

'What are you talking about? Caroline doesn't play cards.'

'You should spend more time at home, Ruthie. You might learn a little about what your wife does do.'

Richard decided not to react. He wouldn't shout, as he wished to, 'Don't call me Ruthie, and he wouldn't tell him to speak with more respect for his wife, and he wouldn't tell him to get out of the house, although that would be effected. 'You are right. This business I'm involved in does take me away too much.' He helped himself to coffee and sat at the end of the table. The bloody cheek of the boy, sitting at the head of the table too. No doubt if the post had come he would be opening that with the letter-knife. Tommy put down the paper untidily and smiled. The pouches under his eyes were attractive in such a young man: he looked debauched but saveable. Richard could see what the ladies found desirable in him.

'Where was it your business took you last night?'

'London. I'm investing, not much, in a British Car Syndicate. Might be worthwhile, bit of a gamble. And what about your gambling? Who did you play with last night?' Richard was exasperated.

'Cathal, Ralph Wittenham, a friend of his, Branley—'

'Wittenham? Good God, Tommy. That's very high stakes. I hope you know what you're doing.'

'I did have rather a good IOU from Ralph, but sadly, last night, he reduced it by a couple of thousand.'

'You don't think it strange, Mamma, that the children don't like him? Even Elizabeth? She who would like the attention of the entire world?'

'I don't know what to say, Richard. Like you, I don't want him in my house, he's so . . . upsetting, so disruptive. I'm sorry, darling, but when he's using the Abbey as his headquarters, when you're away, well, I'm pleased. And I know I shouldn't be.'

'I was intending to give him Home Farm, or a life tenancy and the income, but now it's out of the question.'

'Oh, no, of course not.' She had felt it her duty as a mother to protect Tommy, and had hoped that all the unpleasant decisions would be made and carried out by Richard. But any thought of Tommy staying in Findlesham, at Home Farm, made her drop her motherly façade. 'He would turn it into a – a gambling den or a—'

'Bordello?'

'Or an inn!'

'Well, that's enough to be going on with.'

'What do you suggest we do?' she said pathetically. 'Buy him a house in . . .' She tried to think of the least accessible county. 'Northumberland? Give him an income? Try to break his trusts? He is never going to take anything up, the Army or the Church. I have talked to him about getting a living somewhere.'

'Pity the poor parishioners.'

'And as for the Army, well, we could buy him a commission in a regiment I suppose but—'

'Again, what regiment would take him, when told that his family wouldn't be responsible for his debts?'

'What then?'

Richard picked up one of the enamel patch-boxes sitting on her dressing-table and examined the inscription, *When this you see pray think on me though many miles you distant be.* 'Have you missed anything, Mamma, since he has been at home?'

'Oh, Richard. How sad. Yes, I had hoped it wasn't him. You too?'

'Yes. Quite a few little items. Some of the silver is missing. I've "mislaid" cufflinks and a lovely little Della Robbia – he probably sold it for nothing. I would rather he had sold it back to me!' He picked up another of the little boxes, green with an inscription in pink, *Love and be happy.* 'You should give him this,' he said, holding it up. 'But I think we act on this,' showing her the former.

'What shall we do?'

'A certain amount is already done. I have seen a solicitor and we are no longer legally responsible for his debts. Some of them I have paid however, but not his gambling IOUs. My plan is not to break his trusts again. He should have the opportunity of living properly, if he decides to. Who knows, he might change in five or ten years.'

'And then again he might not.'

'I'm going to make over to him the income from the Shropshire property you brought into the family.'

'All that mining stock?'

'Yes, until his trusts mature, on the proviso that he stays out of the country. That is a kindness, really, because whether he accepts or not, the legal notice about the debts will be published and he wouldn't enjoy that sort of notoriety. He doesn't mind being known as a rakehell and womanizer but the ignominy of public knowledge of his failure to honour his debts would hurt. And I've instructed all the staff that his presence here is not welcome.'

'Isn't that rather cruel?'

'Very cruel, I would say. I thought this would be the last resort until I realized it *was* the last resort. It isn't a question, is it, of high spirits, or youthful irresponsibility? He is a corrupting influence.'

Ann nodded. Was he worried about Caroline, more than the children? 'His drinking sets a bad example.'

'If you're thinking about Caroline, she doesn't need a bad example. Sorry, Mamma, I shouldn't have said that. She's a good mother to the boys, at least, and is liked by everyone on the estate. Oh, Christ! This whole thing is absolutely bloody! Sorry again. I hate doing this to

Tommy and to the family.' He was still holding the little box, looking around the room as if he had never seen it before, surprised to be in her bedroom, with the remnants of breakfast on a tray.

'Would you like that? Would you like to give it to Caroline?'

He smiled and kissed her affectionately. 'I would like it.'

They were sitting quietly together outside the cottage, comfortable with each other, both enjoying the music, though neither paying close attention, Algernon admiring the sound of the flute, and thinking of the flautist, Mary the piano and the pianist. All the windows were open, letting in the warm, sweet-smelling air and letting out the sounds of Schubert. Algernon beckoned Mary to sit nearer, pulling at her wicker chair. She leaned towards him expecting him to speak, but he took her left hand twisting the gold ring on her finger.

'It isn't my old . . .'

'I know,' he said with difficulty. 'I hope nobody else does.' The music ended and, with great relief, he coughed. 'Artists! They take every cough, every sneeze as a personal affront, and amateurs,' he tipped his head towards the window, 'they object to one's breathing, using anger as a cover for inadequacy.'

'Sh, sh. They'll hear.' He coughed again. 'Is that hay fever, Algy, or your summer cold?' Her concern was concealed by a bright smile.

'Would you accept a summer fever?'

'No more than a hay cold.'

'How are you getting on with your recorder, Mary?'

'Not so well that I wouldn't welcome coughs and sneezes to drown it! I like playing it, though. Do you know I can catch the pony with it? Both she and the donkey come trotting up to the fence if I stand over there and play it.'

Algernon gazed out over the idyllic scene, lush green fields rolling away to poppy-studded wheat. 'Is a donkey a good substitute for a cow?'

'Joe Hogg gives me all the milk and cream I need, enough to make butter as well, so I exchanged the cow for Dolly.'

'The donkey?'

'Dolly, the donkey, yes. She's company for Terpsy.'

'Terpsy?'

'The pony. Terpsichore. She was bred from Little Dancer.' A spasm of pain crossed her face. 'I don't want to forget George. It would be wrong to, well, bury the memory of John's father. Do you see?'

'I do see.' He patted her hand, the music resumed and they lapsed into silence. Mary rearranged the rug on Algernon's lap and the parasol fixed to the back of her chair. In the late afternoon some of the flowers wilted a little, losing their brilliance in the shadows formed by the slowly setting sun. Geraniums softened from a sharp scarlet to a softer, muted red, blue delphiniums faded to the colour of forget-me-nots, but the night-scented stock and nicotiana – planted in clumps of varying white under the window – asserted themselves, filling the air with their scent.

★

'What has been heard from Tommy? I notice no mention of him from Richard at luncheon.'

'That is because . . .' She paused and announced importantly, 'We have had a very serious disagreement about him – a fight!'

How touching, Algernon thought. 'A fight' was a proof of the relationship, reassuringly prosaic. Something normal. 'A fight? I am very pleased for you, Mary. But why about Tommy?'

'It was so horrible, Algy, letting everybody, the whole world, know about his debts. How could he? It was printed in things that people buy. Whatever Bertie might do, or did, I would never betray him like that.'

'I doubt if your mysterious brother would ever find himself in the position to borrow vast sums of money on the strength of your family name and then saddle you with his debts. What would you think if he could, and by so doing, you lost this house?'

She turned her head away from the garden, farmland, little stream and distant thatch of the Hoggs' farm to examine the sun-golden bricks and long windows of her beloved house. 'It would be terrible, I love it so, I can't imagine not being here – *it* not being here. But I would put Bertie first.'

'Absolute twaddle! Good gracious, Mary, I thought you had grown out of such sentimental peasant thinking. This time next year who will have remembered, or care, about young Thomas Fiennders and a bad debt or two? Just think of what what has happened already in 1900. The Boer War continues.'

'But Mafeking was relieved.'

'Quite so. Man has flown. Imagine that! Imagine the Zeppelin.'

'July the first, George's fortieth birthday.'

'Mary, I will remind you that George is not, or was not, here to enjoy his fortieth birthday. Look, you have made me cough—'

'I'll get you some water. What an interesting year. And the Olympic Games in Paris too.'

'Women competing for the first time. That will be of considerably more import than an unpleasant young man's peccadilloes.'

'Ah, and the young prince dying. Poor Queen Victoria.'

Holding his handkerchief to his mouth, he coughed again through his laughter. Had she been teasing him? In part, perhaps.

'Do you really think I'm a peasant?'

'I do. The very best of peasants, all that is good and true, as well as silly and sentimental.' He put up a hand to touch her face, neither peasant nor patrician, just beautiful. 'It is no wonder that he loves you – Richard. Get me that water.'

She carried the tall glass of cool water through the stone-flagged hall, treading softly, but unable to resist a peek into the parlour. They had been playing something delicate and mournful but Richard heard her and, glancing over his shoulder with a grin, changed to a sprightly mazurka. She whispered, 'Sorry,' and crept out into the sunlight. The piano could still be heard, the jaunty sound drifting through the window, the flute silent, when she realized that Algernon wasn't asleep. Lifting his head she saw the trickle of blood from the corner of his mouth.

How appropriate that the music was Chopin's. Was that thought sentimental? She didn't wipe her eyes; her tears dried in the sun.

Why should she feel so guilty? She had been very good to him, only a second cousin, after all. There had been a time, it was true, a few years only, when she had been less kind: no financial help, no gifts of wine, no horses loaned, invitations to dinner less frequent, but when Thomas had died their friendship had resumed. He had been welcome at the dower house with Francis – who didn't appear to be here, tactful of him – and Caroline had entertained them often at the Abbey. She had nothing to blame herself for – and yet . . . There was Issy's husband, the Hon. Freddy Boring, as Algy called him, officiating at Algy's funeral in Algy's church. *He* had been given the infinitely more valuable living of Findlesham, which had been all but promised to Algy himself. The ritual of the funeral continued. She hardly noticed it, standing, sitting, responding automatically. At her age, friends and relations were dying. There were more funerals than christenings, it seemed. The church was full, with an overflow in the porch and the little lane outside, as it had been in his lifetime, with the same worshippers, and all were there willingly from affection and respect. Would it be so at her own funeral in St Michael's? ANN ELIZABETH FIENNDERS BELOVED WIFE OF THOMAS R.I.P. She shivered. She could see Richard looking at her with surprise. It wasn't cold.

★

'Thank you, Mary, but I don't want anything.'

'Nothing? Nothing to eat or . . .'

'Nothing. I just want to sit here. I am pleased to be here with you and when I know it is all over I will eat, drink and talk, I expect, but for now just sit quietly with me, please.'

She leaned back in her chair and closed her eyes. It was one of those curiosities in life: Algernon's closest friends couldn't be at his funeral – it wasn't 'correct', they both knew that. Correct or not, she didn't want to see Richard in public with his wife. Sally had gone and would report on all that she considered important – what Lady Caroline and Mrs Fiennders wore, how many wreaths and who had gone to the ale-house after. She would know *that*, because, she said, she was old enough to go to one and be respectable.

It was September the second. She had woken this morning alone. Richard wouldn't be here until tomorrow, September the third. He hadn't been here since August the thirty-first. After washing, drinking her tea, making the bed, preparing lunch for herself and Francis, she had sat at the dressing-table and slowly and methodically manicured her nails, then burnished the little silver tools with a piece of chamois leather. The small patch-box, Battersea enamel, *Love and be happy*, sat on the centre of the table. Inside it Richard had put a beauty patch, not one of the tiny dots that ladies had used in the olden days, but a piece of black cotton big enough to cover the end of her nose. Francis stirred. She peeped at him through half-opened eyes. He uncrossed his legs and stretched them, then folded his hands and stretched his arms above his head. She waited for him to speak, but he settled back, still staring, sightless, out of the window. She moved her hands from the arms of her chair to her lap, flattening them over her stomach. Over the years of talking to women, she had listened to their gossip, the exchange of hints and mutual advice, what to do before, during and after. How to avoid falling for one, what to do if you had. How to tell before the month came round, what the signs were. If you missed a month, was it too late to do anything? How to bring it on. What was the difference between just missing a month and being *in* the way? The lore about it was immense: 'Never lie with a man at the new moon', 'Don't eat for six hours before', 'Don't let him eat for six hours before', 'Don't *you* eat for six hours after – it starves the baby', 'Drink pints of water before', would that drown the baby? 'Don't do it lying on your back', 'Go for a walk after', 'Jump up and down after'. There was logical advice as well, like, 'Don't let it happen inside you'. And the advice if all of this failed was as extensive: 'Hot baths', 'Gin', 'Walking up hills', 'Cold baths with mustard', 'Hot baths with feverfew', 'A sponge soaked in vinegar inserted', 'Run up and downstairs backwards', 'Purgatives', 'Pints of salt water', 'An infusion of rue'. On and on and on. If she did everything, it might well work. Smiling, she touched the tip of her nose.

'It isn't that comical, Mary.' He had been watching her, worried by the vertical frown lines that kept appearing between her eyebrows. Even with her eyes shut he could see the anxiety mark her face.

'Richard thinks it is. He says if the brim of my bonnet was two yards round, my nose would still poke out!'

'Are you all right, Mary?'

'Are *you* all right?' She touched his cheek. 'So hard for you, dear Francis.'

'Yes, but good to be with you. I think I *would* like something to eat now.'

'Good, I have a baked ham.'

'Some funeral baked meats – but they won't furnish forth a marriage table. What is it, Mary?'

She was pale and shaking. 'This is a terrible time, a bad time to ask, but I can't think of anything else. I was sure this morning, it was September the second.'

'It will be September the second all day.' He gave a little laugh which she ignored.

'They say you always know. I didn't know exactly but I've thought it was possible – no, probable. Oh, Francis, we have been so happy, more, but something has always been there, lurking, waiting for us—'

He took her shoulders firmly and said, 'I think I know what it is, Mary.'

But she babbled on, still trembling and inarticulate. 'I'll have to go away. Where should I go? Oxford? London? Which would you prefer? I want to be pleased about it, and I don't want – I hate the thought of leaving the Pightle, and you're the only person who could, but what about Sally? How could I think of all this today? I should think of you. I should think of Algy.'

'Mary, be quiet. Be quiet or I will pick you up and shake you and that might damage the baby.'

That quietened her but only for a moment. 'The baby? You know?'

'It is obvious. Please, let us get our lunch, a glass of wine and—'

'Obvious? Does it show?' She patted her flat stomach. 'Not in that way. Lunch!'

She fetched the ham and potatoes, pickled beetroot and bread, while he laid the table and opened the wine, poured it, drinking his own in two large gulps and refilling the glass.

'It is a very appropriate day, in fact, to talk about our future – hush! Algy and I have discussed this very thing many times and what should be done about it.' He piled his plate with slices of ham, helped himself to potatoes and took half the jar of beetroot. 'It's extraordinary. I am ravenous. Maybe *I* am eating for two.' Mary followed his example with the wine, but spluttered on the second gulp. He reached across and took the glass from her. 'You don't need that, dear girl.'

She wiped her chin and replaced the bright red-checked napkin on her lap. 'No, I don't.' They stared at each other across the table. 'Francis, will you marry me?'

'Of course,' he said carving another slice of ham. 'I would be delighted. But . . .' he looked at her sternly '. . . I don't want a long engagement.'

A very small wedding, as she had told Mrs Fiennders, very small. Emma Bowden had been at the dower house letting out some of Ann Fiennders' clothes. With Davis gone, and not replaced, she had been up there quite a lot, good money so no bother. And with Dot doing all, well, most of the housework at Keepers Cottage these days, she had time on her hands. A wedding in that quarter was unexpected to say the least. And why? Mary had all she needed now; if she was lonely, she had only to say. Emma herself would be happy to keep her company on visits and trips. That trap was very comfortable.

'A very small wedding, Emma? What a surprise! Not that the wedding will be small, but that there will be one at all.' Ann laid out a russet wool tight-bodiced dress. 'This also needs releasing just a little. Dr Henders says corsets shouldn't be worn too tight, especially if one is an active woman.'

Or, if one is a fat woman, Emma thought, smugly running her hands down her own narrow hips.

She was getting scrawny, Ann could see, a mistake, that, very ageing. A small wedding, damnation! Two spare men gone, poor old Algy, and now his friend. Mr and Mrs Francis Clarke. Foolish of him, he could have done better than that. An irritation still, the girl, but those slender, boyish looks *would* appeal to a man like that. But there was other news of a brighter sort. She flashed a charming smile at Emma Bowden – she could afford to be gracious – everything at Fiennders Abbey had suddenly improved. Certain fears that she had had were unfounded if what she had guessed was true, and with Tommy gone – where was he, Africa somewhere? Sugar plantations. Did they grow sugar in Africa? And Maud living in London . . .

'There isn't much to let out here, Mrs Fiennders.' Emma showed her the lining where the seams had been strained to tearing point.

'No, indeed.' Impulsively she bundled it up and thrust

it into Emma's arms. 'You have it, dear. Russet isn't your colour, but you could wear it at "the small wedding".'

It was when they were on honeymoon – all three of them – safe, lost in the crowds of London, that Richard had told her about Caroline. His mother had guessed, and, too pleased to keep it to herself, had hinted archly at the 'good' news. He had observed his wife discreetly. It would explain her recent overtures, which had been repulsed by him as tenderly as possible; his happiness didn't require her sadness or shame. It would also explain the new control of her drinking. The overtures had not only been sexual, she had attempted to regain their friendship, recalling memories of times past; but it was painful, the pressure of feigned nostalgia.

He had confronted her with his suspicions in what used to be *their* bedroom but was now used exclusively by her. She was wearing a slippery satin pink nightdress that revealed the protuberant stomach and defined navel of a pregnant woman. He noticed that the pink material didn't clash with her gingery-red hair, but looked ugly against the mottled pink of her skin. He had offered her a divorce. 'Surely Andrew will want to claim his own child? We can all talk about this reasonably, I am sure, if only Louise Osmund knows. She *must* know. Why else does she spend so much time away? It will shock our parents more than our friends. This is the twentieth century, after all.' He wasn't really surprised when she slapped his face in what was growing to be her inevitable response to his lack of reaction. It was deserved. He had shown no anger, no shock, and no distress. Remembering his own forthcoming fatherhood, it was difficult not to laugh at the humour of the situation. He realized it must be galling for her to see her husband receive news of adultery and its consequences with a smile.

He had not smiled when reporting it to Mary. The pregnancy of his wife had tainted his pleasure in that of his mistress. 'Everything will go on as usual. The child will be presented as mine. I don't even know if Andrew knows. I don't like it, but I will accept it for now, and it certainly frees me, us, from any guilt.'

She lay in his arms, her head on his shoulder. The noise of the traffic filtered through the heavy curtains. 'Not altogether,' she said softly. The news had made her feel a little sick; the long line of loveless marriages, infidelities and ill-kept secrets pulled at her conscience. But, as Francis had said later, a divorce would have made no difference to her. She never could and wouldn't want to be the mistress of Fiennders Abbey.

'It's difficult to know, Mary, when to call. You keep yourself to yourself so much these days.'

'Well, I *am* married, you know, Hanny.' The noise of the men working on the barn nearly drowned their conversation. She closed the bedroom windows.

'Ah, mebbe you are newly wed, but you'd shut yourself off before that. I'm not criticizing, love, but – oh, Lord! I remember that!'

The manicure set lay open on the dressing-table, the silver glinting in the sunlight. She laughed. 'If Sam knew what I'd done – before his time, though – to get that to you . . . That's really why I've come, Mary.'

'To do your nails, Hanny?' Her voice wasn't cold, but it contained a warning.

'No reason, Mary, to talk like that. I'll say my piece, and if you want, I'll be gone and won't talk of it no more.'

'I don't know what *piece* you have to say, Hannah, but I would appreciate you not—'

'I'm your sister, woman, and younger, yes, but at our age it don't figure.'

'*Doesn't* figure.'

'Yes, so stop being all schoolmarm with me and listen. There's only one thing I don't know but what I can guess at, though, all else I know. You and Richard Fiennders have always been sweethearts – don't interrupt. I've seen him in olden days, look at you and you at him. I know the mannycure was from him, and of course it was plain it could come to nothing, or so folks thought. All knew, Mary love, that you and George was over before it took.'

Mary averted her pinched, angry face.

'We reckoned – Sam and me – you'd have a good enough life teachering and with the shop after George—'

Mary interrupted impatiently, 'I did. I had a good enough life after George died. So what is it you're saying now? You always were a good story-teller.'

'No, I wasn't. I was good at sums. It's simple, no story-telling, and nothing I've said, to no one.'

'*Anyone.*'

'Yes – let me finish now! You took up with him since you got this cottage. Maybe before.'

'No, not before.' She had forgotten her sister's guile.

Hannah smiled broadly. 'After, then. Thank you. You married Mr Clarke, who is *not* the marrying kind, if you get my meaning, because . . .' she took a deep breath, 'because, Mary Bowden, *you* are having a baby. And that there barn . . .' she gestured out of the window, 'is being made into a snug little home—'

'A snug little school-room and study, for my husband.'

'A snug little *home* for Mr Clarke! And if you're not with child you must be at the butter and cream, noon till night, for you've grown up here,' she cupped her breasts, 'and look like a proper woman.' She thought better of that. 'Nearly.'

Mary shrugged her shoulders, defeated.

'Good. Er . . . I've lost my drift.'

'Really, Hanny? I'd have thought you'd lost your breath.'

'No, so, let's say you're two months gone, yes?'

'Yes.'

'I'll come and see to your lying-in, no midwife needed, no midwife to talk then. You being here, out of the run of things, no one need know straight way *and* you're fortunate, for it's my thinking that young Dot is with child too, and that will take the eye off you.'

'Dot? Ma and Pa's first great-grandchild!'

'Your first grandchild.'

'Do I look like a grandmother? Oh, Hanny. What a thing, all these babies!'

'And that brings us to the last thing. There's been talk on and off, up at the house, of all going not so well, for a time now – you hear it from the kitchen-maids and the gardener's boy, the young groom, the forester, talk of carryings-on, hot temper, but nothing you could pin down. Then, sudden-like—'

'*Suddenly.*'

'Yes, all think all is well, for m'lady is to have her fifth. I'd be that sad, Mary, if he – if Master Richard . . .' She trailed away, awkwardly.

'It's all right, Hanny. But I can't talk of it.' Mary's smile was enough to convince her sister. 'It isn't my secret, you see.'

'I do see. A secret told isn't a secret no more.'

'*Any more.*'

'Yes. I'll be gone then for now.' She turned back from the door. 'Are you happy now, Mary?'

'Yes.' She sounded surprised. 'We are happy now, Richard and I . . .' Later that day as she watched him leaving, vanishing into the wood, she lit the first oil lamp of the evening and saw the echo of a lamp being lit in the barn. Then she finished the sentence silently, '. . . and I think we will always be.'

1990

Roper, sons & roper. The brass plate had been polished
that morning, the stone steps washed and chalked, the
night's detritus from the nearby pub and take-away kebab
house swept away and only a faded scrawled graffito,
Windelsham boys suck, spoilt the immaculate façade of the
old house. The faint smell of stale urine, being added to
night after night, was probably impossible to eliminate.
Neon strip-lighting visible through all the windows
showed that the whole building was used as offices. A
disembodied voice filtered through the grille under the
bell. 'Mr Clarke? Push the front door now, please, and
make sure, if you will, that it shuts behind you. We're on
the second floor.'

Richard knew that he was being observed as closely
as he was examining the photographs lining the walls of
the office.

'Yes, it's been more than a hobby with all of us
Ropers. The law might well be the hobby and photog-
raphy the career! We were all good enough to be professional.' He said this calmly, as a matter of universally
accepted fact. 'For instance, Mr Clarke.' He led him away
from the modern photographs, in narrow steel frames or
mounted unframed on clear plastic, to the wall behind

the large desk, where sepia-coloured photographs hung in Victorian mahogany frames. 'This is your grandmother, Mrs Jackson as she was then, before she married your grandfather.'

He coughed, cleared his throat, tapped his nose, rocked back on his heels and squinted slyly at his visitor who, feeling he ought to respond, raised his eyebrows quizzically, looked at the floor, kicked away a non-existent piece of fluff, raised his shoulders to his ears and said, 'Putative or progenitive.' A performance, he thought, that would not disgrace a BBC half-hour sitcom.

'Quite so. Now then, you see how modern my great-grandfather's ideas were? He was recording the refurbishment, the rebuilding of your house, The Pightle. He used Mrs Jackson as a focus for the arch of the doorway, the transom, but her head as you can see is turned away. Clearly he didn't want it to be the portrait of a woman – oh, no – but the portrait of a house!'

Richard nodded his agreement. 'Very avant-garde. Though might she not have looked over her shoulder at the last minute? Er . . . no . . . well . . . silly of me,' he corrected himself hastily.

Mr Roper's expression of hurt and disbelief was followed by a condescending smile. 'We both come from artistic families, but our talents take different directions.' He added, 'I have all your compact discs. Fortunately there aren't many – so expensive, you know.'

'No, there aren't many.' Richard felt apologetic. 'After all, I'm hardly Sviatslav Richter!'

'You are not . . . he. *He* isn't English.'

What could he mean? That there was a conspiracy

among record companies not to record English concert pianists? Richard sat in the chair indicated.

'So, to work.' Herbert Roper sat behind the large partner's desk. 'I *should* advise you to save your money consulting me – compulsory purchase orders are seldom overturned – but in this case I am willing to advise you without fee, because—'

'Really, no. That's not—'

'I – am – outraged. I – am – disgusted. I – am – filled – with – despair . . .' he thumped the table for emphasis with his fat little fist '. . . that this wretched country should even think of destroying that house, that barn, that wood, that pond. I am lost for words!' He had risen during this speech, not that there was far to rise, and waved a pamphlet under Richard's nose. 'I am legal adviser to NMAFF – No Motorway Access for Findlesham.' He frowned. 'Not a very good acronym, I'm afraid.'

'Very refreshing, Mr Roper. It says what you want it to say. I sometimes think the acronym comes before the cause.'

'How true. Thank you.'

'If you want a catchier one, you could call it NAFF – No Access for Findlesham.'

'Too late.' The solicitor sighed. 'It's probably all too late. It would have helped if you had taken up occupancy when the tenants left. I say that more in sorrow than in anger.'

'Yes, but at the time I had concerts in Prague and then Venezuela.'

A deeper sigh accompanied, 'Such a pity you can't get work here. The Sheldonian in Oxford. They put on very nice concerts.'

'Perhaps, when all this is settled, I might—'

'So much to settle.'

'Yes. At least I'm meeting my aunt Kate at last, this afternoon. I'm going out to Home Farm. Try to make her see reason. She'd be much better off at Fiennders Abbey.'

'Very difficult. But there is a strain of parsimony on both sides of the family. It comes down through the female sides, inherited like that hair.' He gestured to a photograph on the side wall. 'Your grandmother again.'

Richard rose to look at it.

'That hair is almost white. She was lovely, ageless; I mean, she could have been born today. So slender. My grandfather was more than a touch in love with her – that has been passed down too, inherited.'

'Does that mean that *you*'re in love with me?'

They both laughed, the little round man clapping his pudgy hands. 'Let me give you this before you go.' He handed over a thick file of legal documents. 'My daughter copied these papers, everything pertaining to you.'

'Your daughter?'

'Yes. She's "*and Roper*". My father is "*Roper*", my brother and I "*Sons*". Do you see?' The intercom buzzer rang. 'Miss McKenna? Please push the door and make sure—'

A little laugh could be heard and a shouted, 'I know!'

'One of the committee of NMAFF, an experienced demonstrator.'

'Then I must go. An experienced demonstrator wouldn't be good for my jet-lag. I'll call you, Mr Roper, and tell you how I get on with my aunt.'

'Don't be hard on her. She's a survivor, but ninety, well, that must be considered.'

Richard passed Miss McKenna, member of NMAFF, on the stairs. She was wearing the obligatory black. Black leather boots, heavy enough to last the lifetime of a farm-labourer but that would last only as long as the fashion. Her short, tight Lycra skirt was also black, as was the cotton T-shirt printed with the ambiguous message WORK TO RULE. Her hair, too, was black, framing a pale face, enlivened only by the eyes which were as blue as a kitten's.

'Hi!' she said, pulling the black rubber back-pack out of the way, but otherwise ignoring him as she clumped up the stairs.

He looked back after her, disappointed that he couldn't quite see up her skirt. He wondered if her knickers were black too.

Where the town of Wellsbury ended, or was supposed to, Findlesham began, as one county gave way to another. Which was responsible for the endless ribbon development, straggling in a long line to the horizon and beyond, was unclear; the boundaries had changed so often and all the political parties had had their share of power. No one had a monopoly on bad planning. The development had started slowly in the late forties and accelerated in the sixties. By the time most of Findlesham was declared an Area of Outstanding Natural Beauty the damage had been done. The houses nearest the town were now all rooming-houses and bed-and-breakfasts – or small hotels as they preferred to call themselves – their front gardens cemented over and packed with cars. The only sign of vegetation was the weeds that poked through cracks in the cement, dusty dandelions lending a splash of colour, the yellow relieving the dirty grey uniformity. The beauty lay well behind the houses: fields and meadows, brooks and woods, changed but still quintessentially English in their small domestic detail. Nearly all the old barns had become houses, the conversions eliminating most of the details that had made them attractive. Hedges had been ripped out to make larger fields and replaced, if at all, with barbed-wire. Here and there, pine trees and other fast-growing evergreens stood where oak, beech and ash once flourished and new crops brightened the landscape. Huge swathes of oil-seed rape, of a yellow so intense it looked like an explosion in a paint factory, grew beside the more traditional fields of wheat and barley.

Richard lowered his window, hoping to smell the scents of the countryside glimpsed through the gaps, but the fumes of the traffic greeted him as they would in London, New York or Paris. His driver, a local man, more than pleased to be hired for the day, was driving a beautifully kept old Wolseley, which smelled of leather and polish. Not 'any old polish', as he had explained, but local beeswax obtainable from the shop – 'booteek', he said – down from the garage. The honey from the bees was also available, as were china beehives made locally by a potter who shared converted stables with other crafts-people.

'Craftspeople'. 'Crafts' was said with scorn, and 'people' was spat out. 'Craftspeople, you know, not crafts-men, that's what you have to call them, so's not to offend the craftswomen.'

Richard caught his eye in the driving-mirror and made

what he hoped were suitable noises indicating an amused fraternity. 'Let the little woman have her way.'

Although only a few miles, it was a slow journey punctuated by traffic lights, pinch points, stretches of red tarmac leading to 30 m.p.h. signs and all the usual paraphernalia of failed attempts to control traffic. A filter-left lane was heralded by a gigantic sign,

BERREFORD – GOLF!!! KEEP LEFT.

The club-house was visible, set on the edge of the greens: a huge, ginger brick building with maroon wood window-frames and a shallow, pitched roof, looking like a giant misshapen cottage as designed by a child – the ubiquitous architecture of rural supermarkets.

'We're not behind the times here, d'you see, Mr Clarke. There, look . . .' The driver pointed to another road sign,

SUPERSTORE – KEEP RIGHT.

'Not that it's what I'd call a superstore, not as big as the one outside Oxford. New it is, since your dad's time, anyhow.'

'This is all new, isn't it, since his time? All this.' Richard waved a hand at the bumper-to-bumper traffic. 'All this must have been farmland.'

'And woodland. This here part of the dual-carriage-way was a thicket once, thousand years old, they say. The supermarket's a big help, though. My wife does our weekly shop up there and a big monthly do at the cash and carry. That way we saves time fiddling around in the little shops.'

'Save time, Bill? For what?'

'The wife, see, she works in the business, takes the calls, a secretary like, does the books. Very good with figures and when we're pushed for drivers, she does that too. And when the new access road starts and the service station, well, my trade's going to drop off at the garage. Won't be selling so much petrol. We'll need— Excuse me, Richard . . . sir.' He picked up the ringing mobile phone, flourishing it ostentatiously. 'Hello, hello?' He shook it impatiently. 'Can't hear a bloody thing.'

Richard leaned over the front seat. 'I think you're supposed to pull up the aerial,' he said.

'Ah, yes. Right you are, of course.' Tugging at the aerial he steered an erratic course, accelerating through an amber light, slowing at a green one and changing lanes without using his indicator.

Richard gripped the centre arm-rest. 'Perhaps I can help, Bill. Why don't I take it?' He grabbed the phone, extended the aerial and answered it. 'Hello.'

'Thank you, sir. Tell them we'll be at Home Farm in about ten minutes.'

As they approached Richard could see a motor-bike leaning against the hedge, the owner's helmet dangling from the handle-bars, as the Wolseley bumped slowly down the unmade-up drive.

'She's as stubborn as ground-elder, Miss Kate. I asks you, why not make up this here path? Nice bit of tarmac, wouldn't cost too much. And why don't she get a garage? The dairies would make a lovely garage.' He manoeuvred the car round a deep rut, cursing. 'Bugger me if I don't tell her I won't bring the Wolseley down this again. I've got meself a perfectly good new second-hand four-wheel-drive, but she insists on this and you know what, sir, Mr Clarke, Richard, sir?' He couldn't make up his mind. It was awkward like, them being cousins, sort of, in a way. He pushed his thick stubby fingers through the dry blond hair that sprouted from his head like wheat stubble. They were second cousins, twice removed, his dad had said, though to his way of thinking, second and twice removed added up to fourth and that wasn't very close. Cousins, though.

'What? And by the way, Bill, Richard is OK by me.'

'Right you are, Richard, but . . . er . . . it'll be "sir", when Miss Kate's in the car.'

'If you think so. Now then – what?'

'What? Er . . . Richard?'

'*What* were you saying about the car and . . .?'

'Oh, yes. She only likes this car but even this I have to leave out of sight. I honk on the hooter, see?' He gave two blasts. 'And I wait. And when she's ready, she bangs the gong, I drive round the back and she gets in.'

'Whose is that, do you know?' They pulled up behind the motor-bike.

'Not a Harley-Davidson or a Yamamoto, oh, no.'

'No, I can see that. I mean, who owns it?'

'It's young Tess's, by the looks of it. Her gets on well with the old lady, always has done, and now they've got—'

'Oh, the "demo demon".' He got out, closing the door with a satisfying thud, without slamming it. Bill smiled and nodded, approving his care. 'Let's say an hour, Bill, then we'll be going for a drive. She wants to show me something.'

'Everything, more like. Take as long as suits. I'll stretch my legs.' He gestured to the hill beyond the house. 'Just half-way up, that'll do me. Sparrows' Dice is steeper than it looks.'

When Bill Jackson had trudged about half-way up the hill, he paused in the weak spring sun and gazed about him. Home Farm, with its straggle of outbuildings – dairy, cow-byre, stables, granary and barns – looked like a doll's house. All it needed was a large hand to lower into the picture cows, a horse, a farmer in an old-fashioned smock and a dairy-maid with wooden buckets. He settled under a spreading beech tree, leaned back against its broad trunk, and took a pipe and tobacco from his pocket. Good opportunity this, a nice smoke; not welcome in the taxi, his pipe, not welcome anywhere really, even in the Bull –

No pipes or cigars in the dining room,

it said. He tamped down the sweet, clover-scented tobacco into the bowl of the pipe and took pains to light it, shielding it from the slightest of breezes. He had got it going nicely, the thin trail of smoke echoed by the broader trail from the farmhouse chimney, when he slowly fell into a heavy sleep.

Reading the names carved into the grey stone cross, they had forgotten the old woman. She sank back onto a convenient gravestone and slipped her aching feet out of her shoes, misshapen by swollen joints. She twisted round to look at the headstone. It would be as well to check that she wasn't sitting on a relative or ancestor. The name had worn away and all she could see was *Spinster of this Parish*. Ha! An accurate description of herself. The grave-yard was screened from the crescent of terraced council houses by a thick fence of spinach-green cypress. Now, the tenants who had demanded this protection from the dead couldn't see the church either. Poor fools, she thought. All that was visible of the houses from where she sat were the television aerials, stuck like clusters of silver twigs to the roofs.

'Aunt Kate?' the young man called, the humour and confidence gone from his voice. 'Are you OK? Not too tired?'

Pulling on her shoes she padded through the unmown grass to join them at the war memorial. LEST WE FORGET *1914–1918*. She repeated the words and laughed. 'I thought that quite unnecessary at the time. Who could forget? But we did. Look.' She pointed to the back of the cross and a second set of dates above another list of names, *1939–1945*.

'I see what you mean now, it was all just . . . chance. Did you know all of these people?' He traced some names with his forefinger.

'Most of them.'

'Nice.' The girl spoke for the first time, swishing her long dark hair over her shoulder. 'Nice that they're all together.'

'What do you mean?' She was beginning to irritate him. He hadn't wanted her here, pushy, opinionated little piece. Typical 'new' woman.

'Well, there's no class system. Upstairs and downstairs all muddled up.'

'How do *you* know?'

'I've heard my gran talk about it. I remember the names.'

'You see, Aunt Kate, *she* didn't forget, Tess's gran.' He looked back at the cross, ashamed of his irritation in the presence of this. Reading the names, he spoke them aloud, with Kate accompanying him as a soft echo.

James Adams.'

'Farmhand, good bowler.'

'Thomas Baring-Kimball.'

'Aunt Issy's eldest.'

'Daniel Chalker.'

'Chair mender, last cottage.'

'James Coffield.'

'Son of the motor-car man.'

'Juniper Corrigan.'

'Farmhand, old Juniper's grandson.'

'Will Corrigan.'

'Brother, pot-man at the Bull and Butcher.'

'Ephraim Elkins.'

'Cow-man at Home Farm.'

'Josiah Elkins.'

'Shepherd at Home Farm.'

'Charles Fiennders. Oliver Fiennders. Adam Fiennders.'

Nothing accompanied these names.

'Lancelot Henders.'

'Doctor's son, wicked name, isn't it?'

'Edward Hogg. Joseph Hogg.'

'Joe Hogg's boys, from Old Coddlestone Farm.'

'George Jackson.'

'Dot and John's eldest, he shouldn't have gone, lied about his age.'

'*Alfred Nichols. Martin Nichols.*'

'Sons of the groom, stable boys, Flora's brothers – she married Billy Jackson.'

'*Michael Quinn. Matthew Quinn. Patrick Quinn.*'

'Aggy Quinn was a wonderful mother, Mary was a good friend.'

The girl pressed her hand to her mouth to stop herself crying.

'*James Rigger.*'

'Horse breeder. There are still horses round here bred from good stock of his and his father's.'

'*Robert Reade.*'

'Son of the young gardener and your great-aunt.'

'*Stanley Sharp.*'

'Innkeeper's son.'

'*Gabriel Shippon.*'

'Helped his father with the milk cart.'

'*Jeremiah Turner. Zachary Turner.*'

'Sons of the estate carpenter.'

Richard turned away. He wished the roll-call was ended. 'Was your mother here? Did she tell you all about—'

'*I* was here. Some of us sheltered over there.' She pointed to the church porch.

'Oh, it was raining?'

'Of course. The dedication ceremony took hours, or so it seemed to us young ones. My uncle Freddy took it, couldn't get through the prayers, Aunt Issy's husband. He didn't actually cry, kept stopping and blowing his nose. We pretended amongst ourselves we thought it funny, but nobody did. It was bad enough to be dead, mouldering in the earth. If that had to happen, we all wanted to moulder here with friends and parents, not there, in France and Belgium. And then so many people were sniffling, not only the bereaved but others – cottagers, farm people, the Bexley-Wrights – her, I remember – they were crying because their children had escaped. *That* was what I meant about the accident of birth, not the silver-spoon-in-mouth privileged birth. If men didn't fight, didn't die, it was because they were too young or too old.' She fiddled with her hair, tucking wisps of pale grey behind her ears and tilted her head towards the church. 'We girls were all in long dark cloaks with big hoods, mittened and booted, some with muffs. Little white faces in shadowy shrouds, is what we looked like. The boys stood out more, more individual, grey or black suits mostly, carrying their hats. In spite of a long winter they all looked healthy. The poor were out in all weathers working, and the rich, well, they were out too, riding, hunting, shooting, whatever. And . . . and . . . it wasn't much more than twenty years some of them would have, before they had given up *their* lives, "To the Glory of God and Their Country", and made the girls widows.'

'Are you OK?' Tess put a hand on the old lady's shoulder.

'Yes. Sorry to be so morbid.' She patted the girl's cheek. 'I remember your great-grandmother, Teresa. They were a bit left out of it being Catholics, not their church.'

'Yes, she said it all felt very awkward. As well as sad, I mean.'

'You see, there was the undercurrent of what it had done to the family. The Family. The Fiennders'. And everybody was there, had to be, and some had never been together before. Mary, your grandmother, was there.' She examined him, looking for physical signs of the Bowdens, but they were more obvious in the female line. 'She stood apart in her little group, thinner-looking than ever in black. There were other groups, fanning out from the cross under large umbrellas.' She screwed up her eyes, trying to remember. 'It was like Seurat's *Sunday at Grande Jatte*, as if painted by Munch.'

Tess nodded. 'Good, what a terrific description.' Richard didn't conceal his surprise. 'I'm not a bloody ignoramus, you know,' she added indignantly, 'just because I live round here. Sorry, go on,' she said to Kate.

Kate continued as if she had been speaking through the little spat. 'Decent enough, not a time for gossip and gloating. The two boys were there, of course, some knew, most suspected. Ann Fiennders, careful to avoid the old gardener – Maud knew all about that.' Laughing, she shook her head. 'And what was it Philip Larkin said? "Sex was invented in the sixties"!' She took a few steps through the long, tangled grass, flinching at the nettles, to a gravestone topped with the carved head of an angel that had rather large wings sprouting from its back. She laughed. 'He didn't get the proportions quite right. These wings would have sunk her, not taken her off to the heavens.' She tugged feebly with arthritic hands at the thick ivy as gnarled as her fingers. 'Uncle Richard read something about the future and trust, and the young who would do a better job than their forebears in running the world. He looked over at us in the porch. Didn't want to single out his two boys, you see, or one of them.

335

I should have a word about this, it shouldn't get this neglected.'

They joined her at the graveside, pulling at the glossy, dark-green ivy and peeling away the white flowering columbine to reveal the epitaph,

SACRED TO THE MEMORY OF MARY CLARKE.
BELOVED WIFE OF THE LATE FRANCIS
AND OF THE LATE GEORGE JACKSON
ET
RADIATUS OTIOSUS OMNINO FIDELIS

Richard knelt on the cushion of moss, cleaning out the inscription. 'What does it mean? I took Latin, but I've never heard this.'

'It isn't a saying as such. It means, loosely, "Radiant, free, always faithful".'

'How odd. I mean it's lovely, of course, beautiful, but a strange inscription for a tombstone.'

'No, it isn't,' the girl said excitedly. 'Don't you see?' She grabbed the old woman. 'Who died first, her or Richard?'

'Mary.'

'Oh, to be loved like that. And to love! We're not capable of that today. We can manage the radiance, the freedom, but you can forget the always faithful – forget it!' She pulled at her Lycra skirt as if embarrassed by its brevity. 'The only part we get right is the fucking. Oh, sorry.'

Kate ignored the perfunctory apology. 'You get the "fucking" part right, do you? I *am* surprised. Judging by the amount of articles in newspapers and magazines giving advice, the books on sexual fulfilment, classroom lectures on intercourse, not to mention videos portraying the entire act, I'd have thought that was the last thing that came naturally to your generation.' She sank back onto a handy stone coffin after first inspecting its dedication: GONE BUT NOT FORGOTTEN. 'Better than "forgotten but not gone", which is my living epitaph.'

Stunned, Tess and Richard returned to examining the stone. Behind them Kate muttered, 'According to *Cosmopolitan*, you don't even know how to masturbate.' They exchanged an awkward smile.

'So, Dick, have you figured it out?' Tess asked.

'No. And nobody ever calls me Dick.'

'Yes, they do. I read an interview with you in the *Guardian*.'

'Nobody who knows me—'

'Look.' She took his finger and traced the initials of the Latin. 'R-O-O-F, right?' She turned to the old woman. 'On that stone plaque in the church, Richard Oliver . . .'

'Ormerod.'

'Thanks, Fiennders. See? R.O.O.F.'

'Tessa, that − is − beautiful! Thank you.' He jumped to his feet and hugged her.

'Brilliant!'

'That was why your father was called Rufus.' Kate smiled at his enthusiasm, the first time he had been so unguarded. 'If he had been a girl, she would have been called Ruth. Maud told me.'

'Didn't you know any of this? Didn't you care? It would have been quite easy to find out. Extraordinary.' Tess gave him a tiny push, exasperated, the added 'a' to her name an irritation to her as much as 'Dick' was to him.

He regretted the impulsive hug: her familiarity and criticism were annoying. 'I did care and I suspected something, but my father's response to questions was invariably, "It all happened a long time ago". He – my mother and he – thought my curiosity was unhealthy and they both hated gossip. Both of them a bit formal and almost repressed, you see. Especially him. Maybe that's why he married so late in life.'

'Hardly gossip.'

'And when he died and some of the odd financial arrangements came out, well, I was working all over the world and I had no contact with anybody here.' He shot an apologetic glance at Kate. 'Except for Roper, of course.'

'Why do you want contact now? Why do you want to save the cottage? Money?' He ignored Tess's aggression and, squatting at the foot of the grave, he smiled at the inscription. 'Something I found in the cottage yesterday. Some *things*,' he added softly.

The cupboard hadn't been opened for at least fifty years. Layers of plaster, paint and lining paper had concealed it, just another part of the uneven walls. Successive tenants had decorated lazily and only the empty thud of his magazine swiping a fly against the wall had made him suspicious. Tapping the area with a hammer and using a knife in the cracks, he had found the cupboard. A faint aroma of camphor and lavender escaped as he opened the door. The smell danced briefly around the room, like a prisoner released after solitary confinement. The clothes were immaculate as if washed, starched and ironed, brushed, pressed and polished yesterday by loving unseen hands. They were his grandfather's, of course. He had only to examine the inside breast pocket of one jacket:

Turnbull & Asser. Jermyn Street.
R. Fiennders, Esq.

There was even a tail-coat there, no different from the one *he* wore for work, his dress shirts, too, were made at Turnbull and Asser. When his father had spoken about The Pightle, what had he said? A museum, a repository, a museum – to love?

He lay back on the high bed, his hands behind his head. The view couldn't have changed, shortened perhaps by the growth of trees or widened by judicious felling, but the same distant roof-top of a farmhouse, the irregular pattern of fields sown with different crops; sitting higher, he could get a glimpse of the pond, surrounded by reeds and iris and busy with wild mallard and domestic white ducks. It was then that he saw the beam. The long, supporting beam, thick, round and honey-coloured, above his head. There was something scratched, no, carved, deep into the wood. Letters. Initials? Graffiti? He stood on the bed, wobbling. Neatly incised and dark with age was the inscription – *R – M. MDCCCC.* His grand-parents on this bed . . .

He leapt off the bed, feeling coarse, an intruder. The

dust from the plaster and paint made him cough and he opened the window wide. Holding his handkerchief to his face he wiped away the dust and the tears.

'Are you all right, Richard?' The girl's voice was soft. She was standing above him. 'You're crying.'

'Am I?' He felt his face. 'Oh, yes. How odd.' Standing, he looked at the two women, one over ninety and the other – twenty? Twenty-five? Both from here, of here, part of the jig-saw puzzle. He didn't want to piece together any more today. 'Look, would you mind if I didn't come back with you? I'd like to go for a walk. I'll walk back to the Bull, OK?'

'That's a good idea, Richard my dear. There's a foot-path from the kissing-gate.' Kate pointed across the churchyard. 'It leads up to the village if you turn left into the wood, and to Fiennders Abbey, the park, if you turn right. And we should get back or Jackson will have woken up and found his beloved Wolseley gone.'

'Yeah, right, though we stuck the note on the front door.' Tess was disappointed. 'So, when are you going, then, Richard? Or aren't you? Are you going to join NMAFF and fight? Or are you off giving recitals? Is Rome expecting you? Are you to display your talents in Vienna?'

'I have a recital at the Wigmore Hall next week.'

'Oh, I see! So this visit wasn't happenstance then, it was expedient.'

'Christ, you are pedantic. You sound like a bloody school-teacher.'

'Hardly a surprise, is it?'

1919

Francis was watching for Richard's return. Across the yard he could see the light from the cottage shining through windows, the curtains still open. Mary must be watching too. Watching and waiting. The rain had almost stopped, but the drizzle that replaced it was as cheerless, grey water, grey as the sky; even the fields were grey, reflecting the clouds, and the pond was only a darker grey. There was nothing to be expected from Richard's visit. His proposition was foolish, a last-ditch attempt to correct the sad farce that the war had created. He heard the horse crashing through the undergrowth of the wood, beyond the sodden fields, twigs, boughs and branches brought down by the recent storms, and turned away from the window. Naïve, maybe, but correct to use the horse. It drew less attention than the trap or the motor car. That people had known for so long they had lost interest didn't stop Richard behaving like a gentleman, protecting Caroline and Timothy at Fiennders Abbey and Mary and Rufus here. But whatever he had to tell Mary, Francis knew that this must be the last chapter. Thank God the boys were away, Rufus at Cambridge and Timothy at Oxford.

Richard dismounted and put the horse in the stables,

gave him a quick rub-down and put the saddle and bridle in the tack-room, tasks that would be done for him at the Abbey by old George Nichols. He hung his heavy, wet raincoat over a drying frame and wiped his damp face with a handkerchief. He was hot still from the memory of the embarrassing conversation with Andrew Osmund. Why hadn't he guessed? He had thought Louise Osmund was a fool. Fooled. But think of the fool *he* was.

'Oh, my dear old fellow, please don't go on. No, no. Nothing in it. Oh, Lord, Richard old chap. Can't see how you could think . . . Gallantry, one might call it, all that hand-kissing stuff. And compliments to the ladies, well, always done that, they like it, and well, Caroline more than most, don't you know.' He laughed unhappily. 'Course you do. Oh, God, really, so awkward, don't know what to say. Louise has always known, thought you did. Not *told*, of course, just got the hang of it.'

Richard had listened to his tangled, clumsy protestations, humiliated by both his false accusation and by a realization of what might be the truth.

'She was away, Louise, a lot, yes, but she hates the country, you see, hunting, shooting, doesn't like any of it. Thinks the country is for growing food, which she likes to eat in town!' Another laugh cut short, punctuated his endless gaucherie. 'Oh dear, oh dear, and then there's you and your whatsit . . .' A cough, a shrug accompanied an offensive raise of the eyebrows. 'What a mess! How could you think, though, even so, even if true? I mean, rotten show all round. I couldn't have taken Timothy into the family. Got to see, Richard, the die is cast. Fiennders can't belong to . . . can't be anything other . . . I mean, looking at it from the point of view of blood, is it so bad?' On and on he had burbled, incoherent with embarrassment. His own loss, the elder son, hadn't destroyed his family. He was able to talk of that death in terms of bravery, valour, sacrifice for King and Country. There was a younger son.

Richard cut short the meeting brusquely. 'Thank you, Andrew. I deeply regret that I have mistrusted you and . . . and, I thank you for your forbearance.' He left before any further words of sympathy could add to his embarrassment.

She came flying out of the front door, holding a shawl over her head, skittering lightly over the cobblestones. 'Richard? Richard? There you are. What happened? You've been so long.'

He held out his arms and folded them around her, kissing the top of her head. 'Mary Bowden, are you really fifty-something? Is this hair white or grey? Is it true you're a witch? Or did you just bewitch me?' Pulling her hair out of its pins, he held her head and slowly kissed her forehead, eyes, tip of her nose and then mouth, letting his hands travel down, caressing the familiar but still desirable body. 'You don't think we're too old to be lovers here in the stable?'

She murmured, 'Not too old, my love, too cold, maybe.'

The rain was quite heavy again, but the two shadowy figures crossing from the stables to the house seemed impervious to it. They walked, arms around each other, heads together, as if it was a morning in spring and the warmth of sun came from the skies not the chill of rain.

Francis drew the curtains and returned to his fire and the letter he was writing – to his son. No wonder the boy was lonely, or a loner. His parents' life with each other was all-enclosing; everything else was an appendage, including Rufus.

'You laughed? Richard, how could you? No wonder she struck you.'

'Well, she didn't exactly, the book missed me and knocked over her looking-glass.'

'Broke it?'

'Broke it.'

'Seven years' bad luck.'

'Only seven? Surely she deserves more than that?'

'Why did you laugh? It's so sad, so terrible, to be betrayed by your own brother – Tommy . . . Oh, Richard, his name, Timmy – it was deliberate . . .'

'Oh, quite, like us, like Rufus. I laughed, because . . . look, Mary, this is difficult. It isn't right to talk about . . . well . . .'

'Your wife.'

'Yes, my wife. Hell, how odd that sounds. I never use the word, except when we are away. *You* are my wife, or *ma femme* or *meine Frau*—'

'Richard! *Why did you laugh?*'

'It was at myself, I was relieved, actually relieved, to be cuckolded by my brother. It means that – that Fiennders Abbey will still be occupied by a Fiennders. It's so, well, *ingrained*, this family thing. And she, poor woman, thought that this deep, dark secret would "undo" me, instead of which I welcomed it.'

She sat up in bed, hugging her knees, frowning. 'My father understood all that. He used to tell us about the muniment room, all the deeds and papers.'

'Yes, our fathers got on well, didn't they? But I bet yours didn't believe in primogeniture. After all Bertie did not become keeper, did he?'

'I'm not sure I believe in it, Richard. And . . . have you thought what *you* have done?'

'By breaking up the estate?' He sighed. 'Oh, yes, my love, I've thought. I've thought and thought.'

'I can see how practical it is – the first-born son getting it all, keeping the estate together, but it is so unfair on the others, especially a younger son.'

'I'd have thought Issy would have suffered the most. After all she is the eldest.'

'No, not really, it's different for women,' she said. 'We're born knowing the superior claims of men.'

'Mary! I hope you never said that in front of your ancient Aunt Biddy!' He pulled her back into his arms as she flinched from the rumbling of a distant storm and the random jagged flashes of lightning. She relaxed under his soothing hand. 'It's all right, no danger, beloved, it's a long way away, a long way, nearer Oxford.' Sleepy, she turned on her side. He followed, an arm still holding her.

'Good. But I'm glad that you're here.'

'So Rufus and Timothy are cousins, of sorts.'

1990

'I know what it is about you!' He was relieved. There had been a nagging question-mark in his head. Why, or what, was odd about her? 'Aunt Kate.'

'Yes, dear?'

'You wear trousers. You're the only . . . er . . .' How should he put it? 'You're the only elderly woman I know who wears trousers.'

'Ah, well, Richard, when I *was* elderly I didn't. I started wearing them when I was old, too old to care what people thought. Now then, you choose. "Rusty Nail", "Dry Martini", "White Lady", "Manhattan", "Rah Rah Rut"?'

'What on earth is that?'

'Rye whisky, Pernod and bitters.'

'Bloody hell! I'll settle for a dry martini. After that lot it seems as innocuous as lemonade.'

'Olive or twist of lemon?'

'What about a tiny onion?'

'That would be a Gibson. You asked for a dry martini.'

'OK. Neither.'

'Straight up or on the rocks?'

'Rocks. How do you know all these cocktails? Misspent youth?'

'Rather well spent, I think – no, it was all around me when I worked, don't forget.' He was ashamed of his ignorance. They had talked constantly of the past, but only as it had affected him. 'Kate – is it OK if I call you Kate? I thought with you calling your mother Maud . . .'

'Kate is fine.' She mixed the drinks expertly, pouring his over ice into a tumbler that could have been a give-away at a petrol station, and her own into a delicate Y-shaped glass on a stem with no ice.

'Delicious! Perfect! You could be a barman at the Ritz.'

'I think the bar at the Stafford Hotel is accepted as being the Utopia of dry martinis.'

'Look, I'm sorry, but I've got to ask. "Work", you said. What work?'

She was surprised. 'Didn't you know? I was a singer, accompanied myself on the piano. A "cabaret artiste"!'

'What!'

'Here, come into the back room, I'll show you. Funny your father didn't say.' She led him into a sitting room that ran the length of the house, with long windows at both ends. 'I wrote some of my songs, but mostly I played whatever touched the heartstrings of sentimental drunks at three a.m. My hands are too arthritic now, especially the right. I can hardly play a note.' She lifted the lid and played a few bars of Ravel's piano concerto for the left hand, segueing into,

"They asked me how I knew, our true love was true,
I of course replied, something here inside, cannot be denied.
Now laughing friends deride, tears I cannot hide –

dum de dum de dum – dah de dum dum dum
Smoke gets in your eyes."

It was a frail, raspy voice but not unattractive. 'That always got them in tears, then they'd order another bottle to cheer themselves up.'

'Good Lord, it's an old Steinway, beautiful. You've looked after it, it's been tuned.'

'Your grandfather gave it to Maud in 1899, I think, when she first moved to London. She played very well.'

'Sit down, play some more.'

'You play.'

'I will, I will, but I'd like to hear something of yours.'

'They were silly, slight things, risqué for those days, full of innuendo, teasing.'

He beamed at her. 'I'm thrilled! I have a Bohemian aunt!'

She lifted the seat of the piano stool. It was stuffed untidily with a mixture of photographs and sheet music. 'Here I am.' Shyly she held out a photograph, a portrait of a young woman with white skin, huge kohl-rimmed dark eyes and a thin, wide mouth. Her hair, cut in a short bob, was black with a straight, heavy fringe.

'You look like that film-star – Louise Brooks – or what's-her-name, that society woman with a funny name, or was it her daughter?'

'Emerald Cunard? Nancy Cunard?'

'Yes. That's it.'

'That was Maud's idea, so that I didn't look like me. Changed my name as well.'

'To?'

'I'm embarrassed. Oh, all right – Kitty Kat.'

'Kitty Kat? Perfect. I love it. If it wasn't too late I'd change my name – something like Frankie Fine!'

'That would hardly help your career, it sounds like a crooner. Ricardo Finskovski would be more useful.'

'True, too true. Oh, what's that?' The vroom-vroom of a motor-bike could be heard, followed by the sputter of an engine cutting out and two loud toots on a horn. 'Is that her, the demon-demo schoolmistress?'

'Don't sneer, Richard. She got a first at Edinburgh and a postgraduate degree, more than you did at Cambridge.'

'What's she doing here? Does she drop in like this all the time?' He was jealous. Stupid, really, but he wanted to keep this newly found eccentric relation to himself.

'She stables her horse here. They don't have stables or any land, the McKennas.'

'She doesn't strike me as the pony-club type.'

'Oh, no, none of that. She rides, likes it. Jim Rigger let her have the horse cheap. It's a beautiful mare but very difficult, temperamental, no good for children or beginners.'

'I'm just taking Ginger out for a quick ride before it gets too late, Kate – Oh sorry. Didn't know anybody was here – no car.'

She was wearing black, of course. Black stretch jeans, leather jodhpur boots, a black polo-neck sweater and a black velvet riding hat, from which tendrils of blue-black hair escaped. Rather too fetching, Richard thought, those wisps of hair, to be entirely accidental.

'I walked over.'

'From the Bull and Butcher? That's a good few miles. Do you want me to give you a lift back after my ride?'

'Thanks, but no. Why do you call it the Bull and *Butcher*? It's just the Bull.'

'*Now* it is, I suppose, but it was the Bull and Butcher for hundreds of years till some animal-rights group defaced the sign, only a couple of years ago. They blocked out "Butcher" and the painting so the Sharps changed the name. But we all – the locals – still call it its proper name. Sure about the lift? It'll be dark, not easy, those footpaths, for a stranger.'

'A stranger' irritated him. 'Quite sure. I have a torch and Aunt Kate is making me dinner.'

'*That* I am not, Richard. I'm giving you dinner. It comes from All The Trimmings. Don't worry, it's very good.'

'Our posh deli and take-away, in old Findlesham.' Tess pushed back the strands of hair under her hat. 'It is good, expensive, though. OK, I'm off. 'Bye, Kate, 'bye.'

Through the long side window he saw her lead out a dark, glossy horse, its coat almost as black as its owner's hair. It was tossing its head and pulling at the rein. 'Ginger? Bloody funny name for a horse that colour.'

Kate laughed. 'It's bred from a mare called Gelsey and that was bred from one called Margot, I think, and before that Tiny Tapper and so on – they've always had names to do with dancing. And the Sharps don't own the Bull any more,' she added inconsequentially. 'They sold it to a chain, they only work there now. I miss the skittle alley.'

'It's good though, Kate, and quite good food.'

'What is the chain called, odd name – Prestige Pubs? Lovely Locals?'

'Much worse. "Innteresting Inns".'

'Oh, Lord!' She leaned against the piano, closing her eyes. She was tired. 'I'm going to sit down, Richard, in the living-room. You wander around the house on your own. Dinner will be ready in about half an hour.'

'Before I do that, I'd like to talk to you.'

'About the house?'

'That and other things.'

She had expected this. He was going to tell her that he was doing it all for her sake, that she would be better off at Fiennders Abbey.

The sharp features of her bony face were more prominent with fatigue, he noticed, as she settled in the comfortable chair. A large grey cat noiselessly jumped on her lap, its claws kneading her legs until it settled down, forming a cushion of fur.

'Another martini?' she said.

'No, thanks. You?'

'Not for me. I can't drink as much as I used to.'

The fire was unlit, but laid with twists of newspaper, sticks and a mixture of logs and coal. Both sides of the inglenook were stacked with logs and there was a brightly polished brass bucket containing coal on the right.

'This must be warm in winter.' He sat across the hearth from her on an old leather ottoman. He was embarrassed and didn't know how to start.

She saved him the problem. 'I know, strictly speaking, this is your house, Richard, but . . .'

'Loosely speaking, too, Kate.'

She stared at him, unsmiling, her hands nervously stroking the cat.

'Don't look so worried, Kate. I want to ask you a favour.' The cat mewed a protest as she rubbed its ears carelessly. 'Look, I'm really ashamed of bothering you with those letters – about leaving. You might laugh when I tell you why.'

'I might not,' she said grimly.

'I didn't mind *you* being here.'

'Even though I was a squatter?'

'Hardly that! But I didn't want you to install a husband or—'

'A lover! A *partner*, that's what they're called these days. I think I *will* laugh.'

'You see, if you had . . . when you . . . well . .'

'Died?'

'Yes, all right, died, it would be hard to get the, er, person evicted.'

'Well, really, Richard. I know I've just about stolen the house from you but I wouldn't have put you in that position. I do have *some* family feelings. What about the favour?'

'Yes, the favour. First I would like to come over and practise every day, then I needn't go back to London until the concert. Then, if you're agreeable, I'd like to keep a couple of rooms here for myself, perhaps put in another bathroom. What do you say?'

The cat was quietly purring now under her gentle, even caresses. 'Yes. Good idea. It will save you some money. Let's have dinner and then we'll go upstairs and choose your rooms.' She pushed the cat off her lap as she stood up. 'The *poulet basquaise* will be ready and I've made a salad.'

'Sounds delicious.'

She crossed the hall into the kitchen, her heels clicking on the flagstone floor. 'We'll eat in here, all right?'

'Splendid.'

As she knelt at the oven of the old range, she said, 'All you've lost from having me here is a bit of rent.'

Fifty years of rent, he thought. 'Let me help.' He knelt at the range with her. 'Aunt Kate, did smoke ever get in your eyes?'

She handed him a thick cloth. 'Careful, it's very hot.' The corners of her thin mouth curled. 'Oh, yes, there was something here inside that could not, did not have to be denied. Occasionally. But only once seriously, and when it ended laughing friends did deride.'

'What happened?'

'It ended when the war ended. He returned to his family in America as I expected. And now, Richard, you will have to help *me* up, as well as the *poulet basquaise.*'

It was dark when Tess arrived back at the farm. Even in the cold night air she was hot, perspiring and tired, but Ginger, who was flecked with patches of sweat like foam from detergents that floats on a stream, would need rubbing down and calming. Come to that, *she* needed it too! She had ridden the horse fast, galloping her up the front face of Beacon Hill then across towards Little Bewdley, skirting the huge cement-block barn with the corrugated iron roof, blaring out disco music, where some kind of mini-rave was taking place – attended, no doubt, by her young sister Kelly. They had circled back through the unused old commons, slowing the pace to a canter as they adjusted their eyes to twilight. The land was covered in bracken and hawthorn. The bushes protected oak saplings which, as they grew, would overshadow the hawthorns and they, no longer needed, would die away. The environmentalist working for NMAFF had shown her that, as well as all the rare wild flowers growing in the meadows around The Pightle. That the house, woodland and land – an Area of Outstanding Natural Beauty *and* a Site of Special Scientific Interest – might be buried for ever under a blanket of concrete was nothing short of environmental murder, he'd said. Very emotional. She'd found him attractive at first. They'd been to the pictures together at the multiplex off the new roundabout between Wellsbury and Gadstone Magna. He had chosen the film, something about gorillas and an improbably beautiful young woman whose life's work was protecting them. Afterwards they'd had dinner at the Indian vegetarian restaurant in the pedestrian precinct in Wellsbury, drinking tea with it, no wine. He was nice, and it was all very worthy, but you'd have to be mad about a bloke to put up with that again – and she wasn't.

The gallop had been good for both pony and rider, working off excess energy, or excess something. She left Ginger settled peacefully in the stable and walked quietly round the back of the house to get her bike. Through the partly opened side window she could hear him playing the piano. Must be him – Kate could never manage this. She didn't know what it was, only that it was beautiful, and that she had to stop and had to listen. All very romantic. Pity he was such a self-centred, cold, conceited pig. You could tell that from the photo on the compact disc she'd bought of Chopin's twenty-four preludes – all that tousled brown hair, wayward genius stuff. He was good-looking in a way but not as good-looking as all that. The music ended. The piano lid was shut. Kate was talking. Silently and swiftly she walked back to her bike. Better not start it here. Best to push it down the track till it was out of earshot. It took a few revs to get it going, sounding noisier than usual in the silence of the night.

'Tess! Tess!' The beam of a torch preceded the shout. 'May I change my mind about the lift? You were right about the footpath. I'm not used to such total darkness.'

'It's one of the best things about the country. Nowhere else — no city — has real night.'

He could hardly see her: the light from his torch lit her face but only just. The hair had escaped from the crash helmet again falling in wisps above the blue, blue eyes. Perhaps he had misjudged her vanity.

'Get on. You can wear my hard hat, strap it tight, tuck your legs up and hold on.'

'Hold on where?'

'Where do you think? Haven't you ever ridden pillion before? Below my tits and above my hips.'

He was still laughing as she steered the motor-bike through the small double roundabout and over the traffic humps into Old Findlesham Street.

'What's that funny-looking Chinese dome thing there?' He had to shout.

She braked suddenly, causing him to disobey her previous orders.

'Sorry about that, Tess, but you did stop rather suddenly.'

'Wouldn't be the first time, anyway. That's the bus shelter. Built in eighteen eighty-something to commemorate Victoria's Golden Jubilee.'

'A bus shelter in eighteen eighty-seven?'

'Oh, well, originally it was just a roof put over the village pump to protect the cottage women. Do you want to have a look?' They sat in the shelter, which was dimly lit by one of the imitation gas lamps that lined the street.

'Is that the famous All The Trimmings next to the garage?'

'Yes, it used to be a real village shop and post-office but the Jacksons couldn't cope with that and the garage and the taxi service, so they sold it to Liza Osmund, who tarted it up and turned it into a mini Harrods.'

'Useful, isn't it, if you haven't got a car and can't get to Waitrose, or you want something special?'

'Yeah, but if you haven't got a car it means you haven't got any fucking dosh, doesn't it, and if you haven't got any fucking dosh, you can't afford All The Trimmings.'

'Do you swear like that in front of your pupils?'

'No, I don't. Though they swear like that in front of me. OK, I've got to go home, got lots of essays to mark. Do you want me to take you back, or do you want to walk?'

'Where do you live?'

'We live in a council house over there, beyond the wood.'

'You live with your parents still?'

'Not *still*, again. I had a studio flat in Wellsbury, not far from my school but, well, my dad was made redundant – he worked at Coffield's, the car place outside Oxford – and they'd just put a deposit on the house, they had a "right to buy" at the height of the boom and the mortgage went up, et cetera, et cetera, so I moved back to help out.'

'Drop me here. I'll walk on to the Bull.'

They paused at the window of All The Trimmings. It was tastefully decorated with white china bowls of various sizes, filled high with limes, lemons, green almonds and nutmegs. On the shop door was a notice:

FINDLESHAM PRESERVATION SOCIETY

April 3	Hedge Laying
May 4	Basket and Broom Making
June 2	Visit and Talk. The Medicinal Properties of Herbs. Reades Nurseries.
July 5	Webbs Farm. How to make Goat Cheese. (Bring the Kids!)
August 7	Candle Making
September 8	Gleaning Competition in aid of the Library.
October 4	Open Day in the Craft Studio. Demonstration of Weaving and Natural Dyes.

It was signed *Liza Fiennders Osmund*.

'*Fiennders* Osmund?'

'Distant relation, I think – several times removed. A great-great-great-something or other of your granddad's daughter by Lady Whatsit, his wife.'

He frowned, trying to work it out.

'We call her Liza Do-a-lot because she never stops organizing things. And people. Fêtes, fund-raising, petitions, protests . . .'

' "Do-a-lot", oh, I get it, "Liza Doolittle", *Pygmalion*.

I hope the relationship is distant enough for me not to have to call.'

She laughed. 'Oh, very Jane Austen.'

'Maybe, but as I appear to be related in one way or another to everyone from here to Wellsbury and beyond . . . where do they live, the Osmunds?' He lowered his voice. 'Above the shop?'

'Course not. He's something in the City – not much of a something, otherwise I couldn't see her running a shop. They live in Keepers Cottage. Fabulous position, down this road for about a mile and then left down Drover's Lane. It's a cul-de-sac, only their house and Old Barn Cottage.'

'I suppose I'll see them at the NMAFF meeting Saturday.'

'No, you won't. She's the NIMBY from hell!'

'Nimby?'

'You *have* been away a long time, Not-In-My-Back-Yard. *She*, head of the Findlesham Preservation Society, lobbied for Findlesham by-pass to go through Swainshill, three miles out of the way so they wouldn't hear the noise from their house. It's on this side, see, and when the motorway access fight started, Drover's Lane was one of the possibilities, so naturally, The Pightle was her choice. And, you should see the house now! Two bow-front windows downstairs, dormer windows in the attic, a "Victorian" conservatory stuck on the side like a glass bunion, and carriage lamps by the front door, which is mock Georgian!'

'Isn't that rather snobbish of you?'

'I don't care. I don't know much about architecture,

but I know what I hate.' She pulled off her hat, shaking down her hair and rubbing her scalp.

'You have got a temper.'

'That's the Irish in me.' She grinned.

'Is McKenna an Irish name?'

'Certainly is, and so is Quinn, that's a family name too. Look, I must go.' She started to push the bike along the road. He followed, holding the handle-bar on the other side.

'If you're not doing anything tomorrow, Tess, would you like dinner?' In the darkness he couldn't see her smile and nod. 'I'd love to talk to you some more about . . . everything. You know there's a Quinn — a beneficiary — in my grandmother's will.'

Disappointed at the reason for the invitation, she quickened her pace. 'Let you know in the morning, all right?'

'Sure. I'll be out in the afternoon anyway. I'm taking Kate over to Fiennders Abbey.'

'You shit,' she hissed. 'You absolute self-centred little shit.' She pushed the bike at him, knocking him down. 'That poor woman! Throwing her out of her house. At *her* age. What's more, you slimy toad, you fuck-pig, I doubt legally if you can do it. She's got squatter's rights, or something, and you can wipe that stupid smirk off your nasty little face.'

He pushed the bike away and jumped to his feet, laughing through his protestations. 'She's going to visit some friends, for Christ's sake. She's calling on the sick and aged, like some Lady Bountiful from days of yore. She'll probably take some soup from All The Trimmings!' He rubbed his shins, wincing, and brushed the front of a rather greasy jacket, then, examining his hands carefully, he spread them out, flexing the fingers.

'Bloody hell, Richard, I am sorry. I thought—'

'I know what you thought.' He continued flexing his fingers. 'I've had my face slapped a couple of times, but I've never had a motor-bike thrown at me before. What do you do for an encore?'

'Are they all right, your hands? I'll kill myself if you've hurt them.'

'Why don't you kill yourself anyway, do the world a favour? No, no, they seem to be OK.'

'I heard you playing tonight. I listened outside. Really, it was so beautiful. You're sure they're all right?'

'Yes.'

'What were you playing? I didn't know it.'

'The last piece was Brahms' "Liebeslieder", transposed for piano by himself.'

' "Liebeslieder"?'

'Love songs.' He started to sing but a window was pushed open in the nearby Juniper Cottage and an unseen man shouted, 'Some of us are trying to get some sleep. Go and do your courting in the bus shelter – like all else do.'

'You don't sing very well,' she whispered.

Billy stopped the car as near to the gates as he could get. A discreet sign in faded gold lettering read, *Fiennders Abbey. Short- and Long-Term Rest Home, FRCPS Approved.*

'What does that mean – FRCPS?' Richard helped his aunt out of the car.

'I'll wait here, shall I, Miss Kate, sir? It means that it's reliable.'

'But what does it *mean*?'

'I don't know, Mr Clarke, to tell the truth.'

'Then how do you know it's reliable?'

'Oh, shut up, Richard. Both of you. Yes, Billy, wait there. *In* the car. Sleep if you wish, but don't move.'

He walked her up the gravel path to the large double front door, where a hand-written notice hung askew on the wrought-iron door knob: *Bell doesn't work, please use knocker.* He examined the door. 'There isn't a knocker.'

'You're supposed to use that poker.' A rusty brass fire-iron was sitting in a cracked terracotta flower-pot in the corner.

'How much do they charge here?' he said, thumping the door.

'Three hundred and fifty pounds a week. Minimum.'

'I don't believe you. You're just saying that in case I get ideas about leaving you here.' He put his arm round her and kissed the top of her head. 'I think I'd rather put up with you.' He left her with her friends: Mrs Smith — by her accent a local woman — thin and jolly, so stooped that had she had any breasts her chin would have been resting on them, and Glendora, an ancient vision in turquoise with eye-shadow to match, like Kate a one-time 'artiste'.

Crossing the stile onto a footpath, Richard looked back at the ugly, untidy conglomeration of buildings that hid the house. Most had been thrown up during the last war when the house was requisitioned; flimsy pre-fabs that had served as administration offices, storage sheds and latrines. They had been painted a shade of green that clashed with every natural green of plant, grass and tree. The stables were now garages and the tack-room concealed the oil tank. The beautiful building with its clock-tower that had once held the carriage was festooned with hanging baskets, the high arched door holding a painted wooden sign declaring it in sloping script to be *Ye Olde Coach House.* Which, Richard thought, was self-evident. For such a big house the gardens were comparatively small and mostly laid to lawn; grass that was studded with clover, moss, couch-grass and other weeds. The flower borders were narrow: daffodils and narcissi were dying off and being replaced by french marigolds and red salvia. He turned his back on the depressing scene and followed the footpath through the growing wheat.

The Sharps at the Bull had told him that all, or nearly all, the land for miles around was farmed by Agrilea plc, although a lot of it was owned by individual farmers. It was the only way to farm profitably it seemed. Any smallholdings were run as either organic or 'hobby' farms. The path led through a young plantation, the saplings protected by plastic tubes, into the usual beechwoods. Occasional white arrows had been painted on the trees marking the right-of-way, but on seeing ahead another vast expanse of unhedged fields, he decided to trespass – on what would have been his own land. Twisting tracks made by red deer and muntjacs led through the undergrowth, and four-wheel-drive vehicles had scarred broad rides. He passed a wire-netted enclosure, which was waiting for pheasant chicks. So, the car tracks must belong to the gamekeeper. Instead of the welcoming, beckoning white arrows, other signs were nailed to the trees:

PRIVATE. KEEP OUT. NO RIGHT OF WAY.

He wasn't the first trespasser: a lone rider had followed the broad track, probably using the fallen trees as jumps. He surprised some red deer grazing. For a second they exchanged startled glances, then the animals vanished back into the wood in graceful leaps and bounds.

It was an odd place to have a hut – rather an elaborate shape, too. He couldn't think what purpose it served but it would do to shelter in from the rain which had just started. The windows must have lost their glass years before; there were no fragments lying around, inside or out. The smell of old woodsmoke mingled with that of mildew and mice. A pitter-patter in the roof was further evidence of mice – the rain wasn't heavy enough to make that sound. Nothing was stored here, no bales of wire, sacks of pheasant feed, axes, saws or garden tools. The style of architecture was too elegant for that of a utilitarian shed. It could have been a gate-house – but to where? A medieval house lost, its foundations gone in ploughed fields? Hardly. This was made of wood. If the house hadn't survived, why would this? Another mystery to solve – one to replace that which Kate had solved today. He sat on the floor with his back to the wall, not fancying the frayed armchairs covered in little dots of mouse droppings, with rusty springs showing, coiled like a jack-in-the-box about to leap out.

He had been so absorbed in his own immediate background that he hadn't thought of, or questioned, Kate's parentage. In Findlesham she was known as Katherine Fiennders. When his father had spoke of them, mother and daughter, which was rare, he had called them Maud and Katherine and he knew they had moved to Home Farm in 1940 to get out of London during the war. Kate had taken Richard up to the first floor and let him climb the stairs and explore the attics on his own. They would suit him, they were all he needed. The rooms were interesting: sloping ceilings, windows at floor level and space enough for a big bathroom. She had been as delighted as he, and showed him what they now referred to as *her* floor. The bathroom first, big and draughty with an ill-fitting window. A claw-footed, deep bath in the middle of the room, a small wash-basin and a lavatory with a high cistern and a chain flush. The floor was covered with cracked white lino. 'I'll do this up for you,' he'd said.

Her bedroom came next. He couldn't remember all the details of the room; only the dressing table remained sharply in his head. Old-fashioned, not antique, kidney-shaped, with a triple mirror. It belonged to a still feminine woman. A scent bottle, *circa* 1940, glass, with a gold tassel, redolent of violets, sat next to a glass bowl containing pale pink face powder. The powder was still used, traces of it dusted the glass surface and the swan's-down powder puff rested lightly on the bowl. A manicure set lay open for frequent use, its old leather slotted with exquisite pieces of ivory and silver. And a photograph in a square silver frame stood at the back. The frame was *art-nouveau*, decorated with silver fronds creeping round it like sea-weed. The photograph was of a dark-haired, attractive, unsmiling woman, dressed in a simple, high-necked, ankle-length dress, with a child. The child was about eight years old, with an oval face out of which stared large, apprehensive, brown eyes. Her hair was loose and straight, held off her forehead by a broad ribbon. It was blonde hair, so pale it was the colour of milk.

He had picked up the manicure set carefully. 'This is so pretty. Who is it, the photograph?'

'Maud.'

'Yes, I guessed that. Who is the little girl?'

'Me.'

He continued to examine the leather case and laughed, uneasily. 'But you have . . . had *black* hair. Louise Brooks.'

'That was a wig, for work.'

'Is this very old? Victorian? Oh, yes. "*Anson & Brooks, High Street, Windsor, by appointment VR MDCCVIII*".' He gave her a quick glance. 'I don't understand.' He fingered the creamy chamois and rubbed one of the little silver tools. 'I have seen photographs of Grandma Mary – Roper has some.'

'Of course. Old Roper took that.'

It was possible to see the likeness between the old woman sitting on the bed and the little girl in the photograph, but to compare it with the photograph of the young woman hanging on the wall in Roper's office? The colour of the hair, and the eyes too. They were similar. That was undeniable, especially the hair, but the face, though attractive and interesting, was not as beautiful.

'MB? Kate, who was MB?' He held back the corner of the soft leather where the initials were embossed.

'Mary Bowden.'

'*MDCCVIII*. Eighteen seventy-eight, yes? She was about thirteen. How could a keeper's child afford . . .'

'Richard gave it to her.'

'They knew each other, then?'

'Always. As children, always. He was at Eton and—'

'Ah, I see! He got it in Windsor.'

'It was about then the mothers started to worry. Richard was kept away – Scotland with cousins, Florence . . .'

'And she?'

'She was pushed into marrying the smith, George Jackson.'

'That's horrible. Bloody hell. How old was she?'

'Just fourteen.' She shrugged and made a contemptuous little snort. 'And that was when all the trouble began.'

'Fourteen. Unbelievable.' He sat on the bed next to her. 'But why do you have this?'

'She left it to me – Mary – because I have the same initials.'

'Not KF?'

'No, Richard. Really, you are remarkably obtuse. My initials are MKFB. My father named me Mary after his sister, whom he adored, my mother chose Katherine, some joke about *The Taming of the Shrew*, Fiennders was used as camouflage and Bowden, well, that was legal.'

He had held her hand, sitting on the bed, staring at the photograph on the dressing-table, remembering that his father hadn't known or wanted to know, isolating himself from the past and his family, immersed in work, ostrich-like, burying his head in language – how many did he speak, fourteen? More? Marrying so very late, when both *his* parents were dead and Francis, too; one child, himself, enough for academics. And he, too, had inherited this detachment. Thirty-five and no connections, no friends, just acquaintances, working relationships and lovers. Lovers? Attractive convenient bodies. No home even, hotel rooms and a service apartment in New York when he wasn't working or travelling.

She squeezed his hand, reading his thoughts. 'Rufus was a very bright man, you know. His work in the war was supposed to have been important – vital.'

'Didn't he live with you, your father? Didn't people notice?'

'He spent time with us, but not all his time. He loved Maud, I'm sure, and me. It was easier earlier on in London, so large and anonymous, and by the time we came here so much had changed, people moving, people dead, that it wasn't noticed. And Albert was always a loner, odd, an odd-job man. Jack of all trades. Good with his hands, a craftsman – chair-caning, stone masonry. He lived in the woods near West Wycombe for quite a while, working as a bodger. *He* made Mary's tomb.'

'The angel with heavy wings?'

'Yes.' She patted his hand. 'Let's get going.'

Replacing the manicure case on the dressing-table, he dipped his finger in the face powder. 'I'm pleased about Albert. That means you're my aunt twice over, a *very* close relation.' He dabbed the tip of her nose with the powder. 'You have remarkably good skin.'

'For a woman of my age?'

'Any age.'

'It's buttermilk, an old family recipe.'

According to the Ordnance Survey Map, if he returned to the footpath, or bridle-path as it was, crossed the field and circled round the edge of Cannons Copse, taking the tunnel under the crossroads, a path led to the back of the council estate where he could cut through to St Michael's and have another look at the church. Half-way along the rutted track, now muddy, he looked back at the hut. It could be a folly. A hundred years ago when some of the trees were still saplings, it might have been seen from the Abbey. Ladies could have had tea there, playing house, strolling after luncheon, caught in a summer shower. As he had, they would shelter from the rain. Or maybe it was a romantic trysting place. He would never know. But these were all definitely part of the Abbey's original grounds. What had been a park was now all under plough, with the occasional magnificent oak tree relieving the monotony. A stretch of tangled, thorny briar studded with buds promising wild roses had been part of a formal garden once, the roses not wild but cultivated, lush and heavy-scented.

His trousers were wet from the long grass in the only meadow on the walk by the time he got to Pickaxe Close, and his shoes were heavy with soil and clay. Pickaxe Close? Not even near! The estate was a uniform group of semi-detached and terraced houses with the narrow car-filled roads used as garages, and the garages used as workshops. It was late afternoon and curtains were not yet drawn. Every downstairs window showed the flickering light of television. A narrow alley led him to the front of the church. The notice-board said it was a group parish and services were only held here one Sunday in four, the other villages sharing the Reverend Fred Baring and the curate, the Reverend Charles Caird. The services were in Little Bewdley, Up Riddings and Great Giddesly. He wanted to see his grandparents' graves again, then he must hurry back to pick up Kate.

He touched the heavy wings of the stone saint, Albert's loving, if clumsy, tribute to his sister: 1865–1941.

She had been seventy-six when she died and still beloved of R.O.O.F. But in death they had been divided – Richard Oliver Ormerod Fiennders lay in the family mausoleum with Lady Caroline Fiennders, having survived Mary by just one year.

1940

'It took George and John and me hours to get here last time. Do you remember the traption?'

'Well, oh, well I remember it!'

The car was parked so close to the hedge that he only just managed to squeeze himself out of it. 'Here, let me give you a hand.'

She looked up at him, smiling, as he helped her out over the running board. 'Cheaper to come in the old traption than this. It's an early form of rationing, putting the price of petrol up. Two shillings a gallon!'

'One and elevenpence ha'penny.'

'Same thing.'

'If it does get rationed, Richard, if the war goes on, should we get a Coffield and sell this? It would be more economical to run.'

'Get a Coffield, maybe, but not sell this.'

The dark blue Daimler had nearly overtaken the occupants of the stables in his affections. Young George Nichols, too, he cared for it, washing and polishing it after every use. He even suspected him of treating the tyres like horses' hoofs, removing stones and lumps of mud.

'All right, Mary, my love, where is it?'

Little Wittenham Lane lay at the foot of the two hills,

the Wittenham Clumps. Further off lay a third large one, Brightwell Barrow.

'There.' She waved vaguely.

'Oh, no! We'll never do it, Mary. You were only twenty-five when you came here before, fifty years ago!'

'Not *that* one, the smallest one. You saw it on the map, Castle Fort. We can take it slowly, pause at the wood, rest half-way up—'

'Collapse at the top.'

She set off ahead of him. He had stopped to admire the fifteenth-century tower of St Peter's Church and the odd crooked chimney sticking out of a cottage down the lane.

'Wait for me!' He pushed his glasses up the bridge of his nose. From behind, her determined little figure looked like that of a child. She was wearing dark brown stockings and sensible brogues, a fawn corduroy knee-length skirt and an old tweed hacking jacket. Her hair, streaked milky-white and grey, hung down her back, tied with a brown velvet ribbon. He remembered her as a ten-year-old – at six – always her slender legs encased in thick black wool stockings and heavy boots.

'Come on, then.' She held out a hand, which he took, shortening his stride, and they walked till they reached the wood. Down in the village they could see the rise and fall of the roofs of cottages, houses, church and barns. Thatch and slate, stone and timber. The lane was made a cul-de-sac by both the river Thames and the little river Thame, but a footbridge crossed the water leading to a path across the meadows, through the remains of the old fort and into Dorchester. They could just see the figures of two women carrying straw shopping baskets.

'Race you to the top.' Not a question, a statement. She did. 'Sit down?' she said, panting, cheeks flushed.

'Phew, yes. Marvellous view, isn't it?'

'Marvellous. Nothing much has changed since . . . since then.' She had come up here alone, leaving George and John by the river, and thought only of Richard, and now . . . She kissed his cheek, lined and weather-beaten.

'And when did Aunt Biddy discover it?'

'She was taken as a young girl in eighteen fifty.'

'I don't suppose much has changed since then – a road widened, a few cars, that red blob . . . either a pillar-box or a telephone box. Nearly a hundred years!'

She wasn't listening. Twenty-five she had been, George's thirtieth birthday. His last. They had fished, George and John, and she hadn't seen Richard for ten years. She pressed her hand to her heart, it was beating so hard.

'Was it too much for you?'

She didn't reply.

'The climb, Mary, was it too much?'

And then it was another ten years before . . .

'What?' Her anguished face alarmed him. 'You're not well, are you? I'll run down, ask in the village, there must be a doctor. I'll borrow a horse and cart.'

'No, no. Oh, I'm sorry, I was thinking how much I missed you.'

'Then?'

'Yes.'

'But, my love, we have had years to make up the loss.'

'Oh, yes. Forty, last New Year's Eve,' she said precisely. They made their way to the far side of the hill where she remembered the tree with the carved poem to be. Those twenty years apart had been full of work, bringing up John, and the pleasure of friendships, Miss Crewe, Aunt Biddy, Sally, Hanny, but nothing in her life had been so painful as the day-to-day living without him. The only comparable pain was the grief at the death of her father, and that was a natural pain which had subsided with time and been absorbed into her memories. Other deaths had different pains; shock at the loss of the young people in the last war was bearable because it was shared. Yet others had died – in due time, after a good allotted span – or that's what they always said at funerals. Even Richard's mother – she tried not to laugh.

'Thank God, Mary, you laughed. You were looking so gloomy. Why are you laughing?'

'I don't know, well, I know *what* I was laughing at, I can't think why.'

'Share it.' He leaned back against a dead tree, an oak blasted by lightning, its bark burnt black, and took her shoulders, kissing the brown tip of her nose.

'It was about your mother.'

'Poor old Mamma.'

'Not at all. Not "poor old", she had a long and *full* life.'

'And a very interesting end!'

'Yes, poor old Sam, more like. Too old to make a convincing love object.'

'A grieving Romeo!'

'And your mother dressed up as a barge-woman, only everything made of fine lawn.'

He smiled, shaking his head. 'Typical of Mamma.'

'Can you imagine the lock-keepers as they took the barge through, hurling a rope, "Take this, my man", and when I think of all we went through trying to protect you! Old Dr Henders and Albert and me getting her off the barge, getting her back to the dower house.' She didn't mention Robert Henders and Albert putting her down on the tow-path, shaking with laughter, while she held Sam Reade, comforting him. 'Then finally, when I'd dressed her in her nightgown and bed-jacket and we'd got her into bed, you appeared, supposed to be the mourning son . . .'

'Morning sun? Oh, Mamma never thought I was that.'

'M-O-U-R.'

'I was teasing. Of course I knew she hadn't died there. What was the gardener doing, lurking outside with red-rimmed eyes? What were *you* doing there? You hadn't been in the house since—'

'Since I used to black the grates. It was lucky Hanny was on the telephone exchange at the shop otherwise everybody would have known. I was the only one Sam felt he could trust. I was the only one he knew . . . knew!'

'I'd known for years. Caroline told me in one of her alcoholic rages. She thought I'd be mortified.'

'I suppose, as usual, you laughed.'

'I did. All right. Where is this tree? I'm exhausted.'

'It's somewhere here, near, I know.' She circled a large beech, running her hand around its bark. 'Here! Here it is! Still here. Look, Richard, darling, look. Stand in front of me, trace the letters with your fingers and look.'

His fingers followed the etched letters:

> *'As up the hill with labouring steps we tread.'*

'True,' he said, 'it was a labour.' Continuing to feel the letters, he read,

'And yonder there, where Thames' smooth waters glide
In later days appeared monastic pride.

'Hm, "monastic pride", that could apply to Fiennders Abbey. And me.' She placed her chin on his shoulder:

'And awful doom award the earthly great,'

then put one hand, protecting over his, protecting it.

1990

They had all met in one of Roper's offices; the Coffield Conference Centre had been suggested but Herbert Roper dismissed the idea, 'Waste of money.' He wanted to keep the meeting small – and orderly, if possible. There were only about twenty NMAFF members present, 'The hard core', Kate said, a representative from the sympathetic Council for the Protection of Rural England, John from the environmental protection organization, and himself, sitting at the back, as an interested party. Very interested. Roper had spoken well, keeping his speech moderate and sticking to the legal position though his face was flushed with emotion and he was unable to control his excited little leaps. As he mentioned each item of the property that would be destroyed, he flung an arm at an appropriate photograph. His gestures were theatrical, Richard thought. Perhaps he, too, should have been an 'artiste', like Aunt Kate. A younger man took his place in front of the desk. Not a natural speaker, he used notes and shouted about the Government's disgusting attitude to the countryside. Carried away, his theme took on capitalism in general, farmers in particular and their responsibility for the destruction of rural England. He didn't finish with a stirring rendition of 'The Red Flag', as might have been expected, but a surprisingly well-sung version of John Betjeman's parody of the most famous of the harvest hymns:

> 'We spray the fields and scatter
> The poison on the ground
> So that no wicked wild flowers
> Upon our farm are found.
> We like whatever helps us
> To line our purse with pence;
> The twenty-four-hour broiler-house
> And neat electric fence.
>
> All concrete sheds around us
> And Jaguars in the yard,
> The telly lounge and the deep-freeze
> Are ours from working hard.
>
> We fire the fields for harvest
> The hedges swell the flame,
> The oak trees—'

Some people were joining in and others laughing when he was interrupted by a determined Tess.

> 'And if we lose on arable,
> Then bungalows will pay.'

'Just a minute, just a minute, excuse me, Darren, but who hasn't got a telly here? Who doesn't want a Jaguar or a BMW? Before we sit in judgement on farmers, we should ask ourselves a few questions. Yes, they've exploited the land, but encouraged by *us* and the Government so that *we* can have cheap food. We all take part –

right? If we want to do something about our environment, *we* must take responsibility. We should buy decently produced food even if it costs a little more and encourage others to do the same.' She stopped suddenly and sat down. 'Anyway, that's got nothing to do with the motorway access and the destruction of one specific site, which we are here to protect.'

The young man grumbled a bit but gave up when Herbert invited John, the environmentalist, to speak, introducing him as a 'caring scientist'. He, too, spoke well, calmly putting the case for no extra access roads at all. 'The damage done to the cottage, barns, woods and meadows of The Pightle will be total and irrecoverable but the damage will spread to every hamlet and village for miles around. They will be used as short-cuts by commuters, lorries and all heavy traffic. Lanes will become roads, roads will become highways and the villages themselves will become noisy polluted islands of unwanted houses.' That was greeted by fervent applause. Ways of lobbying the Government and attracting the attention of the media were discussed and a rather beautiful young woman, her hair plaited and coiled around her ears, wearing a long paisley dress and a shawl, added that the site was a confluence of vital ley lines and as such should be a national monument.

Richard waved across the room to Tess. He hadn't seen her since she'd driven him back to the Bull; she hadn't called. Just as well – he didn't want to get involved with a local girl. Awkward if he was to live here either at The Pightle or Home Farm. His vanity was piqued, though, at her lack of response. He wasn't usually spurned. Still, he would be seeing Lillian on Wednesday.

'That was good, Tess. I was amazed.'

'What at? My defence of farmers or that I didn't swear?'

'Both. It was *surprising*, you speaking up for the farmers, but *amazing* that you didn't call the bolshie young man a fuck-pig.'

'Well, I come from a farming family, see, only farmhands, and I only call special people fuck-pigs.'

He grinned. 'I'm flattered.'

'Yeah, well, see you.'

A pretty little plump woman with a bunch of leaflets bustled up and stopped her leaving. 'Oh, Tess, if you could distribute some of these at the school – and you, Mr Clarke, is it?'

'Yes, Richard Clarke.'

She put out a pudgy little hand. 'I'm Anne Roper.'

'Oh, "And Roper".'

'No, *Anne* Roper.'

'Yes, I know, I meant *and* Roper – as in, "Roper, Sons, *and Roper*".'

'I like that, Mr Clarke. I think I'll change my name. Now, will you leave some of these at the reception desk of the Bull?' She didn't wait for a refusal. ''Bye. Don't forget Dad's having a word with you and don't keep him long. My mother will be waiting dinner. Jill! Jill!' She thrust more leaflets into the arms of the beautiful woman in the paisley dress and shawl, who was already burdened with a handbag, a shopping bag, a briefcase and a laptop computer. Tess zipped up her black leather jacket, tucking the leaflets under her chin. 'Sorry I didn't call the other night, Richard,' she mumbled. 'But when I got to—'

'Not to worry, just as well, I could get addicted to your pillion.'

She watched him leave the room with old Herbert, on the way up to his office, were they, discussing 'business'? She had discussed 'business' there, too. Damn. She *had* called but he had gone out, and leaving a message at the Bull was like having an ad in the *Findlesham Weekly* and putting it on the Internet.

'That particular legacy was the money bequeathed to your grandmother by the school-teacher Sarah Crewe, part of which was used to buy The Pightle. She left it in her turn, and for the same reasons, to Teresa Quinn's daughter.'

'Tess's gran!'

'She was thus able to become a school-teacher.'

'And spawn a long line of school-teachers!'

'Indeed, and very honourable it was of her, but then she was scrupulous in meeting her moral debts.'

'And the Webbs, why them?'

'Long story, Richard, but again an obligation. It was a little inheritance from Aunt Biddy, Bridget Jackson, that Mary felt belonged to the daughters of her friend Sally Webb.'

He was standing at the window, NMAFF members were in the street chatting, but no Tess. A Saturday-night crowd was parading up and down, in and out of the pub, the pizza parlour, the Chinese take-away, the kebab van and the video shop. 'Why don't I make an appointment to see you next week, Herbert? I'm sure you want to get home to your family.'

'Thank you, most kind. Steel yourself, my boy. I'd be very surprised, as I said, if the minister changes his mind. And demonstrations can go wrong. Get Rent-a-Mob in and the media will use them rather than us. You'll find public apathy turning into—'

'Antipathy?'

'Ha! Very nice. My word! What's that?'

The sound of a crash from the stairs below had been followed by an angry shout of 'Bollocks!'

'Miss McKenna, I presume.'

'I'll see if I can help.'

Herbert Roper watched from the landing as Richard sped down the stairs.

'Are you all right?'

She was sprawled upside down on the stairs, surrounded by leaflets and the contents of her bag.

'It's those hobnailed boots.'

'It's the fucking worn-out carpet.'

'You're not hurt, then, I take it, Miss McKenna?' Herbert called. 'I won't worry.' He shut the door on the scene. Richard Clarke could see to that.

As he helped her up, Richard observed that, yes, she did wear black knickers.

'Bloody hell, I'm going to have a bruise. I'll be black and blue.'

'Blue will make a nice change.'

'You looked up my skirt. I saw you.'

'Not far to look. Did you come on your bike?'

'Course.'

'Well, you're not going home on it. You'll be very shaky.'

'How do you suppose I'll get home? And where do you propose I put my bloody bike?' Although said with her usual belligerence, she was quite happy to be relieved of responsibility – and she *was* shaky.

'I'm going to drive you home and we'll put the bike in the back of the station wagon.'

'What?'

'I hired it. Wanted to take some stuff from The Pightle over to Home Farm.'

He looked at her profile in the car. She was paler than ever. Her nose, he hadn't noticed it before, had a high narrow bridge with a slight bump on it, not unlike the profile of Nefertiti. 'Are you crying?'

'Not much. I'm tired, I think. It was a hard week. Kids can be tough.'

'And it was a hard fall.'

'And I'm hungry – didn't have time for lunch.'

He pulled off the road into a lay-by, parking between a caravan selling teas and hot pies, and a flower-seller.

'Why have we stopped? Don't worry, I'll be all right.'

'Will you?' He turned her face round. Crying had made the blue of her eyes more intense, cerulean. He closed his eyes and kissed her. Imperceptibly her mouth opened, but he held her head away and said, 'I should give you dinner.' He got out of the car quickly and ran back to the flower-seller, returning with a tin bucket full of narcissi and daffodils. 'Here.' She took the bucket, balancing it on her lap. 'I bought the lot, he's thrilled, he's going home. Why are you laughing?'

'I thought . . . I thought . . . Oh, Christ! I've spilled the water on my skirt.'

'Let's pray it doesn't shrink.'

'I thought, well, when you said "I'll give you dinner" . . . Oh, shit!'

'If you don't stop laughing . .'

'Here, you take them – and you jumped out of the car, I thought you were going to buy me a hot pie.'

'No, I'm going to buy you dinner at the Colcroft Arms. It's supposed to be very good. It's in *The Good Food Guide*. There can't be much water left in the tin. Take the flowers and shut up.'

The room was lit mainly by candles – real cream-coloured beeswax – on the tables and some in pewter sconces on the walls alternating with electric candle lamps. The furniture – tables, chairs and sideboards – was all old, highly polished and unmatching. Well-placed mirrors, again all different in both size and framing, reflected other guests. Tess was facing the room, but Richard could see as much in the gilt rococo-framed mirror on the wall behind her.

'It's a good wine list. Would you like champagne first or a cocktail?'

She grinned. 'Wow! Champagne, I suppose, how wonderful. But what if I don't like it? Could I still have a cocktail?'

He nodded, smiling. How sweet, her honesty. 'Certainly. Have you never had champagne?'

'Only some funny sweet stuff one Christmas at Father Dugan's.'

'And you didn't like it?'

'Not much.'

'That shows you've got a good palate.' He beckoned the waiter. 'A bottle of the Laurent Perrier 'eighty-five, please, and a bottle of mineral water, still. I'll keep the wine list till we know what we're eating.'

Her whole ensemble was black as usual but she looked lovely. 'You look marvellous, Tess, beautiful.'

She was wearing a black silk sleeveless dress, cut to the collar-bone. The dress was wide but of such soft material it fell in gentle folds against her body. Her Lycra skirt and sweater might be more revealing, but this was, in its subtle way, more appealing. Somehow she had managed to pin the masses of wavy hair to the top of her head, making the most of her long white neck, around which was tied a narrow piece of black cord holding one pear-shaped jet bead.

'The last time I came here, well, it was the first time too, we had the set lunch and half a carafe of the house white.'

'We?'

'A bloke from the school – or – none of your business.'

'Would sir care to try the champagne?' The waiter presented the bottle for approval and carefully removed the cork.

'It didn't pop,' she said.

The waiter ignored this and poured a little into the crystal flute on Richard's right. 'It isn't supposed to pop if it's opened properly, and it was.' He sipped and nodded to the waiter. 'Delicious, thank you.' He gestured to Tess.

'I think Miss McKenna will approve as well.' He nudged her foot under the table, remembering the inches high stiletto heels and the knee-high socks. Extraordinary, but it worked. On her, anyway. 'Right, what do you feel like? To start with, tuna tartare with lime and coriander? I might have that, or griddled scallops with a turnip cake?'

'Richard.' She took a roll from a basket lined with a white linen napkin. 'Oooh, this is good. Olive and rosemary – all very trendy, isn't it? Just like the *Guardian* on Saturday. Look, I want to ask you something. Why did you stop kissing me in the car?'

'Tess, have you no social graces? That's the sort of thing you talk about after a few glasses of wine. Like having a row, always wait till after dinner. I'm definitely having the tuna.'

'Me too. But why? Why did you stop?'

'I don't believe in taking advantage of damsels in distress.'

'I'm serious.'

'After the tuna, I'm going to have the *magret* of duck with a Madeira reduction . . .'

'Sounds like a sale.'

'So if you have that or the lamb, say, we can have a bottle of claret.'

'Why?'

He stretched across the table and kissed her. 'Now, for Christ's sake, what are you going to have?'

'Liver with caramelized shallots and mashed potato studded with horseradish.'

'Good girl.' He studied the wine list.

'This is nothing like Father Dugan's stuff. I won't need the cocktail.'

'I'm pleased to hear it.'

She drained her glass, looking round for room for the bottle. 'Where is it?'

He signalled the waiter, who gestured to an ice-bucket sitting on a side-table. 'It's near, sir.'

'Even nearer would be better. Put it on the table, will you? We're alcoholics. And we're ready to order.'

'This is fabulous. Do you eat – go out I mean, a lot like this?'

'Yes. Don't forget I travel all the time. I have to eat out.'

'Don't your girl-friends cook for you – bloody hell!' Looking over his shoulder, her eyes widened. 'Don't look now but . . .'

'Don't look *where* now? And why?'

'The Osmunds have just come in. You know, Liza Fiennders Osmund and her husband.'

'Oh, I see, yes. I can see them in the mirror, I think. Red-faced woman, reddish hair, and tall, thin, drippy-looking man, lank hair, balding.'

'*Exactement!*'

'You speak French?'

'Have to. I'm a teacher, don't forget. Obviously you do.'

'Also have to. Italian, German, Spanish, too, and some—' He stopped at her murderous look. 'It's nothing, it runs in the family. It's what my father did.' They ordered their food, the waiter leaving, suitably impressed by the request of a bottle of Pichon Lalande 1982. 'Tess, why would that annoy you, my speaking—'

'It doesn't annoy me, mate, it infuriates me. I'm jealous.'

'Jealous of what?'

'Your background, your talent, your freedom, your fucking *sangfroid*!'

'I'm not sure *everybody* heard that, Tess. Would you like to speak up a bit?'

'Tuna for madame – tuna for sir.' The waiter filled the champagne flutes, anxious to indulge the rich alcoholics.

'Bugger, the Osmunds are sitting too near to talk about them.'

'You're full of surprises, Tess. Such gentility. Kate's already told me a lot about them, anyway. He was a Lloyd's Name, that's why money's tight. Sad about the daughter.'

'Yeah, drugs always are. It's a bit of a problem at school. Not coke, though, only grass and speed and E. And there's not much they can do about Ann Osmund's habit 'cos Liza drinks like a fish – that runs in their family like languages do in yours.'

'OK, the tuna?'

'Mm, terrific. Sorry I shouted.'

'Listen, when I came to pick you up this evening, I parked round the corner like you said. I was early. I walked to your house, stood opposite and watched through the curtains. The television was on, a couple of kids were watching. An older man, I guessed your dad, was checking the pools. A young man was reading and writing at a table.'

'My brother, he's at agricultural college.'

'A really lovely-looking woman came in, smiling. She was carrying a tray.'

'Supper, toasted cheese.'

'Your brother tidied his books, everybody sat round

the table. They ate. They talked. They laughed. Nothing like that has ever happened to me. I was an observer. I felt excluded. Lonely. Jealous.'

At her insistence, he had parked again round the corner from thirty-four, Harrow Place, which lay between Plough Street and Hurdle Lane. The houses and streets all looked exactly the same with not a farm implement anywhere in sight.

'In medieval times, this was an old settlement, then *your family* uprooted it and put it to grassland.'

'You know, Tess, you don't have a chip on your shoulders, you have a bloody great baked potato!'

'Got a bruise on my shoulder, and on my hip.' She massaged her elbow. A little too much to drink, Richard thought, though they had finished neither the champagne nor the claret. Tess had been impressed by that.

'Shows you're rich. *My* idea of being rich is throwing away butter before its sell-by date.'

'I'm going to walk you home, it's late, even if it's only to thirty-two Harrow Place.'

'In a hundred years, these will be the good old days. And in five hundred years, this will be the Middle Ages.' She rubbed her knee and peered at him out of the tangle of hair which had escaped its pins. 'Still don't get it, Richard. Why – did – you – stop – kissing – me?'

'All right. I'll kiss you. I'll finish the kiss.' He had meant it to be tender, sweet: 'You are young', 'We are different', 'Life is strange'. But again her mouth opened and he responded. He thought of her knees, and the bruise. Where was it? On her thigh, no, her hip. He had noticed the vein on the inside of her knee, blue. Where did it end? His hand found the hem of her dress and lifted the soft silk, tracing where his imagination took the vein. The smallest of sighs greeted this, his hand touching her. He opened his eyes. Her legs had parted a little. Putting one hand behind her head he lowered her back on to the seat and started to unzip his trousers. Her legs were open now, long, white and beautiful. There was a bruise on her left knee. He bent to kiss it but when her body arched towards him, waiting for him to enter, he knew that he simply didn't want to. Not this way. Not now. If ever. He held her, saying nothing, as she repeated, 'Why? Why not? Why?'

As promised, he walked with her to thirty-two Harrow Place. As her desire and anger faded away, she was left with embarrassment. 'I've had too much champagne and everything,' she said.

'Me too, Tess. Get up late – you'll still be shocked from the fall. Go in. I just want to make sure you're safe home.'

The front door closed quietly, no lights went on, everybody was in bed in thirty-two Harrow Place. Everybody was in bed in Plough Street, Hurdle Lane and Pickaxe Close.

Only eleven thirty. And a moon. He would like to know the house at night, as they had done. Mary, Richard and Francis. And his father. Walking down the lane he looked back to where the pick-up was parked. In this light, in the green-black shadows thrown by the trees, it could almost be an old trap, without its pony. Not unlike the oddly shaped one in the garden at the back of the craft museum where the collection of old farming machinery was displayed. 'TYPICAL OXFORDSHIRE TRAP *circa 1890*', said the attached card.

The house, its long windows lit by the high moon, looked occupied. Somebody could have stayed up, waiting for him to come home. A series of light clouds drifted across the moon, the windows darkened and the welcome vanished. The garden, though overgrown, was still winning the battle against encroaching weeds and grass, and in spite of the compulsory purchase order the farmland on two sides was ploughed and sown in neat rows. Only the fields that were 'set aside', beyond the little orchard, were unkempt. Stony, choked with nettles and thistles, abandoned. What pride could a farmer have in earning money for not farming? Kate had tried to explain it to him, but he refused to understand or condone the millions of pounds paid by the Government for millions of neglected acres.

A darker cloud obscured the moon completely and for a few minutes he lost his bearings, isolated in the blackness. Suddenly a brilliant beam of light appeared penetrating the dark and obliterating the night. A jeep, or a four-wheel-drive something-or-other, was approaching along one of the old deer tracks. It stopped abruptly just beyond him. A man in a tattered old anorak leaned out of the window.

'Everything all right, squire?' It was a London accent, confident, cheery.

'Just doing a bit er lamping, see. No harm, eh?'

Richard noticed two guns sitting across the lap of another roughly dressed man in the passenger seat.

'No hunting around here, see? So, we gets paid for a bit of shooting. A few foxes for the farmer, right? And – nudge, nudge, wink, wink – a deer or two for us to make it worth our while. Can't have the poor old farmer lose his sheep and chickens, can we? All right, squire?' he repeated.

Richard shrugged, perhaps it was all right. He must ask somebody about it. The jeep bounced on, the light retreating, and he found his way back to the pick-up. The jeep hadn't been a Land-rover, it was a Coffield Cub.

'I wouldn't get a Coffield on principle. They done me out of my rights in nineteen fourteen or fifteen, thereabouts.'

The traffic all the way from the bypass had been solid, moving in hiccups, the double stream of cars constantly overtaking by inches and then dropping back. Occasionally, an impatient driver would cut into a lane moving at a moderately quicker rate, only to be left with an impotent rage as the lane he had moved from accelerated and he was left behind.

'Nineteen fourteen, Bill? You weren't born.'

'No, but if I had been, I wouldn't have sold my father's birthright.'

'An impossible proposition, anyway. How long is it going to take?'

'You'll get your train, Richard, don't you worry.'

Young or old, man or woman, the drivers' faces all displayed the same mixture of emotions – frustration, irritation and despair. The sound, though, changed from car to car. On Radio Two, Jimmy Young was giving advice punctuated by light pop music; *The World at One,* on Radio Four, was receiving party statements, instead of answers to questions, from politicians; a concert of Haydn from St John's, Smith Square, was on Radio Three, and other stations offered numerous variations of modern rock and pop. One middle-aged woman, in glasses and a haircut that made her look like an old schoolgirl, was using her journey to learn French. As she drew level he heard her say, '*C'est combien, un kilo de pêches?*'

'Five thousand pounds they got. Kept a copy of the cheque they did. "Pay Flora and William Jackson five thousand pounds". There's a photo of them holding it, him all smiles and her looking over her specs, scared like.'

'Lot of money in those days, Bill.'

'That was then and this is now and I should be worth five billion, and now we can hardly manage.'

'Isn't there any other way, a short cut?'

'Hold your horses, Richard. We could turn off and go through Edgecombe and the Industrial Estate, but that would add five miles. I swear you'll be at the station with time to spare. In any case, a Coffield wouldn't have the same sort of appeal as this or the four-wheel drive.'

The traffic had started to move a little faster as cars filtered off to the right at a crossroads ahead and Richard sat back.

'I only suggested the Coffield because it would be cheaper for you to run.'

'And thank you for your kind thoughts, sir – Richard.'

They were ninth in line at the lights. They would either just make it at the next change, Richard calculated, or they would not. Probably not. Bill was scrupulous about amber lights.

'It was here, you know, at this crossing, that it happened.' He had lowered his voice suitably to match the gravity of the information. 'Before the dual carriageway, before the right filter light, before traffic lights at all. And that's another reason not to have a Coffield. Respect for the dead.'

The traffic started inching forward then slowly accelerated but, as predicted, when the lights turned to amber, Bill stopped and put on the handbrake.

'I thought they were in some beautiful old Daimler or Bentley,' Richard said. He sat up, looking right and left. It was a crossroads of four dual carriageways. The right was signposted to 'WELLSBURY, AVOIDING LOW BRIDGE' and the left 'HEMSDUTTON, M4 AND THE WEST'.

'No, it was the war, see. They used the little Coffield to save on petrol coupons.' He gave a deep gloomy sigh. 'Nobody's fault. Nobody going fast, bad luck, bad timing. Before seat belts. They took her to the Cottage Hospital, Memorial Hospital, really. Paid for by old Coffield after the First World War.'

The lights had changed, they moved off. Richard twisted round for a last look.

'Pity they weren't killed together. Awful for him. Poor man.'

'Nobody's fault. They had no chance – big army lorry. Nobody's fault.'

In the train which, as Bill had sworn, he caught easily, that little phrase rang in his head: 'Timing, it was all timing. Nobody's fault.' He had heard that before in the history of his grandmother's life and death.

★

Kate knew he had seen them. They had bought tickets in the back row to avoid his notice, but he had definitely seen them. In the first half, the cellist, Lillian Gerlinka, had been playing as much for Richard as the audience, especially in the Schubert sonata, but now he was studiously avoiding her attention, glancing at her only when conducting from the piano. In the interval, Tess had questioned Kate about the cellist.

'Not his accompanist, dear, she's a soloist in her own right, excellent, really excellent.'

'And Richard?' Tess had been to amateur concerts at local churches, listened to classical music on the radio and had compact discs of her favourite works, but she felt she hadn't enough knowledge to have opinions about performers. Brilliant and lousy, they were clear, but . . . 'Richard, Kate, is he excellent?'

'Oh, yes, he's superb, a brilliant technician with a great soul. I knew from listening to him practise that he had technique – I didn't know about the soul.'

'Kate, do they travel all over the world together doing this?' She had figured out a story for herself to answer all the questions – he wanted her but, because he was a decent sort, wouldn't go through with it because this cellist, Lillian Whatsername, was his girl-friend. Very romantic she looked, long dark green velvet dress with a white Puritan collar. Very Slav, those slanted eyes and high cheekbones, and hair so straight it must have been ironed, light brown with a hundred and fifty quid's worth of highlights.

'No, they work well together, but they both have successful solo careers and play with other musicians too.

Lillian often plays with her husband Gideon Gerlinka, the flautist. Here's Herbert. How did you manage?'

The little man anxiously hurried them back to their seats. 'I found a much better parking place just round the corner.'

This was the last piece. She peeped surreptitiously at her programme. 'Brahms Sonata in D Major Opus 78.' Gorgeous! Sublime! Ridiculous to think she had a chance with him. *Vivace ma non troppo*. Vivacious but not too much. No one could accuse her of that. *Vivace* OTT would be more accurate.

The reception at the end was warm and appreciative and they played two encores. After the second, some Americans who had been sitting near the front shouting, 'Bravo,' jumped to their feet applauding. Instinctively, Tess joined them, then Herbert Roper also stood up, with not quite enough courage to shout 'Bravo', so he said it instead: 'Bravo, well done.'

Kate took his arm to lean on and gradually the whole audience gave, what Tess had only read about, a standing ovation. The cellist had been ackowledging the applause with only an unsmiling nod of the head, but now she accepted Richard's hand and bowed graciously to the audience and to him.

A man in the aisle, dressed in a dinner jacket, the assistant manager, signalled for them to follow him.

'How did he know?' Tess whispered. 'Was it my fault, standing up?'

'No. He saw us at the end of the first half, I could tell.'

'Shit! I'm so excited. Oh, I'm too nervous. No, bloody hell, I'll wait outside.'

'Do you think, Tess, that you could discover some little, as yet untapped, well of decorum inside you? Please?'

'Sorry, Mr Roper.'

He was waiting in his dressing room for them, his tail-coat draped over the back of a chair, his white tie unknotted. Lillian had left. If she had been angry in the interval, she was angrier now. He shouldn't have laughed, but to accuse *him* of infidelity – and she a married woman. It was like an opera. Was he doomed to spurn the bodies of beautiful women for ever? They had often made love in dressing rooms in the interval before. It was exciting, dangerous and, in practical terms, it meant they had time for supper afterwards. But when she had appeared in his room after the first half, pressing herself against him – not kissing, that would have smudged her lipstick – then bending over a chair facing the mirror and lifting her dress to her waist, he wasn't excited, only embarrassed for her. Seeing the three sitting in the back row he had been touched by their interest and loyalty. No. He was not going to fuck Lillian and think of Tess.

She stood waiting shyly at the door as Herbert and Kate congratulated him, Kate picking out details of his performance while Herbert, amazingly, kissed him on both cheeks, something he'd learned that artists did from foreign films. 'I'm absolutely sure, Richard,' he said, 'that you could get more work in England.'

'What do you think, Tess?' He brought her into the room. 'Let's have a look at you. What are you wearing?'

She twirled slowly for him. She was wearing black woollen leggings, velvet ballet slippers, a black Nehru-style jacket and her hair was tied back with a velvet bow and plaited. 'Doesn't matter what I'm wearing. I don't quite know how to say what I felt. The music transported me, sorry to sound pretentious, and yet I was always there. You are wonderful, Richard. Kate told me so, but I would have known anyway.'

There was a silence as he embraced them all. Then Kate said, 'We must be going. Herbert is driving us and you must be hungry and want a drink.'

'Yes, I do, I am, but if there's room in the car, could you take me home with you?'

'A pleasure, maestro!'

'I'll have to pick up my case. I'm staying in an hotel off Baker Street, and then we could all have something at the Bull.'

'I'm sorry to have to tell you this, bring the bad news, be the bearer of . . . oh dear, Richard, so sad, and on the night of your triumph.'

Tess cringed in the back seat. Herbert Roper seemed to think that tonight was unusual, an audition that Richard had passed. Fool. The car took the underpass at Acton, which would soon lead on to the M40. Kate, in her sleep, lolled against Tess, muttered, 'Excuse me,' and fell back again.

'It's all right, Herbert. No surprise, not your fault, nobody's fault.' That phrase again. 'Though I do intend to try to stop anything else being destroyed in Findlesham. I have spoken to the Osmunds' solicitor, making an offer for the land that used to be a part of Home Farm. The three-year lease with Agrilea is nearly up and . . . Tess? Are you awake back there?' Richard turned slightly.

She leaned forward between the two men. 'Yes. What?'

'Well, you can help and I think you'll understand. It looks as if I'll be able to buy the land back.'

'Yes, I heard.'

'I'd like to farm it properly, as an organic farm. You know about Agrilea, that's intensive farming, isn't it?'

'As intensive as you can get. Hardly any crop rotation and no livestock. And they spray a lot too, have to – insects and stuff get immune to chemicals.'

'What would I do? How long does it take to get insecticides out of the soil?'

'You could ask Patrick, my brother. He's not only up at the regular agricultural college, he does part-time at a farm approved by the Soil Association too.'

'You'd lose money, Richard. It would be an expensive hobby.' It was all very fine and idealistic, but Herbert considered that the young man, the artist, needed a steadying hand. 'Think of your future. What will you do when you can no longer play the piano?'

'Teach, of course. And I wouldn't think of it as a hobby. It would pay for itself eventually. And, what's more, I *am* thinking of the future.'

'There are lots of organizations you can talk to, like the Countryside Restoration Trust. It would be exciting.' She had been addressing both men when she felt his cheek graze hers. It felt deliberate, but she didn't react, and sank back in her seat.

'You see, Herbert, I feel a certain responsibility. The last war destroyed Fiennders Abbey and the estate, but if Timothy hadn't been killed I think my father and he might have pulled it together again. Did you know that,

Tess?' He looked over his shoulder at her. He was smiling but it was friendly, not amatory. 'They were friends, isn't that odd? Now, I can't make up for what Tommy did and, anyway, I'm not a Fiennders, but . . .'

'Not a legitimate one, but there is consanguinity. Why would the Osmunds let you have the land? And may I say that I'm sad you didn't consult me.'

'They need money and I *am* consulting you, Herbert. I would like you to take over negotiations. Had we won the Pightle case, I might not have pursued it. Without the compensation, I couldn't afford it.'

'I see. Thank you for your confidence.'

'Fuck me, I'm hungry.'

Kate opened her eyes. 'No, no, Tess. *Feed* me, I'm hungry.'

They had left Richard at the Bull after supper and Herbert Roper was driving the two women home. In the tired silence, Kate suddenly said, 'There's a streak of . . . *frugality* is the kinder word but *miserliness* more accurate, on both sides of my family. And I have inherited it.' She sounded quite pleased.

'You have, you have!' Herbert also appeared pleased.

'In olden days, I would have been called a lickpenny.'

Tess laughed. 'You're not that bad.'

'But I'm going to change the habits of a life-time.'

The car turned off the road onto the track, bumping and kicking up stones. 'Will Richard lay a proper path when he moves in?'

'Certainly not.'

'Go on, Kate. What do you mean?'

'I'm going to buy the land.'

Tess's 'What with?' went unnoticed.

'After all this time? You're going to spend some of the money?'

'Yes.'

'What money?' was ignored too.

'I was waiting for a rainy day, but I don't think it will ever be rainy enough for me, so Grandmamma Ann Fiennders' ill-gotten gains can reunify Home Farm. If I do it now and live for another seven years, which I plan to, there will be no death duties.'

'Shall we wait till it stops raining? What do you think?'

Tess had half opened the door of the car. 'It's warm rain, though, and we've got our jackets.' She would rather be out walking with him, talking about the country. Stuck in the car together, she was uneasy.

'Let's wait a bit, OK?'

She slammed the door and sat back.

'Who was that boy who waved to you, back at the watercress beds? One of your pupils?' Richard knew she felt uncomfortable.

'Yeah. Difficult kid, but bright. I got him to volunteer for some jobs in the holidays. Keep him occupied. Helps dig out ponds and things for the Chiltern Society.'

'Single parent?'

'Might as well be. His father works at night, lorry driver, and his mum works during the day on the checkout at Waitrose.'

'So you're probably an anchor for him.'

Christ, this was difficult, just being friends. He'd seen

more of her brother than of her for weeks now. Her life had gone on, same old thing till school broke up, but *he* had moved into Home Farm, and been to . . . all over the place, concerts in Berlin, New York, everywhere. 'Anchor? Don't know about that. He's an irritating little bugger but worth bothering about. You know what pisses me off about my work?'

She was pissed off now he could see, but why? Was she bored?

'I spend most of my time keeping the kids quiet and doing admin. Do you know what I'd like to do? Course you don't, and why should you be interested? I'd like to jack it in and be a librarian. And help kids like that privately, coach them. A part-time librarian. I'd also like to have a good time.'

He laughed.

'I teach partly because I'm honour bound, but if Kelly, my sister, gets on well, she can bloody well take over.'

'Why are you so angry, Tess? You've done so well, considering. So have I, considering.'

'Considering what? Considering you were born to the purple? Even if it was the wrong side of the blanket? Considering you were born above the salt? You go on and on about what happened round here to your lot in the "good old days" but you know nothing, *nothing*, about the lives of working people hereabouts in those times. Did your famous Mary, your gran, collect stones in the fields before dawn?'

'Yes.'

'Did she feed a pig, collect snails for it, give up crusts of bread for it because he was the food for the next year?'

'Yes.' He caught hold of her arm as she was reaching

for the door handle. 'Stop it, Tess. *She* did it, your great-grandmother did it, neither of us did. Come on, then, if you want, we'll walk in the rain.'

It was summer rain, fine and warm. Neither of them put the hoods up on their jackets.

'We'll do the Clumps today, but if you want, some time, they've just opened a bit more of the Thames Path down there, a new bridge. We could walk to Oxford.' Tess looked hopeless, forlorn, scrabbling in her pockets for the walking guide, anxious to entertain him after her outburst. 'It says here that the crooked chimney on that cottage there,' she pointed down the lane, 'was to bring luck to a new house, built on the site of one that was burnt down.'

'More like to make it burn down again.'

She permitted a smile. 'And though only traces of the poem are still there on the tree, it's all in this.' She tapped the guide. 'Kate said your Mary came here.'

'Not bringing the pig, I hope.'

She walked ahead of him up the path cut into the largest hill, leaping over tussocks, pulling the seed flowers off grasses and throwing them into the sky, imitating the bleating of the lambs. Even her walking clothes were black. Black anorak, black T-shirt, black cotton jeans and black sneakers. 'You're really out of condition, you know, Richard.' She waited at the top. 'Or is it your age?'

'I'm only eight years older than you, so it must be lack of condition.' He leaned on the triangulation post, puffing.

'Oxford over there, Dorchester marked, but no Findlesham.' She pointed to an arrow facing west. 'It's there. Shall we scratch it in?'

'Are you a vandal as well as a virago? All right, where's this tree?'

'Not on this hill, on the smaller one, over there.'

They ran down the side of the hill and walked up the other. Because of the rain, the large car park at the foot was empty.

'We have the place to ourselves.'

'Mm, nice.' She consulted the guide. 'According to this, the tree is through the wood on the other side.'

'It's dead,' he said. 'No wonder the bark's peeling off.'

She stood close to the tree, her finger tracing what was left of the poem. 'Here.' She took his hand. 'It's a funny feeling, isn't it? I'll read it out.'

The rain, still warm, was heavier. He tried to shelter her and the guide-book. ' "The summit gained, at ease"? He must have been a strong young man – a poet–peasant.' She could feel his body touching hers. This friendship lark was bloody difficult. 'Apart from that huge field of yellow rape, not that much has changed.'

Her hair tickled his nose. It smelled of air and flowers and health. 'No?'

She quoted from the guide, which was wet and difficult to read. ' "Point out each object." ' She was reluctant to move, to separate their bodies. 'Come round the other side. De dah de dah . . . "the various changes" – look!' There, overwhelming the landscape, were the gigantic cooling towers and chimney of Didcot power station.

'My God, Tess. That would frighten the young poet if he was suddenly reincarnated!'

'Somebody said that all along the Ridgeway, from the

footpath, they look like concrete trees. But they frighten me, in spite of their bulk – no, because of it perhaps – I don't know, it's difficult to explain.'

'Go on, try.' He patted her shoulder.

'Well, they look dangerous, and . . .'

'And?'

She lifted her hair off her neck, surprised. 'I'm soaking.' She pointed to the towers. 'They look dangerous . . . and vulnerable.'

'What a good description. It's perfect.' He was so near her now she couldn't move. 'Are you cold?'

She felt his hand touch hers, resting on the trunk of the tree.

'Your hands aren't cold.' He was lifting her hair. 'It's wet, you're right, soaking.'

Was that the slightest brush from his fingers, or his mouth? Still she didn't move. To be rejected again would remove all chance of friendship. This time, it *was* a kiss.

He slid his hand under her jacket, touching her breast. 'Do you never wear a bra?'

'Not when I'm with you.' She leaned back, feeling him hard against her body.

'I had booked a room for us at the Manoir,' he whispered in her ear, as he unzipped her jacket. 'Intending an attempted seduction.' The jacket dropped off her shoulders as he turned her round to face him. 'But, I can no longer do – your breasts are so sweet – what I feel I ought to do.' He pulled off her T-shirt. 'So, Tess, my darling, I'm going to finish that kiss.'

Kissing, they sank to the ground, she put her hands inside his shirt, feeling the strong shoulders. 'Is it because I'm a Catholic?' She took the shirt off, throwing it aside.

'That I wanted to make love to you in a bed, as opposed to fucking you in the back of a car?'

She wriggled out of her trousers. 'It wasn't the back of the car, it was the front.'

He felt her long legs fold over him as he completed the kiss.

They lay naked in the rain. The grass was wet and the purple-black trees were dripping. Her hair was gleaming, soaked with rain.

'Herbert Roper would expect to take the photographs, wouldn't he?'

'Of us? Here?' She sat up, astonished.

'Would you *have* to wear black?'

'What?!'

'Would you swear not to say, "I, Teresa Mary Mc-Kenna, do not bloody well promise"?'

'How did you know my name?'

'I didn't. Good guess, that's all. "Tess" was bound to be "Teresa" and all good Catholic girls are called Mary.'

'What do you think?' He started the car. 'Check in at the Manoir, have a hot bath, get into something warm – and then fuck in the back of the car?'

'I haven't got anything warm to change into.'

'No. Well, it's back to Home Farm, then. Do you know what Kate is giving us as a wedding present? Some family silver stolen by Tommy that he sold to Maud. Isn't that funny?'

She hit him. 'You told Kate, before you asked me? You absolute—'

He kissed her before she could say 'Fuck-pig'.

The trees were studded with people. Not only the young and brave, or foolhardy, those to whom a fall or a broken leg was not a possibility they entertained, but the middle-aged and elderly, even the old, the ancients, who had been cynically assisted into their positions by the young, calculating that the police would not risk the headlines in the *Sun* or *Mirror*: 'Granny Smith Bruised By Fall', 'Cops In The Copse'. There were a couple of Kate's octogenarians from Fiennders Abbey, fortified with sweet sherry, singing, 'There'll Always Be an England', in counterpoint to the rendering of 'We Shall Overcome' by the middle-aged, and 'Country Feed Back' from REM sung by the young. Little Heather Reade was holding on to Craig Jackson's leg, which was dangling from a sturdy branch above. Her spiky pale-blonde hair stood out against the dark-green foliage and the tiny silver studs in her nose twinkled in the flash-lights of cameras. The Bexley-Wrights from the Old Dower House were sitting sedately side by side half-way up a tall copper beech. She was wearing a flowered dirndl skirt and white blouse, he was in dark trousers, navy-blue blazer, striped shirt and tie. They could have been in their drawing room at home, Richard thought. Cathy Watson from Edgecombe House was wedged in a fork of a strong chestnut tree. She was wearing American work clothes, denim, from the baseball cap on her head, worn back to front, to her jeans tucked into boots, the whole being purchased from Gucci.

All this was a delaying tactic, he knew. Tomorrow the photographers and television cameras would be gone. A gay bishop, an actress, a schoolteacher, a politician, someone would have done something somewhere to delight the press, to fill the front pages. An indiscretion, preferably sexual, with money and drugs as side attractions, would draw them away like a magnet and this idyllic place would vanish. The footpaths and bridleways would contain concrete ghosts.

He saw her sitting on a low branch of a large oak tree, in her usual black – a baggy corduroy smock and long boots. He hoped she would be careful. An evening breeze moved the leaves and branches, half obscuring her face. She looked like the Green Man emerging from the woods. She had been waving to someone, waving goodbye, to the environmental man, who threaded his way through the crowds. 'I'm off. You should be too. It's done, you see, nothing you can do.'

They shook hands.

'Thank you, John, for all the advice and help.'

The man smiled and shrugged. 'Yes, yes, well, goodbye, then.'

'Listen, I'm sorry, John, but I don't know your other name, I mean, your surname.'

'Jackson.'

'Like Bill? At the garage?'

'I suppose so, common enough name.' He waved and was quickly gone.

1991

It was next September when the road was opened. They shooed the chickens away as they walked through the farmyard, turning to acknowledge Kate's wave. The car was parked out of sight behind the hedge, which was already starting to change to its autumnal colours. They set out for Oxford. The slip-road to the motorway was only three miles out of Findlesham. Following the large blue and white signs they turned onto the six-lane motorway from the Pightle Roundabout.

'It's very useful, isn't it? Saves time?'

She placed her hand on his at the wheel to steady it.

All Pan Books are available at your local bookshop or newsagent, or can be ordered direct from the publisher. Indicate the number of copies required and fill in the form below.

Send to: Macmillan General Books C.S.
              Book Service By Post
              PO Box 29, Douglas I-O-M
              IM99 1BQ

or phone: 01624 675137, quoting title, author and credit card number.

or fax: 01624 670923, quoting title, author, and credit card number.

or Internet: http://www.bookpost.co.uk

Please enclose a remittance* to the value of the cover price plus 75 pence per book for post and packing. Overseas customers please allow £1.00 per copy for post and packing.

*Payment may be made in sterling by UK personal cheque, Eurocheque, postal order, sterling draft or international money order, made payable to Book Service By Post.

Alternatively by Access/Visa/MasterCard

Card No.   ☐☐☐☐☐☐☐☐☐☐☐☐☐☐☐☐☐☐☐

Expiry Date   ☐☐☐☐☐☐☐☐☐☐☐☐☐☐☐☐☐☐☐

Signature   ————————————————————

Applicable only in the UK and BFPO addresses.

While every effort is made to keep prices low, it is sometimes necessary to increase prices at short notice. Pan Books reserve the right to show on covers and charge new retail prices which may differ from those advertised in the text or elsewhere.

NAME AND ADDRESS IN BLOCK CAPITAL LETTERS PLEASE

Name ————————————————————————————

Address ————————————————————————————

————————————————————————————————

————————————————————————————————

————————————————————————————————

8/95

Please allow 28 days for delivery.
Please tick box if you do not wish to receive any additional information. ☐